D1527509

The Book of Matthew

The Book of Matthew

A macabre novel of suspense

By Thomas White

McBooks Press, Inc.
www.mcbooks.com
Ithaca, NY

Published by McBooks Press, Inc. 2008

Dust jacket and book design by Panda Musgrove.
Cover illustration composited by Panda Musgrove.
The following images used under license of Shutterstock.com:
Cover images copyright © 2007, Stephen Mulcahey, Alice, and Kirsty Pargeter.

ISBN: 978-1-59013-151-0

Library of Congress Cataloging-in-Publication Data

White, Thomas, 1956-
  The book of Matthew : a macabre novel of suspense / by Thomas White.
    p. cm.
  ISBN 978-1-59013-151-0 (alk. paper)
  1. Serial murders—Fiction. 2. San Francisco (Calif.)—Fiction. I. Title.
PS3623.H5794B66 2008
813'.6—dc22
                    2008004083

All McBooks Press publications can be ordered by calling toll-free 1-888-BOOKS11 (1-888-266-5711). Please call to request a free catalog.

Visit the McBooks Press website at www.mcbooks.com.

Printed in the United States of America
9 8 7 6 5 4 3 2 1

This novel is dedicated to my "quintumvirate," each of them equally culpable in allowing this hair-raising tale to see the light of day:

— Shelly Kintisch, suspense mentor extraordinaire, who slogged through untold manuscript drafts and lengthy midnight telephone calls without rolling her eyes (or so she tells me);

— Margarida MacCormick, my long-suffering best friend, who pulled rabbits out of a dozen hats to allow me to write full-time for several years;

— Jake Elwell, my redoubtable agent, who somehow fished my manuscript out of his floor-to-ceiling slush piles and pronounced it worthy;

— Alex Skutt, my publisher, who was willing to champion a crime thriller occupying the place on the map where it says, "Beyonde Here Be Dragones";

— Jackie Swift, my editor, who pointed out a hundred improvements to a manuscript I had long thought beyond improvement.

To the five of you, I am forever in your debt.

The Book of Matthew

Prologue

By now his screams sounded like the heaving chuffs of a sick cat, so no one could hear him, even from the washed-out trail ten yards away. But someone could still *see* him. *Had* to see him, glistening with sweat and raindrops four feet in midair, stretched taut in agony as if levitated by the branches of the oak overhead.

But then he felt another of those weird *ponks* inside his back. Sometimes they came one at a time, others with a slow staccato *ponk, ponk, ponk.* Each brought a sledge of pain, though it was easing up some as his nervous system began to snuff out. He vomited down his shirt every time he recalled what the freako said would happen next, and so he forced himself to fix on the mottled craters of the bright, bright moon above. And to steel himself for a final scream next time he saw the ghostly coronas of headlight beams from the road out of sight a hundred feet downhill.

He choked out a sob as dark wisps of pitiless cloud wove over the moon again and the icy droplets flicked his cheeks. But then his lips twisted into a grin. At least the rain would chase away the goddamn pig snuffling a yard beneath his feet, sniffing his blood like a wine connoisseur as it dribbled off his mangled wrists.

He sensed the grisly climax was only moments away and tried to distract himself, thinking of things he'd done in his life. First kid in his class to get laid. Winning the gas station football pool three weeks in a row. Standing the whole bar drinks from the reward for spotting that bail jumper. Beating the shit out of that wetback who'd held him up, then getting to testify to boot, his name in the next morning's paper. He'd shown anyone who'd look.

And of course all those famous people he'd met. Barry Bonds. Stormin' Norman. Gilligan. *Eddie Frigging Van Halen*. And that porn star Felicia, now *that* was something. Though she said it wasn't her and got pissed, even with that Betty Boop shoulder tat he'd seen in a dozen tapes. He'd always said, if you wanted to meet famous people, pumping gas was where to be.

He'd be famous tomorrow all right. *Real* frigging famous.

He felt relief as the snuffling ceased. Then he craned his neck downward. The pig was still there. Parked on his haunches not six feet away. Staring at him.

He'd seen a show on *Discovery*. It said they were smart, smarter than dogs. *He knows.*

A second pig grunted out of the brush, planted itself next to its mate and sniffed the air. And then a third, and a fourth. Waiting for the lids to come off the all-you-can-eat buffet.

The droplets came steadier, but then something strange happened: a blink of snowy light out towards the ocean. Then, seconds later, a rolling rumble amid the plinking of the raindrops in the tubs. Funny, you never got lightning in Pacific storms. First time he'd seen it in about ten years.

Maybe it meant the whole thing was a nightmare.

That was it. He'd nodded off in his booth, and Rick would saunter along soon and roust him with the tab. He'd hit the ATM, get a lap dance from Charlene, and forget all about it. He could tell her all about his freaky dream, that she'd even been in it. Girls ate up shit like that, even the slutbags. It wouldn't even be a lie.

He cricked his neck down in disgust. God, he'd have to change clothes.

He grinned. No he wouldn't. The puke's in the dream, stupid.

And then, his skull resonated with the crackling of a tree before its fall. The *ponks* cascaded into a machine-gun burst like a huge zipper unzipping at his spine. The pulleys above him creaked ominously and something in his viscera gave way, something that was never supposed to. Then pain, bubbling pain as squishy stuff sprang loose inside like pipes in an earthquake. His abdominal muscles slowly pulled apart like thick Turkish taffy, and his head and shoulders rose inch by inch toward the invisible, heedless moon. Then the last sound the sicko had said he'd ever hear—the sickening splat as the pigs trotted forward with frenzied squeals—and then the scream he'd marshaled, a howl of indignation at his shameful, ugly death and the monster who had crafted it for a decade.

But there was no sound above the contented rending of sinew from bone. The scream came not from his mouth but from deep inside his head.

CHAPTER ONE

Tuesday, May 6th

Inspector Clemson Yao gazed up at the huge branches twelve feet overhead. Even in the morning, the grove of hoary oaks seemed full of age-old menace, their canopies faded into fog as if the trunks had uncoiled from heaven and gripped the earth. He half expected to see a dozen hooded Druids up to some sort of Druidic no good.

Every homicide crime scene had *some* of that, the sinister "someone was slaughtered here" frisson he got from half a hundred San Francisco venues by now. He even enjoyed it sometimes in that flesh-crawly way Londoners got off on Jack the Ripper tours. But a bunch of spooky trees would perfectly complement the denizens that skittered nightly through his brief snatches of sleep: millipedes with the girth of pythons, roaches like beady-eyed, six-legged footballs. A year ago he'd winched a vaguely human decomp glob by glob from a sewer pipe. Now, one night or so a month, the pipe became home to centipedes like hundred-limbed fire hoses that just kind of smirked at a hollow point.

Tonight they'd be in the trees.

Grady Moore, chief of police of Gilroy, spoke as he doffed the mirror shades he wore heedless of hour or weather. His irises were the color of burnished pewter. The mist muffled his voice, as if the place itself insisted on a funereal hush. "I wouldn't drag you down here, Clem, but it's been three months and not one suspect. I'm like that spider being dangled over the fire in that famous sermon."

Clem nodded sagely. "*Sinners in the Hands of an Angry God*. Always uplifting."

A grimace twisted Grady's leathery features. He'd seen a lot in thirty years in the Salinas Valley, from grisly migrant honor killings to labor rabble-rousers made gruesome examples by feudal lettuce lords, but nothing like this. "Anyway, see the borings in the branches, where he screwed in the pulleys?" He pointed them out, two holes each sunk in two foot-thick branches extending from the yard-wide trunk. "The killer threaded ropes through the four pulleys to a leather belt hitched under the vic's shoulders. Hanging on the other end of the ropes were four huge steel washtubs. Another rope hitched tight round his waist and secured here at the foot of the tree."

Clem looked down. Two steel eyebolts were set in concrete stained an ominous brown. He frowned. "You going to leave this thing in the ground? Put up a visitors' center?"

Grady shook his head. "It's a real old tree, some enviro-gnome has to sign off before we can dig out the concrete. We get two or three gawkers a day."

Clem rolled his eyes. "So when it started raining, the tubs filled with water and hoisted the vic into the tree under his shoulders. Except he was tied to the ground by his waist."

"Right," agreed Grady. "Tubs could each hold five cubic feet of water."

"So total twenty at sixty-six pounds each, that's, umm—"

"Like fourteen hundred pounds hoisting him up. So eventually one of his vertebrae gave up the ghost and he tore in half at the waist. When we found him next day, his northern half was suspended by the tubs up yonder feeding the crows. Feral pigs were chowing down on his southern reaches on the ground there. Nothing in between but his small intestine, strung tight as a bass fiddle string."

Clem shook his head grimly. "And here I thought the little porkers were kinda cute."

"Pig's gotta do. Coroner about shat himself though. And premeditated? Concrete was cured. Means he poured it *months* before. The vic's William Rohde. Nickname Sneezy."

"You've ruled out suicide I take it."

Grady's smile looked like something straight off a Louisiana swamp gator.

Clem continued. "So who'd want to rend him asunder?"

Grady spat out the syrupy remnants of a tobacco plug. "I had a clue, you wouldn't have spent two hours driving down here. Town ne'er-do-well, here all his life. Chevron station manager, single, thirty-two, beered up nightly at Club 602, low-life billiard joint."

Clem nodded. "Guy have a sheet?"

"Busthead bar stuff, DWIs, but nothing that'd have the Cossacks up his ass." Russian Mafia involvement would give the Feds exclusive dibs, something Grady would probably trade his firstborn for by now. They had a big presence on the coast in stolen fuel, "persuading" independent stations to sell it. Not only that, they were renowned for imaginative executions. But even they stayed downwind from Big Oil.

"Yup, Russkies won't mess with Chevron. Leads?"

"Almost nothing. February fourteenth. Huge storm rolling in at midnight, biggest in years, so the killer knew it was time to pull the trigger. Bartender at the 602 said this guy stood Sneezy some beers, left maybe ten. Sneezy staggered out ten minutes later."

"This *guy*? Now *that's* helpful. I'll get right on it."

Grady shrugged an apology. "Place is pitch dark so the losers don't scare each other. Bartender was right pickled himself."

Clem grunted, then paused suspiciously. "Umm . . . Grady, this isn't a gay vic deal, right?" Often the outlanders called in San Francisco Homicide if they thought they had a homosexual crime of passion because they thought of SFPD as a fount of knowledge on the subject. They were indeed, but tried to keep it secret, because it usually meant a week crawling leather bars and illicit bathhouses, duty even the most voyeuristic Vice cops sniffed at.

Grady gave him a sly grin. "Now Clem, would I do that to you?"

"In a heartbeat."

Grady shook his head. "Card-carrying pussyhound, regular at the strips."

"Okay, so how's this involve me?"

"Well, aside from the second opinion, tox is hinky. Mild dose of something called *Burundanga*, weird Colombian import."

Clem pondered. Probably available if you wanted it bad enough, but only from dealers with direct connections to the cartels. A scopolamine powder derived from a jungle shrub, it induced an amnesiac trance like the onset high of the date rape drug Rohypnol, but without the knockout punch. Not popular for date rape, since the vic stayed conscious. But downright nifty if you wanted to inveigle someone somewhere and tear him to pieces.

Clem replied, "Not a grape-picker high, designer stuff. Buyer had to have connections in the city, maybe someone who owed him a favor. Probably had to order in advance. And do his homework; it takes practice. I'll run it by Narcotics. You called him Sneezy? Like the dwarf?"

Grady grinned. "High school. According to legend, whenever he'd get horny, he'd have a sneezing fit. Some cheerleader he was bonking saddled him with it. Stuck to him his whole life like a genital wart. So, inspirations?"

Clem pursed his lips. "Guy have a butler?"

Grady leafed through his notepad and shook his head.

Clem continued. "Well, he sure burned *somebody's* toast to get himself torn in half."

Grady nodded. "Shit, that was the easy part. Died in seconds from blood loss. But he was here for hours, tubs slowly filling with water, increasing the pressure on his backbone. His vertebrae started cracking like walnuts. Coroner got to eighty-six fractures and lost count. Looked like someone worked over his spine with a hammer. Hands bound behind his back with razor wire, arms near tore out of the sockets. He wasn't gagged or taped, had to be screaming in the storm for hours."

Clem's brow knotted in confusion. "Razor wire? Why . . . *Jesus*." His saliva salted up.

Grady nodded gravely. "So he'd bleed nice and slow."

"To fetch the pigs," Clem gasped. "They'd have smelled him when it wasn't raining. What a ghoul. FBI give you anything? Similar MO?"

Grady chuckled. "Squat, 'less you go back like three hundred years."

Clem raised both eyebrows.

"Some Indian pooh-bah in the seventeen hundreds executed criminals the exact same way," Grady continued. "Saved up all his slimeballs 'til the monsoon, strapped 'em all in the trees on this hill same time, like fifty of 'em, then rolled out the bleachers. Rajashtan's own P. T. Barnum."

Clem nodded. "Sure he plagiarized? Could be coincidence."

"Well, there was this sign nailed on the tree, written in that Indian curlicue shit. So first I thought some Hindu ritual killing—*Temple of Doom* stuff—but Feebies said it was written by someone wasn't a native speaker. Grammar was a little off, like he'd worked it up from a textbook."

"Huh. So what did it say?"

Grady spouted some Indian-sounding gibberish.

Clem shot him an impatient scowl. "In English, fuckhead."

Grady gave him a bone-dry smile. "Loosely rendered, 'I'm siiiingin' in the rain.'"

Two hours later, Clem absently bulled through San Francisco's traffic, piecing together the fearsome crime.

The killer had gone to the grove ahead of time. Screwed in the pulleys and hitched up the tubs to the ropes, so all that remained was to fetch and string up the unsuspecting Sneezy. No problem there because of the *Burundanga*. Bogotá's street scum had learned you could dose a mark's beer, and he'd walk off to an ATM with you and hand over his pesos with a shit-eating grin.

He'd done a good job with the dosage. Too much and the vic would be insensate, which took all the fun out of a torture-murder. He'd given Sneezy enough to make him pliable, but not so he'd miss one iota of his gruesome demise. Clem couldn't help but wince. Perhaps the world's leading authority on scopolamine had been Dr. Josef Mengele, who'd been fascinated by the drug's unique ability to subvert the will. He'd supposedly conducted concentration camp experiments to see if parents would kill their own children on command.

The ritual savagery implied a fearsome motive—Sneezy had deeply wronged his killer—but Clem had learned to isolate himself from the hideous veneer of the crime and focus on what bothered him as a cop. And one thing that bothered him was placement of the crime scene. There were several giant oaks within a fifty-yard radius of the CS. Why pick the one closest to the trail and the road and let him howl at the moon? Maybe to tantalize Sneezy with visions of rescue. But if the guy hated him enough to turn him into pig slop, why risk it? As if the killer had some second agenda that had nothing to do with Sneezy.

The killer hadn't hung around for the finale. That would've negated cutting the wrists with razor wire to summon the pigs. They were shy and wily, and wouldn't have approached Sneezy with the killer sitting there. So he'd trussed up Sneezy, maybe had his gloatfest awhile, and then taken off. Probably waited for him to show up on the news the next day. It implied psychopathic sangfroid clean off the charts. He made a mental note to pop Grady an email.

But what troubled him most was something he'd never breathe a word about. Any cop with serious street time had bad dreams. While most never talked about them, Clem dealt with his by making his gargantuan crawlies a cop-bar legend. But all too often, full of inexplicable dread, he dreamed of being drawn by some infernal magnetism down endless spiral staircases of dank, slippery stone dimly lit by cobwebbed, wire-caged bulbs. Finally, he would reach the maw of a labyrinth far beneath the city's subways and sewers, a place terrifying in its silence because even the rats knew better than to venture there.

And he usually stumbled about in lifeless gloom until his subconscious released him to wakefulness. But maybe once a year, he would see the faintest glimmer in some distant cavern, hear the rhythmical pounding of iron on iron, smell the stench of rotting flesh. And then, he would come face-to-face with his most fearsome, yet blackly compelling, nightmare.

In the dark of the city's deepest bowels, a hellish locomotive thing clanked and rumbled down rusted tracks through leagues of tunnels. Its purposes were unknowable to God, its pistons fired through some fiendish combustion by the blood of the slaughtered. At the machine's stern, a hopper belched out bales of gore, accompanied by hollow blasts of a steam whistle. On their clotted surfaces, maggots writhed through fingernails, cartilage, bone chips, and shrunken eyeballs rolling in anguish. Bloodless lips full of fractured teeth twisted in silent screams. Atop the vampiric contraption a tangle of sinuous tubes vanished into dizzying dark. They whipped like tentacles as they sucked down a sludge of flesh, blood and bone, bathed in sickly green light from a row of ornate iron lamps swinging to and fro on stanchions on the behemoth's flanks. Putrescence spurted from beneath the black monster as its wheels heaved and strained, leaving a glistening pool of corruption in its wake. Huge, iridescent bubbles slowly rose from the thick liquid and burst with viscous spatters. Runes like nests of snakes adorned the machine's black metal from stem to stern, a calligraphy so monstrous that its translator would surely be felled into madness.

The Engine. The sons of Cain served it since the days when the city had no civic purpose but to relieve miners of their hard-won gold: the days of the waterfront's Sydney-Town, teeming with parolees from the penal colony of Australia, a square-mile Gomorrah of flophouses, rotgut saloons, and brothels touting live sex shows at a time when New York thought the waltz the height of scandal. A place where churches were banned as a public nuisance, where side streets doubled as toilets or trysting spots. And where, if you tired of sampling the country's most alluring children and potent opiates, you could work your way through rutted streets to watch Dirty Tom MacAlear eat anything placed in front of him for a penny. And where wagon crews passed from one prostrate body to the next, sorting out the living from the dead.

To this day, violent death usually had the banal undertones of yesteryear: grease on the wheels of the city's commerce of drugs, gambling, and lust; an instant's rage fanned into decades of regret by a fog of alcohol; infatuation and hope forged by years of slights into the gruesome intricacies of Murder One.

But what Clem had witnessed in the oak grove was something else. There was rage, of course, and he'd seen plenty before. But here, the eruption was the barest glimpse of the titanic force beneath, like mile on cubic mile of rumbling magma. And more ominously, tempered with a ghoulish, scholarly panache he'd never experienced before: a flair for dealing death that transcended motive, eclipsing the bloody "in your face" stagings of serial killers who sought merely to shock and taunt. This man made a hideous art of slaughter, a compulsion that would not be quenched by a single kill, no matter how ingenious. And for reasons Clem didn't try to fathom, he had few doubts that San Francisco sat astride the killer's volcanic Ring of Fire.

He couldn't ask too many questions about a murder a hundred miles away without raising departmental eyebrows. He would watch the horizon, let mayhem seek him out. But he felt the throb of the ravenous Engine, distant and faint to be sure, but growing louder. And this man did not serve that Engine, but had an implacable hand at the throttle.

CHAPTER TWO

Just as Angie Strackan tidied up her desk to go to lunch, her cell phone trilled. Again the screen glared "Hound of Hell." She made a vampire cross at it but decided to answer. After all, it might be a cop, calling the numbers in Bernadette's phone to let everyone know she had just done a cannonball off the Golden Gate. Maybe a tourist had even caught it on video.

No such luck. The voice at the other end was like a sonic root canal. "Angie! I've been calling all morning! Well, did the Newsomes make that offer? I was *expecting* your call," Bernadette huffed, like a duchess dressing down a maidservant.

"Yes, Mrs. Kelso, it just now came in," Angie sighed into her phone. "$744,000, they almost met the ask." Her jaw tensed to deliver the kicker. "But they only want to pay ten percent down. Banks like to see twenty; it'll be hard for them to get the mortgage."

"Dammit! The house four doors down is a three bedroom, just like mine, and it just sold for a million! And in *cash* ferchrissakes! Just how is it *you* can't get me buyers like that?"

The greenish bile of two months under the Kelso regime rose in Angie's throat. "That house was *not* just like yours! I should know: the broker, Beth Kramnik, is my best friend! Mint condition, twelve-foot plaster ceilings, inlaid hardwood floors, walk-in fridge, the *works*."

She glanced down at the flyer that threatened a perjury charge. "Your appliances aren't 'antiques,' Mrs. Kelso, they're avocado dinosaurs. The striped wallpaper isn't 'stately,' we call it Neo-French Bordello. The lights flicker like a slasher movie. Christ, we can't even get *in* the garage because we can't get the *doors* open! Yet for some inexplicable reason you've concluded this is all my fault. So tell you what: I'll be *happy* to resign! *Happy happy happy!* I'll send you the papers today, in fact." She heard a ragged gasp, hoped it signaled an angina attack, and hung up.

Angie drove north to Union Street for lunch, chuckling at the wail of the phone in her bag. The only Realtor willing to replace her would be a tenderfoot desperate enough to take even the worst listing. Any more-seasoned broker knew that the place was accursed of God. At a light before Union, she fished out the phone, which was just starting another bout of whining.

"Umm . . . Angie? I've been calling and calling," Bernadette pouted. "Now, of *course* I could get another agent to sell that house in a New York minute. But it's messy changing horses in midstream, right? So let's just let cooler heads prevail." She paused hopefully, but Angie let her stew in her own clichés. "So," Bernadette finally croaked, "what should we do?"

Suddenly it was "we." She decided on a last hurrah. "Hmm. Probably this is the only offer we'll get; by now it's what we call 'stale.' So we should just go ahead with the offer, see how they do."

Bernadette sputtered, but relented. Angie continued. "One good thing is that the buyers want to do—and yes, *pay for*—the contracting inspection. They've accepted my suggestion to use Zack Devine. He can come today at four. The Newsomes'll be there, and you can follow along as Zack goes through the house." But only if I wire your jaw shut, she didn't throw in.

Angie cruised only ten minutes before snagging a parking space, handily outmaneuvering an indignant twenty-something and her equally indignant schnauzer. She entered the restaurant. Beth's call, it was a place festooned with Italian flag bunting. A forlorn glance at the blackboard menu next to the bar pegged it as one of those uniquely San Franciscan places that depended on their patrons' naïve passion for fusions of the most absurd sort. In this case it was Sicilian dishes heavy on tofu, curry, and glass noodles that would be pitched out the door of any eatery from Milan to Naples, accompanied by a hearty *va fangul.*

Beth, a spreading, silver-streaked Slavic blonde two years older than

Angie's forty-eight, windmill-waved from a tiny table mere inches from its neighbors. She looked annoyingly cheery.

Angie sat down, blew a strand of jet-black hair off her face, and scowled. "A million-dollar close? Lunch is on you."

"Great, I can spend every night clinking my Krugerrands in front of the TV," Beth moped, flaunting her ability to bend any conversation to her failures at serial Web dating.

Angie changed the subject. "Incidentally, I gave you a referral. A guy called me a week ago about Bernadette's house, wanted to make sure it wasn't a probate. I told him no, Bernadette's mother was the owner, but that she was moving up north to Booneville to live with Bernadette and she'd given Bernadette power of attorney. He asked if I knew an agent to handle the buy side; I gave him your name."

Beth shrugged. "Nothing here."

"Huh. I was *certain* he would call. He knew a lot about the place. Even asked if we'd managed to pry open the garage yet," Angie finished with a sardonic eye roll.

Beth grinned. "Perhaps you mentioned that your client files her teeth into little points?"

Angie averted her eyes. "He *did* ask why it was so overpriced. I might've muttered something unseemly about you-know-who. Honestly, I'm a little worried about Janine, Bernadette's mom. I met her three years back when I sold the house next door, and I've popped in on her a few times since. God, I sure wouldn't want Bernadette responsible for *my* welfare. She's probably at Costco pricing dog food as we speak. But get this: we got an offer!"

"You should be canonized. What's the catch?"

"Ten percent loan," replied Angie, crossing her eyes. "And Zack at four. The inspection will be a howler. Like the fuse box is so old, it's got Indian head pennies stuck in the sockets."

Three hours later Angie forlornly eyed this year's albatross, a down-at-the-heels, three-story, yellow Edwardian with a tiny front yard bordered by overgrown azaleas. She pulled into the narrow driveway up to the garage that formed the first floor. As with many San Francisco houses, it clung to the side of a hill six feet higher in the rear of the house than at the curb, placing the rear of the garage about six feet below ground.

She greeted the apprehensive Newsomes, Zack, and Bernadette, who was as upbeat as a car salesman touting the lot's über-clunker. Her bulk was stuffed in a dress whose seams had to be NASA-spec, making her look like a polyester-clad elephant seal. She worked as a manicurist in a backwoods beauty salon and had made catastrophic use of its employee discount. It looked like they'd permed her with chemicals banned by the Geneva Convention.

Zack, a short, swarthy Sicilian-Irish with a Fu Manchu mustache, began by circling the house, trailed by a conga line of observers. Bernadette hovered over his shoulder and gaped at every slander he heaped on her mother-of-all-jackpots: the yellow paint peeling off in strips; the rusted, leaf-stuffed drainpipes that hadn't drained anything in years; the web of cracks in the stucco that promised early retirement for a lucky contractor.

They now faced the impenetrable garage. In the kitchen, Zack took a rubber mallet and banged on the edges of the door down to the first-floor garage. It was binding at the bottom corner. He banged again, heaving against it. It held fast. He eyed it suspiciously, then hauled back and whacked it hard enough to splinter it into kindling. But it sprang open unscathed.

Zack galloped down into the cobwebbed dark and swept his flashlight across the garage. The oil-stained concrete floor was choked with the discards of decades: several bicycles, a prehistoric washing machine with hand wringer, a console TV that had tuned in on Joe McCarthy, stacks of cardboard boxes, an empty fish tank and stand suitable for a small dolphin.

He studied the rear wall and paused to examine two pipes sticking out of the planks under a window with a broken latch at eye level. Angie felt a twinge of dread. If Zack looked at anything for a while, it was not a good sign.

He clicked on his recorder. "The two steel half-inch pipes under the window may indicate the presence of an underground storage tank." Angie drew breath in horror. A UST.

Bernadette bosomed through the cobwebs. "What, what?" she gasped.

Zack eyed her with the practiced sympathy of a cardiologist. "Fifty years ago, most houses were heated with oil furnaces. The oil tank was often buried in the yard. It had a fill pipe sticking out of the ground for the oil truck and two underground pipes running inside the house to feed the furnace. That's what these are." He shined the light on them. "When the house switched to gas, the tank was often left in the ground. If it's there, you have to remove it before you can sell."

"*What?* Why ever would we have to take it out now? The damn thing's probably been sitting there like a coffin for fifty years! I used to play with my girlfriends up there!"

Angie was incredulous that the youthful Bernadette had any friends. Maybe she'd assembled a retinue of doll dismemberers. The backyard had probably witnessed the medieval-style execution of a dozen head-shaved Barbies.

Zack continued. "It could be a source of groundwater contamination. But let's just see if there's a tank or not."

They clomped up into the backyard. Zack jogged to his truck, hauled out a metal detector, and walked back to a patch of stubbly lawn behind the garage. As he scythed the detector disk five feet away from the wall, it beeped and stayed beeping. Angie winced as Zack droned, "Evidence of a UST, five feet long, three feet wide, parallel to the rear wall starting five feet from the wall."

Bernadette clawed Angie away from the somber crowd. "Okay, so I just need a couple of big, sweaty guys to dig it out, right? That's not so bad. Hell, I can get them up in Booneville for a hundred bucks and beer."

"I'm sorry, Mrs. Kelso, this is the worst thing you could've run into. You need to hire a certified UST contractor. They remove the tank and do soil borings. If there's contamination, they probably have to backhoe the yard."

Bernadette's facial blotches became livid. Her veins stood out and throbbed, as if she'd been afflicted with Ebola. "*And?* How *much?*"

"Umm . . . best case, say four thousand to pull the tank and do the tests. If the tank's leaked oil into the ground, more. A lot more." She paused. "Maybe twenty thousand."

Bernadette let out a spittle-laden shriek and waddled away, jumped in her car, and screeched off in a cloud of burned rubber. The Newsomes took this as a sign from the Almighty and were shortly on the lam. Angie and Zack filed back down the steps to conclude the now symbolic inspection. Zack set to work trying to haul up the frozen rollup garage door.

"It's binding on the frame," he said, beaming his flashlight on the wheels on the right door edge. Welded onto the frame, up against the top wheel, was a slug of steel that blocked it from moving.

Zack shook his head. "Someone sure didn't want this door to open." He paused, looking perplexed. "You know, it was harder to bash open that kitchen door than any I've seen. Come here." He ran the flashlight beam over the steps, then picked up a wedge of wood an inch wide and pointed at the bottom right corner of the door. The wood was compressed upwards.

Zack cocked an eyebrow. "Someone hammered this shim in the door. He blocked access to the garage from the kitchen."

Angie felt her bladder tighten. "So the only way in here was the window at the back wall. The latch is broken."

"Huh. And almost everywhere there's gazillions of cobwebs. But here at the rear wall, just a few. Like someone's been here recently."

"He could've blocked off the garage for years. Looks like the Maurys only came down once a decade to dump stuff."

"Another weird thing." He walked to the left side of the rear wall and pointed out a new-looking piece of plywood. It was just above the foundation at mid-calf, two and a half feet square, tightly fit into the wall between two vertical posts. "This was half-hidden by a stack of boxes. I'd normally say it was done to replace dry rot and wouldn't give it a second look. But now that I'm wondering why someone would lurk around the garage, I'm sure there was no dry rot here." The planks surrounding the plywood were unmarred by telltale water damage.

She nodded. "And strange, it hasn't been nailed in place." She plucked a screwdriver from Zack's belt, stuck the blade between the top of the panel and the plank, and pried the square out.

And gasped in shock and trepidation. Zack's flashlight beamed into the dark of a tunnel shaft made of new-looking plywood extending far under the backyard. The fecund smell of wet earth obliterated the musty odor of a moment before.

"Wow," exclaimed Angie in nervous awe. "I don't think that's supposed to be there."

Zack gave a low whistle, bent, and crawled in. His voice muffled back. "Maybe eight feet deep, then it turns right. But I can't see around the corner." He scrambled out and stood up. "It's not safe. There's two or three feet of lawn dirt sitting on top of it, and some of the roof pieces are bowed. Maybe strained by everyone standing around out there. What I'd like to do is come back tomorrow and shore up the roof. You free at two?"

She nodded. "Just tossing this out there, Zack, but if the tunnel turns to the right at the back, it would probably intersect the UST."

Zack nodded back grimly. "And I'm not sure I want to find out why."

She picked up the panel and began fitting it back in the space. The idea of leaving the tunnel uncovered gave her the creeps, as if whatever was in there might decide to skulk around the garage after they left. But her heart suddenly thudded in her chest.

"Zack. When I pried out the panel, the screwdriver made a mark on the top edge where it bit into the wood. But Jesus. Look at this."

The edge of the plywood was marred with dozens of identical marks.

CHAPTER THREE

Angie awoke to the pink glare of the late-morning sun raking her eyelids through the open drapes, and numbly debated rolling over and risking a napalm migraine. She finally threw herself into the shadows, exhaling in relief as the pain failed to show up. She gingerly unglued an eyelid; the digital clock on the night table glared "11:48" in disapproval. The details of last night's misadventure at her North Beach haunt, Twister, were obscured by alcoholic murk. They stayed that way as her thoughts flew to the ominous tunnel shaft awaiting her. Moments later, she soaped up in the glass shower stall, unable to sponge off the tacky mental residue she always tangled with—at once sensually pleasurable and morally discomfiting—after one of her occasional carnal outings. Terry-robed and sanitized, she entered the living room and switched off the Nat King Cole on endless repeat from the night before. She picked up two half-full tumblers of stale Vodka Collins from the coffee table and carried them to the sink at arm's length to avoid a catastrophic morning-after whiff. Finally, she settled down to defog with her Arabica at the hand-hewn oak table, one of the highlights of the rustic Italian Provincial kitchen that was the pride and joy of the house.

Just before two, she drove to the Maury house to meet Zack, and found a space right in front. Its windows seemed to glower down at her forbiddingly. No matter how many shimmering diamonds and gold ingots she tried to envision, no one could've crawled into that tunnel shaft dozens of times for any but the worst reasons.

She fidgeted in her car, half noticing a white Volvo sedan and its graying matron breezing by, followed by two helmeted bicycle racers. Then a dark blue Toyota hatchback slowed. Its blond, thirtyish driver eyed her quizzically through his glasses before driving on. He stopped again and peered back at her before turning a corner. She grinned at his "Neighborhood Watch" bumper sticker. He probably thought she was casing the place, unaware that it was entirely empty.

With that, Zack's pickup loomed in her rearview. Two flashlights were soon beaming their ghostly way to the back wall of the garage. Zack wedged out the plywood and crawled in, ratcheted up a house jack, then wormed past it. He installed another jack at the end of the tunnel where it turned right.

His voice echoed from inside. "I can see the tank now. But something's really weird." She heard the last jack go in, then a muffled grunt. Two stained workboots appeared, followed by a twisting torso and Zack's sweat-beaded face. "Bad news: I can't get to the tank. The last jack's in the only safe place, and I'm too big. I hate to do this, but you'll have to give it a whirl."

Her throat tightened. "Ulp and double ulp. So what's really weird?"

"Well, I've seen my share of these tanks. They're cylinders, rounded at the ends like a Tylenol capsule. At the end of the tunnel, you can see the face of the tank. But it isn't rounded. It's a big, flat disk, like the bottom of a soup can lying on its side. The bottom half of the face is new steel." Zack hesitated. "And the upper half is Plexiglas, something see-through."

Angie's voice thickened. "To view something inside. Christ, you'd think I'd have learned to stay out of garages." Zack went wide-eyed at her allusion to the terrible events of twenty-two years before, but said nothing.

Anxiety rumbled as Angie elbowed past the first jack, heaved around the corner and flipped the light towards the tank. A bulbous spider scrambled for the shadows. The front face sat forbiddingly five feet away, a circle more than two feet in diameter. The lower half was a shiny steel sheet labeled with faint black stencils, the upper darkly transparent.

As she hauled her hips past the second jack, an unnerving aroma joined those of damp plywood and earth: a raw chemical reek that cloyed from the distant past. She shoved her upper body past the last jack, banging the flashlight on the wall. It dimmed threateningly. She shook it vainly, and as it beamed straight up for the first time, she realized with looming dread that the roof of the last several feet of the tunnel was splashed with bright colors. But crawling on her stomach, she couldn't take it in.

She twisted painfully onto her back. To her shock, her focus resolved on a collage of five fearsome images not two feet from her face. All were of a young woman in pyres of flame, done in crusty artist oils with van Gogh whorls of garish yellow, orange, and red. Three were portraits: a face wracked with anguish, flames licking at her smoldering, blackened cheeks and long blond hair. The eyes, nostrils, and mouths were a *trompe l'oeil* of ragged, gaping holes that gave the sensation of staring through them into a universe stripped of stars.

But the two full-body paintings transfixed her in horror. In one, the woman sat on a chair, head thrown back and flames vomiting from her crimson mouth like a fire-eater. The second was straight out of the hellish visions of Hieronymus Bosch: a face twisted into terror, a naked torso mangled, burned, and bloody. But truly harrowing were her limbs, or what passed for them: her arms and legs seemed to be huge smoking balls of flesh at her shoulders and hips, with charred, skeletal hands and feet protruding like mangled flippers.

Angie battled back the impulse to scuttle out of the tunnel and twisted onto her stomach. Grimly certain that what awaited her was the blackened corpse of the woman in the mural, she wriggled past the last jack. The chemical stench engulfed her, stinging her nostrils. Her lips tingled as she wrenched higher, bumping into the steel tank with an elbow.

As the metallic echo faded, she brought her watery eyes level with the window. Viscous wavelets lapped near the top, the tank filled with a liquid so vile that even a child would know one sip meant death. She fought off visions of it giving way, of torrents of caustic fluid melting her into twitching red ooze. Then she breathed a prayer and pierced the interior with the flashlight.

At first, nothing, as if the wobbly beam were trying to penetrate a coal-black fog.

Then she drew breath. Inch by inch, a pair of silver-sandaled, pink-nailed feet materialized on the floor in the center of the tank. Slowly, they attached themselves to tiny, fine-boned ankles and calves, then to a gown of filmy white silk and sparkly golden sash. Delicate fingers and painted nails entwined in a lap, one finger with a silver ring, another with a gold. Finally, shards of light danced about the features of a wondrous little angel, obscured by tendrils of blond hair floating in a translucent liquid, haloing her high forehead and shoulders. The small of her back rested on an embroidered pillow against the curved rear wall five feet from Angie's face. Her eyes were closed, her brow unfurrowed, her face a mask of dimpled repose.

For an instant, nothing clicked. And then, her olfactory nerves spliced with a dim memory.

High school biology. Formaldehyde. Frogs. Fetal pigs.

Dead flesh. In big steel vats.

She stared petrified as the tresses settled on the girl's shoulders, unveiling her face in the beam. The face seemed to glimmer dimly of its own, giving a lifelike tint to her stony pallor. Angie tried to wrench the light away in fright, to no avail, as if someone had pulled the fuse on her neurons.

Realizing she had stopped breathing, she sucked in a chestful of poison fumes, bringing on a wave of vertigo. Her ears muffled, but then she began to hear mumbles like the echoes of madmen in a hall of dank cells. The face seemed to float in the blackness, throbbing larger and smaller with the cadence of a heartbeat. The features furrowed with the disquiet of nightmare, as if the lids were seconds away from snapping open, unveiling a soul emptied of all but betrayal and madness.

The black void yawned in front of her, stretching into catacombs under the earth. And suddenly, as if beckoned from its lair, another presence loomed, silent and formless. The air crackled with static needles. She felt herself reeled inward, as if she were the victim of a monstrous turn of the tables, the girl fleeing to her stolen world of crayons and jump rope, leaving Angie to drown in the chemical grave. But finally, her fingers pried open, sending the flashlight crashing to the floor and plunging her into darkness.

She choked out a moan as she scrabbled backwards in the blackness. She kicked and clawed her way toward the tunnel opening, the haven that reason whispered was just around the corner but that her fear screamed was miles and miles away.

• • •

Angie flailed her feet out of the tunnel until Zack grasped her ankles and hauled her out. She staggered to a box and plunked down as clumsily as if she were in a suit of armor.

She drew a ragged breath. "Zack, there's a dead girl in there. She's preserved in some kind of fluid, dressed in a nightie. Blond, long hair, eight or nine. And there's this freaky mural of a burning woman on the ceiling."

Zack's face registered shock. "Mary Mother of God. I'm sorry, Angie." He paused. "Maybe natural causes?"

"No, she was murdered. It sounds flaky, but I felt *him* there. Her killer." She shuddered. "Anyway, I know a homicide inspector I bought a house for a while ago. Give me some light?"

Zack pointed the flashlight down at her purse on the box edge, and Angie took out her cell phone. She beat back nausea as memory of the little face loomed, locked her eyes on the screen and keyed in a Y. She'd known him for years, but it had been a while.

Four beeps and a harried "Yao here."

"Clem, it's Angie."

"Hey, great to hear from you! Look, can we talk later? It's a bad time."

She shook her head at the grim irony. "Clem, unless you're carting off vats of body parts, it's a worse time here."

Ten minutes later Clem's white unmarked tested brakes in the driveway. He got out, six gray worsted wool feet of salt-and-pepper buzz cut with a burly weightlifter's frame. His mottled skin was the color of burled walnut. He pocketed the shades he wore during bouts of insomnia, revealing almond eyes with bags like tiny squeezeboxes bracketing a broad, flat nose. His sleeplessness was a departmental legend. After a tough solve, he could often be found snoring in a supply closet he'd outfitted with a cot and a brace of CDs featuring waves, thunderstorms, and crickets, none of which anyone thought worthy of pilfering.

He introduced his uniformed ex-boss, the corpulent, mustachioed Captain Max Frazier, commander of the Sunset District's Taraval Station. Angie eyed them dubiously. Neither stood a chance of crawling to the tank, Clem with his bench-press pecs and Frazier given his obvious adherence to the traditional donut diet.

Frazier stared at her with curiosity. "Damn. Angie Dietrich, right?"

Angie smiled for the first time since she'd entered the tunnel. "Well, Strackan now. Dietrich's my maiden name. Do I know you?"

Frazier grinned back. "I've seen your pic on a cop-bar wall or two. It's still up in Joker's."

"That'd be me. Minus twenty two years of laugh lines."

"Your dad's Brett Dietrich, right? He doing okay? Good cop. Saved my bacon in his day."

"Doing fine. They're in San Diego now, retired."

"I know, I still talk to him like once a year. So a Realtor, huh?" Frazier's eyes twinkled. "Didn't Brett tell me you're a Weekend Warrior now?"

Angie's face burned. She managed to keep up a smile but knew it looked like Botox malpractice. Frazier hadn't touched a nerve; he'd bashed it with a claw hammer. After a criminology undergrad degree at the University of San Francisco, in 1986 she'd entered the San Francisco Police Force. Two months later, she was picking up the pieces of a ruined career, barely escaping prosecution in the city's most notorious police shooting.

She tried for the FBI and ATF, only to be told that they didn't have any slots for Dirty Harriet types. She sullenly drifted through several police-related McJobs before getting her Realtor's license. But at heart she was a third-generation San Francisco cop. She'd spent her youth hearing stories of her grandfather on her father's side, who'd reputedly gunned down looters as a press-ganged sixteen-year-old rookie in the wake of the great quake and fire of 1906.

Five years ago, she'd screwed up her courage and applied for the San Francisco Police Reserve. The program was something of a departmental joke. Most of the thirty unpaid reserve officers were cop wannabes who strutted around stadium events and parades showing off shiny new sidearms. They would be laughed out of any cop bar. But the old guard thought she'd gotten the worst possible rap, and had let her slip in the back door and inch her way into police work. She was now doing ten hours a week on routine uniform narcotics and vice patrols. Only Homicide—her Holy Grail—was off-limits. Clem had tried twice to push through a waiver for her without success.

She ushered them down to the garage, hoping it was the last she'd hear of her career debacle. "You guys can't get in there. You'll have to dig it out."

"Can't backhoe without verifying a crime scene," replied Clem. "I'll go in, we'll pull out the jacks. Tell my wife I love her."

"We can safe it up," interjected Zack. "We need to take some weight off the tunnel."

Frazier tapped Clem's shoulder. "There's some guys on the Taraval shit list who'd be happy to pick up a gold star. Get O'Shaunessey and Burford over here. They're at the precinct."

Twenty minutes later, Angie joined Zack in the yard as he marked the tunnel perimeter with red flags. Clem presented him with two disgruntled bluesuits toting shovels, and Zack set them to digging carefully downward. Angie sat on her haunches, tempted to break the somber mood with an "Alas, poor Morris" when one of them unearthed first the spine and then the complete skeleton of a long-buried pet cat, with name tag and phone number on its decomposing collar.

Half an hour later in the musty garage, Clem zipped into coveralls, pocketed a camera, and snapped on latex. His lips were a grim line, but he threw Angie a wink. "Y'know, Grandma told me that back before the '06 quake, everyone in San Francisco thought that underneath Chinatown was this huge maze of tunnels. They thought half the Chinese were lurking around underground doing inscrutable Chinese things. Then, after the quake leveled Chinatown, they excavated, and guess what? Not one lousy half-ass tunnel. Everyone was really disappointed."

He launched himself into the shaft. A series of clanks as he took down the jacks, then a whispered, stomach-churning "Holy shit . . . Holy, holy shit . . . " White flashes lit up the garage as he shot the crime scene and its macabre tenant. He backed out and stood up, then silently turned away from the group and faced into the shadows of the garage. He remained that way for the better part of a minute before turning back to them. Frazier eyed him questioningly.

Clem exhaled sharply in frustration. "I don't recognize her." He turned to Angie. "I'd know recent missings by sight. She's from way out of town or a long way back. I'd normally like the owner for it, but he died of emphysema a few months back, right?"

Angie nodded. "Emil Maury, Janine's husband. He was eighty-four. On oxygen for three years."

Clem shook his head. "And pretty frail for years before that. Even serial psychopaths take up shuffleboard by sixty. And he wouldn't set it up so he had to crawl through the window. That was so someone else could sneak in."

"So they rented out a few years back, or had someone housesit," replied Angie. "He had to be here by himself a while to build it. A month or more." She recalled a tedious afternoon when Janine had pulled out her photo albums. "Funny, the Maurys had lots of recent pictures from New Mexico. Way more than you'd get from a week in Santa Fe. Maybe they wintered there."

Clem nodded thoughtfully, then eyed Zack. "One thing I did conclude was that I'd love some help from you at the crime scene tomorrow morning. This one's boutique. Can't sign you up as a forensic. But assuming your city inspector's license is current, I'll have Captain Frazier here trump up a roof leak emergency at Taraval. Say fifty an hour for five hours."

Frazier gritted his teeth with amused forbearance at the assault on his maintenance budget, but Zack had spent twenty years crawling around the underbellies of the city's legendary housing stock. He could deduce in seconds what a crime lab might take days to conclude. Angie couldn't help a stab of jealousy that Zack had been asked to sidesaddle a homicide case.

Clem's lips twisted into a flummoxed expression. "How did the killer even know the tank was there? I sure wouldn't have."

Zack replied, "Years back, there was a panic after the city said you couldn't sell your house without pulling the tank. Lots of stuff in the news on how to see if your house had one. For a while, I did a hundred backyards a year with my metal detector. He probably rummaged through the garage after he moved in, realized the tank might be there because of the pipes, same way I did. And this wasn't a union job, so he had construction experience."

Clem flicked a spider off his coveralls as he pondered. "Easy to visit secretly after he moved out. He knew the owners were in their eighties, that they hadn't been down here in years, so he blocked off the doors so he couldn't be surprised. No car, and the old guy could barely get to the toilet, never mind putter around the garage."

Angie nodded. "And he knew nobody'd done any maintenance on the house for like three decades. When I asked Janine why we couldn't get into the garage, she just shrugged." A shiver coursed her lower back. "God, I hope he hasn't done a bunch of these."

Clem replied, "Let's hope not, but my first take isn't serial, at least not an exact replica. You can't just move into another house with a UST. And he's been here within the last month or so. All those visits could mean this one gave him all the jollies he needed."

Angie shuddered. "Of course, no telling what'll happen now that he can't pop in for a viewing."

She took Clem to the corner by the huge aquarium, away from Zack and Frazier. Her voice almost a whisper, she asked, "Clem, this is homicide, right? Looks like there's not a mark on her, but this guy's brain waves would fry a Geiger counter."

Clem shrugged. "Yeah. Least I'm pretty sure."

"Did you feel it? *Him*? I almost peed myself. And that mural . . . "

"Like the guy's right there flipping you the bird?"

Angie nodded slowly.

Clem continued, "Most people can see a crack dealer with an ice pick in his head and find a way to deal with it. Even if it's way nasty, things like motive aren't hard to grasp. But you see a freak's calling card in the flesh, it blows your house down like the big bad wolf. You're sucked into this black hole he's conjured, where you can't recognize any morality or logic. He probably has his own, but it's like looking at yours in a fun-house mirror. The image rolls around in your head like a marble for years."

"Because some part of you is desperate to understand why, so the world makes some kind of sense," Angie added.

"And you may never have that answer," replied Clem. "He may be un-moved watching someone beat a kid to death, yet go postal at the sight of visible panty lines."

"Back in '86, it took me five years before I could look at a girl without thinking of The Beast. And now it's like I'm starting all over again with *this* guy."

"He'd probably like that just fine." He sighed heavily. "Anyway, tomor-row morning the Crime Scene Unit'll be here with oodles of yellow tape.

You won't be showing the place for a few days."

Angie dredged up a sick smile. "Only twenty years and a dog kennel shall rise on this very spot. I guess I should tell Bernadette."

Clem turned to Frazier. "CSU'll have techs here later to drill in and get a sample for hazmat procedures. Gangster turkey shoot just went down in the Mission, so night shift dance card's full. I don't think she's going anywhere; we'll post a guard. Burford?" The backyard digger was still on the Taraval shit list despite his extra gold star.

"Yeah. And tell him to keep an eye out for a machete-wielding cop killer."

"Zack, tomorrow at six? First day's biggest for evidence. After that things get clodhoppered."

Zack nodded. "I assume there will be coffee."

"Not strictly speaking. Reconstruct how he did it before they take it apart. Hammers he used, glue, welding rod, anything recognizable. Check in with Jojo Locsin, I'll be by after I issue statements and stifle collateral damage from City Hall. Times like this, our elected boneheads tend to shit in their beds and kick it out barefoot."

Angie grinned. The eleven members of the Board of Supervisors worked for peanuts, but wielded enormous power, and often hamstrung city operations with turf wars and inane proclamations. One Supe likened it to having twelve mayors. The left wing took special joy in finding ways to pillory the Police Department, with or without cause.

Clem continued, "We'll get an autopsy by nightfall. Let's plan a follow-up for Friday, 11:00 a.m. at the Taraval precinct in Sunset. Better ambience than the Hall of Justice downtown, and I'd rather keep my distance. Once the story hits the streets—and I give it fifteen minutes at the outside—I'll be getting calls from half the tipsters and TV stations in the state."

Angie walked Frazier up the stairs to the kitchen. "Why don't you drop by tomorrow?" he asked. "Say nine. I'll wangle you a pass. Ask for Jojo." He answered her quizzical look with a thin, inscrutable smile. "Just in case any questions come up."

CHAPTER FOUR

Thursday, May 15th

After a night in which the faces of a dozen dead girls loomed in her sub-conscious, Angie reached the crime scene at nine. A blanket of ocean mist blanched the lemon-yellow house into sallow watercolor. Four cranky uniforms held back a crowd of gawkers behind a wall of yellow tape. Three TV vans and satellite gear half-blocked the narrow street lined with twisted, ancient acacias. An anchorwoman primped for her take. Another blue van belonged to the Medical Examiner. Angie's flesh crawled at the sight of her name on the "for sale" sign. No telling how many calls from the press awaited her at the office. A young bluesuit gave her a well-rehearsed stare of intimidation until she gave him her name and asked for Jojo Locsin.

He glanced up curiously at the sign, disappeared and returned, handed her a clip-on badge, and said gruffly, "You break it, you bought it." She deflected a brace of microphones and headed for the back, admitting to a tinge of smugness as the uniform stiff-armed a reporter trying to trail her.

She spotted Clem and Zack on their knees at the edge of the trench. The bluesuit pointed out a thirtyish, lithe-looking man in a shabby brown tweed sport coat, with deep copper skin, longish black hair, and gold wire-rims. He was talking to a tech in hazmats. Under a cloak of fatigue, his features were a pleasing mélange of Latino and South Pacific. He glanced at her clip-on and gave her an expression of half-recognition she knew well from her nights at Twister.

"Hey, don't I know you?"

"Angie Strackan. Wait . . . my Homicide module in the Reserve program, right? Three years back?" She'd attended specialized Police Academy courses to qualify for her Level 1 Reserve status, allowing her to work Investigations.

"Right and right." He salvaged a weak grin. Clem slouched over and gave them a ragged salute. Jojo tipped a nonexistent hat. "Clem, meet the only person from the Reserves who asked if she could case a fresh homicide CS."

"My astonishment knows no bounds. Something with some nifty spatter patterns?"

"I ran it past Jackson, got the idiot-for-asking look." Washington Irving Jackson was chief of the Investigations Division, which oversaw Homicide, Narcotics, Vice, and other specialized units of the Department. A black thirty-year man, he'd been "mysteriously" assigned for most of his career to neighborhoods of color like the Western Addition, much as Clem happened to spend decades in Chinatown and its Han offshoots.

"Well, there you go," Clem said. "She rolled her own. Angie, my sometime partner and favorite flunkey, Division's token Filipino. Whatever you do, don't let him pick restaurants. Jojo, I've been trying to sneak Angie into Homicide for two years. Why don't you give her the cook's tour? Strip club rules: lookee no touchee."

Angie wondered why she was being allowed a tour of an active homicide crime scene. Not that anyone would question her presence. After all, she'd found the body and knew more about the history of the house than anyone in the city. She'd known Clem and his wife, Grace, for three years, going back to their house-hunting days. He was one of the many cops who came to her with his business even decades after the shooting. He'd graced her with several dozen seamy war stories. But he'd never discussed an active case, and she'd never tried to plug herself into one, not wanting to risk her tenuous climb up the Police Reserve ladder.

As Jojo walked her to the trench, the formaldehyde reek rose up in waves. The tank was encrusted with clods of dirt and blackened with age, with red rust spots blossoming from the ancient steel like running sores. A pipe stuck up from the center, suggestive of a one-man submarine. A masked welder worked at the tank face with a blowtorch. She was jarred by the bizarre change in perspective, looking down into the place where she'd been petrified with claustrophobic terror.

Jojo pointed to the blowtorch man. "He's almost done. Then straight to the morgue, nothing in situ. We want her in a controlled environment. Fluid's already drained. Recent pinhole leak where the Plexiglas met the steel, thus the fumes in the tunnel."

Her heart sank as two men wheeled up a gurney. She distracted herself with less visceral evidence. "What did you get off the plywood?"

"Magnifying glass stuff, microscopics later. He removed the cover at least twenty-five times. Of course, he was probably in there a lot more than that while he was living here—didn't need to keep the cover on. From wood fungal activity on the screwdriver marks, most of the visits were a while back. Only two within say the last six months."

Zack trudged up, and Jojo turned to him. "How's the reconstruction?"

"Getting there. First thing he would've done was see if it was usable." Zack pointed out the new welding on the rusting fill pipe. "When they switched to gas years ago, the fill pipe was sawed off and capped under the lawn. So he dug down, found the pipe, sawed it off, and checked inside. In olden days, if they left the tank in, they filled it with cement or sand. If it'd been cement, he couldn't have used it."

So an innocuous decision by a contractor maybe fifty years ago had led to the crime scene's creation. Angie's bowels churned at the thought that she'd driven by a dozen times right while it was happening, chattering on her cell or checking her mascara in the rearview.

"Then he started digging," Zack continued. "Would've taken months if he went underground from the house to the tank, like a prison break. So he dug a trench in the yard, maybe late at night." He walked them over to the stack of plywood. "He removed the old tank face, emptied the sand, laid in the plywood and put the dirt back. Tongue and groove, no nails, no noise. Marine grade, used for boat hulls. Covered it with waterproof tar paper and roofing cement. He put her embalmed body in the tank, then welded steel to the bottom and put in the window. Then filled the tank through the fill pipe and welded it shut. Maybe four weeks full time, not counting the mural."

Angie heard a clank, looked down and turned away. The circular tank face had fallen off, revealing two tiny sandaled feet inside. She moved a few steps to edge the frightful image out of view.

Jojo stepped next to her with a quizzical look, then looked down and nodded as he realized why she'd moved. "We think he embalmed her first in the huge aquarium in the garage, to keep her from decomposing while he worked on the tank. Probably bought it to do the embalming, then kept her in there in fluid until the underground tank was ready. It's brand new, never used. Well, almost never," he added with a grimace.

Angie's gut wrenched at the image of the little girl floating in a fish tank in the gloom while the killer coolly tinkered away.

Jojo continued, "And anyone with a fish tank that big has to be an addict. You'd see other stuff around: air pumps, goofy tank decorations, colored gravel. But there's nothing else there."

A CSU technician kneeled at the tank opening, muttered "Jesus H. Christ," and shot some photos. He nodded gravely at the two burly men with the gurney. As they climbed down with a stretcher, Angie's stomach pleaded with her to get in her car, now. But her feet were riveted to the spot, as if justice demanded that a mother be there to help carry the burden of grief. Angie's only child, her daughter, Jackie, had safely made it to twenty-two. But she briefly let herself imagine pulling her own dead little girl from a vat of stinking chemicals. She fought off the dizzying vision as the men reached into the tank, grasped the girl's ankles, and slid her out.

She was no longer the little angel of first glance. Her bedraggled, matted hair cascaded over her shoulders and face. The white nightie clung obscenely to her frail form. Her skin was not the ivory-hued marble of Angie's chemical delusion, but like rubbery gray potter's clay mottled with greasy, puckered, yellowish wax. Her dimples looked like they'd been acid-etched on her face.

Angie fought back a torrent of rage. The girl's torso was locked in the sitting position she'd been in for who knew how many years. As they adjusted her, her jaw suddenly gaped open, contorting her face into an expression of unfathomable suffering. A mouthful of fluid dribbled down her gown like limpid vomit. One man stood up, leaned over and spat thickly, then kneeled again at the girl's side.

A deputy medical examiner nodded, and they held her legs down, pushed against her shoulders, and tried to lever her prone. But she resisted, as if unwilling to surrender for her trip to the steel table. Angie winced as the girl's vertebrae gave up with an ugly, viscous snap, and they lifted her out. By this time, Clem, Jojo, Zack, and the others had gathered around the trench, the grizzled group wiping at eyes and blinking back tears.

It felt like a funeral. But perversely backwards.

Angie fought back the sensation that her skin had just been scalded off and decided to head for the office to lose herself in some realty. Jojo and Clem silently walked her past the yellow barrier, then the two blocks to her car. As she fumbled for her keys, she saw Frazier bring up the rear. All three were wearing sheepish expressions. Something was coming.

Clem glanced here and there, shifting his weight from one foot to another like a teen working up to a first kiss. "Umm . . . you busy today?" he finally asked.

"About to be. What's with the hangdog looks?"

"You call Bernadette yet?"

Angie rolled her eyes. "I've been avoiding it. She'll go off like Krakatoa."

Clem pursed his lips into a grandma-kiss pucker. "Actually, you can tell her in person. Look, I need a favor. If you can, go up to Booneville and talk to her mom; see if they rented. She's known you a while, and old people respond more readily to someone they know. And it sounds stupid, but Jojo and I need to be within city limits the next two days while they power up the shit pumps at City Hall. It wouldn't do for word to get out that I was gallivanting around the Wine Country right now, police business or not."

Angie couldn't help a thin smile. The city's twenty homicide inspectors had the worst solve rate of any major city in the country. A front-page scandal had just erupted over inspectors starting vacations a day or two after taking a case.

Clem continued. "Of course, you're not Homicide, so anything you get would be hearsay. But right now I don't need a legit statement; I can get it later. I just need to know who to look for. And you need to tell her about the girl in the tank. She'll be a lot more attentive that way."

The thought of being the one to break the news to Janine plowed a furrow through her guts. She finally looked at him askance. "And your il-lustrious colleagues?"

He stifled a smirk. "On the next boat over, drinking piña coladas and watching me bail."

It sank in. Unlike most cities, where young bucks swarmed a challeng-ing case seeking glory, in San Francisco they usually punted, the upshot of the nation's most musclebound police union. Seniority governed promo-tions with an iron fist. Clem often ducked inept colleagues and shoehorned journalists, lawyers, scientists, doctors, and savvy ex-cons into his cases. It cost him occasional ruler raps from Jackson, Clem's main cop-bar buddy for two decades. But Clem's solve rate was twenty points above Division norm, on a par even with Giuliani's NYPD thoroughbreds of yore, and Jackson wasn't about to mess with it too much.

She poked his chest with her finger. "Clem, Homicide's *verboten* for Reserves. I'm not even allowed to type a statement. The union doesn't want any of us working high pay grade slots. And I'm already on the ball courts this month." Routine patdowns for crack vials and baggies. Penny ante deal-ers did much of their business at basketball courts.

"Umm . . . no, you're not. You're Taraval Station, effective today. Some-body or other put in a special request."

Angie started.

"Don't freak, we got your back," Clem continued. "Frazier's up for chief. He can handle any blowback."

She glared at Frazier, his face by now as rouged as a Dodge City dancing girl's. He was in cahoots with Clem. "Clem, the union'll flame-broil me like a Whopper. And you with me."

Clem's face sagged haggardly. "Look at that crime scene, Angie. I'll need a frigging brain trust to get a solve, and most of my colleagues could spend an hour on a childproof cap. And you and I are the only people in this whole department who've come within spitting distance of a card-carrying psycho." He gave her a sidelong, hopeful glance. "And that way, you can come to the case conference at Taraval Station tomorrow. Should be interesting."

She rolled her eyes in acquiescence. It *would* be interesting and prob-ably as close as she'd ever get to working Homicide. Admittedly, it was like the difference between strutting the Bulgari catwalk and doing cheesecake for an auto parts calendar, but sometimes you couldn't fight karma.

Three hours later, Angie was driving the mountain road to Bernadette's house, reflecting on her defunct listing. Two months before, Janine had asked Angie to sell her house after losing her husband, Emil. At the house to draw up the papers, Angie met Janine's only child, Mrs. Bernadette Kelso. She ended up wondering if DNA testing might be in order to prove Janine hadn't been the victim of a disastrous neonatal switcheroo. Where Janine was soft-spoken, Bernadette's voice could grind meat. Where Janine listened politely, Bernadette usually began her sentences in the middle of someone else's. Worse yet, where Janine was a paragon of hygiene, Bernadette often exuded an odor fearsome enough to put a bloodhound into a coma; it was as if she'd coated herself with sink trap grease. That she had ever succeeded in landing a husband was testament to the maxim that there was someone for everyone. Then again, Angie had never met him; he sold auto detailing supplies and was apparently on 98 percent travel.

Although a power-of-attorney Gold Rush was probably on at Janine's expense, Angie decided just to get the place sold and have done. But it was not to be. Angie wanted to price at six fifty to get a brace of competing buyers. But Bernadette smugly showed Angie "comps" for similar houses selling in the low eights. Angie observed that this was for inhabitable properties, drawing daggers from Bernadette that promised weeks of squabbling.

Against her better judgment, Angie overpriced but suggested they spruce up the place. She especially targeted the appalling, striped, faux-velvet wallpaper that covered almost every vertical surface (a daring red downstairs, a memorable sapphire blue upstairs). But Bernadette pronounced it "real antiquey-looking" once she learned that even illegal immigrant painters hired off a pickup tailgate got eleven bucks an hour.

Angie stoically scheduled the first brokers' tour, mentioning that one positive factor (the only one) was Janine's spectacular collection of antiques. Janine was especially proud of a century-old mahogany Queen Anne desk. Like the best cosmetics, show-stopping furniture could work wonders on the most catastrophic properties.

On the appointed morning, Angie arrived toting plates of cheese and crackers, some cheap wine, and a stack of flyers dripping with deceit. But to her shock, she walked into an empty house. All that remained of the furniture was a huge mess to clean up, highlighted by a pile of dead petunias evicted from a planter that had graced the master bedroom. Nearly in tears, she called Bernadette, who'd of course sold everything. "The desk too?" Angie demanded sternly. She knew Janine would want to keep that one splendid piece, clash as it might with Bernadette's high-gloss varnished tree trunks. "Just earn your goddamned keep," Bernadette snarled. It had been that way ever since.

After a dozen dizzying mountain switchbacks, Angie found the driveway and, to her surprise, pulled up behind Bernadette's rattletrap sky-blue Oldsmobile. She should've been working at the beauty parlor. The Kelso residence looked more like three tiny houses rammed together by bulldozers. It had a Dr. Seussian, trapezoidal look, as if the builder's plumb bobs and levels had lost touch with gravity. She banged on the cockeyed aluminum screen door. Bernadette clumped up in a lime-green paisley tent and let her in.

"Huh. Surprised to see you up here. Long drive just to tell me the deal fell through."

Angie took a breath. "Well, it did, Mrs. Kelso. But that's not why I'm here." She related the discovery of the girl in the tank.

Bernadette paled and lumbered over to a knotty pine tree-branch couch. She heaved herself onto it like a sack of wet cement and tsked a few seconds. "Umm . . . guess this doesn't do much for the property. So what's it worth now?"

Angie gritted her teeth at the memory of the dead girl and lowballed to stick it to her nemesis. "Well, no one'd buy it to live there for the next fifty years. But someone would buy just to hold it. Say, sixty thousand." Maybe eighty, but who's counting.

Bernadette's body heaved as if she'd been zapped with cardiac paddles. "What?" Her eyes clamped tight and her head lolled. Angie could almost see the visions of noblesse oblige oozing out of her. "But the insurance . . . " Bernadette sputtered.

Angie shook her head gravely. "They don't insure resale value. There's no damage to the house itself, so . . . "

Bernadette's eyes bulged so scarily that Angie worried they might explode and splatter her with eye goop. "God fucking dammit! This is all your fault! All you needed to do was sell the house! And you go dig up a dead girl in the back forty and cost me half a million bucks! Well, let me tell *you*, I am gonna *sue* your ass for everything you own! And now you can just get the fuck outa my house!"

"I'm sorry, Mrs. Kelso. I've got to talk to Janine. Someone stayed at the house several years ago, while they were away. He's probably the person who buried the girl."

"What? You've already ruined me! And now you expect to traipse upstairs and give my mother a conniption!?"

Angie thought it over. Clem had said she should tell Janine about the homicide to make sure she got her attention. But Janine might be unable to remember anything once she learned she'd been living with a dead girl and a visiting psychopath under her backyard. "Okay. I'll question her, but I won't mention the girl."

"The hell you will! You've got ten seconds to walk out that door!"

"Mrs. Kelso, I'm investigating a homicide. You can let me see Janine, or I can introduce you to someone in lockdown who's done a Hannibal number on her last two boyfriends."

Bernadette sullenly waved Angie toward a stairway.

She climbed the rickety steps and knocked on the door at the landing. It creaked open several inches, and Janine's round eyes peered out, her silvery hair tied back in a tight bun. She gazed up blankly, then beamed. "Why, Angie! You haven't been here in forever!"

Angie grinned. She'd never been there. "Sure haven't. I wanted to see how you're doing."

"Why dear, I'm just fine."

"Janine, there's something I need to ask you." A surprise awaited Angie when she stepped into the clapboard bedroom. The Queen Anne desk stood there in all its glory. Probably the object of a furious tug-of-war between Bernadette and her mother.

Angie sat down next to her on the bed. "Janine, did you ever rent out the house? I was thinking of the New Mexico pictures."

Janine's eyes lit up. "Oh? Would you like to see them? They're right here in the closet." She began to stand up.

Angie held her down by the shoulder. "No, that's okay. I just wanted to know if you rented the house while you were away somewhere."

Janine gazed downward. "Why yes. 2004, four years ago. Umm . . . April. For a year. Emil's brother in Albuquerque had a stroke. We went down to take care of him. He was a widower." Then silence as Janine started to drift away. Angie tapped her shoulder.

"Oh, I'm sorry. I was just thinking about Emil. You know, I really miss him sometimes." Janine smiled weakly.

Angie's throat tightened. Part sympathy, the rest a gentle ache as she wondered if she'd ever miss a man that way. For the moment it didn't seem likely. "I know you must," she said with a sigh.

Janine sighed back. "Anyway. We put an ad in the paper. Emil went down first. I stayed here to rent the place. A blond man. Very sweet and respectful."

"Do you remember his name?"

Janine gave her an embarrassed smile. "Gracious, I sure don't." She knitted her brows. "But I'm certain it was something from the Bible."

Angie rolled her eyes. John, Paul, Thomas. "Well, that helps. Any idea how old he was? What did he look like?"

"I'd say thirties. Glasses. Same height as Emil, about five ten. But on the thin side. He was wearing something . . . medical? Don't know why I say that."

"Did you write a lease? How did he pay you?"

"Oh, I wouldn't *begin* to know how to write a lease. But the payment I remember. He gave us cash for the first three months' rent in advance."

Angie cocked an eyebrow. "Cash? That was a couple thousand dollars."

Janine nodded sagely. "I wanted to fly down to New Mexico right away. I never held with ATM cards: you know they target people like me. I was worried we'd have trouble cashing checks out of state, so I asked him if he could pay in cash."

"And the rest of the payments?"

"He sent them by money order. Including utilities; we didn't want to change them over. He was moved out when we got back."

Angie fought off her anxiety. "Did you write his name down somewhere?"

Janine's tone was gently patronizing. "Of *course*, silly! His name *and* driver's license."

"And when you left for New Mexico, you put it . . . "

"Why, I locked it in the desk, of course, with *all* my important papers."

Angie gazed stonily at the wall. A first-grader could pick a hundred-year-old desk lock.

"So, why all the questions?" Janine continued. "Is anything wrong?"

Angie pasted on a smile. "Nothing dramatic. We found something we think belongs to him."

"Oh, I see," replied Janine and drifted off.

Angie stood up. "Janine, can I check your desk? And over the next few days, I'd like you to remember anything you can about the renter. I'll give you a call, okay?"

Janine looked up and smiled. "Why sure, Angie. Always love to talk to you." She looked away, eyes clouding over. Maybe Alzheimer's, or just that thing that happened to so many people who lost a spouse after half a century: the upwelling of a whole second world, an encyclopedia of remembrances more alluring than the world they lived in.

Angie riffled Janine's papers but found nothing on the renter. When she tripped downstairs, she found Bernadette catatonic on the sofa. Angie kept her distance, to avoid projectiles and because Bernadette's noxious odor permeated the area of the couch.

"I didn't tell her. I also need to know who bought the furniture."

Bernadette countered with a burst of bluster. "That's nobody's goddamn business but mine."

"They need to check for prints. Or you can wait for an invitation from Homicide Inspector Clemson Yao. He won't like having his justice obstructed."

Bernadette shot her a glare of pure malice. But she hauled her bulk up from the sofa, stumped off like some paisley-clad yeti, returned a moment later, and spitefully tossed a slip of paper on the tree-trunk coffee table. "Downtown antique dealer. Bought the lot. For all the good it'll do you. There was fifty people at that estate sale playing touchy-feely. Then the movers."

"Yes, I recall cleaning up after them."

Bernadette slouched behind her to the screen door. "And Angie?"

Angie turned around and faced her.

"You are *so* fired. Bitch."

Toward five, Clem trudged to the morgue. Like most detectives, he usually skipped autopsies; most homicide CODs were painfully obvious and, for a thirty-year cop, empty of the morbid entertainment value of TV crime shows. To boot, San Francisco's MEs had the same lackluster reputation as its inspectors, their pronouncements sometimes worse than useless. Once, over Clem's objections, a deputy had ruled accidental on a seventy-year-old man who fell down a flight of steps, despite finding four older blunt force traumas. He supported his ruling with the maxim that "old people fall down a lot." Clem quickly flushed out the vic's abusive stepson, a collar that had not endeared him to the ME's office.

But he never missed an autopsy on a child. He morosely studied what was left of the girl on the steel table. The cap of her cranium was removed, revealing a cerebrum the color of overripe mushrooms. Her breastbone was sawed in half vertically, ribs pulled back to show her heart and lungs. Her abdominal skin and muscles were peeled back, unveiling a wrenchingly tiny set of visceral organs. No hemorrhagic mayhem typical of the usual CODs under the rubric of BFK (Big Fucking Knife) or BFG (Big Fucking Gun). Instead, her stomach, bladder, and intestines were poked with holes with clean edges, like very large puncture wounds.

Senior Medical Examiner Kathleen Corrigan began her recitation. Her face was obscured behind a plastic wraparound mask. "Caucasian female, eight to nine years old. Preservation is remarkable from immersion in tank fluid. Blood displaced with embalming fluid. No signs of violent death: no wounds, ligature marks, hematomas, blood or skin under fingernails. No sign of sexual assault: no damage to vaginal or anal/rectal tracts, vaginal, anal/rectal, or oral fluid remnants. Not that we'd get DNA—formaldehyde's great for preserving remains but trashes DNA in days. No signs of antemortem restraint: duct tape burns, cloth fibers in the oral cavity, hand bruises from banging on a closet door. No chronic neglect: no malnutrition, dental work up to date at time of death. Anyone's guess on that, say three to ten years ago."

Clem shivered, and not just from the cool of the half-lit morgue. She could've been in that tank longer than she'd been alive.

Kathleen continued. "Get this, we already have liver tox results. Mayor's office sent an aide here this morning to drop off a PDQ nastygram. Guy left his breakfast here too. Puked in my blender."

"You need to get another sign," Clem replied. Someone had just pilfered the one on the tile entryway wall that said "Please Puke In Sink!" as if you were supposed to even if you didn't feel like it.

"Traces of sodium pentobarbital, the drug vets use to put animals to sleep. Four pinhole injection marks on the left upper arm—here—mean homicide. She was basically euthanized. Based on the number of injections, he drugged her up a while—maybe a day—before administering the fatal dose. No blood work, since it was pumped out. We're trying to recover samples from the capillaries, but he was thorough. Not an amateur, Clem."

Clem pointed to the holes in her visceral organs. "What the hell are these? I've never seen them before."

"That's because vics are usually embalmed *after* autopsy, not before. Penetrations from a trocar, a vacuum gadget embalmers use to evacuate digestive and urinary tracts. Nix the stomach contents."

She winced. "Sorry to say, Clem. Signs of prior physical abuse. Spiral fracture of the right humerus, the upper arm, about one year before death, followed by an identical break parallel to the old fracture line two or three weeks before death. Soft tissue damage—heavy bruising—from left and right adult handspans, in process of healing at time of death." She pointed out ten livid blotches that had been hidden by the nightgown's sleeve. "Spiral fractures occur from rotational force, twisting the arm. The bruising means no accident."

Clem nodded. "Marker for abuse. Some abusers just lash out: kid'll come in with a broken arm, next time a concussion. Others inflict the same damage again and again. They get a gruesome satisfaction from the specific torment, like a ritual. Female abusers often follow that pattern. But still a man I bet, based on the strength it took to break her arm."

"Something interesting there. The faint blue coloring in the sclera, the whites of her eyes." She pulled back the girl's lids. The hazel eyes were sunken and wrinkled with tiny folds and ridges, but you could tell what she'd looked like alive. No doubt, she'd been adorable.

Way too adorable to live only a tenth of her natural life.

Clem stifled the rumble of rage and leaned over, spotted the distinct azure tinge and managed a nod. The formaldehyde shredded his sinuses, overwhelming the rancid smell of the morgue. The place was more or less tolerable in winter, when the strongest odor was usually Pine-Sol. But with the coming of spring, decomps and gas poppers started rolling in. And someone had apparently rolled one in within the last 24 hours. While Clem was normally meticulous about his dress, today was Goodwill clearance in fecal brown. His tie was a gag gift with pictures of squad cars whose Mars lights blinked red and blue if he put in a battery. Worst case, he had to toss stuff after a pungent morgue day because no dry cleaner would take his suits.

"At first, I thought discoloration from immersion," Kathleen continued. "But then I found these." She pointed to the girl's skullcap on a porcelain side table and traced a suture with a latexed finger. "Tiny bones in the suture, where the skull plates join together, called Wormian bones."

Clem peered. Her suture wasn't a single irregular line, but composed of a dozen small, jagged pieces of bone locked together like a jigsaw puzzle.

She continued. "Together, the blue sclera and Wormians say a mild case of osteogenesis imperfecta, brittle bone disease. A tendency toward broken bones because of a defect in bone collagen. In the worst cases it's fatal. The baby never makes it out of the birth canal; the bones break apart like twigs. Most of the time—still more serious than her case—it looks like child abuse. Kid'll come in with a fracture, and X-rays show previous broken bones. Parents have their kids taken away and only later, if ever, is it diagnosed. It's not easy to spot in X-rays. Something you have to know how to look for," she finished, with a certain smugness.

Clem straightened and folded his arms skeptically. "You mean maybe she wasn't abused?"

"No, most parents who have kids with this condition are innocent, but the bruising's a giveaway. One point is that most women couldn't inflict this damage on a normal girl, so we'd assume the culprit was male. But here, it could easily be female.

"Judging from the healing of the old fracture, it was put in a cast. Even with long immersion, the skin on the right humerus is paler than the left—see?—so she also got a cast after the recent fracture. No other evidence of abuse: burns, other bruises, scalding, concussion, organ damage, et cetera. So arm-twisting was the abuse of choice. But not an everyday thing, maybe once a year. And only in the last year or so before she died."

"So something triggered it. Or it's someone who wasn't there before."

"Right. With the disease, anything before that would've shown up as other old fractures."

Clem nodded. "The drug. Sodium whatsitsface. Is it controlled?"

"Pentobarbital. Not very. A half-day course in animal euthanasia and you're allowed to buy it. Lots of ranchers keep some around. It won't get you high, so it's not an attention-getter. But something interesting about his using it."

Clem gave her a raised eyebrow.

"Well," she went on, "if you wanted to give someone a 'humane' lethal injection, you'd think, what?"

"Whatever they use for executions, I guess. I saw one, but they didn't hand out menus."

"Right, potassium chloride, combined with an anesthetic and a drug that causes respiratory paralysis. Potassium chloride shorts out the heart. That's what our little heart-stopper Kevorkian's used on his road shows."

"So why didn't our killer, is that the question?"

"Right. Well, the image of lethal injection is that it's humane. But the paralyzing drug may just keep the victim from *showing* he's in pain. The anesthetic isn't effective on all comers, so the potassium chloride may cause excruciating anguish, with no one but the condemned the wiser. So there's a movement in the medical community to change lethal injection to sodium pentobarbital. It's been used to euthanize millions of animals without evidence of pain."

"Well, with that kind of track record, why don't they?"

"It's just a strong depressant, might not do the trick. Talk about a publicity headache. And a painless death for the condemned isn't high on priority lists."

"Right, there's plenty would just as soon see a guy in a hood pickax them on pay-per-view. Including me on bad hair days. So he made sure her death was painless. Because he loved her or cared about her or something."

"Could be. Then again, maybe I'm reading too much into it."

He gave her a sarcastic grin. "Look, I don't see this as some kind of mercy killing, Doc, abuse or no abuse." He eyed the butchered little girl, and his anger flared. "No, she was just so much modeling clay to him."

He sat in his booth at the Internet café, done poring over the procedure for what had to be the hundredth time. But like any effort, a good messy was Edison's ninety percent perspiration. And the messy he'd unearthed a month back—by now christened the Scarecrow messy—was the pinnacle of gruesome inspiration.

He was relieved he didn't have to work from the original, especially in that goofy medieval typeset the Nazis had been so taken with. Someone had appended an English translation. Not that he had any admiration for their loony ideology. But you couldn't match these guys for gut-twisting ritual, from the torchlight processions to the astounding variety of the SS death chambers. Not only that, they'd had that Teutonic compulsion to document the most bloodcurdling details, making its replication a piece of Apfelstrudel.

What was so delectable about this new messy was its unspeakable irony. The executioner set things up just so and let the condemned inflict endless horror on himself, as if dragging his own chopping block to the scaffold like a condemned nobleman in medieval Russia.

He shook his head. Yet another point of macabre Nazi hyperbole: reviving the axe for state executions, with the executioner freakishly attired in black top hat and tails for some Germanic reason. Of course, beheading did have a certain gut-twisting allure as a national death ritual, especially with a few drum rolls and whatnot. And you couldn't touch the stats. There'd been enough noggins hacked off to fill in Lake Tahoe. Hell, one Romanian warlord used to landscape every road with towers of Turkish skulls. And, of course, always grist for some grisly humor. He tried to recall which despot had retained a one-eyed headsman to handle the guys who really pissed him off.

But on the cozier level of person-to-person messies, the decap shtick was pretty humdrum. Done to death, tediously déclassé. That and your average head-chopper was a bottom-feeding lout, a slave to tasteless flamboyance, as devoid of nuance as a hot pants hooker.

Now, you couldn't dismiss the act just because its devotees were such losers. Like watching a porn movie, the first time you saw a severed head, there was an undeniable shock value. But after a while, they all looked pretty much the same. Even during the Reign of Terror in France, they'd probably had to offer free party favors to keep packing 'em in at the guillotines.

And after all, time was always the key to amplifying suffering. In the case of decapitation, the brain had a capacity of only seven seconds of oxygen. Yes, the idea of a head forlornly sitting in a basket thinking "Well, this really sucks" was certainly titillating. But the height of achievement was reached when the messy slowly unfolded of its own ghastly volition.

Like crucifixion. Now there was a messy. Ah, the grandeur that was Rome. Two posts, a few well-placed nails, and voila. Such elegant, Zen-like frugality. The sufferer suffocated as his legs dragged down his diaphragm so he couldn't exhale, locking the poison air in his chest and flooding his lungs with fluid. But it took hours while he desperately bridged up to keep breathing. Crows feasted on his eyes like ravenous tagalongs at an Armani party buffet.

And then they went and ruined a perfectly good thing at Golgotha. Nowadays you couldn't put nail to bone without some over-credentialed FBI moron pegging you for a molested ex-altar boy or a snake-wrangling Pentecostal run amok. You could stick a blinking neon sign over the damn thing saying "Not About Jesus!" and they still wouldn't believe you. And truth was he didn't have anything against Christ, even if Christ probably had a thing or two against him.

Anyway, he might just be able to tweak some new oomph into the head thing. A postmortem embellishment maybe. But just now, he wasn't up to the forklift.

He began to log off, then started. Here he was, mere days away from the long-awaited Scarecrow messy, and there was one thing he'd completely forgotten. Roundly chastising himself, he signaled for another espresso and started a new round of clicks.

Almost eleven years at this. And he couldn't tie a hangman's noose.

It was almost embarrassing.

Unnecessary of course, strictly speaking. The cylindrical winding above the noose — by tradition thirteen times around — was intended to snap the neck in a trapdoor fall, severing the spinal cord and causing instant death. And his Scarecrow messy would be anything but instant. But like a flambé dessert, presentation was everything.

He tracked down a how-to diagram and printed it. Then he paged through a few dozen homicide photos at his favorite limited-access forensic pathology site. Each featured a dreary square knot or granny knot. One yokel had even used a shoe knot, with big bow loops sticking out behind the vic's neck like Tinkerbell wings. You got the feeling she'd flitted around a while before giving up the ghost. Only one Real McCoy in the whole caboodle, and badly tied at that.

Not talking quantum physics here, just Read the Fucking Manual stuff.

People just didn't take pride in their work anymore.

Chapter Five

Angie joined Clem in the Taraval conference room, taking a moment to marvel at its unusual décor; the place was wall to wall with children's crayon drawings and watercolors of policemen apprehending a host of evildoers.

Clem grinned. "They get a lot of class trips."

Just then, a squat, jowly, raven-haired woman in a navy pantsuit marched in, flopped a leather briefcase on the table, and scowled at Clem.

He did the honors. "Doctor Kathleen Corrigan, senior medical examiner. Does not play well with others unless they're dead. Angie Strackan, Police Reserve."

A beam of recognition lit Kathleen's face. "Strackan? As in Roger? Pathologist? Blythe Labs?"

Angie nodded. "My husband. Ex. Sort of. We're on good terms," she added in response to Kathleen's look of alarm at putting her foot in it.

Kathleen sported the barest semblance of a smile. "I talk to Roger maybe twice a month. Mostly on toxins." It sounded like Angie's ex-marriage. Roger was a shop-talking workaholic.

Jojo was the last to enter. "Okay, let's roll. Computer generated," said Clem, flipping them each a nine-by-twelve color pic. The girl had opened her hazel eyes and smiled, her tresses settled in place with computerized brush strokes. "Keep this in house. It hasn't gone to press."

Angie's eyes flashed indignation. He answered her mute question. "False positives. People recall the pic from TV and think they've seen her before when we show it to them. We'll keep it to ourselves a few days to avoid that. Let's start with Doc. She usually has to be somewhere else."

"Clem, we put two autopsies on ice for you. Anyway, I'm mainly here to answer questions."

Angie dipped a toe in the water. "So maybe the abuser killed his daughter?"

"Doubtful," replied Clem. "Yes, first place we look is the parents. But most abuse deaths result from uncontrolled violence. And someone who kills his kid is feeling panic or guilt, not likely to spend a month decorating the corpse. That's the province of a whole 'nother beast: the psychopath, someone spinning out some fantasy. And psychopaths almost never do their own kids; they're too narcissistic about their own flesh and blood. My first take is that the killer was someone else who euthanized her like a dog. He wasn't into sexual predation or torture, at least no evidence."

"But wouldn't the drugging imply sexual abuse?" Angie asked skeptically.

"It could, but I don't lean that way. Partly 'cause no cop wants to go there if he can avoid it, I admit. But no physical evidence. Possible he just didn't leave any, but that's rare on a vic this young. Add to that his posing of the girl. If he's a pedophile, chances are he'd stage her to look provocative. Most rationalize that the kid seduced them. It'll show up if the guy does post-mortem staging."

"But he's presented her as the picture of innocence," replied Angie with a studious nod.

Clem continued, "And it's possible that's what he got off on. But also rare. Some pedophiles feel guilt and might want to stage her that way, like it never happened. But on the other hand, last thing they'd want to do is pop in once a month to apologize."

Angie gave him a dubious look. "Maybe some twisted mercy killing? By the other parent, because she was being abused? Or someone else?"

"I can't buy the other parent. The abuse situation wasn't that desperate. Episodic, maybe once a year, and started only recently. As to a third party, you *do* get freaks called 'Angels of Death,' who mask the need to play God under a mantle of sympathy. But they're big repeaters, and they gravitate somewhere they can do it again and again and no one suspects. Nursing homes, neonatal units. And we don't have a pattern: missing kids with abuse histories. My first guess is the killer wanted a subject—modeling clay—for his tank display."

Angie pondered. "The mural also points at the crime scene as some kind of creepy composition. The girl's an important part, but only a part."

Clem nodded. "PS, there's to be no mention of the mural *ever*. We'll hold it back to flush out false confessions. They'll be doing 'take a number' for something this lurid."

"So why the drugs then? They mean something. The delay before killing her bothers me."

Clem shrugged. "Me too. Maybe hesitation, or something wasn't right with his scenario. Might mean a first-timer."

Jojo took over. "So if not the parents, the key is whether abuse governed his selection. Or because she was blond, or just wrong place wrong time."

Clem eyed him somberly. "The correct answer is 'A.' If there's no tie-in with the abuse, we're SOL. Physical stuff's niller than nil." He paged through the file. "Far as prints? A billion latents from house hunters. In the garage? Zack, old Emil latents off garage stuff. In the tunnel, just Zack and Angie, so the killer wore gloves. Furniture's a dead end. He had months to sanitize the place. Angie?"

She related her discussion with Janine about the mysterious renter.

Clem continued, "Crime took place after he moved in, so April 2004 to 2005. For the killer: No paper trail. No forwarding address to the house, no lease, no security deposit to return, utilities weren't switched over. For the vic: I've gone over missings back through '98, no match. So I'm thinking someone from way out of town. Last night I put the crime scene and her photo on VICAP—the FBI database—to see if we can get something. A crime with the same MO—the means of killing—or signature, other things that individualize the killer. Writing on the walls, cutting off a lock of hair, and so on."

Angie sensed a hole in the logic. "Why assume she'd be reported missing?"

"Even if a parent's the killer, they usually get rid of the body and report. Or make it look like the kid died another way. Only time we often don't get a report is ransom kidnap, don't call the cops stuff. But we hear afterward, and the crime scene's off the chart for kidnappers. Sometimes homeless parents don't report, but she doesn't fit the profile. No dental neglect, no malnutrition. So why wouldn't they report?"

"If they were certain they'd be accused of killing her," replied Angie. "Someone breaks her arm, they take her to the hospital with some story about falling in ballet class, get some funny looks. She disappears a week later. They know the DA's going to grind them into pâté."

"Yes, but without a report, there's too many questions. School, neighbors, relatives. If the cops find out, it's an admission of guilt."

Angie fought on. "Say the killer moves in the house in April. Finds the tank, spots the girl, plans the snatch. By that time, it's June, school's out. Mom and Dad know they'll be keelhauled if they talk. Safer just to rabbit."

Clem rolled his eyes. "Okay, it's possible. First pass, a list of girls who completed what? Second and third grades, left the system in June 2004. But the school district can't spit that data out of its computers. They can barely chug out a report card, from what my teenage daughter says. And we'd get false positives out the wazoo."

"Another route," said Jojo. "If she was in school when her arm was broken, her teacher could've reported it to a school nurse. Schools are required to document suspected abuse cases; they stick out more than skinned knees. And the rent. Janine asks the first three months in cash, then he sends money orders. Why money orders? They're a pain in the ass. Probably to use a false name. You can get them at check-cashing places, and they don't care what name you sign. So by July, when he sent the first money order, he'd done the deed. Rifled Janine's desk, removed the paper with his name and license."

"But how would he know that she didn't have his name or wouldn't remember it while she was in New Mexico? That she hadn't just copied it?"

Jojo shrugged. "Maybe she called to see how things were going, and he realized she didn't have a clue who he was. Fact is, he did the deed, so he probably figured it out somehow."

Clem flicked both wrists, palms open upward in a gesture of resignation. "And nothing from Janine's bank. They traced her money orders to a check-casher, but long gone. Most of those places are fly-by-night."

Angie shook her head in disgust. "How does it just *happen* we can't find his name on one single document? Not even a lousy post office forward?"

Jojo touched a finger to his temple. "Think backwards. After he moved in, when he began contemplating doing the deed, he surmised his name wouldn't be anywhere and that Janine would draw a blank. Otherwise it might never have happened. Even premeditated murders rely on chains of opportunity."

Angie felt a burst of anger at Janine, as if she'd somehow contributed to the girl's death. But she knew it was just impotent venting.

"The aquarium?" asked Clem sadly.

Jojo went over his findings. "Maybe we can track down where he bought it. If we're lucky, he used the Internet. He'd probably use a credit card somewhere in the deal, so we'd have a paper trail."

Clem shook his head. "Not a chance. If he knew his name wouldn't be anywhere, why mess that up? I'm betting he bought it at a store for cash. Worst case, way out of town."

Jojo nodded. "Right, but that tank's way too big for someone to unload by himself. It's about a hundred and fifty pounds. So he had to have a friend help him, or have it delivered. Even if he used a false name to buy it, someone could remember him."

"The whole embalming thing sticks out. You can't just take a continuing ed course," said Clem. "So he did it to keep her from decomposing, right? Me, I'd just buy a big freezer."

Kathleen piped up. "Without embalming, her appearance would've deteriorated as blood leaked through the vessels to the skin, then through the skin into the fluid."

Angie stifled the urge to seek out the restroom, especially with the girl beaming at her from the photo, as if coyly demanding a round of pat-a-cake.

"So a mortuary employee?" asked Clem.

"It's not mortuary work," Kathleen replied. "He didn't use funeral home tricks: sewing her mouth closed so it wouldn't gape open, plastic molds between the eyelids and the eyes so they don't look sunken, et cetera. And the fluid's way off. Parlor fluid is water with dashes of preservatives and cosmetics, but this stuff's hi-test. Formaldehyde's four or five times as much as funeral home stuff. That's why it stewed Angie's brains in the tunnel. Another half-hour and she'd have gotten skin necrosis, meaning your skin dies right before the rest of you does. Formaldehyde acts as a fixative to preserve tissues. But the fluid's also heavy on propylene glycol, which keeps tissues supple. Not found in funeral brew. Without it, over time the formaldehyde would distort the features as they became rubbery. He intended it for long-term preservation, probably came up with his own homegrown."

"Everything else is so exacting, I doubt he'd risk something untried," Angie interjected. "You have the formulation?" Kathleen glanced at Clem, and he nodded. She riffled her file, finally sliding Angie a piece of paper.

"Thanks," Angie replied. "I'll ask my swami about it right now."

She stepped out of the precinct for a sunshine break and strode down Taraval Street, reveling in the vast Pacific panorama and the moist, sweet-salty breeze sweeping uphill. She smiled and waved at the driver of one of the restored 1930s-vintage PCC streetcars as it rumbled by—this one painted in the old Chicago Transit forest green—then pulled out her cell and dialed Roger.

"Angie? Hey! Happy Mother's Day again. Everything okay?"

"I'm at the Sunset police station."

"I knew it would come to this. You perforate a panhandler?"

"Nothing so gratifying. We unearthed a dead girl at that listing I've been whining about."

"Good God, that's you? The banner headline for two days? God, just grotesque." He paused. "I thought Homicide was off-limits. Sure you want to end up face-to-face with another freakoid?"

"They snuck me in the back door. And I'll let them do the shooting this time, cross my black heart. Help me on something?"

"I'm open to negotiations. Free for dinner Tuesday?"

"Uh-huh, but maybe strictly professional." She couldn't decide whether snuggle sex with Ex would be the best thing or the worst thing for her, coming on the heels of her night of seedy licentiousness. Right now it felt like mixing Kahlua and Everclear.

"Someone on your radar? I thought it was busted," replied Roger with a wisp of exly discomfort.

"And out of warranty," said Angie. "No, just healthy caution."

"I'll take my chances. What can I do for you?"

"Embalming fluid."

"I'll have to back order. Anyone I know?"

"No, silly. I need to know about it. Though I do have a candidate," she added as Bernadette's features ballooned in her brain like a nitrogen bubble.

"You've come to the right place. A recent street thing is soaking pot in embalming fluid. It makes it burn slower and makes for a longer-lasting high. They call it 'fry.' We've been analyzing samples to trace them."

"Whatever Weirdo used isn't normal. The ME—Corrigan, she knows you—says it was targeted at preservation." She rattled off the formulation.

"That'd figure if he wanted to keep her looking pretty. Mortuary stuff only has to last a week. It's formulated for rosy cheeks and so on, so the loved one looks sprightly until they nail him up. Gimme a few? And say hello to the doc for me. I need to stay on her good side; she throws us scads of business."

"Just take her to *Texas Chainsaw Massacre*. She'll be tickled pink."

"You think? I'll check the paper." A moment's hesitation, Roger's prelude to a tiptoe question. "Oh. Did Jackie call you? For Mother's Day?"

Angie cringed. "I was away from the phone."

"I told her to call. Anyway, I'll get back to you." Roger's classic MO: appearing supportive but subtly lording over Angie that her daughter was closer to her stepfather than to her own mother. To this day, Angie doubted he was conscious of doing it, even though she'd called him on it half a dozen times.

She let the humiliation recede, walked inside to the conference room door, and inched it open.

" . . . a cannula was inserted into the incision in the carotid artery for fluid insertion. A second cannula was inserted in the jugular vein incision for blood drainage . . . "

Kathleen was in the midst of a blow-by-blow on the embalming as Angie barged in. She took her seat, hoping Kathleen was wrapping it up.

They looked at her with raised eyebrows.

"A few minutes," Angie said. "I miss anything?"

Clem winked. "Kathleen can fill you in later."

"No thanks, I'll skip the details," Angie answered, with a sad glance down at the girl's picture.

"Anyway, we'd been talking about the embalming." Clem grimaced as he eyed Jojo. "I hate to even ask. The blood?"

"There's a drain in the garage floor. Forensics is looking at scrapings from the pipe. Same thing funeral parlors do: dump it in the sewers."

Clem rolled his eyes. "Well, thanks. Now I'll be dreaming about gigantic leeches coming up my toilet. I'll have to put up a sign: *Don't flush tampons! It attracts them!*"

Angie's cell trilled. She stepped into the hallway.

"Got something. It's an oddball. A special formulary to prep cadavers for medical use."

"Oh, Roger, you always say the most romantic things."

"Wows 'em at the bars. Anyway, this potion's meant to stand up to use of cadavers in anatomy classes. They last like five years before they start falling apart. If a body were embalmed this way and kept motionless in fluid, no telling how long it could last. Thirty, forty years."

"Wow. Can they turn it into a night cream?"

"You'd smell like a cadaver. Take a really cheap perfume to bury it. Anyway, duty calls."

"Always has, always will," she replied with a paper-thin smile. "Where do they get the bodies?"

"Unclaimed from the morgues, alcoholics, and druggies. Two years of anatomy and I didn't see one brain that wasn't turned into pudding by gin and smack. The livers were worse."

Angie's mouth formed a moue of distaste. "Where do they do the embalming? Who does it?"

"At school. Say an anatomy prof and a student in dire need of extra credit."

"Thanks, Roger. Tuesday at seven? Postrio?"

"Call it eight."

Her eyes narrowed. The tug-of-war was a hoary tradition. But if she stuck to her guns on the earlier time, she'd end up fielding a sheepish "I'm running late" call at the dinner table.

Angie stepped back in and related her findings. Clem threw Kathleen a smirk. "Doc, just how many of those did you slice and dice in med school?"

Kathleen responded with a cold stare. "I just served them up, I didn't marinate them. That was the kitchen crew. Sorry, yesterday was against the clock."

Clem nodded. "No sweat. Anyway, the killer was probably med school, anatomy. Janine thought he was medical. Maybe wore scrubs."

Angie felt some threads interweave. "Okay. Daddy breaks the girl's arm. She goes to the hospital. The killer's there, recognizes she's abused. Who is he?"

Clem spoke. "X-rays first, so the radiologist or tech. Radiologist often doesn't see patients."

"But only a doc would recognize abuse, right?"

"Not at all. Lots of techs are doctor wannabes, med school washouts. And they cart the files around, page through for coffee room gossip."

"And he's an authority figure," Angie pointed out. "Easy to get her to go with him later, even give her the injection."

Jojo looked hopeful. "You know, we get an ID on her, we could find out which hospital from admissions, even from the school nurse. Then a blond guy, glasses, mid-thirties. Med school or anatomy background. Someone who could know she was an abuse case."

Clem turned to Jojo. "Head for USD. Track down every school nurse here four years ago. Anyone who was a nurse then but isn't in the system now, we'll try and dig them up. If that doesn't work, we'll release the photo to the press and see if a teacher remembers her."

Angie waved a hand. "Can I ride shotgun?"

Clem glanced at Jojo, who winked approval. Clem nodded. "I'll head for the Hall and sneak some help from the *Federales*. Freakoid knows she's been dug up. And I don't have a clue yet what *that* means."

Angie and Jojo hauled down to the headquarters of the Unified School District in the gritty, yet historic, Western Addition. The district was home to some of the city's most grinding poverty and paradoxically—because it was one of the few areas to survive the great fire that followed the '06 quake—to some of its most storied, century-old Victorians. Crack dealers, hookers, and sidewalk squatters plied their trade against a backdrop of patrician houses that would be double the price anywhere else in the city. Jojo had finagled a meeting with the director of health programs, jawboning a gaggle of secretaries and deputy assistants before pleading, "C'mon, help me out here. It's about the dead girl in the tank." A gasp and a miraculous appointment.

Jojo sighed relief as they pulled into the parking lot. "Anyway, hope we don't get the USD third degree. The city's 'progressive' bastion: more *Guardians* per square foot than anywhere in the city." He was referring to the city's ultra-liberal weekly, Angie knew; it seldom mentioned SFPD without allusions to Pinochet's Chile.

They were ushered into the office of Marcie Benjamin, director of health programs, by a mutely disapproving aide-de-camp. Jojo grinned at him and said in his best Martian accent, "We come in peace!" A slim, statuesque black woman pushing forty entered, gave them a surprising smile, and gestured them to two steel chairs in front of a battered wooden desk.

She spoke in a New Orleans brogue. "Sorry about the runaround. It's just we get more dumped on us yearly. Used to be bumps and bruises, polio vaccines, pregnancy tests. Now it's HIV awareness, transgendered outreach, prenatal health seminars, on and on. Lord, don't get me started."

Jojo gave Marcie the picture and explained their mission, but she shook her head in disbelief.

"I'm sorry," she explained. "The nurse program is stuck together with chewing gum and rubber bands. We're staffed by nurse practitioners, they're underpaid and vanish soon as they get something better. Then we have some nursing students. They're gone after a semester of practical."

Jojo closed his eyes with a pained expression. "So a dead end? It's kind of our only hope."

"No, but you're facing some file flipping, and it won't be fun. Come with me."

She walked them to an office choked with rows of gray five-foot file cabinets, and an undersized table, and two chairs that looked like junior-high rejects. "I hate this place. Our abuse files." The room took on a sinister air, the cabinets looming larger and uglier. "Legally you can't see these without a court order, which you'd never get based on what you've told me. But nobody'll squawk. Just don't chitchat with anyone or get sidetracked. Believe me, you'll be tempted to hunt down these so-called parents and carve out their brains with a melon ball thingy."

She rested an arm on a group of three cabinets. "They're alphabetical, where last report was spring 2004. K through 12, so mostly out of your age range. No facial photos unless there was, say, a black eye. So you're basically looking for a girl with a broken arm, which may or may not have been written up for suspected abuse." She paused thoughtfully. "I hate to say it, but your best shot is if she tried to hide it from her abuser and we caught it here. We'd take her to a hospital ourselves. Happens all the time in abuse cases. She was probably scared to death, like it was her fault," she added, her jaw set in cold fury.

She walked to the door, turned, and eyed Jojo grimly. "If you stay in Homicide five years, you'll toe tag ten kids written up in those cabinets. Ten years, you'll arrest that many for killing *their* babies. As Wordsworth said, the child is the father of the man."

Angie's first file set the tone: a six-year-old girl whose feet had been scalded while wearing socks, a technique the scalding set used to reduce telltale blistering. Things didn't get better, and she found herself sandwiched between the need to ignore all else except the folder they sought, and a compulsion to pay heed to each victim.

She caught Jojo's eye. "I'll do better if we chatter incessantly."

His sigh was disconsolate. "I've got two kids."

"One here. Daughter, twenty-two, Jackie. Lives in Seattle." She didn't mention that their speaking terms were tenuous. Like many stepfathers, Roger had been loath to be the heavy. The onus of discipline had been draped on Angie's shoulders like a hair shirt, despite her periodic detonations at Roger. Jackie still favored him with her confidences, and Angie was often reduced to prying the latest Jackie news from his overindulgent clutches. They'd separated without rancor, but it felt like Roger used Jackie's bias to imply that she was more to blame than he for their breakup.

"Boy five, girl three," replied Jojo. "Tony and Melissa."

"So, what's with Clem's remark? About not letting you pick restaurants?"

Jojo laughed heartily. "His verdict on Pinoy soul food. Once I took him to a restaurant on a dare, place my wife, Anna, and I go when we're homesick. Ordered all the outback stuff we don't talk about. Like *dinuguan*, minced pig intestines. *Adidas*, marinated chicken feet. He was barely holding his own. Then we finished with a *balot*, an egg that's allowed to grow a small chick inside. I told him it was a hard-boiled egg. He took a bite, looked at what was left, went tearing for the restroom. I laughed so hard my beer came out my nose."

"So what brought you here?"

"After MacArthur got kicked out of Manila by the Japanese, he sent in covert guys to enlist thousands of Filipinos in the U.S. Army with offers of citizenship. My grandfather joined up and led a jungle war campaign in northern Luzon, the biggest island. After the war, he emigrated. He was one of the lucky ones, because he knew one of MacArthur's aides who could vouch for him. The Americans reneged on most of their promises, mostly claiming 'lack of documentation.' Most Filipinos believe they lost all the records on purpose."

Angie nodded. "I've heard those guys have been fighting for years just to get veterans' benefits, never mind citizenship."

Jojo sported a sour grin. "They're just starting to loosen up now that most of the vets are dead. Anyway, my parents stayed in the Philippines a while, but Ferdinand and Imelda stole my father's business out from under him in the '70s, and they decided to take my grandfather up on his offer of sponsorship. So, here I am, Division's one and only Fil-Am."

Six o'clock rolled around with no results. As they drove to the Sunset, Jojo sighed dejectedly. "I'm wondering if we're banking too much on the abuse connection because it's all we've got."

"You're just burned out, Jojo," she replied, wondering the same thing.

"You're right. I'll just go get some positive reinforcement from my brood."

Angie smiled weakly. "They'll run riot. You're in a dangerously wimpy state."

"That's what my wife is for. I'm something of a disciplinary wuss."

"Ah, so Mommy's the meanie, huh?" she asked with a too-close-to-home edge.

Jojo fielded it. "I exaggerate. But when I was a kid in the Philippines, we had what we call a *yaya*, like a nanny but more so. She was the disciplinarian. Maybe that's the secret."

"Unless you're the *yaya*. So, a happily married inspector? You're trashing the rep. You're supposed to blow off your child support and slug down boilermakers after 10:00 a.m. bloodbaths."

"Hell, Anna couldn't be happier now that I'm not chasing carjackers. Sure, the job gets to you. But hard-boiled, three-divorce boozers actually don't last in Homicide. The diet of scumbuckets and gore gives them too much excuse to shit their insides out and flush."

"So what happens to them?"

"We protect our own, get them transferred. Clem's been Homicide six years. He's pushed two out so far, and he's gunning for a third. Usually when the police work gets slipshod."

"Meaning?"

"Oh, like they blow off leads 'cause they've already decided which hairy slimeball did it. Ignore exculpatory evidence. Defense does their home-work, we get shredded in the cross-exam." The evening mist blanketed the windshield, and he switched on the wipers. He hesitated. "You're probably aware we have the worst solve rate coast to coast. Right down there with Casablanca."

"I'd heard. Some of the worst inspectors, too. Present company excluded."

Jojo winced. "Well, you know that they're picked from a wait list. Clem sat on the list for seven years. No one gets picked because he's any good, like in New York. Been that way more than twenty years. Union didn't want guys getting picked on juice, so now we get clowns who can't Mirandize without a wallet card."

"And you?"

"Exception to the rule. Six years ago we had one Asian in Homicide, Clem. I'm the second, affirmative action. Attrition helps. Some guys fancy the star to pick up cop-bar badge bunnies 'til their first dumpster dive to open a Hefty bag of body parts."

Angie couldn't help a mordant chuckle. "But it can't be *all* your fault."

"Nah, we get more gang kills than most, dead ends. Even if you track down a drive-by gunship, homies lay hands on it first so it'll have two hun-dred latents. And most gang kills are Pee Wees making their bones. The chieftains you *really* want sub it out. Plus we've got the only DA in the galaxy who's sworn never to pursue a death penalty case."

"Guess he's not on too many inspectors' Christmas card lists."

"Not even his own prosecutors'. Most people here oppose the death penalty, but what they don't realize is that it's the mongo bargaining chip for homicide pleas. Scumbags'll eat life without parole to get it off the table. But if defense knows you won't pursue the needle, they'll expect a better deal, so we have to plea down to Murder Two's. The assholes get out faster. The DA's gunning for mayor, that way he can tell the left-wing power brokers he never sent anyone to Death Row. So they go to early out."

"How reassuring. Question: I'm still surprised at being allowed to tag along on Homicide. You guys tend to be even more clannish than other cops."

"You're right, except Clem thinks you're a natural-born ferret. And Frazier feels bad that you got the shaft back in the Dark Ages."

"Trust me, I did. I almost got prosecuted for Man One. Another lefty DA."

"I heard. The union help you out?"

"No, I just ballsed it out, double dared him to try me for ventilating The Beast. Truth is, back then the last thing the union wanted on the force was a woman. It was cop *wives* giving them shit; they didn't want their men partnering with us. And it would open the floodgates. I mean, what next ferchrissakes? A friggin' *homo?*" she finished with her best Archie Bunker accent.

Jojo aped her accent. "Say it ain't so." Despite the city's liberal reputation, SFPD was a stalwart anti-gay bastion, with no openly gay cops on the roster.

"So you guys sure you got my back? I'd be the first person to get drummed out of the Force *and* the Reserve."

"Frazier'd eat the heat; he and Clem go back. Precinct caps are all ex-street. The Department's got closets full of skeletons, and they bite if you poke them. Caps are the keepers of the keys; they've got something on everyone. And Frazier owes your dad big time. Actually it was Frazier who came up with the idea of having you transfer to Taraval so you could fly wingman. Your dad was really torn up that they screwed you over."

Angie could barely veil her shock. Her father—who spent his afternoons trading tales with other ex-beats in a seedy downtown San Diego cop bar—had never talked about the streets, even with her mom. One time, at the age of twelve, she hadn't known he'd put a bullet in a fleeing rape suspect until she heard it from the kids at school the next morning.

And he'd done nothing but mutter platitudes when she'd been bounced. In fact, she'd been infuriated by his lack of empathy and wondered until a moment before if he'd secretly been relieved to see her booted. She knew he'd taken shit from brother officers during her two months in service, and in fact had decked one loutish rookie in a cop bar after overhearing a particularly unsavory remark. In the last decade, the three times she'd brought up the shooting with him had produced awkward silences and a quick change of subject.

Sometimes she wondered how her mother had coped. Cop wives were usually the ones to leave, sometimes because so many cops took the edge off with cop-bar cuties and booze, but most often because their mates shut them out of their world. The excuse of "protecting" them from the street often masked a patronizing misogyny that dated back to the days of the city's infamous Vigilance Committee. But her mom was a staunch German hausfrau her dad had met in Frankfurt at the end of World War II who didn't hold with divorce. Her expectations from life were tempered by memories of corpses rotting in rubble and fresh-faced, uniformed schoolgirls tricking for Spam and cigarettes.

Jojo continued, "Guess your dad never told you. They were partners when Frazier was a rookie. Story goes Frazier got a hair up his ass about this guy'd been boning his own fifteen-year-old daughter and pimping her on the side. He'd tried to nail the pukebag for weeks. Girl wouldn't talk."

"Daddy threatened her, I'm sure."

Jojo nodded. "Anyway, one day Frazier gets a tip from the next-door neighbor that there's a john up there. Frazier and your dad tear on over, john's already gone. By now Frazier's had it. Door's ajar, slimeball's got his kid vacuuming with one of those big upright industrial canisters. He's sitting on his couch in his sweats slurping a beer, smug as a pasha.

"Frazier takes the hose, yanks off the floor attachment, walks over to the couch, jerks the guy's sweats down, jams the tube down on his privates. Sucks up the family jewels like beer foam. Guy's screaming bloody murder, Frazier's got his other hand around the guy's neck, yelling, "What's the matter fuckhead, don't you *like* getting sucked off?" Motor's making that high-pitched whine, like something's stuck in it? Anyway, way Frazier tells it, girl's standing there with this little Mona Lisa smile. Your dad takes her out in the hall and talks to her a minute while Frazier hoovers the guy.

Then he comes back, switches off the vacuum, sends Frazier down to the car to chill.

"After a while your dad comes down, gets in. Frazier buries his head in his hands, whining how he's toast 'cause a rookie up on excessive force in this town won't last a week.

"Your dad shakes his head, says the girl won't corroborate. But he told Daddy Scumbag if he retaliated, he'd be back with the precinct's water-vac. Twelve horsepower."

"Bet *that* cratered the ol' sex life."

Jojo nodded. "Frazier says it hemorrhaged every blood vessel, looked like a little sun-dried eggplant."

"So that's why Frazier owes my father? Doesn't sound like *that* big a deal."

Jojo gave her a wry grin. "Well, there were like eight of those during Frazier's first two years. He'd be taking names in a building lobby if not for your dad."

Angie frowned. "So he was a big excessive force type?" Her father was straight and narrow about that; she couldn't imagine him abetting brutality.

Jojo pondered it. "No. More an old-school cop, got a thing about damsels in distress. Used to run what he called 'wife-beater patrol.' He'd stop at the horse stables going out, get a big bag of horse turds, what he called 'bite-sized.' Then he'd stop by offenders at dinner, check if their wives or girlfriends were sporting new bruises. If they were, he tossed a few turds in the toilet and set the guy 'bobbing for apples.' Crude but effective."

"And he never got brought up on charges?"

"One flush and voila: no evidence. And Frazier was two hundred fifty pounds of scary muscle. Add to that the fact that abusers almost never file complaints; that's one batch of dirty laundry they don't want anyone to see. Anyway, as to why you're here, Clem's also desperate. This is our highest profile unsolved since the Zodiac serial in the sixties." The Zodiac killings were a series of still-unsolved sex slayings highlighted by years of taunting letters. The biggest embarrassment in the Department's history, and one of the landmark cases that led the FBI to enter the serial killer biz. "And if he doesn't get a solve, that's how he'll be remembered. So he's walking around Division with that flesh-eating virus. All he's got is a four-year-old corpse and an old lady who starts making her husband his coffee before she remembers he's dead."

"So why'd he take the case?"

"Mostly 'cause you dumped it in his lap. But Clem also has a tinge of bravado. See, his dad was this Chinatown legend. One of the first Asian cops back when people still talked about Yellow Peril. He died ten years back, and there were five hundred people from Chinatown at the cemetery, almost all of them over eighty. His mom still plays mah-jongg there with the crones. Everyone treats her like some reigning diva."

"Clem included," Angie replied. "I met her at their housewarming party. God, is she one imperious old bird. Once she cuffed Clem under the chin and bawled him out in front of twenty people for using a swear word. It's like she grew up in the Forbidden City wearing five-inch nails."

"So he tells me. She still tells his fortune with *I Ching* hexagrams every time he picks up a new case, just like she did his dad. Anyway, his dad ran the informant network that choked off the last gasp of the tongs during the Depression. They tried to kill him five times, but the hatchet guys didn't have much luck coming back. They figured he had a big-ass demon looking out for him and gave up. So this is maybe Clem's chance to equal his dad."

He pulled up next to her car in front of the station, switched off, took off his wire-rims, and looked at her intently. "So here's the deal. If you want, there's lots of 'help out' stuff on a case like this, like you've been doing. You'd mop the floor with most of our inspectors. Just keep a low profile, okay?"

She nodded, masking her glow at Jojo's compliment, then stepped into the murky Pacific twilight. She was soon clomping upstairs from the garage to the welcome sight of her half-lit kitchen. She wolfed down a pastrami sandwich in bed perusing a mystery, until she blinked her eyes closed and fell asleep with the lights on and a plateful of bread crumbs threatening to tip off the bed.

He glanced at his watch as he folded a week's blue jeans and shirts at the deserted Laundromat two blocks from his garage apartment. Midnight, clos-ing time. He always enjoyed the outing, at least in the afternoon or after 10:00 p.m., when the place was empty. One time he'd toted his basket there at dinnertime and been shocked to find it wall to wall with horny Gen-Xers. One clueless babe—the type who considered scowling men a ringing call to arms—had even flirted with him.

Just as he finished, a dumpy, tattooed woman with a crewcut and nose ring tore through the door, threw open a huge dryer, and pulled out a forgotten pair of red ballet leg warmers. He chuckled as he visualized her ungainly pirouette. Like those dancing hippos in Fantasia.

He sauntered over to the enormous dryer and stuck his head inside. A Draco, top of the line.

Honeypie, perhaps? The most personal of his messies, and he was hesitant about using the ancient Malleus *boilerplate, however grisly it might be. Maybe something completely original?*

Easily managed after closing. He'd seen someone dry a comforter that had to weigh fifty pounds wet, and the motor hadn't batted an eye. Most important, he'd fixed one with his dad once. You could unscrew the panel, defeat the interlock, and crank up the gas hot enough to ignite polyester. And it even took Susan B. Anthonys. You could watch the messy, load in some bucks, and hit the road before the old Czech lady opened up at dawn.

Oh yes, Honeypie would look a sight after three hours flopping around in three-hundred-degree heat and all that milky skin gumming up the airholes. The full-body peel even called to mind a delightful title: the Saint Bartholomew messy, after the disciple flayed alive in Armenia for the conversion of the king's brother, often shown in church art holding his skin like a cape.

The poor sap. One minute you're thinking you've hit the evangelical Lotto. The next, they're skinning you like a mink.

But the whole thing just didn't have legs. One breath of superheated air would turn her lung tissues the color and consistency of week-old gazpacho, inducing death in seconds. Always a problem, that, inducing persnickety Inquisitors in the Burning Times to switch to slower-burning green wood. He could duct-tape her breathing passages, but that would only buy a minute or two.

On the other hand, Honeypie wouldn't have a clue. The piss-yourself factor would be off the chart as she sat there, naked and bound, listening to the coins clink through the slot, knowing only seconds remained until the gas jets flamed and the cylinder began its gruesome roundelay. Still, women could get disappointed when reality didn't measure up.

No, it would be homicidal vaudeville, theater devoid of substance. Couldn't have that.

So Malleus it would be, hammer on hammer, flame on flame. The prescription for Honeypie's grisly end had waited four centuries to be lovingly exhumed from the tomes of a library basement in Marburg, Germany.

But he did like the round and around deal. Where she stops, nobody knows. He'd have to noodle with that one.

CHAPTER SIX

Clem slouched through the door of his sixth pet shop. The odors of puppy-soiled newspaper and fish tank water by now adhered to his sinus cavities. He'd promised Grace he'd be back at noon or thereabouts, and was now solidly in "thereabouts" territory. She'd wanted to overnight at a B&B up north. If he tarried much longer, the atmosphere at the Yao residence would be chilly the rest of the weekend. Well, arctic. He'd spend hours ducking a stony glare that only a hundred generations of Han womanhood could muster. Even his daughter Jenny was starting to master it by now. Grace wasn't one of those self-effacing, "traditional" Asian wives. Then again, he thought with a wry grin, few of them were. They just came across that way until you knew them for a while. Like say a week.

At the counter stood a diminutive, middle-aged redhead with a pug nose and round, oversized eyes like a bush baby's, giving her an expression of fearful vigilance. He flipped pictures of the house, tank, and little girl on the counter and spoke above a din of clanging that echoed from the back of the shop.

"Clemson Yao, Homicide. These ring any bells? It's about the little girl we found in the underground tank. You might've seen it in the paper." Even in North Korea. The bizarre discovery had gotten worldwide play.

She drew breath with a high-pitched squeak. "That's so awful. My God, is that her?"

Clem nodded.

"Jesus. Let me have a closer look." She scrutinized the aquarium and looked up. "You know? That's ours. The stand, that squiggle of scrollwork? We had a local doing the ironwork; that's his. Big tank, too, hundred twenty, most shops don't carry them."

Clem brightened. "The house? Ever deliver there? Say four years back?"

She smiled. "I don't deliver. That's my husband. Back then with our son, but he's in college now." She turned and raised her voice a half-dozen notches. "Mike? Could you come out here?"

A short, beefy, bushy-browed man with a tonsured hairline and olive complexion came out and shook hands. Curly black chest hair spattered with glinting sweat droplets spilled over his tank top. Tufts of fur sprouted from his arms like an old chimpanzee, obscuring a *semper fi* tattoo on each tricep.

He grinned. "Sorry about the racket. I'm tearing out some shelves. Been putting it off."

The woman glanced at Clem and failed to mask a smile. "For eight years."

Mike eyed the picture of the house and looked up, brows knitted. "Y'know? I *do* remember that house. Normally I wouldn't that far back, right? But *this* guy, I mean, he was funny."

"What'd he look like?"

"Shorter'n you, blond, glasses. Long, horsey kind of face, maybe thirty. Shows up early afternoon, right? I had another delivery. Guy gets bent outa shape I couldn't deliver same day, says he'll buy somewheres else. People just aren't that way about fish tanks. I mean, not like a home theater, guy wants it yesterday. So I put off the other delivery, right? Then we haul the tank over there. Then something else weird."

Clem cocked an eyebrow. "That was?"

"Well, you'd figure, he wants the tank that bad, he'd want it in the living room or wherever, right? But we get there, he wants it in the garage. It's all dusty and fulla junk, where he has to move stuff so's we can get the tank in. I mean, fine with me, no steps, right? Tank that big's a frigging gut buster. But strange."

"Anything else pull your whiskers?"

His eye moved to the photo of the girl. His face became somber. "Yeah, I remember her. Cute kid."

Clem started. "She was at the house?"

"No. Well, yeah, there too. But I mean here at the shop."

Clem tried to clear his brain of the bafflement that had just engulfed it.

"She comes skipping in with him," Mike continued. "Then she's oohing and aahing at the puppy cages, right? Broken arm I think. In a cast."

Clem was stunned. Only her father, or another relative or close friend, would dare be seen with her. A stranger would spirit her away. Mike could even identify the house. His "stranger" theory had just been shot out of the saddle.

Clem finally spoke. "Anything else strike you?"

Mike screwed up his face. "Something, like when they're leaving. Can't put my finger on it."

"Did he say her name?"

"Now that I *know* I'd never remember."

"And at the house? Anything?"

"Oh, just when we're leaving, she looks out a window, makes a kid face. Like sticking her thumbs in her ears and wiggling her fingers? Only just one hand, 'cause her arm's broke, right?"

Clem shook off the savage irony of her last hours. "Any date? Name? Off an invoice?" The name would be bogus, but the date would help. He'd probably killed the girl shortly after he'd gotten the tank—the next day based on the injections.

Mike shrugged. "2004, right? I can track it down from the address. It'll take a while." Mike hesitated, then frowned. "This guy. He the murderer?"

"Very possibly. Why?"

"Nothing you can take to the bank. But his eyes. They creeped me out."

Clem raised both eyebrows.

"Hard to pin down. But like you make a joke, you look in his eyes, they're not laughing, right? Just his mouth. His eyes, they were just weird. Like his lids are half closed the whole time? Like he's off in never-never land?"

Like the intoxication of a fantasy soon fulfilled. He'd read about it but never seen it: the adrenaline-soaked, almost sexual languor many psychopaths got before and during what one expert chillingly called "the quench."

Mike had joined an exclusive club. Few people who saw that look lived to tell about it.

Clem tossed the light on the roof and hit the siren. The least the city could do was get him home faster, especially with a potentially homicidal wife tapping her foot by the door.

He was jarred by what he'd learned. He'd have to look at the father or a close relative as the killer.

But then he felt his inspectorly flesh creep. The killer was probably aware that the girl had been abused. Maybe he knew, even *intended* that attention would be riveted on the parents if they reported her missing, to the extent that he could indulge in bravado. And he'd have every reason to be confident. Nine out of ten detectives would already be typing up a warrant application with a fill-in-the-blank for Daddy.

But just maybe, four years after the fact, Clem had almost done exactly what the killer wanted him to.

Saturday brought Angie a mix of tension and respite. The school district's chamber of horrors was closed, as Marcie Benjamin had a conference out of town. She seesawed between relief at the time-out and a grinding anxiousness to resume her first homicide case, and power-walked her neighborhood's hills by the hour.

An aside was revisiting the night at Twister a week back. Three vodka tonics and a ring-removing Jeremy up from Modesto closing a walnut contract. Mid-forties, superb genes, bald spot still small enough to be endearing. More vodka, enough where Tiny the bartender, a towering ex-Minnesota Vikings fullback, gave her a studied glance.

She replayed the cab ride back to her house in the Parkside neighborhood. She'd have preferred his hotel, where she'd have a better handle on pulling the ripcord. But a pat on his thigh as they streaked westward picked up a clunky key in the pocket, the sort handed out by the hundred-buck hostels west of Union Square. He probably didn't want to kill his image as a Central Valley high roller. The ring nestled there too.

A newbie. Seasoned philanderers left such damning evidence behind.

Two years into an indefinite separation from Roger, Angie limited her occasional carnal prowls to married men out of tortuous convenience. She'd found that single men scared the shit out of her. Most especially the hordes of manual-readers, who listened ever so well and oozed honorable intentions like sap from a maple.

She wasn't holding out for Roger. They saw each other every week or two, usually for lunch and occasionally for dinner near his downtown office, where he managed a team of pathologists doing work for hospitals and the police. They bedded down quarterly at his condo after the dinners. Comfy, but hardly compelling. Angie had in fact been crushed when they'd slept together the first time after Roger had moved out; she'd been hoping they'd come crashing together in a whirlwind of exly ardor. But, as they wistfully agreed, it didn't happen. Maybe they'd do the whirlwind thing when they got around to getting divorced, but she wasn't counting on it. Roger had a sort of girlfriend he saw every few weeks, a retired exotic dancer half his age and IQ named Candi (whom Angie christened "Candi with an i"). She'd parlayed some very hard-earned tips into a business selling drapery materials from Italy.

Angie suspected Roger's dating criteria centered on outrageous head and an utter absence of discourse. The opinion was bolstered by a visit to Candi's shop in a decorating enclave sprouting in the abandoned brick buildings of the Warehouse District south of downtown's main drag, Market Street. Candi was a breathy-voiced, doe-eyed traffic stopper with an ass that was probably still spoken about in hushed, worshipful tones in the club she'd worked. Angie decided to buy some drapes and stifled giggles as Candi agonized through three versions of the sales tax before asking her which one was right.

Angie's reliance on adulterers for routine lust-slaking didn't connote approval. Indeed, she considered them bottom-feeding turds, though very good-looking turds. She'd never cheated on her first husband, Clint, Jackie's father, though he hadn't returned the favor. Nor on Roger in eight years, though she'd once been tempted for a month in the idlest manner by a particularly dashing client. She was certain he'd been equally faithful, though she wondered whether he'd first set eyes on Candi at the market after he'd moved out, as he insisted, or snaked around a dance pole in the altogether beforehand. She marveled at the balm of time passed. Had she entertained the notion two years ago, when they were both trying to splint their compound-fractured marriage and fantasizing their escape from it, she would've been cataleptic with jealousy and hurt.

She knew she'd feel a sense of relief someday when she found herself waking up next to a guy who knew important stuff about her, like her phone number. But at the moment, the craving for no-last-names lust didn't faze her. She'd slogged through the never-agains. The wince of self-disgust she initially fought back always faded—early on over the course of a month, and more recently, over, say, a long weekend. Then the night would come when she'd indulge in more than her two vodka tonic limit. And there she'd be, exchanging an "I'm gonna get laid" grin with Tiny, a grizzly bear of a guy who looked out for her those nights as best he could. Once he'd hauled an intended out the back and sent him sprawling in the next-door restaurant's leftovers after he'd tried to give Tiny a twenty to muscle up her drinks.

But being face-to-face with the leavings of a child killer left her troubled at bedding a man whose face she'd have trouble picking out of a lineup. For the second time, she was tied by a thread to a merciless killer. Not like the coincidences everyone risked: "Lady, you have just pissed off the *wrong grocery bagger!*" No, this was a straight line between two points that lodged in her gut like undercooked potatoes.

As if an omen, Sunday was the twenty-first anniversary of the night she'd erased The Beast from the earth. On the first one, she'd been shocked at the procession of squad cars that cruised by her house with Mars lights whirling. Nowadays they were fewer, five or ten over the night.

It was a crime spree that had policemen viewing the world through the crosshairs. In three weeks, the daughters of four cops had been kidnapped, ages ten to thirteen. No witnesses or forensics. A terrifying absence of phone calls and ransom notes. Later it was learned that the kidnapper was a court bailiff who had done two tours in Nam and trained in kidnap techniques under the CIA's Phoenix Program. While cops showed off their pics to other cops in his courtroom, he would sneak a peek, rate the girls on his reptilian ten scale, and jot down the father's name and precinct. Completely under the radar.

It was in this icy atmosphere that Angie started her tour with SFPD. Her partner was named Groucho, a portly twenty-year lifer with a handlebar mustache. One night, he pulled the squad up in front of a dimly lit Victorian in the Haight. A Beast tip had come from a woman named Doris

Manning, who claimed it was her neighbor. Bullshit, like every other tip they'd gotten.

They knocked, and an old woman in a frumpy red housecoat jerked the door open. Her hair looked like Einstein's. "Hurry!" she hissed. "He'll see you!" They moved into the cluttered living room. The place reeked of moth-balls and boiled potatoes.

Groucho began. "Now, ma'am, what leads you to believe that your neighbor is The Beast?"

She looked at him wild-eyed. "Well. One week ago, at 9:00 p.m., I saw him pull up in his driveway. Then he put a big sack over his shoulder and walked around the house to his back door."

As Groucho nodded, her expression was equal parts horror and triumph. "And just *what* did I read in the paper the very next morning? Hmm?"

Groucho raised two bushy eyebrows.

"That girl was kidnapped right out of her playroom!" she finished, disgusted at Groucho's inability to put two and two together.

Groucho's brows knitted together as he intently wrote in his notepad. Angie glanced at it; it was a drawing of a gun pointing at the old woman's head. "Yes, ma'am," he said. "That is indeed highly suspicious behavior. Would there be anything else?"

Doris's eyes bulged with indignation. "What else do you *need?*"

"Frigging open mike night," muttered Groucho as they left. They decided to circle the neighbor's house. As they trudged up the driveway, they heard a crash and jogged to the back. Angie beamed her Maglite at an overturned garbage can, just in time to spot one large fluffy tail trailed by three small ones, skittering away. Raccoons.

Groucho grinned. "See if you can corner them and call Animal Control. Me, I'm headed for Dunkin' Donuts. Back in half an hour."

Groucho slouched back to the squad, and Angie ambled around the back of the house. The raccoons circled to the garage side. By the time Angie turned the corner, they'd vanished. Abutting the side of the garage was a wooden barbecue deck. She bent down and shined her Maglite underneath. Nothing. They'd escaped.

It was then she heard the sound that would echo in her head for decades:

a soft moan, rising and falling in pitch, like the songs of the humpback whales on one of her old Judy Collins records. She shined the beam on the wall of the garage where it met the deck. A patch of stucco had flaked off, exposing boards beneath. She banged once on the wood and listened.

Not one moan now, but several.

Panic thrummed through her as she reached the driveway and studied the rollup door where it met the concrete. It was covered in debris. So the guy didn't park inside the garage, probably in the driveway. She glanced up at the darkened windows. He wasn't home. She tried the rollup door, but it was locked.

She found the back door. A pane was covered with cardboard taped to the glass, easy to punch through and unlock. It would be an illegal search—for a rookie, probably the kiss of death. But someone, or something, was suffering in the garage. Not enough for a warrant, especially since the judges had already approved twenty fruitless house searches and were fed up. If the guy came home now, they'd never get inside.

Angie popped her fist through the cardboard, unlocked, and entered, then pushed the cardboard back and locked again. She stood in a dimly lit kitchen full of dilapidated appliances and wooden cabinets layered in ancient grease. To the left was a door probably leading downstairs to the garage. She clinked the latch and opened. The odor wafting up from the blackness reminded her of a neglected kennel.

As she edged downward on the stairway, she drew her .45 service revolver and called out "Police!" The silence was broken by muffled moans and sobs. She reached the concrete floor and pointed the Maglite into the garage. Then she went numb as she took in the hellish scene.

A circle of ten concrete cinder block stalls, each two feet high and four feet long, surrounded a drain in the center, like piggery stalls she'd once seen at a deserted farmhouse. Above the top of four stalls she saw the arched, naked backs of four girls on their hands and knees, so emaciated that their ribs and backbones stuck out like Dachau victims'. Each girl faced outwards from the drain in the center.

She edged closer. The girls were naked, chained by chafed wrists and ankles to the floor, their mouths covered with duct tape. The stall floors were stained with traces of excrement. She suppressed a heave at the sight of one girl's buttocks splattered with telltale dry white flecks. Judging from the garden hose attached to a spigot on the garage wall, the shitbag probably hosed them down once or twice a day.

She searched for something to get the girls out of the chains and edged toward the garage door. She beamed her flashlight under a crawlspace to the right and saw a huge pile of concrete and dirt. Then, to her shock, she nearly stumbled into an empty pit about six feet deep in front of the garage door, broken through the concrete and into the underlying dirt. It was rectangular, six feet long and four feet wide. A dozen bags of cement were stacked next to it.

Her anger and disgust were squelched by the sound of a car engine. Seconds later, the edges of the rollup door glinted with the glare of headlamps. The Beast was home.

She signaled to the girls that she would hide in the crawlspace. They nodded, eyes reflecting a glimmer of hope. She heard the car trunk close and crouched down. Seconds later, the back door to the house opened and slammed shut. Heavy footsteps moved through the kitchen to the connecting door to the garage, and it opened. Light beamed downstairs from the kitchen.

The first two clomps were accompanied by a loathsome cackle. "This little piggie went to market . . . " Clomp clomp. "This little piggie stayed home . . . " Clomp clomp. "This little piggie had roast beef . . . " She could see his half-lit figure fifteen feet away as he stumped into the garage. He was tall and burly, and carrying a sack across his shoulder. But she couldn't see his face.

He carefully set the sack down, reached toward the ceiling, and switched on a pull-chain bulb. He was wearing a black wool ski mask. He dragged the sack over to the empty stall closest to Angie and stopped there.

"Well, we're up to five piggies." He glanced at the girl next to the empty stall and shook his head sadly. But his lips were pursed into a thin, cruel line. "Though Linda piggie here's down to her last night with us."

He moved around to face the girls. Angie could see the faces of three of them, and the looming figure of The Beast from behind. But she couldn't draw a bead without risking an errant shot hitting the girls.

He moved over several feet; Angie could now see his masked profile. He went into a squat and bugged his eyes at them. His mouth was a mockery of a smile. "Now, we haven't talked about this, but it's *just* the right time. Remember I said you'd go back to your mommies and daddies when we finished our piggie game?"

The girls sobbed and nodded in unison. A sickening ritual. They'd been conditioned to respond this way.

"Well, sometimes people play *jokes* on little piggies. Ha ha ha!" The sobbing increased. "This part of the game is called Piggie Heaven. Now, we know that all piggies go to Piggy Heaven, right?"

The girls nodded desperately.

"Well, tonight Linda piggie is going there!"

Angie nearly fired accidentally as one girl choked out a high-pitched wail through her nose.

He leered at them and spoke over Linda's cries. "But sometimes for something very very good to happen to us, like going to Piggie Heaven, something very very bad has to happen first, right?"

The girls sobbed but nodded. The Beast stood up and circled around the stalls to a shelf on the garage wall about ten feet from Angie. He picked up and brandished a huge hacksaw, looking straight at Linda. His jaw jutted forward. His eyes were now black holes bored in the sockets. This was no sick joke.

The girls' muffled screams galvanized Angie to action. She stood and pointed her revolver. "Freeze! Police!" She exhaled slowly, willing herself not to tremble.

The hacksaw clattered to the floor. He gasped but kept his composure. She could sense him weighing options. He glanced at the pull-chain, but it was out of reach. He finally sneered. "Well, if I was gonna get caught, your timing couldn't be better. None of 'em's dead yet."

She got his drift through a tidal wave of fury that almost buckled her knees. No murder rap. But he was better off than he knew. The illegal search meant that all physical evidence would be inadmissible. And the girls had probably never seen his face. Rage flayed her as she realized that the fucker might just walk. He wouldn't hang around—he'd be under a death fatwa from San Francisco's finest—but he'd soon be plying his trade who knew where.

In four seconds, her father's home brew high-velocity ammo sent six hollow points hurtling out the barrel, blowing ragged fissures through his lungs, trachea, small intestine, pancreas, and colon. HPs didn't normally produce exit wounds, but propelled by something akin to Trident missile fuel, these did; Angie couldn't see them but knew the wounds were the size of nickels as the bullets flattened like pancakes and gouged out his insides. The wall behind him looked like a Jackson Pollock canvas in red.

Through a choking cordite haze, she watched his eyes bulge. He gaped at the ceiling and forced up a viscous cough. A fountain of blood erupted inches in the air from his mouth, and he sagged onto his back. Angie sprinted up and gazed spellbound as a syrupy gasp sent blood welling up to his lips like an overflowing toilet. It finally gurgled out the tracheal exit wound onto the floor. Later she would be shocked when she saw an autopsy photo of his face; rather than the brutish troglodyte she'd expected, with his avian nose, doughy cheeks, and prominent Adam's apple, he looked like a beefy version of Don Knotts.

A shooting review judged the first shot plausible. But the fusillade that followed wasn't, and she was dismissed. The DA decided not to prosecute. In the press, he was adamant that the decision had nothing to do with rumors of a wildcat police strike.

The reaction of the ranks was as expected. Her Academy graduation photo was posted on the wall in every cop bar with the caption, "She got the number of The Beast!" Forensics gave her an award for the largest number of organs scraped off the wall in a cop shooting. She still got Christmas cards from all five of the girls' fathers and from three of the girls. Five years ago, when she went for Police Reserve, she was warmly—if very clandestinely—welcomed.

She didn't know what would come of her unofficial stint in Homicide. But that was where the cream of humanity's monsters hung out. The Ruger .357 revolver her father had given her for her sweet sixteen would be nestling closer at hand than it had for decades. Years ago, she'd wrung her hands a while over ending a human life, even one that stretched the definition of "human" to absurdity. Few cops fired a weapon on the street their whole careers, and she'd learned what most of them had: there was an innate horror in sending pieces of metal tearing through a man's body at the speed of sound that dwarfed the loftiest purpose.

She'd gotten no enjoyment from it and would never do it again unless she had to. But once again, a human monstrosity who wasn't worth the oxygen he breathed stalked the city. And once again, she wouldn't hesitate to splatter organs, blood, and bone on the wall behind him if it came to it.

CHAPTER SEVEN

The phone blared its annoying doodlydo in Clem's dingy, windowless eight-by-eight office. Every few months, he routinely put in a requisition for a phone with a real bell in it. It was just as routinely turned down with a caustic remark clipped to the form that phones didn't have bells anymore. He glowered at it, trying to intimidate it into silence. Then he spied the Virginia area code and the name on the screen. Billy Rankin.

Special Agent William Rankin—Billy to all—was a profiler with the FBI Behavioral Science Unit in Quantico, specializing in serial killers. Clem had sent him a copy of the crime scene file on Friday by courier.

Billy had ridden shotgun on a serial when Clem had made Homicide six years before. The FBI's teaming system under VICAP, the Violent Criminal Apprehension Program, paired profilers with local cops. Now a grudgingly accepted institution, Behavioral Science had had its share of controversy early on, crowbarring its way into high-profile cases to the irritation of grizzled detectives. Earlier profilers seemed more interested in book deals featuring prison photo ops with serial killers they'd had nothing to do with catching. But the deals dried up once it became clear that they were just one more platform for the Feebies to take credit when something good happened and excoriate the locals when it didn't. Even now, their presence on a case was often more hindrance than help, their principal contribution a startling grasp of the obvious.

But Clem and Billy had got on well. Billy had lateraled into Behavioral

Science from the hard-boiled kidnap field investigations unit of the FBI. The aim was to strengthen their ability to work under harrowing time pressure when serials "decompensated," or, as Billy put it, went turbo—when the pace of killing quickened, usually because the killer began to think himself invincible. Billy was not well liked because of his disdain for the psychobabble of his peers, of whom he said they'd never met a syllable they didn't like. He was also the worst-dressed agent in the Bureau. Some said it was a ruse to avoid a promotion that would take him out of fieldwork.

The voice at the other end of the phone line had a deep-south lilt. "Hey. Looks like you woke up with a big-ass scorpion in your jammies." Clem winced at the doozy that had just been added to his summer nightmare catalog. But talking with Billy was an adventure. Raised in Bessemer City, Alabama, Billy toggled at will between Gomerisms and the flair of a Virginia orator.

"Yeah, think I'll switch to my skimpy black things," replied Clem. "Wife's been nagging me anyway."

Billy chortled. "Let me guess. Christmas present. And you've fought her off 'til May."

"Yeah, she got 'em in some shop called Ulterior Motive."

"Part of being married and fifty-something. Got me a collection near-bout. You're fifty-five, right? Thought you'd be used to it by now."

"I'm getting there. So Billy, what sort of reptile am I up to my *tuches* in here? You need to spruce up my file. We're working this one with a Realtor."

"Sounds like your Powell Street Irregulars again."

"Yeah, but she's pretty sharp. Cop kid, Police Reserve. Jessica Fletcher wannabe."

"More's the better, since your colleagues couldn't pop a turd on a flat rock." Billy's indelicate take on Homicide was largely because Bert Heimlich—alias Grunt—had been named lead inspector on the case Billy had worked six years before. Clem claimed Grunt had gone for Homicide because he secretly got off on telling people their loved ones were dead. He was famed for two-hour beer-and-beernut lunches and was rumored to hit on homicide widows. Understandable since he had the face and girth of a walrus and needed the helping hand of a woman's emotional collapse to get laid.

A notorious bigot who heckled black hookers by leering at them and singing "Hi ho, hi ho, it's off to work we go," Grunt had ducked official censure only through the intervention of cronies in the police union. The complaint had come from brother officers. Working girls knew more than anyone about what went down on the street. They were a source of G2 for everyone from the beats to Narcotics, and it didn't pay to piss them off.

On the serial case six years ago, Grunt had zeroed in on a Hispanic friend of one of the vics based on his "intuition." Meaning, the suspect had filed an excessive force beef against Grunt three years before. Thankfully, Grunt mistook Billy's mushmouth talk for evidence of a fellow traveler. He peppered his banter with references to beaners, heebs, and mud people until Billy taped him and wrote an eat-shit-and-die on FBI letterhead to the chief of division. Grunt was yanked, and Clem made lead inspector. To this day, the two circled each other like TV wrestlers seeking the Internal Affairs body slam that would knock the other out of the ring. It was the main reason Clem had passed up several tempting evidence plants lately.

"Anyways, your current killer's not your garden-varietal," continued Billy. "None of the control and domination stuff. Sex, torture, humiliation."

"Yeah, regular altar boy. No gross-out signature shit."

"But this elaborate construction stuff, it just ain't *normal*," Billy fretted, like a father worried about his son dressing his sister's dolls.

"Yeah, it's ritual display squared. Like he was sitting around building a ship in a bottle."

"And no degradation impulse," Billy continued. "Presented her in the best light. Usual bent's to dehumanize the vic, not pedestalize her."

"Tell me about it. Get this, her nightie's brand new. Saks, hundred percent silk. Had flecks of plastic in it from where he clipped off the price tag."

"Not many of my regulars go shopping for their vics, 'specially at the better stores. You'll see something we call undoing, where the guy tries to 'soften' the crime. Often in child killings. But simple stuff like covering the face, nothing like this. And it's not usually a stranger. Kin, or someone he knows. So no chance on Daddy? My call from the bleachers."

Clem sighed. "Everyone else's too, even my wife. I'm going against the grain, but I just don't buy it. Even if I try, all my arrows still point at a stranger."

"Okay, I'll bite. Then she probably represents someone else in his life. Like as not resembled something happened to him or someone he knew."

"Already had that in mind. So he's psychopathic? Even if he didn't turn her into ground round?"

"Well, it's one a those . . . now *what's* that word? Conundrums," answered Billy.

"Umm . . . just what I was thinking. A frigging conundrum," replied Clem.

"I mean, if I was to see this display of remains without knowing mode of death, I'd read remorse. I'd like Daddy for it: her death unintended, the display a twisted atonement.

"But we know it's murder, the most premeditated sort," continued Billy. "If it's a stranger, kidnapping *and* murder, pretty damn psychopathic. But a psychopath's basically incapable of guilt or remorse; it's what defines him. So maybe grief over some other thing happened to him. They can feel grief, though in a narcissistic way—feel sorry for 'emselves. Whether he shreds her up depends on the fantasy got him started. Most of 'em's scary vicious, anger stemming from abuse, humiliation."

Clem pursed his lips. "But we don't see that anger in *this* display."

"Right, but folks don't murder without anger 'less it's their day job. If it's a stranger, anger'll be there, but winging off in another direction. Might could be part of another event in his life—some catastrophe, or another killing—that embodies his underlying anger. Might could be around the same time as this one."

Clem nodded. "He spent *weeks* on that mural with the burning woman. It has to mean *something*. And it's not something good."

"You figure out who she is, you'll know more'n you know now. Speaking of which, when they're done, have the Forensics boys ship it here. There's someone I want to show it to."

"Sotheby's? Psycho killer art has a certain following."

"Later. For now a specialist on oil paints. Dating, provenance, left or right handed. Ask 'em to minimize destructive testing. Now. On Daddy, something's yanking my scrotum I didn't think of before. Killer didn't want her found too easy, right?"

"We *didn't* find her too easy."

"But why didn't he get rid of the pipes?"

Clem banged the heel of his hand on his temple, amazed at his own obtuseness. "Shit. He could've pulled the two pipes, replaced the board, contractor would've never found the tank."

"So *he's dumber'n a pressure-cooked porcupine, or*—"

"He *wanted* her to be found. Didn't want the oldsters to find her. Wanted to *control* when she'd be found, by the contractor." Clem paused thoughtfully. "And then me."

"Control's his middle name. And blocking off the garage?"

Clem grimaced in exasperation. "Not to keep the owners from surprising him; there was no risk of that. To alert the contractor that something was hinky, so he'd look for it. Christ, I feel like Detective Porky Pig."

"B-b-b-because even if the inspector found the tank, they mightn't have found the tunnel—thus the girl—'til the tank was dug up, maybe months or years later. So, 'stead of browning his britches over you carting off his Little Nell, he's—"

"Cackling away. The cretinous little shit. He's playing me."

"Like a Strad. If it's Daddy, and he did the display out of remorse, he wouldn't flaunt it. He'd make damn sure it wasn't found. Also points to a stranger. Question is, where's he go from here?"

"Another girl? I'm thinking not. Okay, hoping."

"Tough call," admitted Billy. "Whether he'll go multiple depends on his need to reprise or escalate the fantasy got him started. Like a fella spends ten years dreaming about carving up the missus. He fillets her, he's happy. Psychopathic? Probably, 'cause he lacks the barriers that separate fantasy from action. But not serial."

"Until he remarries."

"Right. But a fella does freak stuff, something hairier's afoot. He'll surely do something else freakoid, even if not the same thing. So on the one hand, can't discount another girl in a tank. Simplest way to view the crime scene, dangerous to dismiss it. And our philosophy is to work off what the crime scene tells us."

"Even when the result is shit a la mode," Clem chuckled. Some of the

FBI's profiling conclusions became legendary howlers once the killer was caught. Detectives called it 'AWG Syndrome,' the Bureau's tendency to profile every serial as an Average White Guy.

"I've eaten my share," Billy agreed. "So yes, keep an eye out for new missing girls. But the tea leaves say something else may be afoot. Forensics say he visited her a lot early on, but lately only every six months or so. Now, it *could* mean he got him another girl the last year, that his attentions have shifted to her. But if doing her up in the tank was related to some cataclysmic event of years back—and the mural hints at that—might could be his fascination with her's just worn off. Then his jollies switch to her discovery, 'specially after the house went up for sale."

"Christ, I hope so. I don't have it in me to find another dead girl in a tank. Never thought I'd say this to a Fed, but feel like a trip to SF?"

"Chocks away soon as you zip up the next body bag. Throwing the switch on a child killer always gives me that elusive inner radiance. And squares a few debits on the Almighty's shit list."

"That and your next loony might be in Buffalo."

"No joke. My last big stint? Two months, Anchorage in February. Time I left, I was thinking of switching sides."

The morning news showed the yellow house for the umpteenth time. Still the only visual, and the poor sots were beating it to death with a stick. The news director was probably bleeding through his pores. Maybe he should throw them a bone, send them one of those goofy letters with words snipped from magazines, touting himself as "The Mad Mortician." They'd gnaw away on it for weeks.

But today he was reminded of the one thing he'd left behind at the house that he hadn't meant to. That stupid cat. A continual irritation, like a big old hairy wart you kept picking at but that came back every time.

He took heart that it was something innocuous enough to be missed. But if he'd slipped up once, he could again. And there was a more psychic side. As long as he controlled what they knew, then he would be the metronome. But once he couldn't, he might find himself outflanked. The game went to the shuffler of the shells, not to the befuddled guesser.

He drained his coffee, wondering if Yao was on the same track as the media. Thinking that his quarry was skulking about the city like a bug-eyed little Igor, seeking another girl for his embalming pleasure. ▪

That's how most serials worked after all. A tedious lot, and screaming bores at cocktail parties, bending any line of conversation to their pet topics. "Sooo, you're in the online dating biz? Sounds dangerous to me. You know, going out with someone you've never met? Hey, I can't resist asking: Anyone ever get killed doing that? Like maybe strangled with, oh, say, three-eighths-inch polypropylene cliff-climbing rope?"

And all that inane signature and trophy stuff. Homicide's idiot savants, ever lopping off a favorite appendage, writing in blood, pilfering pantyhose, breaking mirrors. Stigmata, cannibalism, scalping, necro-nasties, playing cards, urination. Nipple-biting, eye-gouging, chest-carving, teeth-pulling, hair-cutting, yadayadayada like a naughty boy showing a girl a dead rat.

Sometimes he just felt embarrassed for his poor relations.

To be sure, there were days when it would be a relief to be satisfied with such lowbrow high jinks. Sometimes he woke up feeling more like Sancho Panza than Don Quixote, enslaved to his grandiose inspirations. Like the Pharaoh's chief stonecutter must have felt when the Big Guy snatched the sheet off the model of the pyramids.

Nor was he immune from fixation. He could recall with the detachment of a Buddhist monk his obsession of years ago. He'd park in the dark for hours, ducking as cars cruised by. He'd curse the TV flickering through the curtains until he could worm through the window and be with her in that oddly comforting womb he'd hammered together. Then he'd stare at her unblinking, his face pressed against the Plexiglas an hour at a time. His heart became a jumble of anguish and rapture, interrupted occasionally by the gurgling of the pipes when the toilet flushed two floors up. Twice he'd even fallen asleep, escaping as the eastern sky tinted with the colors of dawn.

But lately, truth was he'd found himself getting a bit bored by her. By his last visit, he'd figured she'd soon be carted away, her remains pared down to bone like a shwarma. He'd felt sadness, but more, determination to send her packing. Doing a replica would be perverse, like Michelangelo sculpting another David because someone had laid into it with a sledge. Wasn't it he who said the work of art was already inside the block of stone, that he just had to unearth it?

No, she was the product of a magical set of coincidences. The fractures, the tank, his arcane hodgepodge of skills. And the statement had been made. He was in a different place now, with a new and fearsome message to flesh out.

Papa's got a brand new bag.

Clem glowered in his office awaiting a call from Rob Lyle in the crime lab. There was no love lost between Homicide and Forensics. Crime lab geeks were often half the age of their detective peers, their labs wall-to-wall with pricey gadgetry while detectives groveled for overtime. Rob's colleagues disdained the intuition of the gumshoes, ignoring the fact that crimes were usually solved because somebody somewhere talked. Add to that Homicide's lack of courtroom pizzazz. The DA would even plead down rather than put either of two tongue-tied inspectors on the stand: one, the infamous Grunt; the other, his crony Pete Finch, aka Mumbles. The DA had nicknamed them both.

Another bone of contention between the two departments was that improved forensics made evidence plants on shitballs you couldn't nail much riskier. Even Clem—an unapologetic planter when it suited—had kept his nose clean lately. Still, a box buried in his garage contained dozens of cigarette butts, tissues, hair follicles, and other DNA bombs, along with latented matchbooks, paper cups, and other goodies he'd picked up in interrogations. Seven plants in thirty years, and not one pricked his conscience. One, a street gang leader who'd dispatched a competitor with a jackhammer, he'd had the audacity to plant twice.

Not that he groused about civil liberties loonies; this was San Francisco, after all. And truth was, he despised the Force's system-sucks whiners. Half of them were incompetent or lazy, avoiding hated court time with stunts like running the siren as they pulled up to a B&E scene to give the guy time to get away. Another third were Dirty Harry wannabes who thought procedures were for the little people. And yes, you could flame out after twenty years of watching burglaries cop to larceny. But truth was, that was all most San Francisco cops and assistant DAs were suited for. Justice was an assembly line, partly because most of its practitioners weren't capable of much else.

But Homicide could be a refuge if you wanted one. Most inspectors didn't like books with no pictures, and did their damnedest to boost their clearance rates with no-brainers. But you could still challenge yourself. He'd been around and knew that top homicide cops almost never left the game if they could help it, even in the face of plum promotions. After retirement, they kept the company of ghosts, often pursuing their most frustrating un-solveds to the grave. He was no different, he knew; half a dozen sad-eyed wraiths would clamor for his attention the moment he hung up his spurs.

And the judicial system behaved better when the topic was murder. Insanity defenses almost never flew except in cop shows. Those few who pulled it off found that being looped on Thorazine in the company of *real* psychotics made San Quentin look like a cakewalk. And these days few ap-peals courts would put a monster back on the street for a technicality.

You had to be willing to take a hit if you colored outside the lines, and Clem did. But planting never replaced detective work, merely augmented it from time to time. And he followed strict guidelines. You didn't plant where there was no motive; it would raise suspicions. You didn't plant to protect a brutal cop. You didn't use innocent vics; their loved ones deserved a clean solve. On the other hand, scumbag vics were big mounds of carrion freely employed to snare the stinkiest buzzard you could.

But while Clem thought the crime lab a necessary evil, Rob, his favor-ite forensic geek, came from a cop family. He zeroed in on the needs of a case like a coon dog, unlike his peers, who could get mired in forensic bloat while Clem had a suspect in the sweat box singing like Sammy Hagar. And he owed Rob for a brace of favors, including some thinly veiled handy-dandy planting hints.

He glared at the silent phone, then distracted himself ironing out the pet shop wrinkle. Even Chief Jackson was offering him side bets on the father, but there were too many inconsistencies. He'd rented the house himself. Maybe his wife and daughter had moved in after, but the neighbors didn't recall a blond girl tramping off to school four years back, just a nondescript guy in a blue car once in a while. And how could he build the tomb with his wife there? Or maybe he'd offed her too, and she was dust-to-dusting under the azaleas along the back fence. Or maybe no wife, just him and his daughter. But then, why kill her? Abusers needed abusees.

And the display didn't fly for an abusive parent. Their jollies came while the child was alive, or, rarely, in the act of killing. The corpse was an afterthought, bringing on shock, panic, or guilt, never macabre creativity. And the mural took it from the greed and anger underlying most murders into the psychic malignancy that could turn the best detective's brain into oatmeal.

But if the killer was a stranger, why wouldn't he buy the tank first, instead of risking capture by letting her be seen? Or tie her up and *then* buy it after he had her if he was the stingy sort? Unless it was chutzpah: taking her to buy the tank he would embalm her in, something as ghoulish as anything Clem could remember.

His phone finally rang. Rob got straight to the point. "We picked up trace bodily fluids. On the outside of the Plexiglas window. Wiped pretty clean, but we got a spot he missed."

"Jesus, Mary, and Joseph," muttered Clem, just as Rob got called away. Maybe the scumbag was jerking off in the tunnel. Bad enough to draw a child killing. The rule was you couldn't draw two in a row unless they were connected, and this was Clem's fifth in six years. Four had been fountains of pain, but like most child killings, easy solves: two more-or-less voluntary confessions from a crack whore and a stepfather; a girl caught in a dealer cross fire; and a boy killed in a hit-and-run by a coked-out lawyer with the cleanest fenders in town. He'd come on like Clarence Darrow until Clem showed him the tiny piece of skin they'd lifted from the hood ornament, inducing him to piss his navy blue Zegnas.

But now he'd have to revisit the same reeking effluvia he'd swum through during child killing number five, an eleven-year-old girl who spent ten days chained to a bed until she broke off a piece of one of the springs and tore out her own throat.

Pedophilia. Maybe it *was* the reason the killer had drugged the girl and put off killing her until the next day.

Clem knew that, like many top homicide detectives, he was driven by a lurid, gut-clenching fascination with the act of murder: its ravaging finality, the demonic jumble of emotions that drove murderers before the act and afflicted them after. Or, far scarier, the icy lack of them. Still burned in his memory was the first time he'd encountered a psychopath: a guy who'd cranked up one night, walked into an ice cream parlor, and shot to death the lone woman working there—a high school grad saving her money for her first semester of college. In interrogation, the shitball had shrugged like a jaywalker as he recounted how he'd made her kneel behind the counter. A dozen cans of cherry vanilla and swiss chocolate were speckled with hundreds of blobs of brain and bone like cannibalistic sprinkles. The crime scene team swore off Baskin-Robbins for months.

Clem's fascination with murder was bolstered by a dissociative chromosome that kept the hatches battened down even in the face of that kind of gore. But a pedophile murder could send it spinning out of the helix. An unsolved serial could turn a cop into an unguided missile who would just as soon take a suspect out in a skiff, chum up a great white, and hang his legs over the gunwale.

Rob got back on. Clem's knuckles whitened. "Rob, the bodily fluids. That what I think it is?"

Rob chuckled. "No, not that. Clear fluid, a little bit of this, a little bit of that, heavy on the salt."

Clem sighed with vexation. "My weekly round of forensic charades. My buddy in LAPD told me every crime lab in the country has one like you."

"Until the detectives take up a collection and have him killed. Sounds like . . ."

Clem bit his lip and went along. "Huh. Lots of salt, right? So just sweat?"

"Close but no cigar. How's a dash of lysozyme grab you?"

Clem gazed at the ceiling. He felt like Watson. "Umm . . . it doesn't."

"Gotcha. The antibacterial enzyme in human tears."

Clem nodded. "Well, no surprise. There were fumes in the tunnel from a leak."

"Nope. Here's one for you: the chemical composition of tears caused by irritation is much different from tears when somebody cries."

"Well, you learn something new every day." Clem hung up shaking his head. Her father, face pressed against the tank, grieving over the daughter he'd murdered? What stranger would mourn her death by his own hand?

• • •

He cradled the eyedropper bottle in his hand, reveling in its potency. The stuff had worked like black magic, slow and insidious. And the coup de grace now just days away. The dervish dance of blood and fire.

The Père Lebrun messy.

Twelve thousand dollars worth of messy.

He wouldn't be there to see it, but he'd have the next best thing. Three hundred extra for the photos. A disposable camera. Just enough resolution to see that mountain of brutal flesh and bone whirling and charring in the pyre of smoke and flame.

And the hands too, of course. Oh yes, the hands would be so nice. The mammoth, bruising knouts that had blackened eyes and gouged flesh purple, now disembodied and Dali-esque on the floor. He'd suggested a video, but they'd declined. Too risky inside prison walls. But a cassette recorder for the screams? No sweat. Another three hundred.

Jesus, the dealer options just killed you.

Still, it was a done deal. But on another topic, he had to wrestle with what to do about the old bitch. Maybe use her to spritz up the Scarecrow messy? An ad lib would be a hoot.

He sported a dry smile as he recalled fee fie foe fuming around for weeks while the house had languished on the market. Truth was, he wasn't even mad at her anymore. After all, his little Cindy had finally been fished from the chemical brew. No harm no foul. But then again, he'd sworn she would pay for making him wait so long.

Then he shook his head in annoyance. If a stone killer couldn't be honest about his little foible, who could? Two years back, out of curiosity, he'd wandered into an abnormal psych lecture at UCSF entitled "Why Would a Psychopath Kill?" The speaker—an FBI pooh-bah who probably fainted at the sight of blood spatters—presented an hour of psychodrivel. Unchecked narcissism. Affective deficit. The MacDonald Triad. Blah blah blah.

He'd staggered out feeling like a Jewish kid reading Mein Kampf. *Everything was so, well, negative.*

And for a month or two he got sucked in by all the developmental crap. Read all the right books, felt bad about himself. Ashamed, even. Self-esteem just shot to shit. Recovered memories, crying jags, bulimia, the works.

God, what a sniveler.

One morning, he almost whimpered into a precinct and turned himself in. And then, he took a good look around. And got really, really pissed.

Hell, most of America's top-billing lawyers and a third of its CEOs were twice the psychopath he was. Some even sported monikers like "Chainsaw." Such rank hypocrisy. Slash thirty thousand jobs and make fifty dead-enders slug down JD and suck gun, you got your own jet. Slash a lousy half-dozen jugulars, you got a T-bone for your last meal.

You could be a captain of industry, wreak havoc, then tool off in your stretch as if you weren't secretly gloating over all those suicide clauses.

Or you could own your own shit and deal your death outright.

That was it in a nutshell. Psychopaths to a man they were.

But like Manson, they just didn't do their own stunts.

Yes, he would do her and do her proud. But not out of overblown vengeful-ness; she certainly didn't deserve that. Great stuff, vengeance, but do the right messy for the wrong reason? There you'd be, huffing and puffing away trying to feel vengeful. And come up with squat. He shuddered. Something like that could set off a tidal wave of self-doubt and eat your lunch, like a golfer who never got his swing back. Just another psychopathic flash in the pan, punching walls every time your betters made America's Most Wanted.

No, he'd do her for the simple reason that he'd found her picture four years ago in the desk. And she looked like a bulldog with impetigo.

Oh, but he was dehumanizing the vic, they'd say. There it was in every pro-filer's Ten Sure Ways to Spot a Psychopath. *A common enough pitfall among the serial rabble. But not for him. For Pete's sake, if they weren't human to you, you might as well stick to misdemeanors and chuck turtles in the trash compac-tor. Talk about your arrested development. Animals were fine when you were a kid, but at some point, you had to put away childish things.*

Not that he didn't wax nostalgic here and there. Especially about the tarantulas.

The magnifying glass he'd gotten for his twelfth birthday quickly became a tool of genocide against the neighborhood spider population. Then he learned from a Mexican schoolmate how to catch tarantulas by flooding their burrows.

His mother blanched when he begged her to allow him to keep one. But she'd just let his sister have a cat and relented as long as he kept it in a tank. She groused about that damn tarantula for two years until he tired of it.

What no one realized was that he'd had not one tarantula, but twenty-five. One after the other. They all looked pretty much alike.

As the school days ended he would quiver with anticipation, at least on sunny afternoons. When summer approached, he rejoiced, not at the coming vacation but at the broiling heat the late spring sun would let him radiate at his latest captive. At first, the huge spider would run maniacal circles inside the tank, even leap at the glass with fangs bared. On a good day he could get it to make a high-pitched hiss that gave him an unforgettable frisson. But after a few introductory sessions, it would cower in a corner of the tank. Its legs would fold tighter and tighter beneath it as the afternoon sun began to shine through the bedroom window, signaling the coming of the terrible fire from above. The one that would over a week fry its legs and palps into hairy stumps, then blind it eye by eye, then finally cook its bulbous abdomen into stinking goop.

He went through so much air freshener that his mother accused him of smoking.

Gracious, what a social calendar the next week or so. The Père Lebrun messy. The Scarecrow messy. The Malleus messy. Yikes.

Patience, patience. He luxuriated in the swelling in his groin, that delicious numbness in his thighs that had begun to bloom lately, when he'd started fleshing out the Scarecrow messy. He'd racked himself for weeks until it was a vision of grisly perfection. Messy messy, oh yes, yes, he thought giddily. Put me in, Coach.

Goodness, maybe too messy? Was such a thing possible?

Naaah, that's exactly what made them so special.

Why would a psychopath kill?

Well gosh gee willikers, why not?

If nothing else, Rob Lyle's forensic brain-burner called for a change of subject, and Clem took some time to ponder Chief Grady Moore stewing over the oak tree killing down in Gilroy. Narcotics had shot blanks on the

Burundanga. Probably a special order through a high-powered connection, not something you rustled up in the projects. Narc squads blanched at the thought of an epidemic, but so far it hadn't hit. Some thought the cartels were wary of flooding U.S. streets with a tool for thieves and rapists. Not out of conscience, since they didn't have any, but for fear of a backlash that would shake the roof tiles off the Medellin haciendas.

It meant he'd never hear anything anyway. If Narcotics ever got wind of someone moving *Burundanga*, there'd be no warrant. They'd just strap on the shoe spikes, stomp him into Alpo, and sell him to a pit bull kennel.

He got on the computer and pecked his way to the VICAP report the FBI had done after Sneezy had been torn in half in the tree. The history of the MO promised a night's insomnia. Maybe for the best. Last night he'd been engaged in some backseat antics with his first below-the-waister of long ago, Amy Chong, only to look up and discover he was putting the moves on a very large tapeworm.

The FBI research spooled down the screen. The place: a prefecture near Jaipur in northwest India. The time: the Maratha invasions of the early 1700s, when Brahmin hordes swept up from the south, killing and enslaving millions and spreading the caste system far and wide. Ruled by one of history's unsung über-sadists, who'd found the traditional means of execution—squashing the malefactor's skull under the foot of an elephant— a bit tedious.

At the onset of each monsoon, the convicts were dragged to the hill, accompanied by jeering crowds and weeping loved ones, and strapped into the trees. The festivities were timed so the rajah could circle the hill in his palanquin the next morning, when the prisoners would be torn in half by the water filling the huge clay jugs attached to the pulleys. Executioners stood by with pails to nudge things along if needed. The rajah would park at a vantage point and enjoy a hearty breakfast, entertained by the screams of the dying.

Clem winced. The reason the killer had left Sneezy ungagged. *I'm singin' in the rain.*

But it was the citation that piqued his interest. The chronicler was a Portuguese missionary whose works were published in a monograph in 1959 and out of print ever since. Clem tried a dozen Internet searches but came up empty except for the innocuous title, which showed up at a rare book site.

Not like piecing together the techniques of Jack the Ripper. Two minutes of Googling would get you all you wanted.

Someone had gone to the ends of the earth to dig up this one.

Noontime found Clem drumming fingers, hoping for word from Jojo. VICAP came up dry, despite his grinding through the two hundred discriminators to enter the crime scene in the database. In fact, he'd had the dubious honor of sending them a CS that bore resemblance to no other in the history of homicide. The analyst told him with a certain gleeful admiration—as if Clem had cobbled it together himself—that it happened only a couple of times a decade. He got the feeling the guy didn't get out much.

His cell rang. "Inspector? Mike Stuart. The pet shop guy."

Clem brightened. The only one who had seen the vic and the killer. Anything from Mike was gold standard. "Hey, Mike, you find anything? I could use it."

"Well, nothing on that invoice yet. But I remembered a couple things I forgot. First is, now I think about it, guy's kind of funny when I'm showing him the tank, right? She's petting the puppies, not going anywhere. But he keeps glancing over at her, back at the tank, back at her again for like five minutes. Like he's nervous she'll take off or something."

Clem's ventricles filled with ice. The killer hadn't been nervous. Otherwise he'd have left her drugged up in the house.

He was measuring her. He'd brought her to make sure he bought the right tank.

He silently pronounced the death penalty on the shitbucket. "Okay. Anything else?"

Mike took a deep breath. "Still got somethin' rollin' around in there. Don't know what it is yet, or why, but I get the feeling it's something you gotta know. I'll call you back."

"Mike, any time, day or night. I mean that, no matter what it is you want to tell me." Some piece of the puzzle was buried in the darkest reaches of Mike's memory. Clem prayed that it would surface in time to aid them.

• • •

Jojo and Angie were at the school child-abuse stacks. Marcie had shang-haied them an assistant, but she didn't last ten minutes before clipclopping away in tears. Angie glanced at the file: a girl whose fingertips had been burned with an iron. But she found herself oddly unmoved. Like working all day in a sewer—sooner or later you stopped noticing that everything smelled like shit.

They slogged into the afternoon. Two p.m. found them sleepily finishing the M's. Jojo hefted a stack of N's and slammed it on the table, signaling his frustration. But five minutes later, Angie was jarred by his whoop bouncing off the walls. She slid over and looked.

Cynthia Nichols.

A report by a Nurse Charlotte Gunder. Angie read the key points aloud. "June 5, 2004, Washington Elementary in the Haight. She was crying and holding her right arm. When the teacher, Diane Stengel, asked about it, she claimed it was nothing, then after more questioning admitted to pain where she'd broken it a year before. Nurse brought her to General." Sounds like we should gnaw this one to the bone."

Jojo called Clem and was quickly off the phone. "He'll meet us at General. Someone'll look up the Nicholses, make some calls. But we should be able to pry the parents' names out of Marcie."

They stopped by Marcie's office. "Jojo, I'll dig up her master file and get it to your office," said Marcie. "It'll have a picture, names and address of parents, school records. The file's in another department, but I'll yank tails."

Five minutes later Angie and Jojo were headed for San Francisco General, the city's only public hospital. Clem met them at the front entrance and led them to the front desk. It was chaotic with staffers, admissions, and tagalongs. He smiled solicitously, flashed his brass at the harried, pinch-faced overseer, and asked if he could speak to the executive administrator, a Doctor Richard Roth. She made a grumpy call. Finally, she peered at him in triumph over neck-chained rhinestone glasses and pronounced Dr. Roth very busy.

Clem put on a blood-freezing scowl, flipped the dead girl's photo in front of her, and spoke sotto voce. "See this little cutie pie? We found her sitting in a tank of embalming fluid. Read all about it." He eyed a newspaper behind the desk. "Ah, you already have. So I can safely say we're on the same front page?"

She nodded glacially.

"Now. The last place we can track her to is guess where? Right here. Accordingly, ma'am, please prevail upon Dr. Roth again to give me a smidgen of his time. If need be, you can tell him there's a reporter at that paper who'll cream his jeans to hear we're on hold because Dr. Roth's so busy."

She gave him a jaded, suit-yourself shrug, as if he were demanding an appointment with the neighborhood cave troll, then turned around and picked up a phone. A moment later, a security guard escorted them to Roth's spacious office on the top floor. At the equally spacious rosewood desk toward the rear, backstopped by a wall full of diplomas and certificates, sat a bearded, balding man with an impressive desk spread. He made a point of scribbling on a memo without looking up. Clem flashed Angie a "looks like we got us an asshole" glance. Finally, Roth peered up theatrically and plodded up to them. His face barely masked irritation.

Clem and Jojo flashed their stars.

"Dr. Richard Roth. Inspector. Inspector." Roth shook hands, then turned to the starless, blue-jeaned Angie and looked her up and down as if a gum-snapping hooker in red boots had materialized in his office. "And you are . . . ?"

Clem interjected gruffly. "Angie Strackan. Realtor."

Angie shot him a grin. He was tweaking Roth, to all appearances successfully. Roth looked affronted, though undecided whether to be affronted over Clem's wising off at him, or, if he wasn't wising off, over the appearance of a lowly Realtor in his sanctum.

"And police reservist," Clem continued. "We're looking for the file on Cynthia Nichols. June 5, 2004." He handed Roth the picture.

Roth didn't give it a glance. "Let me see if I understand. You've just insinuated yourself into my office over a four-year-old file?" Angie was sure he was indulging a bent for puffery. They wouldn't have gotten past the cafeteria unless he knew perfectly well what it was about.

"No, over a dead little girl we just found buried in an underground tank."

"Oh yes, the one in the papers," said Roth dismissively. "It's on the computers. We can go back to '96 by now," he added in a tone implying a feat equal in stature to a moon landing. "You're just looking for the file? No connection with the hospital itself, of course." He jutted his lower lip and raised both eyebrows as if he were strutting the poop deck of the *Bounty*.

"We don't know yet. The killer may have had contact with the victim here. Maybe the radiologist or the tech who did her X-rays. Or whoever put the cast on her."

Roth's pose became belligerent, fists perched firmly on padded hips. "I find that preposterous."

"That may be, but I'll need your cooperation. We'll be as discreet as possible. But this case is already pretty high profile."

"Yes, and so am I. You'll refrain from conducting a witch hunt. The minute I think you are, I'll be on the phone to the mayor, who happens to have had a big role in my appointment."

Clem spoke with mock sympathy. "Don't worry, Doc, I'm sure you'll land the next one by yourself."

Roth went pie-eyed, snapped his mouth open wide enough to admit a dragonfly, and wagged a finger in Clem's face. "I warn you, Inspector," he sputtered. "No half-baked *Pink Panther* antics. You'll clear interviews through me."

"I clear interviews through God. Now, if you can kindly direct us to whoever can yank this file. And you might want to tuck away that finger before it ends up someplace neither of us wants it to."

"I'll make a call. And I mean it, Inspector. You sully the reputation of this hospital and I'll have your badge."

"And you throw a wrench in things and Hizzoner won't let you take a dump in a City Hall restroom. His drones are calling us twice a day."

Roth stopped swinging his testicles and sullenly sat down to make the call, waving them out without a glance. The security guard escorted them.

Jojo grinned at Clem. "*That* went well."

Angie gave Clem an elbow. "Guess what Christmas party *you* won't get invited to."

"No sweat, ours are better anyway."

"Probably we're talking Tailhook caliber. I've got an in now, right?"

"Nah, Homicide's actually a pretty staid bunch. Now Vice, that's another matter. Anyway, assholes like that can crater a case, but only if you let them. There's a hundred people in this city have knock-heads muscle, and a thousand want you to think they do. But most are ten-gallon hat, no cattle."

"You don't think he has the ear of the mayor?"

"I doubt it," replied Clem. "Someone with real juice wouldn't say, 'I'm gonna tell the mayor on you.' You'll just wake up one day with your life blood in a decanter on his credenza."

"But why would he make threats if he couldn't back them up?"

"Oh, he thinks he can. Once at a function I got ossified with the mayor's majordomo, he passed me a few goodies. Like say there's three guys up for some position. Like Roth's, nice, but Peoria far as city politics. The hospital's indigent care, a problem everyone wishes would go away. Position's decided by the Public Health mandarins squatting there forty years no matter who's mayor. But after they decide, they send a notice to the mayor's office before announcing, just in case the guy's got a shitstorm factor. Guy doesn't know yet he's got the job. So this aide, he calls the guy, tells him da mayor's lobbying for him. Lo and behold, the guy's in. So here the mayor didn't do diddly, yet he's got a devoted servant who might come in handy."

Angie laughed. "But he buttonholes the mayor at a function and Hizzoner'll be looking for some more of those great cocktail weenies in thirty seconds."

"By George she's got it!"

They were met at Records by Donna Keppel, a perky young woman with latte-colored skin and Japanese eyes, coiffed in a metallic green and red. With a few plinks, Cynthia's record lasered across her screen. Angie's throat tightened. She'd still been alive when someone had written this stuff up. But not for long.

"Here's your June 5 entry. Brought into ER by a USD nurse, X-ray and cast. Picked up by her father, Thomas Nichols. Radiologist Dr. Francine Roderick. She's still with us. Cast by Dr. Walter Parcell, pediatrician, on loan from UCSF Med School. Lots of our docs are UCSF and work here part time. He retired two years ago."

"Any address or phone on Nichols?"

"Cold storage. I can get it, but it'll take a day."

"Please do. So where can we find Parcell?"

"UCSF would have that; he'd receive a pension."

"Anything about physical abuse?"

She paged through the record. "Yes, notated by Parcell. Aside from the fracture and bruises, the girl seemed terrified about getting the cast. Afraid to show her parents probably. Creepy," she added with a shiver.

"Was it reported outside the hospital?"

"Doesn't look it. The cops are overloaded. There's a certain amount of triage goes on here, so they act on the ones we report. We have an outreach program for less definite cases."

Clem's eyes narrowed. "And this wasn't 'definite'?"

Donna responded levelly. "Inspector, we get babies with cigarette burns on their genitals. A kid with his feet chopped off, for God's sake."

Clem shook his head in disgust. "Understood. Did you know Parcell?"

She grinned. "For sure!" She lowered her voice. "Honest, lots of docs are really full of themselves? Like half the time they'll make a mistake and blame you? He was never that way. Now the cardiologists—"

Clem cut her off. "I'm sure. Anything else stood out about him?"

"For sure. I mean, what a brave guy, given what happened to him."

Clem cocked an eyebrow.

"Oh, you wouldn't know. Ding . . . " She banged her knuckles on her temple. "He's a paraplegic. Got some award from the President. Ten years ago he was in a car accident, lost the use of both legs. But six months later, he was back on duty, only in a wheelchair. People got stuffy, thought he would scare the kids. But they loved it. Every other day he'd tool down the hall with some kid in his lap."

Clem shot Jojo a "scratch one suspect" glance. "And Dr. Roderick?"

"She's been here twenty years, the senior radiologist."

Clem asked the guard to escort them to Radiology. The man looked uncomfortable. "Sir, I can't take you somewhere I haven't been told to."

Clem flipped his badge two inches from the guard's nose. "You've just been told to. Someone gives you problems, I'll be back to shove a corncob up someone's cavernous butt. You reading me?"

The guard grinned. "Loud and clear."

They took the elevator up to Radiology and walked past several offices to Roderick's. Clem knocked, heard a curt "Come in!" and they entered. Roderick sat in the dark in front of a glass backlit wall panel. From behind her, a dozen identical skulls leered back at Angie, but not the skulls she'd seen in X-rays. These showed coral-like brains inside the crania and eyeballs ogling her from the ocular cavities. Clem ignored the macabre display and made introductions.

Roderick caught Angie's eye. "Weird, huh? Nuclear magnetic resonance imaging, MRI. We look inside the brain and find tumors, aneurisms, whatever. It still amazes me." She stood and switched on the light. She was tall, almost Clem's height, a close-cut blonde with touches of silver-gray, and anorexically thin. Laugh lines swarmed her aristocratic features. As she shook hands, Angie noticed a tremor. "Now. You're not on a class field trip, right?"

Clem showed her the picture. "Do you recall this girl, four years back? Duplicate spiral fracture, right humerus, fractures about a year apart."

Roderick smiled apologetically. "I'm sorry. They seldom let us out of our cubbyholes. Patient consultations tend towards major things like brain tumors."

"I was hoping you might remember. It was noted as possible abuse."

She smiled again, though less broadly. "Again, I would just make a diagnosis. That would be handled by ER or a pediatrician. And I see four or five broken arms and, sad to say, one or two abuse cases a day."

Clem nodded. "This girl was murdered after she was treated here. She's the one in the underground tank. I have no choice but to ask the questions."

Roderick let out a gasp. Her chin trembled. "Goodness. I certainly understand."

"How many radiology techs you have here?"

"Seven. Most of them more than four years. One started three months ago. Another two years back."

"Any a Caucasian male, five ten? Blond, on the slim side? Glasses? Thirty, thirty-five?"

Roderick's eyes veiled themselves. She fixed her attention on the skulls and hesitated, framing her words. Her voice was thick and harsh. "Sorry. No one here fits that description."

Clem locked onto her discomfiture. "Dr. Roderick. I'm getting the feeling I'd better ask questions in just the right way, or you'll answer in just the wrong one. I don't make you for a suspect. So how's about we keep things on the level?"

Roderick's eyes riveted on the light board. She spoke in a tremulous voice. "We had someone by that description. Until four months ago. That's all I'll say. If you insist on questioning me further, it'll be with my attorney present." Her jaw trembled uncontrollably, like a toddler deciding whether or not to cry. She stood up with arms and legs akimbo like a marionette under a drunken puppeteer, grabbed her purse, and barged out. Clem asked him to escort them back to Roth's office. They took the elevator to the top floor, only to find a suspiciously Rothless desk.

Jojo cocked an eyebrow. "Curiouser and curiouser. I'm thinking we've touched some non-homicidal nerve here."

Clem cracked his knuckles in the air, as if setting to work. "More like cauterized it with a curling iron."

He glanced to the left of the microwave at the three white boxes, his tip of the hat to haute cuisine. Each contained one hundred bags of what a host of epicures deemed the world's best microwave popcorn. You could only order it from some place in Vermont. The leftmost box held the popcorn in pure form, the central one barbecued, and the box to the right, a cheese variant.

He fired up a package, fished out the bag, and dropped it on the glass-topped coffee table that sat between his single bed and a taupe sofa with dirty white bits of stuffing worming their way to freedom from several seams. He grabbed the kitchen knife and slit the popcorn bag, fetched a dollop of butter, and sat down to dinner. He switched on the TV perched on a corner of the table and watched the evening news, in which he now played a very big part.

But today there was no ramshackle house. Instead, a gravel-voiced Yao announced to a gaggle of microphones that they'd tentatively identified the girl and thought they would soon have a lead on a suspect. A gentle surge of adrenaline tickled his shoulders.

He reviewed his preparations for the next round. He'd changed glasses from his long-favored pilots to owlish wire-rims, making him look more bookish. He was six days into a beard that would erase his most memorable features, his Lurch-like cheekbones. In fact, he'd borne the nickname in school and kind of liked it once it came into routine-enough use to lose the sting.

Early morning three days ago he'd left the Toyota unlocked on a street in Potrero Hill notorious for grand theft auto. It was gone by the time he stopped by in the afternoon. Like the beetles he used to flip on their backs on fire-ant hills, it had been carted away and dissected by a chop shop ring, its innards nourishing a dozen fly-by-night repair shops. He bought an ancient burnt orange Subaru through the classifieds for twelve hundred, signing off the title with his mother's name.

He still had more than fourteen thousand, even after the twelve grand he'd shelled out for the coming Père Lebrun messy. It was hidden in the tiny closet under a false floor he'd constructed that would give way only if you pressed two corners simultaneously. He was rather proud of his design and had even thought about applying for a patent.

His landlady was a stout mulatto Brazilian pushing seventy who spoke only halting English. Since he'd paid her six months in advance for his five hundred square feet on a quiet edge of the Castro only five blocks from his last place, he'd only seen her twice. Another plus was that she didn't have a car and let him park in her carport out of sight of the street

But best of all, she didn't have a problem with the bird.

More than a pet, the bird was his boon companion. He'd bought him as a fledgling three years ago off an old codger in the Mojave. A shrike common to the California deserts, he was also known by a darker nickname: the butcher bird.

His dull gray, speckled plumage and long, dagger-like beak wouldn't merit a mention among bird-watchers, what with California's astounding wealth of herons, pelicans, and the like. He seemed perfectly innocuous, feeding on insects, or, preferably, on mice and small snakes.

Innocuous, that is, until a large spiny cactus was placed in his cage. It was then that the little fellow earned his fearsome handle. Programmed by some ancient, diabolical instinct, he would deftly skewer his prey alive on the *cactus spines, leaving the creatures to twitch and writhe for hours while he dined on favorite tidbits at leisure. He liked his meat fresh; after a captive finally died, he would never touch it again. He had christened the bird Vlad, after the Romanian Vlad the Impaler. The medieval warlord was infamous for dispatching thousands with the same grisly technique.*

No matter how many mice and snakes he tossed in the cage, Vlad would catch them and mount them as long as there was space left on the cactus. His record was up to eight mice and three snakes. His handling of the snakes was amazing. In less than a minute he could nimbly wind the living serpent round and around the cactus, as if stringing Christmas tree lights. In between snacks, he would sit contentedly on his perch and watch the display of wriggling captives, admiring his handiwork. Sometimes they sat together for an hour or more, quietly enjoying the gruesome spectacle. At those times, he often felt that Vlad was the only creature on earth who really understood him.

Seeing to Vlad's feeding was his only regular outing besides the Laundromat. By now he knew every pet shop in the city that carried the bird's delicacies. He rotated carefully, since the kindly shop owners assumed their little mousies would be enjoyed as pets, not slowly eaten alive by an avian sadist.

He shuffled over to the closet that housed the toilet and shower, and studied himself in the little mirror on the door panel. He tweaked at the beard with trembling fingers, urging it to come in faster. He couldn't help a smile. Soon his own mother wouldn't know him.

Or want to.

CHAPTER EIGHT

Tuesday, May 20th

From out of a roiling black and gray mist, the room began to materialize, slowly taking on discrete shapes and colors. It was perhaps twenty feet deep by fifteen wide, and dimly lit by four wall sconce tallow candles, two on each of the longer walls. Water dripped in a dozen places from the low slanted ceiling, and collected in a channel carved in the floorboards that led to a small drainpipe where the floor met one of the walls. Here and there, especially around the channel, he spotted suspicious dark blotches on the dry-rotted wood plank walls and floor. Dozens of thumb-sized cockroaches jigsawed patterns on the walls and ceiling and flitted through the air with low-pitched whirrs. Wooden shelves lined the wall to his right, while the other walls were equipped with huge, rusted, iron eyebolts spaced every three feet. He moved closer to the wall to his left. Hanging from pegs were ominous-looking cast-iron implements: shears, pliers, saws, cleavers, awls like those used in sewing leather, but for some reason much larger. He brought his face closer to them; they were covered with clots of drying gore.

As if drawn by some unearthly force, he stepped farther into the room and slowly walked up to a large barrel in the corner where the left wall met the rear one. He drew breath; it was full to its rim with severed, desiccated arms, hands, and legs. He furtively looked to his right at the shelves; they were stacked with dried-out ears, toes, and noses. He saw another barrel in the other corner but could not bring himself to approach it.

He turned and now saw what appeared to be an operating table in the middle of the room. It had not been there before. He gingerly stepped toward it, his eyes refusing for a moment to focus, not wishing to realize what he was looking at.

But finally he could not battle back the vision. Wriggling against leather straps that held her down was something that he thought had once been an old, fat black woman. Her arms and legs had been amputated, and long strips of her skin had been peeled off her torso in a circular pattern, making her look like a human caterpillar as she wriggled to and fro.

She slowly turned towards him, revealing what was left of her face. Her jaw had been pried off and the rest of her facial bones had been smashed and broken, but seemingly not in a paroxysm of rage. Instead, it seemed her face had been purposely disfigured to resemble a cathedral gargoyle. Flaps of skin had been partly flensed from her temples and cheeks, and sewn tightly to her cheeks and forehead to heighten the effect. Her eyes now opened and seemed to beg for death.

He heard the slow creak of the door at the far wall as it edged open, and he held his breath in terror. His eyes teared as the room filled with dazzling light, and his knees begin to buckle as the sunshine framed a tall, thin, long-haired woman in silhouette. The torturess Delphine.

Slowly she approached him, extended a delicate hand, and touched his forehead. For a moment he was paralyzed, then he lashed out desperately at it, and tried to turn and run. But he was glued to the spot as she kept running fingers over his cheeks and temples.

An insistent voice broke in. "Clem! Clem! It's Grace! Wake up!"

He slowly emerged from the nightmare as Grace continued to brush his forehead. Her almond eyes and high forehead and cheekbones edged furtively into view under the soft light of the lamp above the headboard. She was biting her lower lip in apprehension. Finally he exhaled deeply with a "whew!" Grace's exhalation matched his own, but, he was sure, with a tinge of annoyance. "Umm . . . sorry about that."

She leaned forward and kissed his cheek, then settled back on her pillow. "It's okay. By now I've pretty well solved your left jab. So where were you? You remember?"

Clem shuddered at the memory. "The attic of Delphine Lalaurie. The nineteenth century's most notorious murderess. New Orleans in the 1830's. She tortured dozens of her slaves. I was reading about it last night."

Grace pursed her lips. "Clemson, you need to get another hobby."

He winced as he shook his head. "Clemson" meant trouble. "Job stuff, actually. She was horribly creative in her work, reminds me a bit of the cases I'm seeing now. The guy in the tree, the little girl in the tank."

"Spare me the details." Grace took a deep breath. "Clem, it's been six years. And I admit I was ecstatic when you got the star." It was true. Homicide cops almost never got shot at. "But this stuff is running once a week. And that's just the times you wake me. You're like a Vietnam vet with PTSD fighting the Viet Cong every night." She kissed his cheek again. "Look, it's not me I'm worried about, even the occasional uppercut to the jaw. It's you."

Clem grunted. Obviously there wasn't much he could say.

Grace continued, "Frazier's got a good shot at chief. Even Jackson's a dark horse, so to speak. Frazier'd back you for deputy chief, and Jackson would make you chief of division, right?"

Clem's stomach churned, but he nodded dutifully. "Neither's a shoo-in, but yeah."

"Okay, I'm never going to ask you to retire, but I really need some quid pro quo here. If one of them makes chief, you agree not to find some way to sabotage your own promotion. Okay?"

Clem gazed at the ceiling and said nothing. She took his chin in her hand and turned his head toward her. "Do *not* force me to recruit your mother on this. If I'm not mistaken, she already thinks you're being pursued by some sort of nine-headed bird."

The thought made his bladder tighten. "I never thought she actually believed in it. *Jiu tou niao.* She used to terrorize me with it as a kid. '*What?* You don't clean room yet? Nine-head bird come take you, feed heart to babies!' 'Don't play with your *gui tou!* Nine-head bird come, bite off!'" He paused. "And if neither of them make chief?"

But Grace had her head buried in her pillow trying to stifle peals of laughter. "*Gui tou?* Turtle head? *Turtle head?*"

"That's what she called it. Like the way a turtle's head looks when he sticks it out of—"

She punched his arm, still giggling. "I got it, I got it." Her eyes twinkled. "So should I switch to saying *gui tou?*"

"Sure, if you never want to see it again in a state that would be useful to you. And if neither of them make chief?"

"I'll keep my mouth shut for one year unless I think you're going to shoot people from the top of Coit Tower. We'll revisit the issue then."

Clem shrugged. "Probably the best I'll get anyway. Okay, deal."

"Trust me, it *is* the best you'll get." She paused and smiled slyly. "In fact, under the circumstances, you would be well advised to make me something of a peace offering."

"Umm . . . what's that?"

She snuggled up to him, reached under her pillow, and held up a pair of nearly transparent black briefs.

Just as Clem had the Hall of Justice in his sights, his cell phone jingled and the screen lit up. For the moment, it was the most unwelcome name he could imagine. Chief Jackson never called him before work on routine stuff, only when he wanted Clem to handle a homicide. They were blessedly few at 8:00 a.m.; the business of murder didn't really kick into gear until after noon. But, what with his being tied up in a notorious child killing, it meant that whatever he was about to tackle would be anything but routine.

Clem let it ring six times to signal his displeasure, then pushed the button just before it switched to voice mail. "So why don't I want to answer this?"

Jackson chuckled. "Thought you wouldn't for a minute there. Make a pit stop at Pacific Medical Center. See Doctor Hal Richards in Neurology."

"You know, in case you haven't noticed, I've kind of got a full plate at the moment."

"I noticed. By the way, you track down the father yet?"

"No, the only Thomas Nichols here now is nineteen, black, and gay. Looks like Papa flew the coop."

"My money's still on him. Anyway, you can hand off this one to a moron once we get a handle on it."

"So what makes me so special?"

"It's a world-class freak show over there. You've always had a sort of yen for the grotesque."

"Thank you for thinking of me. Care to run through the grotesqueries before I walk in?"

"You're about to boldly go where no inspector has gone before. Remember that doc who got waylaid jogging two months back?"

"Vaguely." A weird assault case. Doctor Alan Simmons, a resident cardiologist at Pacific, had been on a run just after dawn on the deserted trails of Stern Grove in the western part of the city. Someone had come up behind, headlocked him, and dosed him with chloroform. He woke up ten minutes later hidden behind some bushes just off the trail, none the worse for the experience other than some nausea and a neatly bandaged injection wound on his neck. No robbery motive; the guy'd had his wallet with him on the run, and it was untouched. The hospital had given him every tox screen known to man, but came up empty. "So he's been murdered?"

"Need you ask? The modus operandi appears to be . . . now where the *hell* did I put that?" Jackson shuffled papers theatrically.

"Spare me the drum roll, dickhead."

"That's Chief Dickhead to you. Ah, here it is." Pause. "A tapeworm."

"Shit, I forgot my meds this morning. A little voice in my head just said 'a tapeworm.'"

Twenty minutes later, Clem was standing over a hospital bed with three somber doctors, looking at a very tall, very handsome, and very brain-dead cardiologist on life support.

Clem eyed the youngest doc, a jowly, sleepless-looking blond man in his thirties with a receding hairline and the beginnings of a paunch. He was already not aging well. "Okay, Doctor Richards, one more time from the top. What killed this guy was . . . "

"*Echinococcus multilocularis,*" he replied with a certain academic smugness.

Clem shook his head in annoyance. "Not the echino part. The other part."

"A tapeworm larva."

"That's what I thought you said. So the murder weapon was a tapeworm."

"A larva. Well, a whole bunch of them. But not just any old tapeworm. Sort of the Marquis de Sade of tapeworms."

"Umm . . . dare I ask?"

"Well, it's not uncommon for normal tapeworm larvae to nest in the brain, especially in Third World countries. They're pretty harmless except when they begin to die because the body's immune system starts to attack them. They start to, well, wiggle around a lot."

"Wiggle around." Clem choked back nausea as he jotted a note in his pad.

"Right. It can cause severe convulsions."

He was fighting them off just hearing about it. "But it's usually not fatal?"

"Rarely. Sometimes the larvae block up a space in the brain that allows cerebrospinal fluid to pass from the brain to the spinal cord. If it's blocked, the brain's making fluid, but there's no way for it to get out. So fluid pressure builds up in the brain. It's called hydrocephalus."

"So why don't the larvae turn into tapeworms and munch the guy's brain?"

"The larva has a kind of trigger that allows it to grow into a tapeworm. If the space it occupies is too small, it spends its life as a larva. The interstices in the brain are too small for them to become tapeworms."

"So not like in the intestines, where there's all the room in the world."

"Exactly. But this tapeworm will make your blood run cold."

Clem eked out a thin smile. "I'm just dying to find out why."

"Well, first of all, it's very rare. Doesn't normally occur in the lower forty-eight. Only place I've seen it is in Alaska, among the Eskimos. *Multilocularis* only infests certain foxes, mostly way up north. Sometimes the sled dogs eat a fox and get infested. Then they pass it to humans."

Clem nodded. "Not too many dog teams in San Francisco. So this multi-whatever shouldn't be here. What's so fiendish about these babies?"

The doctor shook his head in amazement. "Well, instead of just sitting there in the brain nice and quiet, these things go crazy. They subdivide and form giant cysts. Each contains hundreds of tiny larvae. Those cysts spin off daughter cysts. And unlike normal larvae, these cysts eat brain tissue like tumors as they grow. When they're ready, they burst open and unleash hundreds more larvae."

Clem stopped taking notes. He wasn't likely to forget what he was hearing.

"This is an MRI of his brain. We shot it two days ago after he went into a seizure," an older doctor continued as he held a large black X-ray film up to the light. Clem scrutinized it in horrified fascination. The dark brain corals were riddled with maybe a hundred pea-sized white spheres.

The slow steady beep of the heart monitor suddenly seemed the height of perversity.

The doctor nodded toward the bed. "Two months back we screened for every toxin we could think of. Even if we'd shot an MRI back then, we wouldn't have seen these things. But by now, like a third of his brain pan is filled with tapeworm larvae. The condition's called alveolar hydatid disease. The mortality rate is more than fifty percent."

Clem choked down his bile. "Okay, I think that covers it. No chance this guy just ate some bad fox tartare?"

The young doctor's face became grim. "Inspector, in Alaska, the victims were infected by a single larva. The cases took years to develop." He nodded to the victim. "This guy took two months."

Clem's throat clutched. "Meaning?"

"Meaning the only way this could happen would be if the victim were exposed to hundreds of larvae all at once. Thus the wound in his neck. The killer injected them into a carotid artery, and they made a beeline for his brain."

Angie met Clem and Jojo at San Francisco General. They spent the better part of the afternoon playing hide-and-seek with Roth. Two forays with a guard to his office produced nothing more than an empty desk. A hospital apparently had lots of hiding places.

After the last failure, they retired once more to the lobby. Clem wiped a hand across his face in frustration. But now he gazed curiously at Jojo, who was pacing the perimeter of the lobby.

Jojo returned with a sly grin. "See that?" He gestured with his eyes toward a ceiling-mounted security camera. It was pointed right at them. "When I circled the room, that camera panned on me the whole time. The fucker's got security watching our every move."

Angie nodded. "But I didn't see any in the parking lots. Care to fake him out of his shoes?"

They all exited the lobby to the far end of the lot. Ten minutes later the three of them jogged through the front door and tore for the elevator. A guard halfheartedly tried to stop them as the doors slid closed.

A minute later they entered Roth's office and, as hoped, caught him behind his desk. His eyebrows shot halfway up his forehead as he circled around it. He stood gut sucked in, chin jutting out, and fists balled as if ready to engage Clem in some ill-fated bare-knuckle. "What the hell's this about? Last night I got a frantic call from Dr. Roderick. Whatever you said sent her tearing out of here!"

Clem doled out half a smile. "With you bravely bringing up the rear, I gather."

Roth's face reddened. "I'm not one to throw my weight around, Inspector, but I want you out of here!" Judging from the tiara of sweat beads blanketing Roth's forehead, he was covering up.

Clem gave him an icy glare. "All I did was ask her a question. About an ex-tech. Seems this fellow, who left four months ago, matches a description of the suspect. I'd like to know who he is."

"I'm sorry, Inspector. That's privileged information. If your investigation is based only on the flimsy details you gave Dr. Roderick, I'm betting you can't get a court order. Please don't come back without one. A guard will escort you out." He turned to park himself at his desk.

Clem planted himself in an immobile parade rest. "Doc, you know, under those robes, judges are human beings, with the normal gamut of human foibles. That means they sometimes get stopped for DWI, get caught in a drug sweep or soliciting a hooker, what have you. And funny, you almost never see them on the wrong side of an arraignment. So when we really, really need a court order, like when we're chasing a child killer, it's not that hard for us to get one."

"Oh, we'll just see about that," Roth sputtered. "I'm calling the mayor." He picked up the receiver.

Clem gave him a patronizing smile. "By all means. Oh, but first, tell me one thing Doc, Before you got your job, did the mayor ever talk to you? His Eminence hisself?"

Roth somehow looked pompous and bewildered at the same time.

"No, it was his senior aide. Hugh Warner."

Jojo and Clem exchanged an amused glance, then turned back to Roth. "Be my guest. After that" —Clem pulled out his cell phone and held it up—"my turn."

Roth wavered at the brazen calling of his bluff and edged his stubby fingers away from the receiver. Clem got up, perched on the edge of Roth's desk, and leaned over.

"Let me be plain with you, Doc. I have a hunch I just opened a hamper of dirty diapers I want nothing to do with. Me, I'm just trying to catch a killer with a jones for embalming little girls. You getting me so far?"

Roth exhaled and gave Clem the barest nod.

"Look," Clem continued. "Every department in this city has enough skeletons to fill Arlington. Mine more than most. Now we can get into a 'my dick's bigger than yours' deal. But if I get a court order, it'll focus lots of scrutiny on whatever's buried under the kitty litter. Am I right?" Roth's nod was more conciliatory.

Clem continued. "Now. On my side, I'll waste a couple days I don't have in a pissing contest, and we'll end up pissing blood all over each other." Clem paused. "Let me ask you something. You got any kids?"

Roth gazed up at him curiously. "Boy, fifteen. Girl, seventeen."

Clem nodded. "You know, when it comes to anything with kids, we don't just throw away the rulebook. But we do—shall I say—reinterpret it. Like one time seven years ago, we had a fourteen-year-old boy vanish in the Tenderloin. After some homework I pieced it together: gang kidnapped him on their turf. I tracked down the gang leader to his sister's apartment. He wouldn't tell me where the kid was, just hinted he was scheduled for a Ginzu gang initiation that night. And laughed at me. Like he knew all I could do was haul his ass in. He'd lawyer up, pull his Mr. Clean, be back on the street in time to watch the newbies slice up junior and get their secret code rings."

Clem took a deep breath. "I'm not going to tell you exactly what happened after that, and I assure you, neither would the gang leader. But let's just say that one way or the other, half an hour later, I got that kid out of there. And the gangster was nursing more than his wounded pride. Now look me in the eye, Doc, and tell me you don't believe me."

Angie saw a look in Clem's eyes she'd never seen before, a lupine cold-ness that seemed to suck the light from the room. She felt her flesh creep at the thought of facing that arctic, clairvoyant stare in interrogation. Roth looked away from him with a shudder.

Clem continued. "And if it was *your* daughter we fished from that stink-ing tank, what would you expect me to do with some bureaucrat keeping me from finding her killer? You'd want me to pave the highway with him, am I right?"

Roth nodded grudgingly.

"So we have two choices. You can be a leprechaun guarding his little pot of gold, and I'll pave the highway. And believe me, I *can* do that. I've got my thirty, and I'd have to get caught selling plutonium to al Qaeda to get my pension yanked." Clem paused. "Or, you can be a father, thinking of another father out there who's mad with grief and rage over what a monster did to his daughter."

Roth capitulated with a heavy shrug. "Okay, okay. Four months ago, one of our radiology techs was caught by a doctor doing a lab procedure using an extremely toxic substance. He ignored the safety recommendations for the procedure and endangered the lives of himself and others." His language sounded like a pink slip memo.

"He did this setup on his own? He's just a tech. Doesn't make a heap of sense."

"Well, not exactly. One of the UCSF doctors was doing toxicity research and needed precise calibration standards. He asked Dr. Roderick to supply them using MRI, her specialty."

"And Roderick was too busy to prep the stuff and ordered the tech to do it?"

"Well, it wasn't *exactly* an order . . . "

"And Nixon wasn't *exactly* a crook. Now let me guess. The tech isn't here, and Roderick is. Ergo, the tech went over the barrel, and Roderick got a frowny face in her file."

"It's not that simple, Inspector. This hospital's basically for the city's poor, the only one in fact. Most of our patients have no insurance. Our psych ward is filled with people whose brains have been turned into turnips by booze and drugs. Two floors below us is what the rest of the country calls HIV Central."

Roth took a weary breath. "Inspector, Dr. Roderick is respected nationwide. It's almost impossible for a public hospital like ours to keep top people. Losing her would irreparably damage healthcare for the poor in this city."

Clem nodded. "And now you've got her by the short hairs. So why didn't the tech get a frowny face too?"

"The doctor who caught him wanted a head on a platter. He threatened to go to the state if we didn't fire whoever was responsible. It would've been a monster scandal."

"And you'd be the goat. Look, if this guy's my embalmer—and I'm not saying he is—I wouldn't fret over the detour in his career path. I'll be giving him a lot bigger one. So, who is he?"

Roth pulled a file from his drawer as if he'd had it at the ready. They all circled the desk. A picture was clipped to the right-hand corner. Swedish blond, with short, carefully combed hair and a wan complexion. High, pronounced cheekbones and facial flesh thin enough to be called gaunt. Strong chin, but too strong, almost cartoonishly pointed. Prominent Adam's apple. Eyes brimming with intelligence, but slightly too close together, giving the impression of humorless intensity. Thin lips pursed in a too-serious demeanor, like a Puritan preacher about to call forth brimstone on the flock. He didn't smile too often or too well.

Gooseflesh erupted on Angie's shoulders as she realized she might be looking at a child killer. But then she found herself experiencing a vague sense of recognition. She massaged it, to no avail.

"Robert M. Larsen, Junior," said Roth with a heavy sigh.

Clem laid a hand on Roth's shoulder. "Okay, what else we know?"

Roth paged through. "Birthday, March 16, '76. We get transcripts for medical hires. UCSF '96 through '99. Started pre-med."

"So he's thirty-two. Started college late, twenty."

"Straight A's in non-med stuff: English, history, math. Great in most of the pre-med but got blown out by the biochemistry. Lots do. Switched to med tech, almost straight A's. What with managed care, they do everything but interpret results. Started here five years ago. Before that, four years at a clinic in Burlingame. Clean work history."

"Anatomy?"

"Three semesters. Two A's and a B. Single. Next of kin: mother, April Larsen in Gilroy. No father listed."

"Any idea what he's like?"

"I asked around before the inquiry. Meticulous, didn't make mistakes. Technically best of the best. But he got on the others' nerves—pointing out errors, that kind of thing. Never cracked a joke. Arrogant, like he thought he was a doctor or something."

Angie couldn't suppress a guffaw. Roth reddened but continued gamely. "Kept to himself, never socialized. Surprising though, not following procedures with the toxic."

Angie broke in. "Shouldn't be. Roderick didn't tell him."

Roth shot her a glare. "She swears she did. I'd take her word over Larsen's. And we have a memo with the instructions that he signed acknowledging receipt."

"That he obviously says he didn't. And somehow I doubt you ran it by a handwriting expert. Larsen's an Olympian anal retentive. She may have been busy, forgot to tell him he was working with mustard gas or whatever. What exactly happened?"

"He was supposed to use laminated hazmat gloves and a gas mask, and vent the sample under a special fume hood. He didn't."

Clem took over. "Was he exposed?"

Roth averted his eyes. "Hmm?"

Clem repeated slowly. "Was. He. Exposed. You tested him, right?"

"We . . . intended to test him. It got lost in the sauce during the inquiry."

Right, thought Angie, Roth would've sold nurses into white slavery to get Larsen off the payroll.

"We tried to contact him at his address," Roth continued, "but he moved right after he was let go. We called his mother; she didn't know where. He hasn't filed for unemployment or even come in to pick up a check for some unused vacation."

"Shit," Clem spat out and banged a fist on the desk.

Roth closed his eyes and lowered his voice. "Something else. After he cleared out, the vial of toxin was missing. We're pretty certain he took it."

"Cute. So what are we talking here?"

"Something called dimethyl mercury. Fifty grams, about two ounces, in a special burette."

"I'm not up on my dimethyls. How bad is bad?"

"Honestly, I don't know much either. Not my area." Roth took a deep breath. "But I *can* tell you it's really, *really* bad."

They waited for Roth to have his secretary make them a copy of the file. Jojo eyed Clem. "So. What's your take? You like Larsen for the girl?"

Clem shrugged. "Creepy crawlies, but nothing more. We can show his photo to Janine and to Mike at the pet shop. But a witness ID won't mean squat to the DA after four years, or to me. After that long, people see what they think they're supposed to see. There's nothing—absolutely nothing—that connects him to the girl. We've got as much as we walked in with."

As they left the hospital, Angie eyed Clem suspiciously. "Hey. The thing with the gang leader. Was that true? I'm not judging you. Just curious."

Clem grinned back. "Made it all up on the spot. Actually I'm just a big furry pussycat. Guy's in San Quentin, right around the corner. You can go ask him all about it. I hear he likes visitors."

But despite his relaxed denial, Angie was fairly certain that if she ever took him up on his offer, she would be staring through the glass-mesh window at a man who would shudder at the mention of Clem's name.

Angie nestled against Roger's bare shoulder in the bedroom of his Jackson Street condo and absently eyed the three huge, black-lacquer-framed Ansel Adams prints that dominated the far wall. She'd never cared for them when they were living together—they'd never fit with her taste for decor from the Florentine and Umbrian countryside—but it was comforting to see them here. "Hey, should we get divorced?"

Roger sported the suspicious smile he reserved for her bolt-out-of-the-blue stuff. At fifty, his hairline was receding, but he would wear his age well. He kept in shape at the gym, and she'd hammered him on using cosmetics for years, giving his skin the sheen of someone fifteen years younger. She'd snooped through his medicine cabinet her first time over, and felt gratified that he'd stocked his shelves with pricey moisturizers and other cosmetic gadgetry.

"Umm . . . something I said?"

"Not at all. I was reading about sex with exes. We're supposed to feel this gut-wrenching compulsion, then get all guilty. I mean, the sex is okay, but you know as well as I do there's not one wrench of a gut. And I sure don't feel guilty."

"I see. If we file, we're doing something naughty."

"Right. Then we can get all skittish, like where you won't call. I'll get all torn up wondering why, like if you blame me for something and how dare you blame me when I should be blaming you, like that."

"So I file, fuck the daylights out of you, and then don't call."

She rolled her eyes. "You're supposed to *surprise* me! Now you have to think of something equally bewildering. I think I just trust you too much. Hell, even our outside lays are cul-de-sacs."

Roger grinned and pinched her butt cheek. "So you don't think I'd walk the aisle with Candi."

"It's a legal issue. You're not allowed to sign a marriage license here with an X."

He failed to choke off a smile. "Hey! There's some things I'm allowed to say that you're not."

"Okay, okay. That was mean, I admit. And there's always Arkansas." She gave him a sly sidelong glance. "Did I tell you I bought the most *wonderful* drapes for the bedrooms?"

He clamped his eyes closed. "Christ, you didn't."

"Did." She fought off a giggle and lost.

He pinched her butt again but with more torque. "My God, you're jealous!"

"Not at all, once I figured out you just wanted someone brain dead, not half my age. I'd actually feel kind of bad if you weren't getting standout pussy. As to the drapes, really, I was in the neighborhood and curiosity got the better of me."

"Okay. I shouldn't ask, but if I don't, you'll tell me anyway, only you'll be pissed off to boot. So. What do you think of her?"

"I'm glad you asked. She seems sweet. And young, and beautiful, and most women would sign up with Lucifer in blood to have her ass for a year. Has trouble with the sales tax though."

Roger grinned wryly. "You should see her tell time. So, did you let on?"

"Of course not. I'd never let it get back to you that way. And I don't know what she knows about our quarterly sleeping habits."

Roger laughed. "Don't worry, she doesn't consider you any more of a threat than you do her."

"What? We haven't even filed for divorce, and I'm that threatless?" She pursed her lips and folded her arms across her breasts.

He flicked her hair off her cheek and smiled. "No, you don't understand. She couldn't care less if we sleep together. We're both perfectly happy to see each other every couple of weeks. I think she's after a father figure, but then she starts remembering what an asshole Daddy was. We have nothing in common but pheromones. She's as aware of that as I am."

"And I am. You've at least got the 'and sometimes Y' thing down. Anyway, just a hint: never imply a woman's not a threat if you even remotely want in her pants." She nuzzled him and purred, "Dimethyl mercury . . . "

"Huh?"

Angie had recounted the case at dinner. But once she'd decided they'd spend the night together, she elected to hold off on this detail, lest he get sidetracked by his professional passions. "Our suspect stole a batch from the hospital. The procedure he was doing. Nasty stuff?"

"And how. Mercury in pure form isn't poisonous. Like the stuff from old thermometers, or those maze thingies they used to sell? It's inert; you swallow some and it'll pass right through you. But dimethyl mercury's organic. The body can absorb it into the bloodstream. It's one of the few poisons we call 'supertoxins.' Most are things like nerve gas—stuff that's *supposed* to kill you. In a sense, it's the most poisonous substance known to man: no one's survived exposure. The first people to die from it were the two scientists who first cooked it up in the 1800s."

Angie gulped. "Jeezles. What's it doing in a hospital?"

"It has no medical uses. But it's the best calibration standard for mercury in radiology. Luckily, it's difficult to make, so it's only done by special order from labs like Harvard, and they ask questions before they whip up a batch. Not something you find on e-Bay."

"How does it work? Ingestion?"

"That's why it's so dangerous. The tiniest droplet on your wrist, or even on a latex glove, is absolutely fatal. Ditto inhaling a high concentration. But it's diabolical. You feel just fine for like four months. Then you start getting little tremors. From there, you slowly lose all your senses: first touch, then taste, smell, hearing, sight, everything tanks day by day. Motor coordination follows a steady path downhill to paralysis. Say nine months after exposure, you have the sensory and motor functions of a zucchini. Death's a couple months later."

Angie was aghast. "That's hideous. How the hell does it do that?"

"Basically, it eats the cortex off your brain, disconnecting all the nerves from your body. It takes a few months before the cortex thins enough to produce symptoms. That's why the victim has no idea there's anything wrong. How much does the guy have?"

Angie beat back a tinge of nausea. "Umm . . . like two ounces?"

Roger whistled. "Several hundred doses. In the hands of a disgruntled ex-employee. And possible child killer." He paused, his voice now almost a whisper. "But it's maybe even worse."

"Okay, I give up. What could possibly be worse?"

"Because if he did the procedure without precautions, he's almost certainly been exposed. He read up on the stuff afterwards; that's why he stole it. And if he *did* read up, he knows he's dying."

Angie nodded gravely. "So he could go out with a real bang."

"Exactly. He could paint every car door handle at the Opera House garage during the finale. A half hour later, he'd have a hundred future corpses to his credit."

Angie's throat tightened. "And even if he doesn't have a jones for mass murder, he might take revenge on anyone who wronged him." She thought of Roderick and her heart sank. "In fact, I may know who his first victim is." She told him about Roderick's tremors.

Roger nodded. "Possibly. But what worries me is the girl in the tank, if he's the one who buried her. He may feel you had a role in 'stealing' her."

Angie shook her head. "I doubt it. Clem thinks the killer *wanted* her to be discovered. At least that's what the FBI says."

Roger frowned. "Okay, but outthinking a psycho is Russian roulette. I want to test you for mercury. Usually we test a hair sample; mercury accumulates there. But it takes a while to show up, so I'd rather test your blood. We can go to the lab tomorrow first thing. Even tonight. Unless you'd rather not know."

She sighed. "No, I'd be worse off wondering. But tomorrow's fine. And even if he *was* targeting me, which I doubt, I haven't been home. He'd wait for a sure shot."

"Also, the stuff's dangerous for only about half an hour after exposure to air. He couldn't paint your doorknob at noon and nail you when you get home."

Angie nodded. "And for God's sake, this is all morbid conjecture. There's nothing that says he's anything more than a shafted ex-employee with a bad smile. Now, be chivalrous and go make me a sandwich. All this sex and death stuff is making me hungry."

Chapter Nine

Wednesday, a.m., May 21st

Angie awoke to a hint of light that zigzagged through the skyscrapers to Roger's window. They were both anxious as they gulped down coffee and trotted the deserted blocks to Roger's office in the half-light.

She fidgeted on a chair; a few fluorescent lights dimly lit a maze of gadgetry, computer screens, refrigerators, and glass cabinets. She winced as Roger drew a blood sample, prepped it, and switched on the atomic absorption spectrometer—an impressive-looking box of incomprehensible buttons, dials, and lights. The reds went green, and the contraption began its work with a high-pitched whine. After an eternity, she looked away from the machine and eyed him hopefully. He tore off the printout, stood up, and winked. "Just some very good pinot noir with oak overtones."

They celebrated the renewal of her lease on life with inch-thick pancakes at a bustling spot around the corner. Afterwards, she found herself sporting a bittersweet smile at the realization that it was the first time she'd had breakfast with him in two years, despite nine or ten condo stays. She'd always hightailed it after a cup of coffee, declining his invitations so consistently that he'd stopped asking. Her own unease rubbing off on him.

As she walked to her car, the smile became more bitter and less sweet with the thought that it was the first time she'd had breakfast with *any* man in two years. The realization dealt her a stab of loneliness, coupled with the ickiness she usually kept under wraps. But she knew better than to swear off her one-night stands on the spot (even though they seldom approached an entire night).

No, it was more complicated than just sex. The pull was more compelling, an oddly pleasant queasiness in her intestines, abetted but not caused by one too many vodkas. It felt like she was seeking some affirmation, but on a rational level she couldn't imagine needing that from guys who fucked around on their wives. Even pushing the dreaded fifty, her features—an intriguing mélange of south Austrian peasant stock with a spritz of patrician northern Italian—still turned younger heads; she could snag a high-caliber single guy if she had a mind to. But the thought always gave her a blast of toe-curling vertigo, as if she were teetering at the edge of a well, its stones fading into blackest black.

She sensed that the height of eroticism wasn't in a hotel room amid a flurry of unzipping (though she'd undeniably enjoyed these moments too). It was earlier on, at that juncture when she first knew it was going to happen. Not a conquest deal, especially because husbands on the prowl adjusted their expectations downward at need. She'd more than once, with a certain cold amusement, tracked a philanderer working his way down the ladder after she'd dished him a happy hour cold shoulder. No, it seemed more a languorous delight in that moment when the prospect of sex passed from question to unspoken agreement. And one of those should have been enough, the memory as pleasurable as the event itself. But the needle had somehow gotten stuck in the groove.

All the same, she knew it would be a while before she'd succumb to it. Not because of a change in her feelings for Roger. There were a dozen booby traps lying in wait if she ever ventured back there. His subconscious hijacking of her relationship with Jackie for one, where Jackie seemed to blame her for "losing" Roger. But most of all his workaholism that had so pervaded their life, and the host of things she mindlessly did or didn't do that helped push him toward it. More, she had a sense that sometime she would feel secure enough—maybe less fearful of helplessly watching a relationship she treasured become lifeless and ossified—to have breakfast with someone under conditions less extreme than finding out she wasn't going to die.

Clem fought to stifle a cavernous yawn. "Well, you should be in a good mood then! Nothing gives you more zippity do dah than looking down a barrel and hearing click when you're thinking boom."

"You sound sleepy."

"I've been in insomnia mode, trying to duck this horny tapeworm."

"And you'll break her parasitic little heart. God, men are *such* pigs."

Clem chuckled. "Anyway, did you catch me on the news last night? I announced we had an ID on the girl and that we thought we would soon have a suspect."

"You were on TV? I thought the pooh-bahs usually did that."

"Not if they think the case may crater. Maybe setting me up as the goat if they need one later."

"Big of them. The suspect's really pushing it, though."

"Sure, just part of the game. I need a few days' warm fuzzies with City Hall before they ask why we haven't caught him."

"You thinking Larsen? Sounds like you can't do much with him even if you *do* catch him."

"We can hold him for the poison theft, fuck with his biorhythms. Still no proof he did the girl, but if I get a lot more convinced while he's there, we can always put in a good word with the inmates. Suspected child killers don't do well in county lockup."

Angie cringed. "I imagine. So what's the plan?"

Clem paused. "Tell you what, how's about you see Roderick again? She needs to know she might've been poisoned, not the kind of thing grouchy old detectives are good at. Jojo's having a look-see at Larsen's previous digs in the Castro. It's been vacant, so at least we should get a print set. Also, not trying to be a vulture on the fence, but if she *has* been dosed, I can start thinking about calling in the FBI serial killer boys. They don't need an indictment to play ball. But they've got a two-carcass minimum."

"Kind of a prerequisite for a serial killer."

"Used to be three, but they're on a membership drive. Anyway, try to pick up some tidbits on Larsen. Roderick was rather churlish last time, maybe she'll be chattier now."

"Okay, there in half an hour."

"Call me when you're through. Me, I got ahold of Mama Larsen. I'm going down to Gilroy this afternoon to check into his potty training."

"Look for lots of wingless fly bodies in the tool shed."

• • •

Just as Clem was walking to Motor Pool, his cell phone chirped. He seldom entered a screen name for any witness—there were simply too many of them— but he'd put this one in there. *Mike.*

He poked the button. "Mike. Tell me you remembered."

Mike's tone was somber. "Yeah, I did. But now I did, don't seem like no big deal."

"I'll be the judge of that. Once I nailed someone because his daughter collected Snoopy dolls."

"I'll take your word for it. Okay, Remember I said something's eating me from when they were leaving? See, guy pays up, calls the girl, she comes hopscotching over, right? Clomp, clomp, clomp. So I say something like, 'Guess your dad's gonna get a lotta fish, huh?' She looks up at him, puts her hand over her mouth, and giggles, like it's a secret joke or something."

Clem's pulse rocketed. Before they'd gone in, he'd done the "let's play a game, where if anyone asks, I'm your dad" thing.

Just as he'd thought. The killer was a stranger. With a tumor for a heart.

Clem stopped by UCSF and pried a few tidbits out of HR. The visit netted Dr. Parcell's address, along with the fact that Larsen had had a student job as a lab tech in the anatomy department. A notation in his file cited him for posing a particularly decrepit cadaver as Ronald Reagan in the building lobby during the ex-president's visit to the campus. But just a typical departmental prank. The professor had passed away last year.

Twenty minutes later, Clem was ringing the door chimes of a white and red gingerbread Queen Anne Victorian near Alamo Square, a park uphill from the Western Addition and ground zero for the city's gentrification movement. After the fourth try, he turned to go when his ears picked up the whine of an electric motor and the clank of a dead bolt. The door opened, and an elderly man wheeled into view. He had tousled gray hair, an equine nose, and sunken eyes magnified by black horn-rim glasses with bottle-thick lenses.

"Dr. Parcell? Inspector Clemson Yao, SFPD Homicide."

They shook hands, and Parcell wheeled outside, pointing Clem to a bench. "Unless you'd like a glance inside. I've had some work done, and I can trust you not to pinch the silver." Clem wasn't like Grace, who'd nearly been rear-ended several times making impromptu stops at Sunday afternoon open houses, but he nodded anyway. Probably the only jollies the guy got these days. Parcell did an about-face, and Clem brought up the rear.

What with his profession, Clem had been inside more San Francisco residences than Angie. But homicide was a pastime of the poor, its victims' digs heavy on stopped-up toilets and walls full of vermin. So what graced his eyes made his jaw drop. Queen Annes were often divided into a dozen claustrophobic roomlets, and the grandeur vanished when you walked in. But Clem gazed into a baronial chamber the entire width and half the depth of the house. The plaster cathedral ceilings were thirty feet high, flanked by rows of Gothic stained glass windows in rich reds and blues. Two crystal chandeliers spangled colored light in a thousand directions. The marble fireplace in the distance was large enough to rotisserie a small cow. He walked into the great hall, toeing off his shoes before treading on the wood inlay design in the center of the floor. He steered clear of several ancient Persian rugs, any one of which would make for a respectable trade-in on a Ferrari.

Parcell gestured him to a silk-upholstered sofa, forcing his gingerly traverse of a priceless carpet. Clem smiled thinly. "My wife better never see this."

"After my accident, I decided to have some fun as a distraction, and it turned into a monster. Anyway, you're my first visit from Homicide, though they often ply their trade here." Despite its many renovated Victorians, highlighted by the famed postcard row on Hyde Street, the area surrounding Alamo Square had one of the highest homicide rates in the city.

Clem nodded gravely. "I've put in overtime here myself. This is about an old case of yours. Cynthia Nichols." He handed the picture to Parcell. "Sorry to say, this is the girl we found buried in the underground fuel tank. June fifth, 2004. You noted possible abuse."

Parcell winced. "I *do* remember. In my line of work, abuse cases drag behind you like Jacob Marley's chains. She claimed she twisted her arm falling off a swing. But she was terrified, and the bruises were obviously inflicted. I met her father too."

Clem tensed. "What did he look like?"

"A bit shorter than you, dirty blond hair, glasses."

Just like Larsen. Clem cursed his luck. But Nichols would likely be blond, since his daughter was. And most men were shorter than Clem. So he still couldn't rule out Daddy as the killer. You couldn't take a dead girl's giggle to court. "What else can you tell me?"

"I can tell you what he did for a living. He was a veterinary assistant."

Clem cursed yet again. He now had *two* medical connections. Worse yet, a vet's assistant would have access to the sodium whatever-it-was.

He fought off a burst of pique at Parcell for muddying up the waters. "Just how is it you remember so far back?" he asked with his "skeptical cop" tone, hoping Parcell would recant.

Parcell's reply was firm. "He picked her up from work. He was wearing scrubs, so I asked him. Seemed odd, because people who enjoy caring for animals aren't usually physically abusive. They vent on anything they have power over and usually abuse the animals in their care. They get found out pretty quick."

Clem nodded in resignation. "Makes sense. So you didn't think he was the abuser."

Parcell scratched his chin. "No, also because the girl wasn't afraid of him. I've probably confronted a thousand parents. The loudmouths who threaten to sue are generally the abusers. The sheepish ones—mostly mothers—usually aren't, but they know it's going on and feel responsible. I'd put him in that category."

"Huh. So maybe his wife?"

Parcell gave him a dubious glance. "She'd have to be a strong woman to break that girl's arm with her bare hands. Maybe an older brother?"

"Cynthia had a mild case of what is it? Osteogenesis imperfecta."

Parcell answered with a studious nod.

Clem's stomach suddenly churned. "Doctor. Do you think it's possible that a vet's assistant—someone who watches animals put to sleep every day—might come to believe that his own daughter, in some kind of abuse scenario, might be better off the same way?"

Parcell shrugged. "I'd think he'd try the police first. Or threatening the abuser, or kidnapping. But I've seen way too many demented parents to rule it out."

• • •

Clem drove back to the Hall banging his hands on the wheel. Even though Tom Nichols had vanished without a trace, thirty years of cop intuition whispered that he hadn't killed his daughter, that Larsen was the odds-on favorite. Everything was circumstantial, of course: Cynthia's behavior at the pet shop. The wisp of the creepoid from the hospital visit. The student job. Parcell's conclusions.

But the case had just curdled. Not that he had any doubts, but it never hurt to bounce it off one of the country's leading legal minds. He put in a call. To his surprise, it went straight through.

"Shlomo? *Nu, vie gehts?*" Almost forty years back, Shlomo Tenenbaum had been Clem's roommate for the two years he'd attended Berkeley before Angela Davis did a number on the curriculum. An Orthodox Jew from Brooklyn's Ukrainian neighborhood of Little Odessa, he'd preferred to room with a flaming Goy than to risk getting assigned an apostate Reform Jew. To their mutual surprise, they became inseparable. Shlomo was now a feared Manhattan defense attorney and still Clem's best friend.

"Shalom, Clem. So, how was the seder?" During college, Shlomo's mother sent him enormous parcels of kosher food, "so you should eat right." Even two Shlomos couldn't eat it all, and Clem spent four semesters living on borsht, pastrami, gefilte fish, belly lox, matzoh ball soup, kasha, and corned beef, at first to fend off starvation and later in the throes of what became a lifelong addiction. Even though she was by now in her mid-80s, she still sent Clem a gigantic package a week before Passover. His family was probably the only one in San Francisco's Chinese community that celebrated the Passover seder.

"She outdid herself. But so much! When they delivered the box, Grace asked me if we were getting a big-screen TV."

"Yeah, she forgot and made everything twice. That horseradish cleared your sinuses, huh?"

"It melted through the Tupperware and then the floor of the fridge. Like in that *Alien* movie. So, I'm still Momma's Goy Wonder?"

"No. Now she's decided, you keep kosher two weeks a year and speak half-assed Yiddish, probably a couple *nudniks* from the Lost Tribe of Israel ended up in Hong Kong. So she's asking, do you by chance have a very bad sense of direction?"

"Terrible. So how goes the practice?"

"This week? From hunger, I lost a trial. *Vey*, what *tsurris* I got from that. A little embezzlement deal, open and shut. So I go see this new ADA, he's so young he's still counting pubic hairs. And I can tell he wants to fry bigger fish, wants out quick. Clem, I swear I'm tuning this kid like a Steinway grand. He goes for two years in a country club with bars on the windows and restitution. And like who ever restitutes? So I'm seeing the client, I'm ready to *plotz* I'm so proud."

"And let me guess. He turned it down."

"Looks at me like I told him he's got testicle cancer. Such a *shmegegi*, he'd marry a divorce lawyer so he can get free legal advice if the marriage goes sour. So off we go to trial, it goes so far south they're chasing penguins around the courtroom. Even *he* can tell, the last two days he's praying to God five times a day like a Saudi. Eight years he gets. I told him next time he should try the Blessed Virgin 'cause women listen better. So, what's up?"

"I need a serious *mikvah*."

Shlomo groaned. "That's *mitzvah*, you *schlemiel*. How many times I'm telling you?" It was a joke as old as their friendship. A *mitzvah* was a favor; a *mikvah*, a ritual bath a woman took after her period.

"Okay, so I need one of those." He described the evidence of the case.

Shlomo sighed. "Clem, with the right prosecutor I would *pay* to take that case, just to make him look like such a *putz*. You got two witnesses with a four-year-old ID, and one's an old lady who probably can't handle 'State your name for the record.' Nichols took a powder, so he looks guilty. And even a public defender with a brain hernia would ask Dr. Parcell, was it possible Nichols killed his daughter. Guaranteed reasonable doubt, defense could move for dismissal. You don't happen to have color glossies of Larsen sticking the needle in her arm?"

"Not a one," Clem grumbled.

Shlomo paused. "Umm . . . Clem? What did you tell me about coincidences in police work?"

"That coincidences seldom are."

"And Tom Nichols just *happens* to be a perfect second suspect?"

Clem's heart turned into a ball of tar. "My God. Four years ago, Larsen set a trap. He followed Nichols, figured out what Nichols did for a living before kidnapping and killing Cynthia. *That* was why he used the sodium stuff."

"Exactly. He kills two birds with one stone: gets a flawless corpse for his diorama, and turns your case into *chazzerei*." Pig guts. Yup, his case was pig guts. "Still, there's one thing really bothers me that Larsen's the killer, not Nichols."

Clem ground his molars. He didn't need this from someone whose instincts were wrong about once every leap year. "Okay, what's that?"

"Well, Momma's memory's not what it used to be. Like on Passover, we hide a piece of matzoh, and the kids play 'find the matzoh.' We used to let her hide it, but then she forgets she already did. So for two days she's hiding matzoh. Last year she went through a whole box, my wife's *still* finding year-old matzoh. So Momma's started using memory helpers, they're called, what? Mnemonic devices, that's it. And Clem, even she forgets what she's supposed to remember, she never *ever* forgets the helper."

"Shlomo, is this one of your half-hour Talmudic spiels?"

"Already God may strike me with cholera that you're my best friend. And I'm teaching you now your own Bible? Like Jael, He'll put a tent peg through my head. I'm talking the old lady. Her renter's name was from the Bible. That's how she tried to remember his name. I bet you my Fort Lauderdale condo she's right. And Tom is in there. Thomas, anyway."

Doubting Thomas. The disciple who had to put his fingers in Christ's wounds to be convinced of the Resurrection. Thomas Nichols. And there were no Roberts, Larsen or otherwise, in the Bible.

"Well, shit," Clem muttered. "Okay, but Thomas doesn't jump out at me as being from the Bible. Not like, say, Nebuchadnezzar. Maybe Larsen used a false name with Janine."

"Maybe. But right now, it's a square peg you're pounding in a round hole. You need a nice round peg, and quick."

One of those evil ironies of detecting. If it *was* Larsen, he had superbly covered his tracks, and Cynthia's murder would likely go unpunished. He would need to kill again for Clem to have a shot. And Clem's thirty years told him that the guy would oblige him, if he hadn't already.

• • •

Angie worked her way through the traffic toward General. She recalled the sense of familiarity Larsen's picture had given her. The sensation grew as she let the face, and especially the almost Hitlerian eyes, bore into her cerebral alleyways. But she still couldn't place it.

She called Clem, who was pulling up to the Hall. "I'm having the blondest of moments here. I swear to God I've seen Larsen before. And someplace important. It's driving me batty."

"Yeah, my lumbago's acting up too." He went through his conclusions, especially about Janine and the Bible. "By the way, I just got Larsen's DMV and city parking registration. Keep an eye out for an aging blue Toyota hatchback."

Her legs went numb. "A blue . . . " The realization slammed her like a medicine ball to the solar plexus. "My God," she whispered harshly. "Larsen's the guy. He killed the girl."

Clem was silent for a moment. "Okay, I just pissed the seat. They'll bitch at Motor Pool. I could use an excuse."

Angie's heart pounded. "The afternoon before Zack and I found her. I was sitting in front of Janine's house in my car. He—Larsen, with his weird eyes, everything—drove by, stopped, looked right at me. Then drove away, stopped before turning and stared at me again. Blue Toyota hatchback, say five years old. I thought he was some neighborhood watch type. Took me until now to realize it. He was wearing glasses when I saw him. The hospital picture didn't have them."

"Right, they take badge shots without them. He was probably going by there a couple times a day since the 'for sale' sign went up. Maybe camping out, waiting for something to happen. He was sure to have spotted you sooner or later."

Clem paused. "As usual, nothing that'll indict him. But this same guy scoping you out at the crime-scene-to-be? That's enough for me to want to have a baton-talk with him in a room full of plastic tarps."

Angie couldn't help a wince. "If it's him, that may be the only way to take him out." The hellish shooting back in '86 filled her brain pan. She said, half to herself, "Been there, done that."

There was a moment of silence. "The Beast, huh?" Angie had never talked about it with Clem. Or with anyone for that matter, even Roger. But there was no avoiding it now.

Angie sighed. "Off the record?"

"Record? What record?"

"At the inquiry, I said I just blacked out in rage and fired. But I really didn't." She heard Clem clear his throat, as if he was unsure he wanted to hear this. "Oh, the rage was there, sure. The guy was primordial ooze. He was going to cut up a girl with a hacksaw." Acid bubbled in her throat. "I've always wondered if he would've done her alive and screaming."

"Not something I'd care to wonder once, never mind always."

"But I remember what I was feeling in that fog of rage. I'll never forget it." She paused. "He was maybe going to get off."

"Because the illegal search poisoned all the physical evidence derived from the house search."

"Exactly. And he wore a mask, so the girls had probably never seen his face, even if the DA could get them to testify."

"We almost never get a conviction without physical evidence. And I'd think long and hard before putting *my* daughter through that, especially if he might walk. Lots of parents would say no."

"So even though I was just being the best cop I knew how, it would've been on my head. What would I feel when I read about a bunch of identical kidnappings in Omaha?"

Clem's voice lowered almost to a whisper. "You would've had to hunt him down again and kill him if he got off."

"That, or visualize that hacksaw cutting off arms and legs for the rest of my life. And all this flashed on me the instant before I started pulling the trigger."

"Hmm. So I take it the six shots weren't just about rage."

"Some, maybe even most. But not all. I also wanted to make sure he was dead, dead, dead. Sometimes I think that if I'd had my speedloader, I would've put six more in him."

She shuddered. "Clem, The Beast was really good at what he did. No forensics, no witnesses, no nothing, time after time. In part, that's why I was left holding the bag. He was so good, there might never have been another way to take him out."

Clem pondered it. "With guys that good, usually we have to get lucky, like we did with you. If it's any comfort, I'd have done the same. It's not judge, jury, and executioner stuff. You're a human being weighing two hideous consequences."

"That's kind of what I figured out after a couple of years."

"So why you telling me this? Far as I'm concerned, say three Our Fathers and two Hail Marys."

"What's bothering me is that I'm getting that queasy feeling again in my intestines. Like we're starting to know in our guts that it's Larsen, but we can't do shit. He's probably kicking our coply asses. And all the way down the line, he might just be too good for us."

"Right. And if it *is* him, in the end, like The Beast, he may just have to die for it."

Back in his office, Clem telephoned Billy. "Looks like I might have me an evildoer." He gave Billy a summary of the last few days' events. "We figure Larsen was poisoned at the hospital. He's dying and knows it. He'll be fine for like two months, then he'll start sneezing out hunks of his brain. And he stole a big batch of the poison."

There was a pause. Billy finally spoke. "That weird sound you just heard's my testicles shrinking. Psychopaths are only held back from burning Atlanta by survival instincts. Survival's out the window, Katy bar the door." Billy paused. "Well, on the bright side, if it's an abused girl baked his taters, and he's multiple, he'd need to be somewhere he could find 'em. He's not at a hospital now."

"And he'd need somewhere to *patchke* with her, no one looking in on him."

"That too," agreed Billy. "If he's in SF, he's holed up in a garage apartment, what with the documentation you need to get a big place because of the rents. He'd be a cat covering shit on a tile floor, with the formaldehyde and so on." Clem nodded. Even garages were going for eight hundred a month in the dizzy real estate market.

Clem continued. "If he has other kills to make, I figure the poison becomes a new MO."

"Got to be why he pinched the stuff. Many serials don't follow same MO every time, that's a myth. Just easier to spot the ones always strangle with a bra, give 'em a nifty nickname. The Wonderbra Strangler. Harder to spot the ones like to mix and match, connect their murders."

"But we have a problem. If he's poisoned a bunch of people, we wouldn't have a clue yet. The symptoms don't show up for months."

"Could be. But these guys are their own biggest fans; sun comes up just to hear 'em crow. Lot of 'em collect news stories on 'emselves. We even catch some that way. Mrs. Psychopath wonders why hubby got him a scrapbook with fifty articles on the Cordless Drill Murderer. You'd get a nyah-nyah-na-nyah-nyah thing. He won't miss out on the fun before his Saint Pete interview."

"Especially since it won't go too copacetic," added Clem.

"But on his signature, nothing yet. Don't think we got us an everyday pinkie-lopper though. Something subtler, where signature's clear to him but not others."

"Like a twisted game, where we're supposed to figure it out."

"Yup, I *hate* those guys. And nothing says just poison here on out. Whatever twitters his fritters. And something my thirty-year gut's howling: seems he saw the girl before he did her, maybe even spent some time with her. So he's probably not a random killer, strangling hitchhikers and so on. If he's got other kills, look first at people he knows. Mama, ex-girlfriend, people at work, someone he's at least met before. And if he kills out of some sense of slight, poison won't sate his need to dominate and degrade 'em, too girly-girl. The poison might be a novelty for now. But he could go out with some spectacular mass killing."

"Probably didn't have enough toys as a kid," Clem muttered.

"But with a twist. See, you got serials on the one hand, mass murderers on the other. One almost never does the other. Serials mostly one at a time, a situation they control. Mass murderers build up like Vesuvius, then haul off and bury Pompeii. Mass murder has this implied element of nihilism that doesn't exist for serials."

"Right," said Clem. "Guy does the SWATusi or kills himself after the bloodbath."

"Like there's nobility going down in flames," agreed Billy. "But serials always got 'em an exit strategy. And they surrender quietly, 'cause they think they can beat the rap."

"Right, Bundy was pitching a deal while they were shoving cotton up his ass in the electric chair anteroom," continued Clem. "But Freddie Mercury's got nothing to lose. His brains'll be creamed spinach before they spit out an indictment."

"Yup. But not twenty DB's in a Luby's. It'll have the stealth aspects of the serial. And nothing to lose means it won't be a collar, it'll be a corpse. His or yours, you pick."

Clem started. The second time this had come up in half an hour. "You have the right to remain dead."

"Stake through the heart. Trust me, God'll look the other way. A final issue, Clem. Remember I told you that once we ID the fucker, we're usually ninety-nine percent there?"

"Because they think they're too smart for us to nail them, so they don't rabbit."

"Assuming it's Larsen, you're just getting started. He's on the move, radar deployed. He needed a few weeks when he found out he's dying to get his shit together. But now, he's got unfinished business? He's only got two months."

"If we're right about the poison."

"Even if he *thinks* he's been poisoned. May be a new kill or two out there already we just don't know's his. If I'm you, I'd take the weirdest unsolveds I got, try to connect 'em to this one, find some thread ties 'em together. And just because this kill's clean don't augur diddly. Next one could scarletize the ceiling. He might've done the girl so tidy just so she'd gussy up nice in the tank."

Billy paused, then spoke quietly. "Clem, what we've said comes down to just yet, we don't have us fox turds. But something I *can* venture. You gonna see Mama?"

"Yeah, I toss her salad this afternoon."

"If Larsen's the killer, you see her, you'll pick up the usual childhood nightmare shit, a welter of anger, degradation, shame, what have you. Most child killers aren't born that way. You don't kill a little girl 'less you been shat out Satan's ass and fed to his lawyers."

Billy took a weary breath. "But something else. This man, he's a *proud* man, a meticulous artisan takes an infernal glee in his craft. Turned all his formidable powers to what he wrought in that tunnel, a hellish masterpiece of workmanship and black inspiration, like of which I've not seen before.

"And, my old friend, if he *does* have targets out there, people he *must* kill, and I expect he does, you'll see things'll make Christ deny salvation so the fucker can't sneak in Heaven's back door."

He slipped into the rusted shower stall, still pleasantly buzzed by last night's news report. Not too shabby, Honorable Yao. He'd figured them for a few weeks even to figure out who the girl was, and here it was, just a week after Cynthia—Cindy, actually, as she'd told him with that engaging smile—had taken her turn under the morgue's bone saws.

Most likely they'd tracked her down from the hospital records. They would soon zero in on him if they hadn't already. And certainly, Yao wouldn't be suckered by the Nichols ploy. But he'd never intended it. Yao was savvy enough to deduce not only that Cindy's father had been a dupe but that the good guys had taken a first-round drubbing. Taunting phone calls were kid stuff. An artist let his audience infer genius on its own.

He squeezed some shampoo into a trembling hand. The tremor was more noticeable this morning. In his mind's eye, he could see the tiny globs of metal eating into his brain like grinding machines at the face of a coal seam.

He thought about his visit to the tunnel three weeks back. He'd noticed the tremor then for the first time, strangely empty of grief. Four months ago he'd done the research that told him he was a dead man. He'd seesawed between terror and rage on the one hand and blithe disbelief on the other, because he felt just fine. No weird aches or coughs that foretold a terminal illness. But then memory of the tiny droplet splashing on his wrist would flood back, and he'd rage inside himself again.

That is, until the revelation. When he'd come to understand all.

He'd always known the shadow at the borders of sleep that loomed when all grew silent, announcing itself with a sound like the slow tap tap tapping of a huge brass pendulum.

It wasn't some Sunday-school imp with horns and a pointy tail. No, the predation boiled with flares of slick, reeking disease, a tumor exulting in its own corruption, arcing the heavens and swollen to a girth beyond galaxies. And heedless as the procession of a Hindu Juggernaut, rending its zealots into shattered limbs and gore as they threw themselves under the idol's huge, creaking wheels.

Souls? Mere gobbets of cosmic snot.

What mattered was matter. The blood and the bone.

And he had slowly imbued himself with a calling, to emulate the power that rendered the blood of the universe into clots of pus. But he was no lunatic doing the bidding of dogs or demons. No, he was a creature of unshackled will, with a mandate to peel the gangrenous skin from the earth.

And then, four months back, he'd learned it was he who would die. He staggered about in a fog of irony, wondering if the toil he'd endured was just some cosmic exploding cigar. But miraculously, the night arrived when he sensed again the silence, and then, the ominous tap tap tap. His body curled around itself like a strangling vine as he realized that the leviathan had emerged for him, for the last time, throbbing with hideous majesty.

He awoke full of omnipotence. He had not been struck down by the reaper with a droplet of death. He was to become that reaper. When the time was right, he would strike at will, the Black Death made flesh. With a touch, he would vent destruction on hundreds, his quarry clueless that their brains would slowly turn into rotting putty.

But before that, the way would be expunged of rot. Those who had so wronged him would be first. They would bray and bellow. They would be his angelus, chime his hours with their sobs. He would howl with exultation, Hell's gatekeeper ushering in the damned. He would pay homage to their flesh. And then they would stink the dying stench. Stink like the shit his father shoveled up his nose day in, day out on the plasma display in his brain.

Chicken Soup for the Soul.

And then, wonder of wonders, the "for sale" sign went up. Before then, he'd thought about popping Yao & Co. a letter revealing the tomb and throwing down the gauntlet. But it would've been tawdry self-promotion, like a bad poet posting his tripe on Internet bulletin boards.

So he'd held off, awaiting the inspection that would turn up the little girl. But then the house languished for months. He fumed by the hour, even putting in a call to sniff out who was gumming up the sale. But the yellow tape finally blanketed the yard like a Halloween toilet paper prank.

As with anything, there was a price. In two months, he would be too disabled to act. His limbs would be palsied with tremors. His sense of touch would fade into numbness. His eyesight would cloud and dim.

But he felt no grief. What would transpire soon would become legend: a series of spellbinding messies, ending in a cataclysm of such exquisite brutality that the planets would quiver on their axes.

Clem couldn't devote much time to the bizarre tapeworm murder and had Jojo give the file a once-over. Jojo paged through it, shaking his head in amazement. The murder was almost elegant in a gruesome sort of way. A far cry from the equally gruesome but far less elegant gang killings in the Philippines known as "chop-chops," where the victim was dismembered and his remains left in a dozen paper bags all over town. Even if you managed to find the guy's head, most of them ended up as John Does. The poorer Filipinos who made up most gang vics—often those who welched on gambling and drug debts—never saw a dentist, and couldn't be identified even from dental records.

Assault had done a fairly thorough job after Simmons had been chloroformed. What with the lack of robbery motive, it implied he'd been a target. They'd interviewed several dozen people at the hospital. As in any place housing a gaggle of colossal egos, doctors despised each other as a matter of course. But they limited their aggression to backbiting among colleagues and in medical journals.

Division had also staked out Stern Grove from dawn until 9:00 a.m. for two weeks, to no avail. Forensics had even given the crime scene a grid walk, unusual in assault cases. Homicide would probably duplicate the effort with the same results. Colleagues would be re-interviewed and the crime lab would take another pass. But they would come up empty.

The only thing Jojo could zero in on was the wallet Simmons had brought with him on the run. But nothing had been taken; apparently it hadn't even been removed from the pocket of his sweats. Simmons had given it a quick look to make sure his money and cards were still there, and that had been the end of it. Forensics hadn't bothered to check for prints; by now, after Simmons had carried it around for two months, it would be a fruitless exercise. But a guy who died with his brain choked with parasites deserved at least that much.

The wallet would probably be at the hospital; Simmons had showed up there one day and never left. A call to the hospital administration proved Jojo right. It was in Simmons's locker. Jojo had a forensic field tech pick it up. An hour later, it was sitting on his desk.

Jojo unsealed the evidence bag, snapped on latex gloves, and tweezed out the contents. At first, nothing out of the ordinary for a single twenty-something: driver's license, American Express, and Visa. A membership card for an exclusive gym contrasted with a restaurant discount card, the kind you slipped in the bill folder when you paid to get one entrée for free. Scrunched-up cocktail napkins with phone numbers for Chloe, Sylvia, and Daphne, each rated on the ten scale: two sevens and a nine with exclamation points. A Citibank deposit slip for four hundred something dollars. Not bad handwriting for a doc.

The wallet billfold was now empty. The photo holder had a clear plastic window but was empty of pictures. He opened it almost as an afterthought and spied a tiny, carefully folded piece of paper hidden below the visible window. Probably just an inspection tag, but he carefully tweezed it open and leaned forward to read the tiny laser-print type. What he saw made him gasp:

The Early Bird Catches the Worm.

Jojo winced at the fierce irony. Simmons had unwittingly carried the killer's sick joke around with him for two months until his death.

Angie threaded the traffic to General, strode up to the desk, and asked for Roderick. A guard escorted her into Roderick's office. She was sitting at her desk, eyes glassy with exhaustion, tension revealed by her quivering jaw. She signaled Angie to a chair.

"Roth told me you know everything," she began, looking away at the credentialed wall with distaste. "And that nothing will go any further."

Angie nodded sternly. "But I'm mainly here to tell you that Larsen may have poisoned you. You should get tested for mercury."

Roderick surprised her with a burst of derisive laughter. "I've been testing myself weekly for four months. As of yesterday, I'm free of heavy metals."

Angie felt chagrined that she'd been off the mark until she realized Roderick would be dying if she hadn't been. "Sorry. I brought this up because of the tremors."

"Incipient Parkinson's. I've had these"—she held up a hand—"for three years. It'll get worse but slowly. Assuming your colleague is remotely competent, I expect to be working a long time."

Angie couldn't help herself. "Yes, I gather people here have seen to that."

Roderick sighed like a mother dealing with an argumentative teenager. "Please. I'm the best in the country at what I do, making half what I could elsewhere. You'd trade that for the welfare of someone who embalms little girls?"

"That stays under wraps. He's only a suspect. And he wasn't when you hounded him out of the building. If it weren't for that, he'd be wearing orange as we speak."

"And I couldn't have known that. How do you think it feels, opening every door—my house, my car—with a handkerchief? I'm sick of it," she spat out. "Anyway, I'm sure he won't try anything. He probably would've already."

Angie continued levelly. "I wouldn't make that assumption. He seems the patient sort."

"I'll assume as I please. I'm sick of living as if *I* were the fugitive. Your inspector buddy's adept at throwing his weight around. Let's hope he's as good at catching criminals. First impressions to the contrary."

Angie blew past her point of no return. "As far as he's concerned, you're worth more to us dead. If we up the body count, the FBI comes in. We could use their help." Roderick's jaw snapped shut. Angie continued, "Now, perhaps you can fill me in on anything you didn't mention last time."

Roderick drew a deep breath. "Truce, truce. Look, Angie, I wasn't born a bitch on wheels. I did something I'm not terribly proud of. And now I'm trying to get through my day with a possible child killer nursing a fairly serious grudge looking over my shoulder. And contending with a disease that, when it gets bad enough, makes little kids cross the street when they see you coming." She averted her gaze and dabbed a finger at each eye.

"I really don't know anything myself," she continued with a jerky shrug. "Joanne Duffy, one of the techs, had some issue with him. Didn't come to anything official." She picked up the phone and called one of the radiologists. Joanne was apparently on break.

Roderick continued. "The guard will take you to the tech break room." She paused. "One other thing, though maybe it's nothing. Four years ago—July or August—he took some sick leave. When he came back, he was like a zombie. Did his work, but you could wave a hand in front of his eyes and he wouldn't blink. It wore off after a few days."

"I'd appreciate if you could dig up the dates. Inspector Yao or I will call you."

Roderick nodded, stood, and switched on her light panel. Angie headed down to the end of the hall with the guard and opened the last door on the right. Two blond women in white pantsuit uniforms were at a table with pastries and coffee.

"Joanne Duffy?"

The taller one looked up curiously.

"Angie Strackan. Could I speak with you?"

Joanne stood up uncertainly and stepped out in the hallway. Just taller than Angie's five-five, on the willowy side, with reddish-blond hair cascading high-schoolishly down her back. Diamond studs whose diameter screamed zirconia. About twenty-five, chock full of Irish chromosomes, with a long, straight nose, a spackling of freckles, and the sort of wide mouth and full lips that turned men into prancing lap dogs.

Angie flashed her Reserve badge. "I'm looking into the disappearance of Robert Larsen after his termination."

Joanne gave her a quizzical look. "Umm . . . Robert?"

"The tech who was let go here a few months ago. Doctor Roderick said you had some sort of issue with him. I'm trying to get some insight into his behavior here."

Joanne grimaced with disgust, her mouth spreading halfway across her cheeks. "You mean Matthew. Christ, that I can give you. What a first-class creep."

Angie's blood raced. "Matthew?"

"Right. Matthew Larsen. My archenemy until he got canned."

"But the name in his file is Robert."

Joanne shrugged. "Could be. But he goes by Matthew."

Angie thought back to Larsen's folder. Robert M. Larsen, Junior. He didn't go by his father's name, but by his middle one. Janine had been right all along.

The first book of the New Testament. The Book of Matthew.

Angie shook off her shock and continued. "So what was the issue?"

Joanne's voice was laden with exasperation. "Oh, it's like every time I was around him, he'd be looking at me sideways. And lunch in the cafeteria: He'd wait for me to get through the line. Then he'd go through, look at where I was sitting like he was coming to this big decision about sitting down with me. Then, he'd sit somewhere else."

"Like he was intimidated."

"Right. Always where he could see me. I'd catch him staring, he'd look away. I used to vary my lunch hour, but he always came in after me. Like he had this supreme crush but not the guts to act. Not that I would've been interested," she added with a floor-to-ceiling eye roll. "Once I even had this hunky doctor sit with me just to drive him out of his skull."

"It probably worked. And this was only directed at you? No other women?"

"Not that I saw. He'd follow me after work too. Never where I could call him on it. He'd walk a ways behind me when I was walking to the bus stop, then turn off. That was the thing: he never did anything where I could file a complaint."

"He was stalking you for a year. Why did it start? He'd been here for years."

"I started two years ago, working nights. Then a day slot opened, so I switched. It got so bad I tried to move back to nights. But they cut a night slot, so I was stuck."

"Okay, I've got a handle on it. Anything else?"

"Well, like a month before he got booted, I confronted him. I'd talked to Dr. Roderick, but they couldn't do anything unless he did something obvious, like touch me. So after one time I caught him doing the staring and looking away thing, I got right in his face, told him to stop it. He denied it. But the way he did it was creepoid."

"How so?"

"Well, you know when you catch most guys at something, there's a second where they're off-kilter? Like they need an instant to flip into lie mode."

"I've seen it all," replied Angie with half a smile, recalling her ex-husband Clint's serial philandering years before.

"Well, there was none of it. He just instantly looked down his nose and called me 'delusional.' I would've slapped him if I hadn't stomped off."

Angie nodded. Psychopaths were superb liars. They had no sense of guilt, and rationalized so well that their lies could become truths inside their heads. Like a rapist who convinced himself the act was consensual even if the girl had blood running out her ears when he left. They were the only criminals who could consistently beat a polygraph. "And after that?"

"He got more subtle. Like in the cafeteria, I'd glance over, he'd be reading. But he was looking out the corner of his eye. And something else: After I dissed him, his face was different. Like his jaw was set so tight you could see the muscles. I bought champagne the day he got fired. The good stuff, eight bucks a bottle," she finished, eking out a smile.

"Ever seen him since?"

"It's creepy. Sometimes on the way home, I'd get this feeling he was out there. Maybe just my imagination on overdrive."

"Or your subconscious picking up danger signals. Look, there's things I can't go into. But there's some chance Matthew could be dangerous."

Joanne's eyes widened. "Dangerous? How?"

"To be honest, we're really not sure yet. You'll know as soon as we do. You have a cell?" Joanne nodded. "Give me your numbers." Joanne rattled them off and Angie poked them into her phone.

Angie handed her a card. "Here's my number. Call me any time. Look, I'm going out on a limb, but I'm worried because you really got his attention. If you see him in a circumstance where it's clear he's been stalking you, call 911. Then get in your car and get out of town."

"Umm . . . I don't have a car," answered Joanne nervously.

"Then rent one. I mean it."

Joanne's eyes glistened as if she was about to break into tears.

Angie continued, "Sorry to ruin your day. Just remember what I told you." Angie patted her shoulder and turned on her heels.

As she walked out of the hospital, she couldn't quell the creeping of her flesh. No way was Matthew finished with Joanne. And any finish Matthew had in mind would not be pretty.

As she reached her car, she called Clem, cursing each ring tone before he answered.

There was a moment of dead air as Clem absorbed the name change. "Matthew. Tell you what, I'm heading out of the Hall to get a pretzel. Daily ritual of mine. Meet me out front?"

Angie pulled up to the Hall fifteen minutes later and parked. The Hall of Justice—"the Hall" to anyone who worked there—was the city's fortress-like complex in a dingy neighborhood that combined courtrooms, police headquarters, the DA's office, forensics labs, the morgue, and anything else that ensured domestic tranquility. The windowless architecture was best described as neo-Stalinist. Across the street was a gaggle of bail bondsmen, along with a parking lot that charged some of the most larcenous rates in the city. It was one of the few government buildings that didn't rate a drive-by on tour-bus routes.

Minutes later Clem and Angie were standing in front of a vendor cart, munching on gigantic warm pretzels slathered in salt and mustard.

Clem wiped the mustard from his lips with a napkin. "Well, that explains a lot. Roth didn't know what name Larsen went by."

"Sure, only the people who worked with him. I see Joanne as a big-time target."

"My Fed crony says Larsen's most likely targets are people he knows, especially anyone who's offended him," agreed Clem.

"That would be her. I told her to get out of town the minute she sees him."

"Sound advice. Psychopaths don't take kindly to rejection. Also, Cynthia's file came in. Finished spring 2004, then vanished. Nada from the parents, Thomas and June Nichols. Jojo went to the address. Renters, bottom of a two-flat house. Owner said one day at the end of June 2004, they skipped town.

So Cynthia was probably dead by then. We've got a court order for phone re-cords, bank stuff, but they probably haven't left much of a trail."

"Probably living a mile up a chained-off dirt road. Time to release her pic to the press?"

"It's going out as we speak, with her name. *Chronicle's* putting out a spe-cial afternoon edition. Last time they did that was 9/11. But be forewarned, it's not unusual to get two or three thousand tips. Bohunks claiming to be long-lost relatives, others saying they're the killer, on and on. One time, I shit you not, I got one from Katmandu. Some fucking guru had a vision of the killer while he was levitating. Said he dropped two feet to the floor, busted both ankles." Clem paused. "Didn't pan out."

"Jeez, hope he didn't call collect." Clem's silence was heavy with annoy-ance. That one had probably worked its way through the cop-bar grapevine to Los Angeles by now. "Clem?"

"Fifty-two bucks in case you're wondering," he muttered. "Anyway, if you're still oozing civic duty tomorrow, there'll be tons of homicidal shit-work. Can't set you up at the Hall, since you're not Homicide, so I'll get you a phone patch at Sunset."

Like most seasoned cops, when outside, Clem rarely looked straight at people he was speaking to; instead, he looked at everything and everyone *but* them, scanning his surroundings for trouble. As he glanced back towards the Hall, Angie saw his jaw tighten. "Christ, my timing bites today."

Angie turned and saw a beefy man nearly as tall as Clem approaching them. He was in shirtsleeves and had saucer-sized sweat stains under his arms despite the cool, misty morning. His complexion was the mottled pink of a habitual tippler, highlighted by a web of tortured capillaries on his bulbous nose. His eyes were too small for his face, piggish and slightly bloodshot. An unkempt brush mustache obscured a good portion of his upper lip and tufts of nose hair jutted from enormous nostrils. His tie sported a long history of coffee stains. Just below it, the shirt buttons above his belt strained mightily to keep in check a massive beer belly, in one spot actually revealing a thin sliver of pale, flaccid skin.

He waddled up to the vendor's cart and ordered two pretzels. Then he turned towards them. "So Clem, ain't ya gonna introduce me?" he asked with a bald-faced leer at Angie.

Clem frowned. "Not a chance. She's not partial to obscene phone calls."

The man put a fistful of pretzels to his chest and said with an expression of exaggerated shock, "*Moi?*" He looked back at Clem, bit off an enormous chunk of pretzel and talked his way around it. Tiny globules of mustard dangled from his mustache. "So how's it goin' on that girl case?" He shook his head sadly, waving the pretzels for emphasis. "Saw her pic. Christ, what a damn shame. I mean, she woulda been freakin' *hot* if she'd a made it another ten years."

Angie reddened and drew breath, prepping to unleash a cannonade of vitriol.

Clem squelched her with a sidelong glance. "Angie, meet Bert Heimlich. Stanford wants his brain after he dies. It might refute Darwin."

Heimlich seemed to puzzle over that for a moment before giving up. "Bet it was her old man. Always is, same as child abuse murders." He grinned at Angie. "Actually I like doin' spankers sometimes 'cause they're usually such easy solves. Ain't that right, Clem?"

Clem elected not to reply. He looked at Angie. "Sorry. Bert's sort of a *Simpsons* version of a homicide cop."

"Hey, I love that show! Never miss it. Seen the movie yet?" Heimlich stuffed another giant hunk of pretzel in his mouth. He eyed Angie and brandished the remnant of the pretzel. "Jeez, who'd a thought a friggin' wetback could bake a decent pretzel, huh?"

Clem gazed heavenward in disbelief. The elderly Chicano cart vendor glared at Heimlich but said nothing. "Hey, don't get me wrong," continued Heimlich. "Just where I come from, we call a spade a spade. Hell, I love a good burrito same as the next guy."

"A good bit more, apparently," muttered Angie with a glance at his stomach.

Heimlich rubbed his belly with a grin that was belied by the junkyard dog look in his eyes. "Well, gotta run here. You two enjoy yourselves," he finished with a suggestive leer.

"I didn't like the look of that last leer," said Clem with a frown as Heimlich headed for the Hall.

"Like Clem and Angie sitting in a tree?"

"Yet another reason I don't want you hanging around Homicide. He wouldn't jerry-rig a rumor on this because it'd come back to him. But he'd do it in a second if he could deny it."

"God, what a pig," Angie spat out.

"Alias 'Grunt.' Don't let that buffoon act fool you. He's a lot smarter than he looks. He just doesn't apply it to solving homicides. And he's spent six years trying to hand me the black spot."

"And you him, I imagine," Angie said with a grin.

Clem nodded. "But he's got more juice than me. Drinking buddies among the crusty old Caucasian union leaders. That's how he's skated on five excessive-force beefs. And he'd sell his firstborn to a brothel to flush me down the IA toilet."

"Hard to imagine any woman letting him spawn with her," replied Angie. "So what happened?"

"He was lead inspector on a case we were working with the FBI. I was junior. FBI got fed up with him, demanded he be pulled from the case. I got the nod, he got a big red X in his jacket. To this day he thinks I engineered the whole thing."

"Which you did, right?"

"*Moi?*" replied Clem with a sly smile.

"So thus my trip to Booneville to see Janine last week?"

"Precisely. Last time I interviewed a witness in Monterey, rumor hit the *Chronicle* that I was golfing Pebble Beach on company time and money. I can't even beat my daughter Jenny at putt-putt."

"So whence the nickname? He former infantry?"

"Hardly. No, when somebody fries his bacon on the stand, instead of saying yes and no, he grunts. Judge has to admonish him to use English every answer. Juries pee their pants, like where they start aping him."

"Must give the DA some serious *agida*."

"He's pledged two tickets to Maui to anyone can bust Grunt to Motor Pool. Jackson gives him mostly murder-suicides so he doesn't have to testify."

"Well, I think I just made an enemy for life. But enough of Grunt. Anything from Matthew's previous place?"

"Clean latents, *no mas*. He was there since April 2005, so he moved there from Janine Maury's house. Post office forwarding shows him moving to this flat from the place he lived in *before* the Maurys', so he never put in a change of address to the Maurys'."

"Strange, he probably didn't know he was going to be a child killer when he moved into Janine's. Why not forward your mail?"

"Exactly. Got his bank records: he closed accounts and cancelled cards four months ago. Everything's PO box. Means we can't establish he was living at the crime scene. Pulled out thirty thousand, so he's not hard up for cash. Oh, we did get one other thing. Found his video store; clerk recognized the pic. Hollywood stuff mostly. But get this: Back like two years ago, for a month or two, seems he went on some sappy self-help binge. Codependency, impulse control, anger management, higher power, I feel your pain. Like one or two tapes every day."

"I'm Matthew, and I'm a psycho killer."

"Hi, Matthew! Then bam, it just stopped. In the last year, mostly one series of horrors, the *Hellraisers*. Four or five times each movie."

"The ones with the guy from Hell? With all the nails sticking out of his head?"

"The very same. And all the hooks ripping people to pieces."

Angie's stomach hit an air pocket. "Sounds like he got in touch with his inner ghoul."

CHAPTER TEN

Clem hit the call-end button with a trembling finger just as he reached the southern outskirts of San Jose on the way to see April Larsen in Gilroy.

Jojo's call had Clem's brain reaching cold fusion. The crimes revolved around each other in his mind like two suns, each caught in the other's gravity. One man's guts turned insides out in a tree, the other's brain turned into Limburger by tapeworms. The MOs bore no resemblance to each other, other than their macabre genius. But the signature was unmistakable.

I'm singin' in the rain. The early bird catches the worm. There could be no doubt: the same psychic furnace had painted the sick humor on each act.

Clem's hands clenched the wheel as the terrible Engine clanked and rumbled through the labyrinth of his brain, spewing gouts of black blood and gore. Just as he'd expected, Sneezy's killer was plying his trade in San Francisco.

Noon found him at the door of a ramshackle brown bungalow on the outskirts of Gilroy. The rusty chain-link fence had long ceased its function. The yard contained two ancient pickups. One of them looked operational, the other beyond the help of even the most wizardly mechanic. It seemed to be sinking into the ground like a mastodon in a tar pit.

A leathery hand jerked the lace curtain from the door's eye-level window, revealing a hung-up-wet female face highlighted by Matthew's craggy cheekbones. Clem heard the clink of locks, and the door creaked open a few inches. The woman was middle height, with hair that had once been blond but had been ravaged into gunmetal gray. An unhealthy sixty, hands sporting a dozen liver spots, knuckles knobby with arthritis, skin a relief map of folds and furrows. She wore a wrinkled blue-pattern shift.

He flashed his badge. "Mrs. Larsen, I need to talk with you. About Matthew."

"He in trouble?" she asked, looking like she wasn't about to believe anything he told her. She continued to stand in the doorway.

"Could I come in? I'm not selling magazines."

"Suit y'self." She grudgingly stood aside. He caught a waft of unwashed clothes and stale cigarettes as he walked in.

"Sorry, maid's day off," she said. At least she had a sense of humor.

"Want coffee? Something stronger? Got bourbon. You guys like tea, I got a bag somewhere."

He actually couldn't stand tea. "Some coffee, thanks. Black." He wouldn't risk a sip, but he'd get a minute to glance around while she saw to it. She gestured him to a red faux-velvet couch with cushions and arms worn pink from use. It was fronted by a small oak-veneered coffee table with a dozen circular stains and a huge cracked glass ashtray brimming with cigarette butts.

He grinned. "Been sitting since San Francisco."

"Suit y'self."

She hobbled into the kitchen, and Clem perused the living room. The furniture was in the same state of decay as the couch, highlighted by a cigarette-burned green leatherette La-Z-Boy across the room from a large TV set, the only item of recent vintage. The ratty beige wall-to-wall was festooned with mouse droppings along the baseboards.

She returned carrying a tumbler a third full of what was probably bourbon, and they sat. She extricated a cigarette from a sleep-scrunched pack of Winstons and lit it with a plastic lighter. She fidgeted relentlessly, tipping the Winston on the edge of the ashtray.

"So what's this about?" she asked, eyeing him warily over her bourbon.

"Matthew's a suspect in a homicide. Now, that doesn't mean he's guilty; we often get a dozen suspects. Mostly just wrong place, wrong time. It means we need to ask questions to clear things up." Clem used this technique with less-sophisticated witnesses, enlisting their aid to help clear the suspect. It worked better than being evasive.

Her eyes bulged. "Oh, that's ridiculous. He couldn't kill someone." She smiled weakly. "Matthew, he's a good boy. Good jobs, visits, sends money. More than I can say for his father."

"And he is . . . ?"

She swigged her bourbon. "Name's Bob. In jail. Salinas Valley State, an hour south. Two years, aggravated assault on an officer, six months to go. Bucket-a-blood barroom stuff. Other guy was a off-duty cop. Got hisself on duty real quick." She glared at Clem as though he'd bribed the judge.

"When was the last time Matthew visited?"

"Hm. Been a while, four months. Calls, but says he's busy, I'm thinking girlfriend."

"He have many girlfriends?"

"Ain't never met a one. He ain't a faggot, don't get me wrong. Found his dad's *Hustlers* under his bed enough times, God knows. Says he has this girl and that, time to time. Just embarrassed to bring 'em here I think." She gestured at the surroundings with her cigarette.

"Any names? Recently?"

"Oh, in one ear, out the other. Last I heard lot about was, umm, Jo something. Jody? Joanne, that's it. Nothing lately though. Like four, five months."

Clem filed it under "creepy." Psychopaths were often compulsive liars, spinning tales that embodied elaborate fantasy structures. "He say where he met her?"

"At work. He's a radiologer, does X-rays. Hey, she get killed? Wasn't Matthew; he was real sweet on her, even bought her these ruby earrings 'cause her favorite color's red. He showed me," she added, adamantly jabbing the cigarette into the heap of butts. Smoke curled upwards in foul-smelling wisps.

"No, it's not her. And to be honest, I'm not at liberty to tell you anything more. Police procedure. You know where I can find him? He moved four months ago."

"Yeah, don't know where. You could get him at work. I'm not sure what's the hospital." So Matthew hadn't told her he'd been fired.

"We don't know either. You don't have his phone number, do you?"

"Said he couldn't get a phone at his new place. Calls from a pay phone."

Matthew's reluctance to have a phone made sense; he was now a fugitive. If he used a prepaid cell, it would be difficult not to give his mother his number, something the police could then track down. And there were pitfalls to using a supposedly "untraceable" prepaid cell; dozens of fugitives had been caught using them. Usually they didn't realize that even after hanging up a call, the phone continued to "talk" to the cellular towers unless it was switched off. If you had the number, in many cases, the phone's location could be triangulated down to a single building.

"He mention anything about where he lived?" Clem asked.

"Not much, said it's real small. Oh, and his landlady's from Rio. Told me that 'cause I always wanted to go to Rio. Ever since I was a girl." She smiled, revealing blackened nubs complementing her tobacco-stained snaggleteeth.

The kettle whistled, and she went to fix the coffee. Clem cased the living room, his attention drawn by two framed photos on the mantel over the soot-encrusted fireplace. Its andirons were almost buried under a pile of ash that was working its way into the living room like a sand dune. One shot showed a plain-faced April Larsen about twenty years back, arm-in-arm with a burly, beetle-browed Scandinavian-looking man about her age, and two kids. One was a gangly, pubescent Matthew, the other a girl about eight with a mischievous smile. Her hair was back-length, a luminous platinum blond.

The next photo seemed five or six years later. Matthew appeared about eighteen. He now had a rangy physique that could mask considerable strength. Mrs. Larsen had worn the years badly, by appearance aging more than a decade. Her husband had gained about fifty pounds. The girl looked thirteen or fourteen, with nascent drop-dead looks. She sported a sullen pout, but Clem couldn't be certain if it was affected. He'd seen that look on his own daughter's face enough times, even observed her practicing it in the mirror, so that he didn't draw conclusions.

Mrs. Larsen returned with the coffee in a discolored white mug, as well as her bourbon, filled to the same one-third full she'd started with. One of those drinkers who believed that if they just kept surreptitiously refilling, no one would notice.

"Matthew get you the TV?"

She eyed it proudly. "Yup. Boy keeps me in good bourbon too, Wild Turkey," she added, gesturing expansively with the glass. "Brings a whole case sometimes," she tacked on with a dreamy expression.

"What's Matthew's father do for a living?"

"Handyman. Carpentry, windows, roofing, plumbing. I always told him he should get his contractor's license, make us some real money for once," she finished with a grimace.

"Matthew work with him when he was younger?"

"Not that he liked to. But Bob was always dragging him on jobs. I was thinking if they could ever get along, they could start a business. But Matthew wanted to go to college. Did, too. Saved money working with his dad, paid his own way," she added with a proud smile.

"Matthew ever have any pets?"

Her face darkened into a belligerent sidelong glare. "What the hell's *that* got to do with anything?"

"Just curious. I'm a dog person. Any brothers or sisters?"

Mrs. Larsen gazed off toward the kitchen. "Had a sister. Claire."

"Had? Is she deceased?"

"Yeah, she died. 2004." Her voice became husky, her throat taut.

"I'm sorry to ask about her, but I have to. What happened to her?"

"Why the hell you need to know about Claire? She ain't even been alive the last four years." She blinked rapidly, staving off tears.

A hurdle. Pursuing it risked shutting her down, but hurdles were often smokescreens thinly masking a need to bare the soul. "I'm sorry. All I can say is that I wouldn't ask without reason."

"Okay, okay." She took a hefty swig and knocked it back with a grimace. "She committed suicide. Four years ago. She was twenty-four." She bowed her head, shattered by it even now.

"She the one in the pictures?"

"Yeah, that's her. Cute lil' kid, wasn't she?" Mrs. Larsen turned away and hid her head.

Clem kept silent until she turned back. "Yes, she was," he replied. "What happened leading up to her suicide?"

"I don't know exactly. Matthew kept up with her. She ran away at sixteen.

Lived up near Modesto." She extracted a cigarette, but it tore near the filter. She spat out an epithet and lit it, clamping a finger on the torn spot. "Look, there's no nice way to say this. She had problems, Claire did. In Modesto she worked as a hooker. In this peep show. Drug problem too."

"And Matthew looked after her."

"Yeah, saw her every few months. Gave her money, tried to get her jobs, gave her his old pickup. Wanted her to come live with him in SF."

"Did you talk to her?"

"She called two, three times a year. Always high, crying her eyes out."

"You go see her?"

"No, Matthew said she didn't want me to see her that way." She lowered her head. "Guess I avoided it too. Like seeing her'd hurt too much. Was like I left it to Matthew."

"So you hadn't seen her in . . ."

"Like eight years," she moaned, her voice high-pitched and strained with guilt.

"She talk about suicide?"

"Yeah, mentioned it once or twice. Matthew said he'd talked her out of it a few times."

Clem paused. "I'm sorry to have to ask this. Did Claire have any history of physical abuse? Sexual abuse? I'm not making judgments here."

Mrs. Larsen shivered, probably deciding whether to show him the door. She finally heaved a wheezy sigh. "Look, nothing I knew about. But . . . okay, like a year ago, Matthew told me Bob was . . . molesting her since she was thirteen, that's why she ran away."

So maybe the sullen expression in the picture wasn't feigned. "Did you confront him?" Clem asked.

"Yeah, stomped off to the prison, hit him 'tween the eyes with it. He denied it. Matthew, *he* said that's how they always react. I ain't been to see him since. Even they called from the prison, told me he's sick. It's him as killed her, not her herself," she finished, her voice choked off by fury into a low-pitched croak.

"Physical abuse?"

She sighed with relief at the change of subject. "Not as I saw. Way Bob grew up, you didn't hit a girl. Didn't hit me neither. But he'd bash Matthew all the time, especially if he'd start crying, he cried pretty easy. Bob'd call him a girl. Once made him put on one of my dresses and makeup and walk 'round the block. Like a queer, y'know, all mincey? Wetbacks was out there howling, like fifty of 'em. Bob said he needed to make a man out of him."

Clem shuddered. Serial killer Henry Lee Lucas had been forced by his prostitute mother to go to his first day of school in a dress. Publicly gutting a kid's gender identity meant rough seas. "He ever do anything serious? Like break Matthew's arm, something like that?"

Mrs. Larsen looked at Clem in surprise. "Yeah. When he was ten. Matthew's crying about something, Bob twisted his arm. He don't know his own strength, 'specially he's been drinking. Surprised he didn't end up in the slammer 'fore this. But with the bar-fight crowd it's honor among thieves: you don't rat. Bob just picked the wrong guy. Busted his jaw too," she added with a peculiar pride.

"He break Matthew's arm more than once?"

"Hm. Nope. Though years later Matthew busted it same place 'cause he went out for football. Bob pushed him into it. I thought it was stupid, he wasn't no damn ball player. Matthew wasn't never too popular at school, kept to hisself. One of the bully types on the team picked on him. He didn't want him on the team. So he tackled him in practice. Twisted his arm real bad where nobody saw."

"Claire committed suicide in 2004. What was the date?"

Mrs. Larsen closed her eyes and exhaled a draught of smoke. "July 25th. Exactly six months after her birthday."

"I'm sorry to have to ask. How did she commit suicide?"

She closed her eyes tightly, and her head bobbed up and down as she began rocking in the couch. Tears flooded her cheeks. "I can't go there, I just can't," she sobbed. Her voice became a hoarse whisper. "Can't. Can't. Please leave. I'm sorry."

He stood up. "I'll let myself out now, Mrs. Larsen. I'm sorry to trouble you. I mean that. Here's my card." He placed it on the coffee table.

He walked to the door, then turned and spoke gently. "Mrs. Larsen, one last question, nothing dramatic. What was Claire's favorite color?"

Mrs. Larsen opened her eyes, still shining with tears. She mustered a faint smile. "Why, red, Inspector. That girl, she just loved anything red, even she was a baby."

Better to track down Claire's suicide via police channels. Clem could cop to a cold-blooded pleasure in breaking a killer in interrogations, especially the ones whose arrogance was exceeded only by that of their hired guns. But a good detective had to know when it wasn't productive to turn the screws, especially on a witness. No point in leaving things where the old lady would meet him with a twelve-gauge next time he pulled in the driveway.

As he maneuvered around the potholes in front of the house, he flinched as a brand new marble started rolling around in his head: the sound of seemingly isolated events coursing toward a maelstrom. Contrary to the claim of most forensics, there was no hocus-pocus involved in intuition—just subconscious stuff that took a while to surface because the brain wasn't roomy enough to keep it on standby. One time he'd pursued a love triangle motive for a murdered woman without knowing why. Only later he realized it was because the blue-eyed husband and his blue-eyed dead wife had a brown-eyed infant son. A genetic impossibility. He'd snoozed through the lecture in high school biology, but it had somehow camped out in a cerebral cranny for four decades. Thirty years of insomnia had taught him that things revealed themselves when they were good and ready to, and not before.

Angie reached her white Spanish-tiled stucco home in the fashionable Parkside neighborhood. With its spacious Edwardians and tree-lined streets, it was uphill and a world away from the rows of cramped, tiny attached houses that made up the huge Sunset district close to the Pacific. The Sunset—the buckle of the city's Fog Belt—had once been a working-class bedroom community in days long gone when the working class could afford San Francisco bedrooms. Now it was besieged by survivors of the dot-com bubble, renters still longing years later for their stock option ships to come in. But the more prosaic business of realty had been kind to Angie. Fifteen years of building a formidable Rolodex in a city where the lowliest detached home started in the middle six figures would have put her well up the hill even without Roger's hefty income. Even working part-time to allow for her police work, she closed on eight or nine houses a year and made close to six figures.

She felt a wave of drowsiness that grew stronger by the minute. It was a culmination of things: the tension of the blood test, the confrontation with Roderick, not to mention her first week of homicide detecting. She jerked the Florentine bedroom curtains closed and buried herself in the quilts and pillows of her Italian wrought-iron bed.

She'd never been able to sleep soundly during the day and found her eyes opening to the sight of the clock display on the night table. One o'clock. She hauled herself out of bed, brewed a muscular cup of coffee, and checked the mail. A Mother's Day card from Jackie, nine days after the fact. The inscription contained a subtle poison: *Look forward to seeing you in June.* Roger had booked an e-ticket so Jackie could fly down for Mother's Day weekend, but she'd pleaded nebulous school commitments.

Angie would see her when she came down for Father's Day.

She shook off the sting and pulled out her cell. There was a message from Clem asking for Joanne's number. She called him back.

"Hey there, Angie. Headed for scenic Salinas Valley State Prison. Saw Mom, thought I'd chat up Dad while I'm at it. He's a resident."

"Big surprise. Jeez, I've been sleeping as if drugged," she said, battling an insistent yawn. "Don't know how you do it."

"Sleep? I don't. Early this morning, a spider the size of a watermelon tried to mate with my daughter. I smithereened the fucker with my bowling ball. I've been awake ever since."

"Umm . . . she's not by any chance starting to date, is she?"

She heard the tightening of a paternal throat. "Well, it was easier when boys had cooties. But it's not so bad. I just remind the horny bastards that every homicide cop's favorite hobby is concocting the perfect murder." He finally interrupted Angie's stern silence with a halfhearted "Okay, joke, joke."

Not likely. "Anyway, you wanted Joanne's cell?"

"Yeah, seems according to Mama, Matthew had him a sweetie pie."

Angie grimaced. "Name of Joanne."

"The same. Seems he even bought her some pricey earrings. But he clammed up after she dissed him. I'll try to get bodyguards for her and Roderick, but you might as well ask for Mercedes squads in this town. Last time they turned me down, I stashed this witness in my garage. Asshole stole my power tools and lit out for Florida."

"One thing I don't get though. He's had two big-time targets. Why hasn't he done anything?"

Clem considered it. "My Fed says he had to retool after he found out he was dying. Psychopaths thrive on this sense of invincibility; mortality's their number one pet peeve. And they often have this fantasy buildup before they do someone who's a 'primary' target. Like maybe he hates Mommy, he'll do a bunch of women just the way he fantasizes doing her. Only later, he does her too."

"Right, he has to get past this huge intimidation. Like Ed Kemper." A six-foot-five giant with a genius IQ, Kemper had long despised his nagging mother. He took to beheading women and having sex with their remains before getting up the guts to dispatch her in like fashion. He capped it by pitching her larynx down the garbage disposal, only to have it spew back out at him, proving his point that she always had to have the last word.

"So he may be in the buildup stage," Clem continued. "Then, he'd establish some kind of symbolic dominance. That's usually butt ugly."

Angie nodded. "Poison's too good for 'em. And Mama-san? Is he building up to doing her?"

"Probably not, she's the helpless boozehound type. That's reserved for your domineering mommies."

"Thank God I never had a son. I'd be nourishing my begonias by now."

"Dear Old Dad's another matter. Beat him, humiliated him. Perfect mulch for a budding serial killer, but not a target unless Matthew puts out a prison contract. With Mom, he calls, visits, sends money, keeps her in liquor, gave her a new TV. I just don't read he's going to do her."

"Too pathetic to be worth it. What else?"

"Well, looks like Matthew got himself two spiral fractures when he was young. It probably 'spoke' to him when he saw Cynthia's chart. And when I asked if he had any pets, mama lost her water. I'm betting animal torture. We had one expert give a lecture: Someone asked him whether any psychopathic killers had a history of childhood animal abuse. He said the better question was, whether any didn't."

She started; it felt as if she was missing some amorphous connection with some earlier evidence. "Hmm. The animal torture yanketh my chain. Get back to me."

"Anyway, biggest thing is, Matthew had a sister, Claire, four years younger, killed herself in 2004. She was molested by Daddy, least that's what Matthew told Mom. Ran away at sixteen. Matthew looked after her. Lived around Modesto. I saw a pic from when she was seven or eight. Long blond hair, reminded me of Cynthia enough to give me butterflies."

Angie felt woozy. "Umm . . . Joanne. Ditto long blond hair, down her back like a teenager."

"Huh. Matthew told Mama that Joanne's favorite color's red, not something he'd be in a position to know. I asked her later what *Claire's* favorite color was, one guess. Wouldn't surprise me if Joanne looked like Claire did as an adult. On her better days anyway. She was a hooker, lots of drugs."

"So the tank was some monument to Claire?" Angie speculated. "Taking her back to a time before she was a sexually abused, drugged-out hooker?"

"Could be. But Matthew built the tomb a month or so before Claire committed suicide in July 2004. Wouldn't surprise me if he built it *afterwards*, as a reaction. But before?"

Angie pondered. "Maybe she was going downhill. Like he knew she was a goner."

"Also, Mama freaked when I asked how it happened. Probably not your everyday Gillette job. I'll check it out tonight."

"Funny. Roderick said Matthew took off some sick days in 2004, like July or August, came back like the walking dead." The line went silent. "Clem? Still there?"

"Sorry. Something my Fed buddy once told me. Psychopaths never have 'real' relationships. They often have a whole set of synthetic emotions that *look* normal. Guy'll plaster his cubicle with pics of his kids, but would he run into a burning building to save them? No, he'd trip and sprain his ankle. Like Matthew with his mom. Plays the good son, but like he doesn't help her with her booze problem; he buys her bourbon by the barrel. He's in complete control."

"And it lets him put the screws to Daddy," added Angie. "Finds out he molested Claire, tattles to Mom."

"Right. Wouldn't surprise me if it was similar with sis. Like Mama mentioned he looked after Claire. But he also convinced Mom not to visit her. The best way to manipulate people is keep them from talking to each other. I do it every day in interrogations. A psychopath's constructs crash and burn when the people who know him start comparing notes."

"So maybe when Claire committed suicide, he lost a relationship where he pulled the strings. And later, he runs into Joanne. Wants to set up the same deal, but she sends him packing."

"And gets herself on the mother of all shit lists."

The drive north was a bonus to his mission. The Golden Gate had been wreathed in fluffy clouds. And now, the rounded hills of the Sonoma wine country were working their way from winter green to summer golden brown. The dry grass was drab up close. But at a distance, the hills looked amazingly like enormous mounds of baked bread.

He'd worried that the Subaru would self-destruct on the road trip, but it was holding its own. The suspension was almost gone; if he hit a bump at thirty, the car would start shaking like an overloaded washer on spin until he pulled over. But highway speeds didn't faze it.

He'd even taken Vlad along, The bird riveted his gaze on the hills, proba-bly in rapture at the gazillions of critters awaiting impalement on those grassy slopes. A month from now, he'd come back and release him. Not many cacti, but Vlad could do perfectly well with a good stretch of barbed wire. He de-served better than a dollop of birdseed in the pound.

And to think they said psychos were heartless. Just another bad rap.

At the northern edge of the hill country, he pulled over to stretch himself at a rest area nestled in a grove of ancient oaks. He ambled a quarter mile around the grove, then gasped as he stood at the foot of one of the largest trees.

The Maharajah tree. He was looking at its twin.

He circled it twice. No mistake, for he'd studied that tree in Gilroy for hours. It was as if some bird had carried a doppelganger acorn two hundred miles north and dropped it.

He smiled as his thoughts flew back three months, to Sneezy's night in the tree.

For more than ten years, since the night when he'd stopped at the bar to use the toilet and recognized that almost-forgotten face, he'd known Sneezy's day would dawn. And it had been that night a decade ago that had set him on his chosen path: to become the world's grandmaster of the ways of anguish.

And grandmaster he was, forty-two handwritten leather notebooks proof of his erudition, a compendium so fearsome that a century hence it would be mentioned in whispers. He could see them in his mind, each page vacuum-sheathed in a zero-humidity vault, perhaps in the bowels of FBI headquarters, or in the hands of an appreciative collector.

The da Vincis of Death. He'd even tried the writing backwards thing, but it had gotten too tedious.

The bone grinders of KGB founder Beria's dungeons. The death furnaces of the East German Stasi, reserved for those guilty of treason. Excerpts from the diaries of Chinese torturer Lao Guo, force-fed his own flesh by a princess whose lover he'd dispatched the same way. The horrific ramblings of London's executioner Jason Hardy, hacked into offal by a mob after an execution so sickening that even the bloodthirsty crowd had cried out for mercy. Toxins rendered from algal scum, Afghan mushrooms, and tiny Indonesian crabs that could liquefy muscle into goo, turn a spinal cord into strands of linguini, or explode a liver like a blood squib. Tiny fish from Borneo that swam up the urethra and shot spines into flesh, drowning victims in their urine. Ants of the Brazilian Pantanal whose bites swelled a hand to the size of a catcher's mitt. Sap from Malaysian tree vines that turned the eyes into pits of gore if one chanced to look up in the rain. More than two thousand pages.

But for the crème de la crème, he thanked Dominican Brother Heinrich Kramer. Assigned the task of ferreting out members of the infamous Society of Witches by Pope Innocent VIII in the 1400s, he'd penned a handy Witchfinding for Dummies. Published in thirty editions over two centuries, it spent ten thousand weeks on the medieval version of the New York Times Best Seller List.

Malleus Maleficarum. The Witch Hammer.

Bite on that, Danielle Steele.

Not that Malleus dealt in the oh-so-gory details. Indeed:

> Now a surgeon cuts off rotten limbs, and mangy sheep are isolated from the healthy; but a prudent judge will not deem it safe to bind himself to one fixed rule in dealing with a prisoner whose silence he is unable to overcome.

No, the passage for which he was beholden to Kramer was this one:

> And while she is being questioned on each point, let her be
> frequently subjected to torture . . . and while this is done,
> let the Notary write down how she is tortured, what ques-
> tions are asked and how she answers.

*He grinned at the irony. Nowadays, your everyday hardworking torturer—
and he'd been privileged to meet a few—got twenty to life. In days of yore, you
got an office staff.*

*And most of the records had been burned by Church officials who didn't
want such stuff on the shelves. But hundreds still moldered in libraries and
archives throughout Europe. Over the course of three trips to France and
Germany, he'd managed to dredge up more than a dozen zingers.*

*Including the Big Kahuna that would climax Honeypie's ferocious
Malleus messy. He hadn't even known what he'd happened onto at first; his
Latin was limited to handy keywords like "red-hot iron." He went through four
translators before finding one financially desperate enough to complete it.*

*Of course the whole deal hadn't started out that way. For years just a day-
dream here, a night at the library there, schmoozing over the most grisly fate he
could vent on Sneezy. But the momentum had built like a planet accreting on
the flotsam of space. In the end he'd shelled out thousands, even vacationed in
armpits like Azerbaijan and Paraguay to amass the most vile of the vile.*

*At first he'd thought it mental masturbation, even half-heartedly tried to
put a halt to it two years back. But Sneezy's dilapidated green van was always
there at the 602, a beacon keeping him to his path. To cull and catalog, and
finally to select the messy from the hundreds he'd unearthed.*

*The Maharajah messy. He'd awaited only the revelation three months ago to
know it was time. Time to become, not passive savant, but master practitioner.*

*And finally, the wondrous night at the tree. His excitement had grown as
the weather report detailed the coming storm. He'd trembled as he screwed the
pulleys in the branches and threaded the ropes to the tubs. Then he'd driven to
the bar, dead certain that Sneezy would pick this one night to be absent. But
he'd exulted as he pulled into the parking lot and saw the van.*

*The Burundanga worked wonders. After standing Sneezy beers, he waited
in the parking lot until Sneezy came out weaving like a punch-drunk boxer.*

Did he want to try some outrageous Colombian? Of course. Sneezy would've said yes if he'd asked him if he wanted to eat marbles. In the grove, a couple of prodigious hits and Sneezy collapsed down in the grass and nodded off. He was oblivious as the rope circled his waist and the belt hitched tight under his shoulders. He didn't come to until the tubs winched him into the tree and the razor wire started drawing blood from his wrists.

He sat down in front of Sneezy and told him everything that would happen to him. And then he told him why.

Remember the piss, Sneezy? Remember the piss?

He remembered the piss. Oh yes, he remembered the piss.

Clem processed into Salinas Valley State, known to residents as Soledad. His flesh crawled as he worked past the forbidding guard towers and checkpoints, and not just because he'd pulled some stunts that in theory could land him a stint there. Soledad was California's most violent and haphazardly run prison, at one point infamous for chewing through seven wardens in three years. Lockdowns were the norm rather than the exception. Its water wells were poisoned by its own septic tanks and the runoff of pesticides from the agricultural juggernaut of Salinas Valley. Charles Manson had been its most distinguished tenant. Even the cons had objected to his presence and had tried more than once to burn him alive. He'd supposedly kept guards attentive by giving them signed photos, which still had cachet on the autograph market and kept them in beer money.

Clem was ushered past a room packed with roughshod women waiting to see sons, husbands, and boyfriends. The chunky blond guard checked him in over the din of a squabble between visitors and a guard over the perennially empty tampon dispenser in the bathroom.

"Y'know, Bob's a weird case," said the guard. "His old lady used to visit once a week, but she ain't been here in forever. He's sick, so even we called her, she still don't show."

The guard led him past the steel-meshed front desk cage to a VIP visiting room. He stopped on his way out and lowered his voice. "I'll tell you up front. Bob, he's taken a beating lately."

Clem cocked an eyebrow.

"When he got here, he didn't pay heed to the sacred Soledad pecking order. Three months back he dissed a Mex. Turns out the guy's in line for Nuestra."

Nuestra Familia, the Mexican gang that controlled the trade in drugs and other contraband in Soledad. Members wore red rags, as bandannas or sticking out of a pocket; you learned that the day you got your prison blues. The wannabe didn't have his rag yet, Larsen had been caught unawares.

The guard continued. "Now Bob's sick, payback's a red-eyed bitch. Never gave us any shit, so we try and keep him in isolation." Most prisons had a block for "at-risk" cons: convicted cops, pedophiles, child killers, suspected snitches, those who ran afoul of the gangs. They lived in dread of a prison riot, when they would be slaughtered to a man as in the infamous New Mexico State Prison riot almost thirty years before. Blowtorches were the traditional implements of choice.

Clem nodded. "But in Soledad, you want something, there's fifty ways to get it. I'm surprised he's still alive." Nuestra was "blood in, blood out." You killed to get in, you died to get out. The wannabe probably needed a corpse to be awarded the coveted color.

The guard shrugged. "Depends on your definition of 'alive.'"

Clem sat down on a gray steel chair that matched the table, the walls, the ceiling, and the riveted floor. Through a wire mesh window, he saw the blue denim of an inmate down the corridor, accompanied by a green-clad guard. The prisoner was walking with a shuffle, as though he were in chains. But he came through the door with not an anklet to be seen.

Clem looked at him in astonishment. His right leg wasn't working, and he dragged it behind him as if he'd had a stroke. Ditto his left arm, which hung limply at his side, devoid of movement except for the fingers, which clenched and unclenched with their own rhythm.

Clem gazed at his face. He could recognize the balding, sixtyish Robert Larsen—all three hundred pounds of him—but only barely. His flabby jowls were swollen with bruises. His rheumy left eye was almost closed, the eyelid barely fluttering each time he blinked. On the other hand, his blackened right eye blinked too rapidly, as if he had a piece of grit in it. His lower lip jutted forward and rolled side to side like a cow grinding grass, spilling rivulets from the corners of his mouth and twisting it into a permanent scowl. Two of his front teeth were missing, the ragged lividity of the gums suggesting they'd just been knocked out. He reeked of urine and body odor.

The guard helped him into his chair. "I'll be outside. Bob, you behave yourself, hear?"

Larsen looked at Clem curiously with his one functioning eye. "Whassis about?" It was a fight for him to speak. His enunciation mimicked the patterns of the deaf, the letters T and D in especially short supply.

"I'm here about your son. San Francisco Homicide."

His working eye spasmed into a rapid-fire blink. "Huh? He get hisself killed?"

"We're looking at him as a suspect. Just routine. I saw your wife, figured I'd talk to you too."

"She . . . she coming to see me?" he asked hopefully, like a child.

"I have no idea. I understand she thinks you molested your deceased daughter, Claire."

His jaw trembled violently. "N-No. No. I didn't. Never," he replied, vehemence building in his voice. He sucked in a breath with the hollow sound of someone wearing scuba gear. "Okay, I ain't never been the greatest husband. I admit, I mess around with a few good-time girls. But I never touch her, not Claire. Matthew, he was lying. He get back at me for all the shit I give him before, what it was. But he said he would tell April the ta-ruth. And I keep calling her and she hang up. So I guess he lied again. Again." He hung his mammoth head in misery.

"When did this happen?"

Larsen didn't look up. "'Bout three months ago."

"You talk to him on the phone?"

Larsen gazed at Clem, his operative eye showing surprise. "No, he come visit. I shock to see him. And not too happy. I always thought he lie to April. Almost took a swing at him. But I didn't want to lose visitation, case April come see me. I hope she will. I think I'm 'iying. D-dying." He hung his head again. Spittle cascaded from a corner of his mouth from the effort of pronouncing the ominous word. He wiped his jowls clumsily with his sleeve.

"Why did he agree to tell April the truth?"

"Bygones, bygones. He said."

"When did you start getting sick?"

"Four, five week ago. Got bad real quick."

"Been to the prison doc?"

"Yeah, five time. Even somebody from outside come see me. Can't figure it out, never seen nothing like it. I think I'm dying."

"It's possible you *are* dying, sir. So I'm going to ask you again. I'll never discuss this with April. You didn't sexually abuse Claire? You swear?"

"God's my witness. I'm finish soon enough, I know. Never touch her. Even never hit her. I admit, I beat holy shit out of Matthew bunch of times. But not Claire." He buried his head in his functional hand. It spasmed, squeezing his swollen cheeks.

Clem thought Larsen was being straight with him. He decided to change the subject. "So you're having a tough time in here I gather."

Larsen clumsily pointed to his face. "Maybe once a week. That part I used to. I fuck up, I admit. But ain't that as bother me." Larsen's eyes glazed over.

"So what does?"

"When they get bored. They say I Dead Man Spazzing," he finished, his mouth contorted into a sick grin. But then his face screwed up with fear. "Something special they say. From Nuestra."

Clem shuddered. "Special" in a prison wasn't good. "That all they said?"

Larsen shrugged, but his working eye filled with foreboding. "I ask around, see if anything going on. Nothing. Well, one buddy work in motor pool, mechanic. Say Mexes put word out they need a tire, next few days. Big one like eighteen-wheeler. They got a water truck with tire that big. So guy ask 'em where they want it, can't just roll it down the cell blocks. Don't worry, they say, don't need to move it, Mexes want it right there."

Clem felt the blood drain from his face.

A giant tire.

Big enough for Larsen's enormous girth.

The motor pool. Gasoline.

The grisly retribution reserved for informants (and more often nowadays, those accused of witchcraft) in the townships of apartheid South Africa. The tire was jammed over the torso, doused with gasoline, and set ablaze.

Molten rubber cooked the victim's lower body while the flames roared above. Usually his hands were chopped off so he couldn't free himself.

The necklace.

Clem kept a poker face. "Okay, Mr. Larsen, that'll be enough. Sorry to trouble you." He signaled the guard to take Larsen away.

"Tell April. Please. I *never* done that, *never*. Dying, tell her, please," he cried softly, twisting his immense head back towards Clem as he limped away on the arm of the guard.

Clem's stomach churned as he went to the security desk. "You tape visits?"

The guard eyed him curiously. "Sure, SOP. Keep 'em a year."

"Larsen. His son visited him three months ago. Can I see the tape?"

"Put in a request if you want it for evidence. Warden ain't back 'til tomorrow. But you just want a look, well, one hand washes the other. I get murdered in SF, I'll call you."

The guard spent a minute on the computer and found Matthew's visit. February 5th. He brought the tape out from the library and spun forward. "Roll 'em. No audio, just visuals."

Clem started the video. The view was from a ceiling camera diagonally above. Matthew sauntered in, clad in a light jacket and leather gloves. The experience was jarring, his first real glimpse of his elusive quarry. A guard brought in his father, this time in the prime of health.

Their body language was a study in opposites. Matthew removed his gloves and leaned back, one leg casually crossed over the other, while his father sat across the table looking spring-loaded. Suddenly his face contorted and he rose half out of his chair, as if he were going to sail across the table and lay into his son. But he glanced around and sat back down. Larsen gaped as Matthew continued to talk. Then he spoke, shaking his meaty palms held upward as if begging. Matthew pondered, theatrically resting his chin in his hand, then spoke again.

Matthew stood up, drew on his gloves and turned to leave. Then he turned back to his father and held out his right hand. Larsen stared suspiciously at it, and then leaned and shook it. The room guard sprang forward to prevent the contact, not permitted even in VIP rooms. Matthew did a "reach for the sky" in apology, and the guard waved him out in annoyance. Larsen glanced down and rubbed his thumb over the fingers of his right hand, as if he'd gotten something sticky on them.

Clem rewound the handshake. The deadliest of weapons had snuck through the metal detector on the fingers of Matthew's glove. Yet he was still in good shape—well enough to be driving a week ago—while his father was a month from a fatal coma. He'd dealt his father an enormous dose, maybe with an ampule and a membrane in the lining to protect himself. And condemned him to a terrible death, leaving him defenseless among men whose brutality was their measure.

And the *coup de grace* the necklace, so fearsome that Haitian mobs had taken it for their own. Coroners often made themselves scarce when the call went out.

Clem turned to the guard, who was immersed in a newspaper. "Prison doc in?"

The guard gave him a quizzical look. "Why, you sick?"

Clem stifled a smirk. He would perform a triple bypass on himself before seeing a prison doc with a malady. The prisons were havens for physicians cashiered elsewhere for malpractice. "I just need to talk to him." The guard shrugged and paged him.

A saggy, balding man in coffee-stained green scrubs soon entered. He took Clem's hand with the hesitation of someone unhappy to be at close quarters with a cop. His eyes bounced off Clem and darted around the room like a ferret's, as if he were expecting manacles with a side of Mirandas. Maybe some loosey-goosey prescriptions back there somewhere.

"Inspector, Dr. Ron Langley. What can I do for you?"

"You need to test Robert Larsen for mercury poisoning. There's enough inside him to kill a herd of hippos."

Langley's sallow face morphed from relief to amused skepticism. "I don't mean to contradict you, Inspector. And I admit my specialty is shank wounds. But mercury poisoning? Nothing here he could get it from."

"His son poisoned him with something called dimethyl mercury. In the visiting room, three months ago. I saw the tape."

The guard looked up from his paper, startled. Probably because Matthew shouldn't have been allowed in the VIP room. It was reserved for inmates to meet with attorneys and the cops. But for fifty bucks a guard might look the other way.

The doctor whistled. "The symptoms *could* arise from heavy metal poisoning. But we didn't look at that." He scratched his chin. "Funny. His son called two weeks ago. Heard his father was sick. I started describing the symptoms, he begged off. Never heard back."

So Matthew had called to make sure the poison foray had worked. Clem turned to the guard. "You get calling-party numbers on incomings, right?"

"Yup, we block cell phones, and if the caller ID's disabled. And record incoming numbers."

"Can you figure out when that call came in? Then we can get the number he called from."

Clem didn't discuss the necklace with the man. The guards had their own gangs, operating under a regimen of tight-lipped *omertá* that would do a wiseguy proud. The Soledad guard gang was called the Green Wall, founded after the assault on the guards. They might be in on Matthew's plans. He wrote out a report, sealed it in an envelope, and gave it to the guard to pass to the warden.

Then he set out for the city. He dialed Billy, got voice mail, and told him to book his ticket.

Larsen hadn't molested his daughter. He was your basic lout and would respond with defensive bluster, not feigned sincerity. And it would be difficult to maintain a false front in the face of his impending death. But most prostitutes were molested as kids. If Claire hadn't been abused, why had she run away to sell herself in the flesh pits of Modesto?

And the necklace wasn't according to Hoyle. Cons and their jailers maintained an uneasy (and often profitable) coexistence. Murders were done low profile so as not to encourage outside scrutiny. But a guy burned alive Soweto-style could mean major grief, maybe even another warden. The two rival Mexican gangs—La Eme and Nuestra—held sway in the prisons all the way to east Texas. They weren't likely to shit in the kitchen without reason. And Nuestra wouldn't help a wannabe on his kill. For some reason they'd reserved Larsen for their own devices. Not only that, an execution that elaborate would require at least one of the guys in green to go grab a smoke at just the wrong moment.

Probably a thousand dollar smoke. There was major *dinero* chasing this deal.

Matthew had a contract out on his own father. And Nuestra hadn't come up with the necklace.

Matthew had.

Angie puttered around the house, trying to zero in on what it was she was supposed to do but hadn't. She finally remembered she'd intended to call Janine and glanced at the clock. Just after two. Bernadette was filing nails until six. She dialed the house and felt a burst of relief at Janine's hello.

"Janine, how are you?"

"Me? Why, I'm just fine," she answered levelly, as if she couldn't lock on to who Angie was.

"I was calling to see if you remembered anything about your renter."

"Why, Angie! Yes, yes, glad you called. Actually, I was going to call you, but . . . oh, to be honest, I forgot. You know how I am these days."

"That's okay. Did you come up with anything?"

"Well, Angie, you're not going to believe this, but I just now saw him! Half an hour ago! Now, isn't that just the strangest coincidence?"

Angie wondered if Janine was experiencing dementia. "You just saw him?"

"Why, yes! He came to visit me. Oh . . . wait . . . and what you said you found at the house? I'm sure you told me, but I can't remember what it was. Anyway, he said don't worry, you can keep it, he'd get another one. Now, wasn't that nice?"

Angie felt the beginnings of dread. "Umm . . . Janine. You're saying that your renter from four years ago came to visit you. For certain."

"I know, dear, you think I'm seeing things. But it's true! Said he was in the neighborhood, wanted to drop off something of mine he accidentally took years ago when he packed up."

"Janine. You're serious, right? Your renter—his name is Matthew Larsen —gave you something? What was it?"

"Matthew. Yes, *that's* it. From the Bible. Well, it sure isn't anything I remember. One of those snowflake thingies, you turn it upside down and it snows inside? It's from Tijuana, one of those gag souvenirs. I mean, it hasn't snowed in Tijuana in a hundred years, right? Of course, we were in Tijuana before, when we went to San Diego. But I don't remember we got one of those. I mean, well, maybe we did."

Angie gripped the phone so tightly that her fingers cramped. "Janine. Did you touch it?"

"Well, yes, dear," responded Janine, with a tinge of irritation. "Of *course* I touched it. Turned it upside down. To make it snow."

Angie's heart rate doubled. "Janine, I'm driving there now. I feel horrible I didn't tell you before. But I never figured he'd come after you. Janine, Matthew is very, very dangerous. Did you tell him anything about Bernadette?"

Janine gasped. "Well, yes, he asked about her. I said she worked in town. At the beauty parlor."

"Janine, call Bernadette. Tell her to come home now and to look out for anyone who looks like Matthew." She heard Janine mumble a confused assent.

She cursed herself for not telling Janine about Matthew. She thought she'd been so goddamn smart, even after Clem had said to tell her about the dead girl, and here the old lady was, almost certainly poisoned. She tore down to the garage and fired up her Honda for the three-hour trip. A week in Homicide, just one lousy week, and she'd gotten someone killed. She banged her fists on the wheel as the garage door opened and screeched her tires reversing into the afternoon sun.

Bernadette was spread-eagled in the chair at her manicure table, half dozing, when the bell at the top of the door jingled. She looked up groggily, saw the blond, white-coated man in the wire-rims standing at the counter, and shook herself awake. Probably asking for directions. She hadn't had but two manicures all day. And four bucks in tips.

"What can I do for you? Manicure?" she asked jokingly. Booneville men didn't go in for manicures too often. Or even haircuts.

He smiled broadly. "Yes, ma'am. Just what I had in mind in fact."

Bernadette hauled herself to her feet and gestured at the chair in front of her table. "Well, you've come to the right place! This here's the only manicure for fifty miles!"

She prepared the bowl, plunged in his left hand and started working on his cuticles. He piped up. "I'm not from here. But God, I love San Francisco. Great restaurants."

"*That's* for sure. I love to go to the Wharf and eat seafood. Especially Dungeness crabs! Mmmmmm!" she exclaimed, licking her lips.

His eyes lit up. "Oh? I'll have to try them."

"Get some for me too! I could eat 'em 'til I'm sick! So, what brings you up these parts? You a doctor? What with the coat and all."

"Yup, Jim Vance. Radiologist. Moving to San Francisco from Ohio. I was visiting a clinic in Santa Rosa, thought I'd take a drive north."

"Bernadette Kelso. Soooo, moving to Baghdad by the Bay, huh? Great city." She paused pregnantly. "Got a place yet?"

"I've just started looking. No agent, just went to some open houses on Sunday. Boy, things are expensive."

Bernadette's heart thudded like a tympani. "Well now, they sure are, aren't they? Happens *I'm* selling a place down there. My mom used to live there, house I grew up in. But she wanted to move up here after my dad died a few months back. So. What exactly you looking for?"

"Oh, with prices these days, thought I'd get a place that needs work so I could get it cheap. I'm something of an amateur contractor."

"Hmm. Well, tell the truth, my place might could use someone like you. And I might be willing to work out a good . . . deal." She quelled the frog hopping in her throat and gave him her best you-me-and-the-lamppost look. "Y'know, selling the damn place's been a pain in the neck. My husband and I, well, we have loads of money. Stock market. I'm kind of a wiz, if I do say so myself." She threw him a huge stage wink. "I just work here so's I have something to do. By now, I just want the place off my hands. Damn nuisance."

"Oh? I'd think it'd be a cinch to sell."

She shook her head in disgust. "Silly me, I signed up this agent didn't know her ass from a hole in the wall. Friend of my mom's. I wanted it done and over with, but she overpriced. And of course, what did I know? So it just sat there. I finally fired her and took it off the market. I'll go at it again, but I won't hire another goddamn agent, that's for sure."

The phone rang. The stylist picked up, waved at Bernadette, and mouthed "Mother!" Bernadette waved her off.

She turned back to the table, scrutinizing him like a cobra. He was giddy as he continued. "Well, maybe we can work out a deal, right? Get an attorney to work the papers and clear the title. If the price is right, I can pay cash. We could wrap it up in a week."

Bernadette's heartbeat had her wondering what arrhythmia felt like. "Hmm. Well, place'd get six on the market. But I could go, say, five fifty, even five if you can do a cash deal in a week. It's a three bedroom. Edwardian," she added, hoping he wouldn't ask what that meant. "In Forest Hill Extension, one of the best areas."

The stylist waved insistently and mouthed, "Important!" Bernadette pointed in irritation at the table and mouthed "Customer!" The stylist shrugged, got back on the phone, and then hung up.

Bernadette looked back at him. He was positively gushing. "Wow! That sounds just outstanding! I really need to get a look at it. Any chance we could get together Friday morning? Day after tomorrow? I have to fly back to Cleveland in the afternoon."

She thanked her lucky stars that the little girl's picture had just been released to the news; she'd caught it at noon, and not one shot of the house, only her picture. And the cops were probably finished with the crime scene. But if she needed to, she'd yank that goddamn yellow tape off yard by yard before he got there. "I can do that. Say nine?"

"That works. Look, why don't you give me your cell? But you can be darn sure I'm going to be there! Gosh, I can hardly wait to see it!"

As he left, Bernadette's parting smile morphed into a leer, her lips peeled back from her teeth like a rat in rigor. What a rube. She'd need an attorney on the quick. It was a slow afternoon, a good time to hunt one down. She could draw up the papers by Friday with fill-in-the-blanks. Once that mountain of money poured into her account, she'd be gone. By the time he found out what he'd bought into, there'd be nothing left of her but a cloud of smoke, like Road Runner pulling the vanishing act on Wile E. Coyote.

Maybe the right time to leave it all behind. Mother, husband, her rickety piece-of-shit house, everything. With that kind of cash, you could live a long time up north, or in Arizona, or western Virginia, or who knew *where* all.

God, the bozo had even given her an absurdly big tip. It was all almost too good to be true.

As Angie rocketed through Marin County to the northlands, she screwed up her courage and dialed. "Clem, I think he's just killed Janine. Maybe Bernadette too."

"Good God. What happened?"

Angie related her conversation with Janine. "And it's my fault. I didn't tell her about the girl, that Matthew was dangerous. God, I'm so sorry."

After a moment, Clem spoke. "Well, it's true I said to tell her about Cynthia. But as to it being your fault, look, if he was going to get them, he was going to, unless they moved to freaking Siberia. Fact is, it could've gone a lot worse if she'd tried to call the cops. I'm sure he's got a nasty Plan B."

"Well, thanks for trying to make me feel better, but I don't. They didn't have the option of protecting themselves. All because I was a smartass know-it-all."

He sighed. "Look, Angie, one thing you learn quick is you can't protect everyone. I've had three witnesses wake up dead after I talked to them. One was a twenty-year-old girl. Look at Joanne. We both know she's A-list, but chances are I can't get her diddly. In this town, you need something really out there, a suspect who threatens a witness. There's a chance she'll be stone dead a month from now. And best you can do is attend the funeral, feel shitty about it, then move on."

"I feel shitty about it. Damn shitty."

"Well, you just found out this stuff doesn't work like Miss Marple. Now get it together. I want gnashing of teeth, I'll ask. What else got said?"

Angie's face burned. She was furious at Clem for his callousness but took a deep breath. "Okay, I told Janine we were looking for him because we'd found something of his at the house."

Clem chuckled grimly. "Massive understatement. And?"

"He told her we could keep it; he'd get another one. Meaning he's hunting another girl?"

"More likely a little psychopathic humor. Best he could probably do is kidnap and kill a random girl. I don't think he's done that. Chances are nil we'd have *another* missing with no report. And I just don't think he's the random sort. Did you call the locals?"

Angie gritted her teeth. "Half an hour ago. The desk sergeant asked me if I'd been drinking."

"I would too. Their stock-in-trade's Wine Country DWIs. I'll give it a whirl, but I doubt I can get more than a unit to stop by the house."

"So why target Janine, maybe Bernadette?"

Clem paused. "Maybe letting me know he can reach in there on us any time he pleases. Psychopaths can be funny about cops. They're often fascinated by them. Sometimes they want to compete with us, show everybody they're smarter than we are. Other times they feel this sense of collegiality, like we're each other's alter egos. Sometimes they show up at cop bars trying to strike up a conversation."

"Okay, but how did he track down Bernadette's house?"

"Well, he could probably get her address off the Internet. And remember, he rifled Janine's desk. All he needed was a birthday card."

Angie's thoughts flew back to her lunch with her Realtor friend, Beth, and her foot goosed the car another ten miles over the limit. "Clem. God, I think I've actually talked to him."

"Huh?"

"Someone called me two weeks ago about the listing. He wanted the name of an agent. I gave him my friend's name, but he never called. He knew a lot about the place. Said he'd seen it at an open house." Her heart thumped in her ears. "And asked if we'd managed to break into the garage yet. I thought he was just being snide."

"So he wanted to find out why the house wasn't selling."

Suddenly her heart sank. "Umm . . . Clem, he asked me why the price was so high. I . . . may have gently alluded to greed on someone's part."

"Someone named Bernadette. Not up there with his motives for Roderick and Joanne, but psychopaths can be cantankerous little buggers. Anyway, go see what's what. Leave the snow globe up there, you're not a Forensic. I'll have the provincials pick it up later."

"Okay. So what did you find out about Daddy Larsen?"

"Matthew poisoned him a few months back. Right in the visiting room. He's dying. And it's not pretty."

The thought of Janine going the same way stung Angie with a new bout of guilt. "And I think Matthew put out a contract on him. A way hairy one," Clem continued. "Probably a few days from now."

"We're talking serious closure."

"Also, I don't think he abused his daughter. Matthew made it up to get back at him."

"No surprise. But *something* wrecked her train before she was old enough to drive."

Two hours later, Angie pulled up in front of Bernadette's house and was confused not to see the hideous blue Olds. She strode up the steps and banged noisily.

Janine came to the door and gave her a stern look. "Now you tell me what's this all about."

"Janine, where's Bernadette? She was supposed to come home."

Janine shrugged. "I called, got one of the other girls. I said it was important, but she was with a customer. Then I called later and she was out."

Angie walked over to the couch and sat down. Janine sat next to her. "There's something I need to tell you," she said tremulously. "Matthew may have poisoned you. In fact, I'm sure of it." She eyed the snow globe on the coffee table. Any other time she would've grinned at the radioactive kitsch: a skyline of neon-lit cantinas with a mariachi band sporting yard-wide sombreros on the blue background. But now, all she could do was curse Matthew's grisly sense of humor.

"How could he have poisoned me? I'd think I'd know about it, wouldn't I?"

Angie reached for it, then started at her oversight. She walked around the table and inspected the back of the globe. "It's introduced through the skin and takes a long time to kill."

But now she felt bewilderment as she brought her face inches from the globe. No telltale smudge. The stuff was thick and oily, four times heavier than water because of the mercury content, and could only be removed with a solvent.

She shook off her confusion, sat back down, and related Matthew's theft of the poison, staring at the floor, unable to look Janine in the eye. "I don't see anything. Maybe there wasn't any poison. But I feel so guilty. I knew Matthew was dangerous. But I didn't tell you because I was worried you'd go into shock and not be able to help me. I'm so sorry." She narrated the discovery of Cynthia's tomb and the hunt for Matthew, flushed with embarrassment.

Janine stared at the wall in silence for a moment. She finally turned and patted Angie's back with a painful smile. "Look, Angie. Being eighty-one isn't like being forty. Especially when you've buried your husband of sixty years. You hope for some great sunsets, that you don't fall down and break your hip in a thousand pieces, and that you have a nice, peaceful death at some point or other. I mean, *look* at me. I'm a city girl living a left turn from nowhere with a daughter counting the days 'til I breathe my last."

Angie gasped. Janine gave her a thin-lipped smile. "Angie, Emil wasn't in the ground a day before Bernadette started on the power-of-attorney thing. But I couldn't take care of the house anymore. I had no choice.

"So you think I'd be wringing my hands if I was going to die a year from now? I almost wish you'd been right. From what you've said, there are lots worse ways for an old lady to die. Seeing Emil spend three years clutching an oxygen mask taught me that," she said with a shiver. "And one of those ways would be to cower in my room while Matthew broke in and cut me to pieces."

Angie rallied with a weak smile. "Okay. So, Bernadette was tied up? She's probably all right then. Matthew may be after her. I think that's why he came here and talked to you. He wanted to find out where she worked."

"The second time I called, she'd gone out, said she'd be out the rest of the day. Something about finding an attorney."

Angie grimaced. Probably to see if she could sue for the dead listing. Ridiculous, but no telling how low a country lawyer might stoop to get a breather from easement spats. "Okay, I'll call her on her cell. I'd send the police after her, but they think I've hit too many wineries. So what did he look like?"

"I didn't recognize him until he told me who he was, but he was wearing a beard. Short, like he'd just started growing it. And no glasses, like when I saw him four years ago. A green windbreaker. Black jeans."

Angie thought back to his hospital photo. "The beard would disguise his craggy cheekbones. Did he have a car?"

"I doubt he walked. He parked up the road, so I couldn't see it when I came to the door. But I did catch a glint of orange through the trees, so maybe that was his car."

"Hmm. Meaning he got rid of his blue Toyota."

"I suppose. Anyway, dear, it's you I feel sorry for. Finding that girl under my lawn must've been horrible. And to think all I'd thought I'd saddled you with was my loving daughter. So were you there when they dug up the tank?"

"Yup. But after the initial shock, it was kind of fascinating, all the forensics and everything." Angie didn't care to discuss the grotesque images still haunting her, and changed the subject. "By the way, when they were digging, they found Speckle."

Janine stared at her vacantly. "Speckle?"

"Your cat. Buried in the yard. Had a collar on it. With the name Speckle."

"Well, dear, it certainly couldn't be *our* cat. Emil was allergic."

Angie started. Matthew must have buried it. The cat had been interred in the lawn above the tunnel. That's why the cops had run into it. He'd buried the cat after he'd built the tunnel, probably because the ground was already turned. She thought of the collar again. The tag had a phone number on it. Could be nothing: maybe the cat had just meowed its last in the backyard, and Matthew had taken care of it, the same as anyone else.

But the discovery troubled her. Maybe that was why something rang her bell when Clem had mentioned the animal torture. She slowly brought the scene back into recall and went over the odd arrangement of the cat's remains, something she hadn't considered while thinking of popping the "Alas, poor Morris" joke on the two cops.

When they'd been digging carefully downward, they'd first run into the cat's spine. Speckle had been buried squatting on his haunches, not lying on his side or curled up, as anyone else would bury a dead cat.

She wasn't sure, of course, but she couldn't escape the conclusion that Speckle had been buried alive.

• • •

Clem pulled into the Hall parking lot at five. He got on his computer and found Claire quickly in the registry of deaths. July 25th, 2004. Committed suicide on the edge of a small town at the south end of the Central Valley, Auburn, an hour and something south of Modesto. He remembered the case. It had been horrific enough to make the papers for a day or two.

Claire had burned herself to death in the cab of a pickup truck. She'd pulled off a highway exit onto a dead-end dirt road, locked the doors, rolled up the windows, doused herself with gasoline, and set fire to herself. A California Highway Patrol spotted it from the highway, half a mile away.

They'd tentatively identified her by the plate, registered to Matthew, who'd told them he'd given Claire the pickup several months before. The Auburn cops ruled it a suicide, though they'd routinely checked out an alibi on Matthew, who'd been visiting his mother in Gilroy that night. The autopsy was inconclusive; there hadn't been anything left but bone and gristle.

There could be little doubt that the burning woman in the tunnel mural was Claire.

Jojo popped in. Clem grinned. "What a moron. Don't you know how risky it is to waltz into my office after five? You may never get home."

"Anna's taken the kids to visit an auntie in Sacramento. They'll overnight if Tita Marie breaks out the brandy, which she will unless she's been run over by a Humvee. So I'm batching."

"Okay, ever been to scenic Auburn? I want you to chat up da *police* chief down there. Take a gander."

Jojo leaned over Clem's shoulder. "Whoa, that's her? I remember that one. I'll see if I can arrange a meet." Jojo disappeared and was back five minutes later. "The chief'll see me. Grudgingly. I get the feeling he doesn't want to see this one woken up."

"Small towns just hate nasty suicides. Bad for the bucolic image."

After Jojo left, Clem paged through his messages. One was from Mike, the pet shop guy. He'd found the invoice, made out to one Andrew Keyes. The invoice date—probably the date of Cynthia's disappearance—was June 14th. The last day of school, a half day.

She'd probably died the day after. He'd remember June 15th a while.

Next, he pulled up some references on the quaint art of necklacing from the FBI database and the Internet, including a report on the spread of the practice to Haiti, where it reached a peak under President Aristide. The Haitians had nicknamed it *Père Lebrun*. You had to hand it to these guys for their grim humor. Père Lebrun—Papa Lebrun—was a happy-go-lucky tire dealer in Port-au-Prince whose TV ads featured him doing a spiel with his head sticking out of a tire. His name was now the most famous in western Hispaniola.

The Haitian link had a ring to it. Nuestra wouldn't know from neck-lacing. If they could, they'd farm it out, probably to someone with a Père Lebrun or two on his resume. And while stateside Haitian gangs were a south Florida deal, there were a hundred thousand Haitian-Americans living in California. Most were from previous immigrant generations, before the boat-loads washed ashore in Miami-Dade County under Carter. But there were a few demon spawn who'd been part of the ferocious Haitian gang scene that raged on the streets of their shattered capital. Probably one or two in Soledad, happy to take a refresher course and pick up a couple large to boot. He'd check with the warden tomorrow.

He dialed Joanne. She was leaving the hospital, and they agreed to meet at her favorite café on Valencia Street, near the apartment she shared with a med student who was never there. Clem told her to look for the biggest, meanest-looking Chinese guy she'd ever seen.

He found the place and parked in front of a handy hydrant. She waved at him from a booth. A fresh-faced Irish lassie look, not like Claire's Scandinavian package. Claire's features were sharper, her eyes more almond, her mouth more brooding than Joanne's, her lips not as full. But enough resemblance so he wasn't surprised Matthew had zeroed in on her. Or that anyone would, he thought with a languorous grin.

He sat down. "You hungry? Want a danish? Dinner? Anything eight bucks or less. My department's not much on expense accounts."

She smiled. "No, the coffee's great, but the food's shaky."

"Okay, I won't keep you. Angie Strackan talked to you about Matthew."

Her smile vanished and she looked away. "Yeah, scared me half to death."

"Well, better that than have you thinking all's right with the world when it isn't. The news isn't all bad though."

Her eyes widened in curiosity.

"What I'm saying isn't for public consumption," Clem went on. "We're certain Matthew was poisoned at the hospital. He's got call it six, seven weeks where he's dangerous. After that, he couldn't squash a cockroach. So you can outlast him as long as you're careful."

Her face twisted into a look of frustration. "And just how am I supposed to be 'careful'? I can't very well sit in my rocking chair with a shotgun across my lap."

"Well, sending you up the river for shooting the super isn't what I had in mind. For the moment, see if you can find someone to give you a ride to and from work. Put a dead bolt in your door. Don't walk around any deserted places, especially at night. And I'm trying to get police protection. Actually for you and Dr. Roderick. But it's a long shot."

"Why is that?"

"Because we don't have evidence that you're in danger. Not the kind that pays for overtime."

"Well, do your best. But why's he so dangerous? I mean, he stalked me, but it's not like he's killed anyone, right?" Clem looked down at his coffee. She repeated herself suspiciously. "Right?"

"Wrong, I'm afraid. He almost certainly killed the girl we found in the underground tank."

She clapped a hand over her mouth.

"And poisoned his father," he went on relentlessly. "And maybe the owner of the house where we found the tank. An old lady."

Joanne gazed down, picked up her spoon, and began stirring her coffee. She continued stirring and stirring. She finally spoke. "I *wondered* why Homicide was springing for my latte."

"We're not known for glad tidings. Just an idea, but any way you can take a sabbatical? Say a month and a half? It'd take him an hour to tie his shoes by then."

She thought for a moment and shook her head. "Inspector, I live paycheck to paycheck. I've got eighty bucks in my savings account and a hundred before they switch off my credit card. I'd lose my salary for a month or more and still have to pay rent. And pay for staying somewhere else. My folks live here and all my relatives are in the area. If I stay with them he could still find me. And I wouldn't want to put my relatives in danger. Well, except this one cousin maybe." She smiled wanly.

"Well, dial 911 if you get spooked. I'll ring you tomorrow about the protection."

"Okay. Hey, there's one thing I'd like you to answer if you can. Why me? I mean, I'm considered pretty and all, but that's not what this is about. Or he'd just bird-dog all over the hospital. A big hospital's Disneyland for boys, all the RN's, candy-stripers . . . "

"I think you remind him of his sister. She committed suicide four years ago. A hooker, heavy into drugs."

"How flattering." She lost herself in thought for a moment. "Umm . . . there's something I should tell you. Just a vibration I picked up. I thought of it after I talked to Angie."

"Anything you've got."

"Okay. Right after I told him to take a hike, I was picking up all this barely suppressed rage." She paused. "But it changed, like over a few weeks. I've been trying to pin down where I'd seen that look before. And I figured out: When I was ten, I saw a leopard at the zoo. He was just sitting on his haunches in his cage, staring at me with those weird yellow and black eyes. I was frozen to the spot. And I knew what he was saying to me with those eyes. That I was prey. No big deal, just the way it was. That it was my role in life to be his meat."

Clem spoke quietly. "Coolly predatory."

She nodded. "I had this morbid curiosity about leopards for years. Ever hear the old sop, man's the only animal that kills for enjoyment? Some leopards, if they get in a cattle pen, will kill every animal in there even if they only need to eat one."

"The mass murderer of the animal kingdom."

"Like people, you never know. Once they found three leopards that had lived in a busy Indian train station for years with no one the wiser."

Clem left Joanne still absently stirring her latte and headed home, bone-weary. He wondered if he should risk sleep tonight. He was sure to run into the carnivorous Amazonian stag beetles soon. Last time they'd savaged his neighbor's toy poodle, Munchkin, beyond the most skillful taxidermy. Then again, he hated that dog.

As he hit the Market Street traffic heading west of Twin Peaks, he mulled over Matthew's retribution against his father. He couldn't help a certain grudging admiration. The elaborate contract—enlisting a Mexican prison gang, the guards, probably even a subcontractor—was the height of premeditation, and, he admitted with a wince, completely ingenious. The necklace could be pulled off even within the confines of a prison and had a ferocious eloquence to it.

The height of premeditation. The concrete at the oak tree, poured months ahead of time.

A ferocious eloquence. Billy had said to look at his weirdest unsolved.

Matthew. Sneezy. Each thirty-two. Each raised in Gilroy.

For seconds the tenuous connection threatened to vanish. Anything might loft it into the void: a pretty woman crossing the street, a car horn. And then his head filled with the resonance of a finger rimming a brandy glass.

The memory that wove everything together was innocuous but monstrous in portent, one of those vaguely Confucian things that Chinese went to their graves secretly hating their parents for. An ill-fated high school crush he'd had on Betsy Hsu, captain of the cheerleaders. Although Clem was tallest in his class, his mother had forbidden him to go out for basketball and demanded he focus on his studies. The scene remained riveted in his brain forty years later.

As she'd heard him out in the kitchen while lopping the head off a plucked duck, Clem watched the wrinkles slowly crawl back and forth across her high forehead like a phalanx of earthworms, a sure sign that she was silently plotting a counteroffensive.

"Hah!" she finally spat out, glaring up at him and rhythmically waving the duck's head like a little red Mao book. "You see even one Chinese guy on TV play basketball? Too short. If I want son do that, long ago I go to Congo, marry biggest Watusi I see. But I ever do that? No I don't. Only sport Chinese good at? Kung Fu stuff. And only guy ever make money in Kung Fu? Bruce Lee."

She stuck up a forefinger. Clem blanched; this gesture was usually the prelude to a tale of some distant relative (most likely fictitious) who had come to some dire end.

"Your fourth cousin Liong in Hong Kong try make living Kung Fu. Work tourist show, break cinder block with head twice a day, five bucks. Then they play joke, pull switcheroo with block use cement make skyscraper. Liong bash head on block, don't break. Crowd boo. Liong bash bigger, dent brain. After that don't eat food, only crawly bug. Wife disgust and leave. Only work he do? Mop floor. Hand him mop, mop all day. Take away mop, he stop. Father get him job at zoo. Then one day exhibit live scorpion, maybe hundred. Liong come in night to mop, eat every one. Next day, head swell up like beach ball and explode."

But her satisfaction with the successful riposte suddenly faded and she eyed him suspiciously. "Wait. This about Hsu eldest daughter again, right? Cheerleader? How many times your father tell you, think with head on shoulder, not *gui tou*."

Thus died his shot at Betsy. Because, like most cheerleaders, she only dated jocks.

He dialed Grady Moore in Gilroy.

"This about Sneezy, Clem? Hope you have something. I'm gazing down the barrel of early retirement here."

"Don't work on your putt just yet. You said Sneezy got his nickname from a cheerleader. Was he by chance a football player?"

"Could be, but talk to my dep. Gilroy born 'n bred, a year behind Sneezy in high school. Hold on a sec . . . "

The deputy picked up. Clem repeated his question. "Yeah, defense, cornerback," replied the deputy. "Not good enough for college ball, though."

"You remember Sneezy harassing some kid? Blond, with glasses?" Clem asked. Jocks invariably zeroed in on some weakling in the herd and made his life a living hell. In his Chinatown school, they'd proclaimed one kid gay on the flimsiest of evidence and kept him close to tears until Clem had a burst of compassion and called a halt. They'd backed off. Clem was the biggest guy in the school, and his dad the kind of cop you didn't want having a chat with you in the alleys off Stockton.

"Oh, God knows. Hey, there's always some doofus they pick on, right?"

The deputy sounded uncomfortable. Guilty, even.

"Let me guess. Your jacket have a big letter on it too?"

The deputy sighed. "Basketball and track."

"And you were in on the torture sessions?"

"We all were. Nothing I'm too proud of now, mob psychology thing. We called him Lurch."

"So what happened with the football team?"

"He tried out. No one thought he'd make the squad, but he had these long, dangly arms, so coach had him try out for wide receiver."

Who was covered by the cornerback on the defense. Sneezy.

The deputy continued, "So Sneezy bashed the shit out of him two or three practices; kid just wouldn't throw in the towel. Finally Sneezy got him where he pulled his arm behind his back and slammed him to the ground. Broke his arm."

"And he was off the team." The only way the Dad from Hell would let him quit. "But I'm guessing that wasn't the end of it."

"No, Sneezy figured it was open season. And we all went along with it, until one day, Sneezy came into school early and siphoned a milk carton of piss into Lurch's locker. Got all his books. Kid came in and slipped in front of his locker, just lay there on the floor in Sneezy's piss. Cried his eyes out in front of everybody, finally got up and ran out, didn't come back for days. We never told, but we all sort of backed off." The deputy drew breath. "My God. You don't mean—"

"Yeah. I mean. And after that?"

"It got worse. Sneezy was going with this cheerleader. She booted him when she heard about the piss. And told the other girls about his sneezing fits; that's when he got the nickname. He got the ice treatment from every girl in school. Didn't even go to the prom—no one would go with him."

"So no more pompom nookie, he's the school pariah, and guess whose fault it is."

"Exactly. Sneezy took to tailing Lurch home and beating the fuck out of him 'til he got caught by a patrol car and warned."

The scenario fell deftly into place. Matthew figured out that Sneezy went to the 602 every night. Prepared his execution site at the tree. Then came into the bar the night of the storm, jogged Sneezy's memory. Stood him beers, hit him with the bygones routine. After half a dozen free Budweisers and a *Burundanga* chaser, Sneezy must have seen Matthew as his brand-new best bud. That is, until he learned too late that Matthew intended to feed his organs to the local wildlife.

You couldn't help a twinge of sympathy for Matthew. What he'd done was the most fervent fantasy of high school doormats the world over.

"Jesus H. Christ." The deputy paused. "You know, I joined up at nineteen. Not long after, I ran into Lurch downtown. He walked away really fast, like he was scared of me. I caught up with him and told him I was sorry for all the shit we dished on him in school."

"Who knows, it might've kept your keister off the old oak tree. Put your boss on." A few seconds of country hold music and Grady picked up. "I'll fax you a photo," Clem said. "See if you can get an ID from the bartender." He explained his take on Matthew and Sneezy.

"Shit, a twenty-year-old motive? I'll double my Prozac dose before I hit the DA with that one."

"We've got dibs here. I make the same fellow for a doctor here, though I don't have a clue why he did it and probably never will. And for a little girl four years back."

"My God, not the one in the tank?"

"The very same. But it won't see an indictment. I'm gonna gouge the fucker's eyes out with my shoehorn and go from there."

Grady paused thoughtfully. "Damn. It's the perfect shape. I need to remember that."

In the gloaming dark, Jojo pulled in the driveway of the Auburn police chief's picket-fenced house. As he rang the doorbell, a TV blared a sitcom from the living room. He wondered if anyone would hear him. But a heavily made-up teenage girl edged open the door, then rolled her eyes in exasperation. She'd been expecting someone else, maybe a boyfriend. He introduced himself. She rolled her eyes again and took off to get her father. He found himself wondering whether teenagers' eyes ever got stuck in the rolled-up position, so they couldn't unroll them again without some kind of eye surgery.

The chief came out a moment later. He looked fifty, with thin, graying hair, dull three-decade cop eyes, and a belly that evinced a taste for off-duty beer. He looked Jojo up and down suspiciously, but in an inflated way, as if trying to impress a city boy with his astute powers of observation. Jojo proffered a hand, and he took it with one of those bone-splintering grips that some men considered a token of manliness. Jojo gripped back likewise.

"Jack Trance." He stuck his thumbs in his waistband as he slouched down the porch steps. "Everybody's watching the tube. Quieter out here." Trance plopped down squarely in the middle of the steps like a yard-wide, pot-bellied Buddha. Jojo couldn't sit down without violating every tenet of male personal space.

"Now, what can I do for you on this Claire Larsen thing?" Trance asked, leaning forward far enough that Jojo listened for a seam ripping stem to stern.

"Her brother Matthew is a murder suspect. We want to get a handle on what happened with his sister."

Trance nodded as if he'd been expecting it all along. "Happened 8:00 p.m. After the firemen got it put out—they were on another fire, she was toast anyway—we got a look at the truck. Doors were locked. Green eight-year-old Chevy pickup. She was in the driver's seat, keys on the floor under her feet. Five-gallon gas can on the passenger side. When she lit up, vapor blast blew out the passenger window. Both of 'em were rolled up when it went off; rubber seal came out melted on the window."

"Strange way for a woman to suicide. Usually they don't do anything with a bad cleanup job."

Trance shrugged. "We worked it with Modesto. Long-time hooker, two soliciting, two possession. Didn't have a pimp. Lined up johns working sex dives, mainly this peep-show place on the edge of town. Owners expect the girls to work off the clock, but they don't take a piece. No drug debts, cash and carry."

"The peep owners didn't take commissions off the girls? No one she could've cheated?"

"Nope, big no-no. Vice can't shut 'em down: freedom of speech. But they go on the take, they're promoting prostitution. Vice plants girls every now and then to keep 'em straight. Anyway, from what her mother and brother said, she was always talking suicide."

"So why'd she drive seventy or eighty miles to dump it in your lap? Why not in Modesto?

Trance answered with an indifferent shrug. "Good question."

"She had drug connections. Why wouldn't she just gulp a mouthful of downers?"

Trance's pique began building steam. "Christ, I'm supposed to know what's running through the mind of a suicidal, doped-up whore?" He launched a ballistic hawker six or seven feet into a hapless arborvitae. Jojo got the feeling he practiced.

"Okay, okay. So you saw Matthew and his mom?"

"Alibi was clean. He arrived at her house in Gilroy about nine. No way he could've done it and got to Gilroy by then. Would've taken him near two hours."

Jojo was perplexed. "How'd you track him down? We had trouble with that."

"Got an SF address off his plate, but he'd moved. Got a forward off the post office. Don't sound like CIA razzle dazzle to me," Trance snickered.

Jojo started. When he'd checked, the post office had shown Matthew's address for the year he'd been at the Maury house as his previous one. Matthew must have forgotten about the mail forward until Trance's deputy knocked on his door, then realized it was evidence tying him to Cynthia's killing. So he'd gone back to the post office, told them they'd screwed up, made sure they removed the change of address. The last paper trail gone.

Trance continued, "Then we met Matthew and his mom in Gilroy. Morning three days after, so what, the 28th?"

"Right. What was Matthew like?"

"He was shocked, almost couldn't talk. He wasn't faking. I've seen fakers before."

"I'm sure. He was staying at his mother's?"

"No, he'd left late the night of the 25th back to the city. Couldn't get a phone number, so my dep went to his house morning of the 28th. He was in no condition to drive. I had my dep bring him to Gilroy, met them there."

"And April Larsen alibied Matthew?" asked Jojo with a barely suppressed grin.

"Yeah. She was sure it was nine. And she was real torn up; she wouldn't fake-alibi her son for killing her daughter. So what the hell's so funny, junior?"

"My boss saw her this afternoon. Let's just say she likes her bourbon. Early and often."

"Look, you little smartass, I saw the goddamn guy. He was almost comatose. I been at this a long, long time, lots longer than you. I got a sixth sense when someone's shitting me."

Jojo decided to shred him. If the pompous jerk had been in the zone four years back, Matthew might be rooming with his father in Soledad. "Yeah? Well, when your dep visited the bereaved, there'd been a dead girl in a tank under his yard for a month. Your sixth sense pick that up too?"

"Shit. Just shit," Trance spat out, shaking his head and looking chastened. He was certainly familiar with the case.

Jojo spoke in a conciliatory tone. "Look, Jack, I'd like to see where it happened. I'm not trying to fuck up your rep. This guy's killed people in the last few months."

"Yeah, yeah, I'll take you. Ride shotgun?"

"I'll follow you, head back from there."

The chief hauled himself up and revved his cruiser. He led Jojo through a maze of streets that grew less and less inhabited. The houses were spread farther apart and became more dilapidated, until the last street turned into a gravelly road lined by dense trees blanking out the night sky. After a backbone-jarring mile, Trance made a sharp right into a road of rutted, loosely packed dirt, lined with brush so thick it scratched at both sides of the car. The only light came eerily from their headlights.

They bumped along five hundred feet, the trees giving way to stiff, low-lying scrub. Finally, they circled to the right of a tree-covered hillock, and the road died out in front of a tiny, ill-kempt graveyard. It contained thirty or forty overgrown gravestones and monuments, surrounded by a spiked wrought-iron fence with wide gaps where it had fallen over or rusted away. Most of the discolored marbles were topped with crosses, their inscriptions barely legible, all dating from the early 1900s. Jojo got out and viewed the headlights and red taillights from the highway about half a mile behind the cemetery. The wind blew stiffly through the meadow, creating a rustle in the scrub and gently bowing the few gnarled, stunted trees. He buttoned his jacket against the chill. The chief was already out with his flashlight.

"Creepy place," Jojo exclaimed. "I take it this doesn't make the list of Auburn's prime make-out spots. So what's the story here?"

Trance pointed his beam to the left of the cemetery. "Used to be a wooden church here. Methodist. Brick foundation's underneath the brush there. See?" He beamed his flashlight at the ancient masonry walls barely visible in the overgrowth. "Cemetery's the churchyard. Church burned down ninety years back. Land's still Methodist, but never built there again. Weird story."

Jojo was not surprised in the slightest. "I'm all ears."

"Oh, according to legend, the minister and his wife, they had a big falling out. Moved here from Ohio to take over the parish after seminary. She hated it here, decided she hated him too same time. Told him she was leaving, taking the kids back to Ohio, wanted a divorce. He dragged her here that night, soaked her in gasoline, locked her in the church, and set fire to it. They found her with her hands clamped to the metal skeleton of a stained-glass window. Had to saw 'em off at the wrists to get her off. Found most of her fingernails stuck in the door where she tore 'em off trying to claw her way out. Every organ incinerated except her heart, they found it between her feet, really tough to burn. He disappeared with his kids. Some said down to Mexico. Tent revivals." Trance gazed down at the ground, as if something had just occurred to him.

"How quaint. So where was the pickup when it burned?"

"Where I'm parked. Looking at the foundation."

Jojo aimed his beam and gazed at the spot, immersed in melancholy. He shook it off and looked around. With the hill behind them, no one traveling the gravel road would be able to see here. The only view was from the highway.

Jojo pointed in the distance. "So CHP spotted the fire from there. How long would it take to get here after they saw it?"

"Say ten minutes from the far side, going left. Going right, maybe twenty, 'cause you'd need to exit, get back on the highway the other direction, then exit again, and get back on to catch the exit before the fire. The gravel road we were on leads to the highway access road, half mile past where we turned onto the dirt road. But the gravel road's not marked, so from the access road you'd have to know to take it. Then find the dirt road, which isn't easy."

"And with that hill there, it'd be impossible to spot the fire, even two hundred feet down the road."

"Right. Almost no traffic this way anyway."

"Are there trails leading off this clearing?"

"Four or five of 'em. Like that one." He pointed out a barely discernible break in the brush.

"Pretty easy to walk ten minutes and vanish."

"Yup, and no houses half a mile any direction. Closed off this one though." He pointed his flashlight at a chained gate with red and white barber pole stripes blocking one of the pathways. "Couple old wells off that way. Kid fell in six months back. He was okay, just broke his arm, but we blocked it off. So, you see everything you needed to?"

"I'll look around, but you can get back to your family. Last question: The pickup. Car heaven?"

"Yup, scrunched. Keys may be around somewhere, but God only knows. And thanks, I'll hit the road. Look, Jojo, sorry about being an asshole before. I'm getting a bad feeling about this."

"Don't sweat it. I come up with something, we'll hand it off. You can reopen yourself."

Trance shook hands with his annoying crunch-grip. "Thanks. And keep an eye out. They say this place is haunted."

Jojo crunched back. "Some of my best friends are ghosts."

Trance reversed into the brush and tooled down the road into the dark. Jojo walked to his car and switched on the fog lights, then kicked through the brush overgrowing the church foundation. He sat down on a mound of crumbling brick and gazed across the moonlit meadow.

Trance didn't know who he was talking to. *Americanos* were pikers when it came to ghosts. In the Philippines, away from the bustling cities, the cane cutters of the lowlands and the charcoal makers of the mountains bought black candles and fetched the amulet-waving *mambabarang* when their children caught fever. Evil demons called *aswang* stalked jungle and beach by moonlight. Hideous giants, the bare-chested, foul-smelling *kapres*, squatted in the high trees smoking huge cigars, waiting to make victims of girls passing underneath.

He recalled the spirit tales of his craggy-cheeked *yaya* in the bedroom after she stained her teeth red with *bunga* juice to heighten the effect. He smiled at memory of the stifled shrieks of his sisters that their mother pretended not to hear, since she'd admonished the crone not to scare the children with her mumbo jumbo: the *tamawo*, red-eyed corpse eaters who could smell a person dying, who trailed the wakes and hid under deathbeds, who made human flesh taste like pig and fed it to the unsuspecting to turn them into their like. The terrible *mananggal*, beautiful maidens who discarded arms and legs by night, sprouted bat wings and grew needle tongues, who ate unborn babies out of pregnant girls' wombs, who would feast on your intestines if you slept with your belly exposed. The *tiyanak*, babies who died and became grotesque spirits of the wood who would lead you astray to starve in the forests. The *engkantadas*, fallen angels who looked like maidens, who would punish you with sickness for bathing in the river or picking an orchid without asking them.

And though a practicing Catholic raised in Americanized Manila, he'd stood vigil at his *yaya's* viewing as she'd begged him to before she died, to make sure the corpse-eaters didn't get her. And she'd taught him as well as any cock-fighting, rum-drinking *provinciano* how to act when there were ghosts around: softly say *tabi-tabi po* three times so you didn't surprise them, because they didn't like surprises. Then stop breathing, eyes wide while they decided whether to show themselves. And if they came, all you'd see might be a sparkly ripple in the moonlight, the faintest corona darting in and out of view, a voice of muted anguish above the moan of the wind.

For half an hour, he peered among the gnarled oaks as the wind whistled and the chill sent needles through his clothing. Just as he was ready to give up and start for home, he saw it: a tiny shimmering orb flitting among the farthest trees. Its color was the blue-black of lapis lazuli, so invisible against the shadows that he rubbed his eyes to be sure. It vanished, but moments later darted back into view. Then it stopped and slowly divided in half, as if one had been hidden behind the other. He rubbed his eyes again. They were still there, now absolutely still, as if waiting.

Yes, there were ghosts out there. Two, to be exact. The ghosts of two burned and brutalized women, condemned to haunt this lonely spot by the rage of two men, men of such unspeakable evil that even the most fearsome *aswang* would cower before them.

Tabi-tabi po . . .

CHAPTER ELEVEN

Thursday, May 22nd

Just after 9:00 a.m., Angie met Clem for the first time at his claustrophobic office. She threaded through the day's pick of handcuffed brigands emptying from squad cars in front, and worked her way past the metal detectors up to Clem's floor. Through some bureaucratic sleight of hand, Clem had the only office in Homicide. The other inspectors and staff occupied a sea of battered gray metal desks outside his door. Clem sat behind his desk on the phone and gave her a salute. His eyes didn't focus but darted around like water striders. The insomnia was going tertiary.

He hung up and yawned hugely. "Sorry. Last night I had to kill a wasp the size of a freaking turkey vulture. It tried to lay eggs in my mother so they could hatch and eat her alive."

Angie nodded in sympathy. "I *hate* when that happens."

He eyed her hopefully. "So, you here to turn yourself in for criminal negligence? I could use the collar."

"No, looks like Matthew didn't poison Janine. And she told me it was better she didn't know anyway." She related the basics of her visit.

"Thought you were fielding crank calls at Taraval today. It's 'take a number' for morons coast to coast."

She could hardly have missed the little girl's photo when she'd untwisted the rubber band from the *Chronicle* as she sipped her coffee. The article pegged the prime suspect as a former hospital employee, also suspected of the Gilroy oak tree killing. They discussed Clem's conclusions about Sneezy and the dead cardiologist.

"So you're letting out the Matthew stuff, even without his name."

Clem nodded. "Leakology 101. As my FBI buddy says, I want him feeling like a cat in a roomful of rocking chairs. Maybe he'll put off whatever he's got planned. Especially since I'm more likely to dig up a hundred carat diamond in my yard than get police protection for anyone. And I want it out there that we don't think it's the parents; they'll be more likely to surface. So what brings you here?"

"The cat we found in the backyard, the phone number on the collar. By the way, he's driving something orange now. Matthew, that is, not the cat."

"Okay, I've got two flunkies fielding calls. Let's jog down to Evidence and find little Felix."

Jojo walked in and gave Angie a wink. "Well, I'm betting someone killed Claire." He recounted his visit to Auburn.

Clem cocked an eyebrow. "Matthew?"

"My take. He went to Modesto, subdued her, drove her to Auburn, torched her, and walked out by one of the trails. Had his car stashed on one of the streets."

Clem leaned back in his chair. "Sucks for motive. I'd figure a drug or pimp murder."

"But the locals say no foul play by the sex and drug denizens. And there's one thing that really points to Matthew." He told the story of the minister and his wife.

Clem nodded. "Your average pimp isn't nearly so poetic. And that could explain why it happened more than an hour from Modesto. So the mural would represent her murder, not her suicide. Still, my kingdom for a motive. Without it, not a word to the DA." He grinned at Angie. "Last time I brought him something like that, I got this in interoffice mail." He reached in his drawer and held up a paperback copy of *Grimm's Fairy Tales*.

"Believe me, Clem," insisted Jojo. "She wasn't just looking for some picturesque spot to do the deed. No way she could've happened to find that place."

Clem's expression darkened. "And?"

Jojo mumbled something.

"I didn't catch that."

Jojo's face reddened, and he sighed in resignation. "And yes. The ghosts told me."

Clem shot him a withering glare, then frowned at Angie. "Every other case it's tappy tappy toe . . . "

"That's *tabi-tabi po*," Jojo corrected with annoyance. "So you don't surprise them."

"God forbid. Amazing how many ghosts here speak Tagalog. But does he ever *once* get 'em to make a frigging statement?"

Angie shook her head in sympathy. "Problem witnesses. They tell you that in school."

"The worst," Clem grumbled. "Don't get me started."

Angie suppressed a smile. Clem wouldn't dare ridicule the spirits, since it was gospel truth to his mother that San Francisco was overrun with them. He'd told Angie he'd gone well into his teens certain that girls thought him a troll, because his mother never failed to disparage his looks so the ghosts wouldn't kidnap him. That he'd never been snatched merely proved her right.

And old habits died hard. At their housewarming party, Clem's wife, Grace, told Angie that she'd first been drawn to Clem's piercing eyes. Clem's mother glowered at Grace, then shrugged at Angie and said, "Same exact eyes his great-uncle Chu, work on railroad. Get cataract, then one night go pee, fall in horse trough, smash skull, and drown. Wife and children in China then no money. They marry off daughter to rich ugly man to support family. Year later, she have son look like bullfrog. Ugly man blame her, kick her out. Family broke again, wife buy too cheap smelly fish. Week later all poison dead. All 'cause of great-uncle Chu's eyes," the crone finished, hobbling off in triumph.

Clem turned back to Jojo. "We're off to look at a dead cat. You coming?"

"Umm . . . context?"

"Spring clearance at Animal Control. Thought I'd pick up some for the office."

They signed in at the cavernous evidence room and found Speckle's remains in a box of siftings. Angie looked over the little skeleton and the collar that encircled the vertebrae. The leather had wasted away, but the copper tag was still legible under a blue-green patina. She popped the seven-digit number in her cell and dialed, but it came up out of service. She keyed in San Jose and got a curmudgeonly old man. He didn't know, or want to know, anything about Speckle. Finally, she tried the Central Valley and got a sleepy-voiced woman.

"Funny, you guys calling again." So Forensics had probably tried already. "It's not me," she said, stifling a yawn. "But I forgot I had this roommate; she moved out two years back to live with her boyfriend. Bridgett. Maybe she knows something. I have a number." She gave it to Angie.

She dialed and a man answered, "Yo." A television blared a talk show in the background.

"Hello, I'm looking for Bridgett?"

"Umm . . . what about?" he asked, as if screening her calls. She went through her recitation.

The man finally grunted. "Okay, just a sec. There a reward?"

Angie rolled her eyes. "Umm . . . I don't know of one." He grunted again and half-held his hand over the phone. The TV turned down, and a woman took over for Mr. Yo.

"What's this about Speckle?"

Angie introduced herself. "I'm looking for anyone who knows about a cat named Speckle."

"Bridgett Westin. Well yeah, I know about him. God, did you find him? After all this time?"

"After a fashion. Unfortunately, buried in a yard in San Francisco. But this is part of a homicide investigation. I'd like to know what you can tell me about him."

She hesitated, probably at mention of the police. "Well, he was my friend's cat. But she died. Claire Larsen."

Angie's blood raced. "Bridgett, I need to talk to you, today. Do you have some time?"

"Umm, yeah. I don't work 'til tonight." The man spoke up in the background. Bridgett covered the phone, then got back on and lowered her voice. "Okay, my boyfriend says if you're the cops, we should get a reward. Look, Angie is it? Can you swing, say, twenty bucks? That'll keep him happy."

"Sure, no problem," Angie replied, gazing cross-eyed at the ceiling.

"Thanks, it'll make my life easier. I live in Modesto." She gave Angie directions.

"Two hours from now? We can grab lunch."

"Okay. But I still get the twenty, right?"

"Yes, yes, you still get the twenty." She got off the phone to find Clem edging toward a nearby emergency exit door. She scowled and held out an open palm. "Twenty bucks."

Clem took a few noontime calls, stifling machine-gun yawns and munching on a gristly burger. One was from the desk guard at Soledad Prison with the phone number Matthew had used. Clem took the opportunity to transfer to the warden, but his secretary claimed he was busy. For the third time today. The guy—a certain Bud Fallon, with all of two months in the Soledad driver's seat—didn't seem concerned. Clem handed Matthew's number off to the phone company for a location and called Jojo to his office.

"See what we can get off Matthew's landlady being from Rio. I think there's some Brazilian civic association here."

"Can we release his photo? Helpful if I can pass it along."

"I checked. 'We'll get back to you.' Have the sketch artist whip up a rough. Glasses. Dig up the Brazilians, give it to their officers. No name, I doubt he's using his real one anyway. That way I won't get french-fried by Legal."

"We might get something," replied Jojo. "They're a close-knit group. Latin Catholics, everybody knows everybody. Like Filipinos."

"Also mention he's probably driving an orange car. Not Hashbury Day-Glo, nothing that eye-catching. Like a dark orange."

The answer came in from the phone company. Clem looked up at Jojo. "Huh. Matthew used a pay phone, edge of Castro and Noe Valley."

"So he goes back to his old haunt to call, or he didn't go that far when he moved."

"Perps using pay phones don't generally travel too far. What they do is use a bunch so they don't get staked out, but not far from where they're holed up. Check rental classifieds from right before he moved out of his last place. When was that?"

"January 18th," responded Jojo. "Paid off the lease. Claimed a death in the family; he was moving back home."

"He'd get a garage. He'll want to conserve cash. And impossible to rent a big place now without employment references, polygraph, et cetera. Garages are more easygoing 'cause they're mostly illegal. Check video places too."

Jojo took off. Clem called Roderick and crossed his fingers. "I'm following up on some dates for Matthew's absence from work in 2004."

She sighed. "Yes, yes, I have them. On the computer." She paused a moment. "Sick days July 25th through 28th. Four days. Returned the 29th."

"What were his normal hours?"

"Days, eight to five."

Matthew hadn't just taken off after Claire's death, but also the 25th, the day she died. The Auburn cops hadn't checked, or they'd have grilled him.

"While we're on the subject. Can you check June 14th? Did he take another sick day?" The afternoon Matthew had gone to the pet shop with Cynthia.

"Well, he was absent, but it wasn't a sick day. A scheduled vacation day."

"Scheduled? Like how scheduled? Can you tell when he put in for it?"

"Yes, yes . . . he applied and got approval June 6th."

Acid rose in his gullet. Matthew had planned the snatch the day after he'd seen Cynthia at the hospital, so he'd targeted her instantly. He'd set it up for the last day of school, a half-day, probably met her leaving school.

"Thanks. I wanted to tell you personally: even though he hasn't made a move on you in months, I think you're still in danger."

"Well, then please do me a favor and go catch him. Or do you limit yourself to telling people they're in danger? Nice work if you can get it."

Clem counted to three. "We're trying. I've also put you and Joanne up for police protection. I can't guarantee anything, but I'll let you know soon as I hear."

"Well, how gratifying. I mean, here I was under the impression I was worth more to you dead. So the FBI can join in."

Clem bit his lip. No wonder she was being so chilly. Angie's interview techniques had all the subtlety of a cruise missile. "Well, that's not exactly what I said to her."

She sighed, and her tone became conciliatory. "It's okay, Inspector. I have to admit I deserved that comeuppance."

"And the FBI is already in it. He poisoned his father with mercury. And I think he's taken some pretty violent revenge on other people. I don't want to get into the details, but poison would be the least of your worries."

"That's sobering." She paused. "Look, I admit Matthew has every reason to hunt me down. I totally screwed him over. I wrote a memo with the procedures and flat out forgot to give it to him. By the time I remembered, he'd already done it and gotten caught. And the stuff had been decanted into a burette, so there was no warning label."

"And the signature on the memo, confirming that you gave him the instructions?"

She paused. "Well, let's just say it's not hard to find good forgers in the hospital pharmacy biz."

"And Matthew never confronted you?"

"His hospital privileges were revoked the day it happened. And I've had a guard walk me to and from my car at work ever since it happened." She paused. "Sometimes I almost wish he *would* confront me. It's any decent doctor's worst nightmare to cause someone's death through sheer stupidity, even a psycho like Matthew."

Clem nodded grimly. "Believe me, I know the feeling."

"And I feel even worse because I had a chance to at least own up to it and didn't. To be honest, if I had it to do again, maybe I'd let myself get blackballed, finish up in some shoehorn clinic in Tulsa. But this is the way it is. So. What do you suggest I do?"

"Well, if it's possible, I'd get out of town a month or two. I imagine you've got accumulated vacation."

"Yes, like nine months. But nothing works that way."

"The building will still be on its foundations when you get back. Unless the Big One hits."

She chuckled for the first time. "We've had an earthquake retrofit up for bond approval ever since the last Big One in '89. Problem is, I've got several brain tumor patients who will be on death's door if anyone screws up their MRIs in the next week. Which anyone here but me probably would. And Roth'll scream bloody murder."

"I'll cuddle up to Roth if need be. If you get spooked before then, worst case you and Joanne can camp out in my garage, long as you promise not to filch my power tools. And Doctor, if you decide to take off, think about taking her. He's been stalking her. She can't do it herself; she's living hand to mouth. Hell, she might even be good company."

"A good deed. What a thought. I'll avoid the temptation to walk off with your table saw, but I'll talk with Roth when he's back. He's at a convention for three days. But you already know that, right?"

"Umm . . . I do?"

"Oh. I assumed it was you. Roth called me on his cell, said someone from Homicide called his office this morning, didn't leave a name. He asked me if I knew what it was about."

Clem's stomach plummeted in a burst of wind shear. Clem and Jojo always left their names unless it was dangerous to do so.

It had to be Grunt, dogging his case again. He'd snuck a peek at the file and was sniffing around to dump on Clem later: incompetence if he didn't get a solve, procedural lapses if he did. Last time, Clem had encountered a crime scene cat who'd been dining on his ex-owner for two days and kept darting in for nibbles. He finally collared the man-eater with a can of Friskies from the kitchen cabinet. Grunt filed a complaint—compromising a crime scene—but had been laughed out of IA. Roth probably wouldn't say anything, but Grunt was still a little too close to raising questions at IA about Clem's rescue of the kid from the gang leader years ago. And Grunt's union cronies would try to force him into retirement on the flimsiest pretext.

Then again, even if the rescue came to light, it would probably be little more than annoyance; the gangster was way too smart to corroborate. Any cop would consider Clem's actions justifiable, and retribution on the street would be fearsome once the gang leader left San Quentin.

But more to the point, the gangster would be canned Spam if Clem ever dimed him to the kidnapped kid's father, a man who'd personally hacked the heads off a dozen enemies, swirled them in pitch, and used them as tiki torches to light his patio.

He shuddered. The guy—who ironically went by the absurd moniker of Uncle Haha—owed him big. But there were people whose marker you just didn't want, no matter how much you might need it someday. Curse the paperboy in the wrong company for trashing your peonies, and you might find his innards delivered to you in jars like leftovers from a Pharaoh's funeral. Thankfully Uncle Haha lived an hour south of Modesto, well out of earshot.

"Dr. Roderick," Clem finished, "best you and Roth talk to no one but me, so things don't get confused. And very important: if you decide to disappear, tell me. I don't need to explain why." Clem hung up roundly irritated. It seemed the best he could do to help people was tell them to leave town. He felt like a pathetic old sheriff galloping up and down the street howling that the James boys were headed for the bank, not a homicide inspector in a well-heeled city.

Angie found Bridgett's down-at-the-heels Modesto suburb and parked in front of a soot-encrusted brick fourplex. There was a green dumpster to the left, choked with so much refuse that the lid stuck half-open. A few bottles, two pre-owned disposable diapers, and empty Chinese food cartons were scattered in front, evidence of a rejected bag-toss. The brown lawn was highlighted by a gigantic concrete birdbath full of what looked like thirty-weight motor oil. Any bird idiotic enough to splosh around in it would emerge looking like a victim of the *Exxon Valdez*.

She picked out Bridgett's door, downstairs closest to the dumpster. Bridgett opened and gave Angie a circular wave with her palm. She was about Angie's height, five-five, with ringlets of jet-black hair and a voluptuous figure overstated by black stretch pants and an eye-searing, pink, low-cut T-shirt, both worn tight as a spinnaker in a gale. Early thirties, with eyes that had the self-protective look of having seen too much too quickly when young.

She wrinkled her button nose and gave Angie an apologetic shrug. "Landlord's late on the garbage bill. Last time they pulled the dumpster, and we were stacking stuff on the ground. You think it smells bad now . . . "

Angie grinned. "Oh, I do. Let's find someplace with a more appealing aroma for lunch. Suggestions?"

Bridgett pointed out an old-fashioned diner half a block away made from a giant aluminum trailer. They took a tattered booth. The grease-stained menus were the size of newspapers, listing several hundred items. The twenty items under "Greek Specialties" probably denoted the background of the owner, and were likely the safest bets.

Bridgett eyed her with unconcealed excitement. "Can I get an appetizer?"

Angie gathered she didn't get taken out much. "Go for it."

"I just love these fried mozzarella sticks. And they give you a shitload. I'll get the cheeseburger."

Angie chose the stuffed grape leaves. "Now tell me about Speckle. And Claire."

Bridgett averted her gaze. "Well, if you're the cops, maybe you know how Claire made her living. Look, I can't get into trouble for what I tell you, right?" She waited, and Angie shook her head. "Okay. Claire and I, well, we used to trick together. Bill was one of my johns, decided to 'rescue' me." She rolled her eyes in amusement. "Basically means he gets laid for free now. I'm a waitress. Anyway, I showed her the ropes. Big sister deal. In a twisted sort of way," she added quietly.

"I'm not judging you. I doubt most working girls trick because they want to."

Bridgette smiled wanly. "You got *that* right. Anyway, she was sixteen when she got here. I got her fake ID so she could set up johns at the peep I was working."

"How did that work?" Angie found herself curious in a lurid sort of way.

"Oh, they develop this fantasy deal watching you. Then, when they finally go for it, you can get like twice the street."

"And the owner knew about it?"

Bridgett answered with a sardonic laugh. "Hell, it was in the job description. Off-premises, of course. Word gets around, horndog grapevine. They just said we couldn't take the lead. And if you were any good, you didn't need to. You'd build up regulars pretty quick. To where you could blow off the slimier ones," she said with a little grimace.

Angie grinned. "They all sound a bit slimy to me. Did the owners take a cut?"

"No, they could get shut down." She smiled thinly. "Of course, they took their cut in freebies. You went along once in a while, or you'd find your-self on day shift. Sometimes I think that's the reason those guys get in the business. For the perks," Bridgett finished as the waitress brought the moz-zarella sticks and Angie's grape leaves.

"Same with some Vice cops. So that's where Claire worked?"

"Yeah, the owners liked her. Good-looking, blond, hot bod, pouty bad-girl look. She got lots of 'em to trick who never would've otherwise. 'Happily' married types who went in for a peek."

Angie smiled thinly and said, half to herself, "I know about those . . . "

Bridgett looked at her curiously. "Hmm?"

"Another time. Back to Claire."

"Anyway, it's too bad. She could've saved money, gotten out of the life. Like I did," she continued, shaking her head as she bit into a mozzarella stick.

"But the problem was . . . "

"Dope. I mean, we all did, like coke if the john anted up," she said with a nostalgic smile. "But Claire, she'd go on a bender, we're talking a week. Owners wouldn't let her work or she'd pass out in the booth. Usually I'd front her; she was good for it."

"So what set her on the binges?" Angie asked, and swallowed a grape leaf.

Bridgett glanced away, clearly uncomfortable. "Umm . . . look, this is getting into some pretty personal stuff about Claire. I thought this was about Speckle."

"It is. Part of a homicide investigation."

"So who are you investigating, to where it turns on a dead cat?"

"Claire's brother, Matthew."

Bridgett's face filled with disgust. "Lurch. The scumbag."

Angie looked at her questioningly.

"The fucking scumbag. Lurch. His nickname in school. Claire told me." Bridgette looked down at her mozzarella sticks as if they'd turned into dog turds. Finally, she asked quietly, "Will he get executed if you catch him?"

"No, he's been poisoned, he has seven or eight months to live. But he'll be a twitching vegetable long before that."

Bridgett sighed, seemingly in relief. "Then there is a God."

The grape leaves churned in Angie's stomach. "Guess I've opened Pandora's box. We'd heard he looked after Claire. That's off the mark?"

Bridgett's face brimmed with incredulous anger. "Looked after her? Hell, he was her number one john."

Angie cringed from head to toe.

"He'd come down with a big bag of coke or smack, get her started," Bridgette continued. "Shit, he didn't even do them himself. And she liked the stuff so damn much, she'd give in."   '

"Why would he give her the drugs?"

"Because she hated his guts so much it was the only way she'd talk to him. Then he'd get her doped up." Bridgett lowered her voice to a harsh whisper. "And just use her," she finished, brushing away a tear. The waitress plunked down the cheeseburger and walked off. Bridgett stifled a retch, finally dredging up a limp smile as she gazed down at her lunch. "Doggy bag."

"She'd take the drugs," Angie pursued, "even if she knew Matthew was going to do that?"

"At first, he wouldn't do it when he'd give her the drugs. He'd show up again a day or two after, once she was in her bender. When he finished, he'd leave a pile of cash. Couple hundred."

"So when did this start?"

Bridgett grimaced. "The sex? When she was thirteen. First only once in a while, after school in the house. Their parents worked. Sometimes outside somewhere, like if she didn't come home 'cause he'd been getting that look."

"And she never told her parents?"

Bridgett sighed. "He told her he'd kill her if she told. And just so she knew he'd do it, he killed her cat."

Angie's legs went numb.

Bridgett continued quietly. "He'd already been caught torturing a cat by a neighbor, and we're not talking cans on a tail. The cat died. His father grabbed him by the hair and made him clean out Claire's cat's litter box. Then he tied Matthew to a chair in the backyard and spent like five minutes smearing the shit all over his face, up his nose, in his hair, right in front of Claire and her mom. He didn't stop 'til Matthew was puking blood. Claire was certain he was going to die.

"Anyway, day after Claire threatened to tell, after school he dragged her out in the backyard in the rain. He had her cat—Mittens I think?—in this produce box, where she could see his nose poking out. He punched her a couple times 'til she was on her knees throwing up. Then he kicked the box in this hole and kicked the mud in after it. And told her that if she dug up Mittens, he'd take her out in the fields that same afternoon and bury her alive, same as he did the cat. Said he had a nice spot dug up and ready. Then he left her there, screaming in the mud, went inside, watched her through a window."

"To make sure she didn't dig up the cat. Jesus," Angie spat out.

Bridgett nodded, her eyes moist. "Anyway, Matthew lived at home for, I guess, two years after he graduated. Said he was saving money for college, working with his dad."

"But really so he could keep doing Claire," said Angie.

"Uh-huh. Claire left home soon as she thought she could handle the streets. After she ran away, he left home too, started college. She called her mom, told her she was in Modesto. Begged her not to tell anyone, but he wormed it out of the old lady. One night Claire's working, up pops the screen and there's Matthew. Didn't say a word, just popped in tokens for two hours so the attendant had to come empty the machine. She just kept dancing, didn't want to get fired. But she told me she mouthed 'fuck you' in his face the whole time," Bridgett finished with a smile of admiration.

Angie fought off the urge to cut short the interview. "So he started in again."

"Yeah, showed up more and more often. Wanted her to move to the city and live with him. What bliss *that* would've been, huh? Told her he'd never been with another woman. Like he was 'saving' himself for her. After a while, she like adjusted to it. Really sick. He'd show up with dope and money, she'd just let him do his business and he'd leave. At that point, she was on a bender more than not. Like 2003, early 2004."

"You ever meet him?"

"Yeah, once. He gave me the willies. I was at her trailer. She went to use the john and he just stared at me—like telling me to leave, right now, without saying it. I was out of there in two minutes, let me tell you. His eyes, they froze my blood into Popsicles. And believe you me, I've seen some creepy eyes in my life." She shuddered. "Anyway, we got drunk one night, and she told all."

"And Speckle? When did she get him? And why was your number on his collar?"

"Like two years before she died. So what, 2002? Wandered into her trailer park." Bridgett grinned ruefully. "She never could keep her phone connected. So I let her use mine. Cat had good people sense too. Claire told me he hissed at Matthew first time they met. After he left, Speckle plunked a turd in front of the door. Like giving Claire his verdict."

Angie smiled. "There's times I could use a cat like that. Claire died in July 2004. Was she going downhill before that?"

Bridgett knitted her brows. "No, in fact the opposite. Like three months before she died, she had this big falling out with Matthew. He'd done something that just went too far, though she never told me what, even I asked her. And remember, we're talking two hookers here, right? Anyway, she screamed at him, called him a pervert. He tried to calm her down, she threatened him with a kitchen knife. After that, she didn't hear from him. Except one day like a month later, he left his pickup at her trailer park, taped the keys to her door with a note said he was giving it to her, even put some insurance in her name. She never drove it though."

"Did she talk about suicide?"

"Well, yeah. But it was like she was one of those types who talk about it but don't do the deed. Guess I was wrong. Still surprised me though."

"Why is that?"

"Well, the way she died," answered Bridgett with a shiver. "I mean, why would you *do* something like that?" She collected herself. "But also, 'cause when the Matthew stuff was at its worst, she'd have been more likely to do it. After she sent him packing, it was like she felt good about giving him the boot. She saved a little money, even opened a savings account. That was a big day. I went with her. She was so proud of that. Said it made her feel almost like a real person," Bridgett finished, wiping away a tear.

"So it didn't make sense she'd commit suicide."

Bridgett looked down at her cold cheeseburger, lost in thought. "No. Especially now I think about it. Like, first I felt all guilty, but now I don't know what to think."

"Guilty about what?"

"Well, after she found Speckle, when she'd talk about suicide, she'd get all gooey. Ask me to take care of him if she killed herself, she'd call me and tell me to come get him. I mean, maybe that was a way to protect herself, like I'd come talk her out of it. But really, I think that little cat meant a lot to her."

"Especially after what happened to her first cat."

"For sure. Well, the night she did it, I was working a john. My answering machine was broke. I thought she called to tell me to come get Speckle, but couldn't. I went to her trailer after I heard, I had a key, but Speckle was gone. I put up posters, but nothing. I figured she gave him to someone else. Hope he had himself a good little cat life," she finished with a tiny smile.

"I'm sure he did, Bridgett." There was no point in telling her the ugly truth. "And why don't you know what to think now?"

Bridgett turned pale. "Because I just now figured out why she never drove the pickup. God, I don't know why I didn't think of it before." She bowed her head. "Maybe I just didn't want to know."

Angie felt an uncomfortable tingle in her shoulders. "Why didn't she?"

Bridgett's voice became husky. "Claire ran away at sixteen. I taught her to drive. One of my regulars, he had a second car, lent it to me. God, she was such a klutz behind the wheel. Like she couldn't hit the brake and the turn signal at the same time." She wiped at her eyes, then raised her head and locked eyes with Angie. "I glanced in the pickup cab first time I saw it. And now I think about it, I'm sure there were three pedals."

Angie nodded. "A clutch. Meaning it was a stick."

"But the car she learned on was an automatic. She'd never driven a stick in her life. Angie, she *couldn't* have driven that pickup, even if she wanted to."

Clem sifted through the Cynthia calls. So far, more than two hundred had flooded into the 800 number. Most dripping with good intentions but useless, some from get-a-lifes claiming they'd killed her, or asking if there were any full frontal nude shots.

The false confession troops were also out in force. They didn't even rate an inspector, just a paunchy, pencil-chewing uniform who ended each interview with a jaded "We'll get back to you." Clem eyeballed the rejects as they skulked by, each as crestfallen as an out-of-work actor who's just flubbed the audition. He even waved at one failing his eighth shot at stardom: a gaunt, shock-headed derelict everyone called Boo Boo because his voice was a ringer for Yogi Bear's sidekick. Last time, Clem had asked him dourly why he didn't just go the fuck ahead and kill somebody. The guy'd broken into tears and buried his head in his hands.

The phone rang. Chief Jackson. "Sorry, Clem, you got turned down for protection."

Clem fumed in silence. Bigger cities like LA had divisions that did nothing but protect witnesses and other likely targets. In San Francisco, the service depended on the mayor's public appearance schedule, since he had a tinpot dictator's taste for shows of force that sopped up bodyguards like a sponge. He probably sent himself his own death threats.

"Now why am I not surprised?" replied Clem. "Any boots worth licking?"

"Already licked. Can you put 'em up?" Jackson's wife had extorted a new bedroom set after the last time he'd housed a witness, a crotch-scratching, flamboyantly flatulent, two-hundred-pound biker mama named Gasbag.

"I offered Roderick my garage. No go without the pillow mints."

"Thanks for trying. FYI, Hizzoner's office make bad juju. What with Cynthia's pic on every news show on the planet this morning. CNN, BBC, TV Kazakhstan . . . "

"Sorry. I'm skipping my personal growth classes."

"We'll miss you at yoga. I've got a thumb in the shit dike for now, but not if he chalks up another kid. That'll have the goblins out of their caves." San Francisco had legions of activists waiting in the wings to make hay off any perceived incompetence in the Police Department.

"My chicken bones say not another girl. But it'll be somebody."

Jackson grunted and hung up. The phone rang again. It was the cop working the Cynthia calls.

"Hey," Clem said. "Got me a nibble?"

"Guy says his name's Nichols." She paused. "Tom Nichols." They hadn't released the first names of the parents, only Cynthia's name.

"Put him on." Clem heard the phone transfer, then silence.

"Mr. Nichols?"

"Yes. I'm Tom Nichols." He had a rumbling, unsteady voice.

"Where you at, Mr. Nichols?"

"I'm—well, I'm in California."

"Care to narrow it down a bit?"

He hesitated. "Out east. The Sierras." The mountains on the Nevada border. Clem glanced down at the phone. The area code checked out. He probably couldn't use an anonymous prepaid cell, since most of the Sierras didn't have coverage.

"Good enough. So why you calling?"

"I saw Cindy's picture in the paper this morning. I—well—I feel like I should tell you what happened." His tone was funereally grave. Most cranks went in for cheap histrionics.

"Now that you know we don't think you killed her. Yeah, Mr. Nichols, you probably should. Not big on punctuality, are you?"

"I—we ran. We were afraid."

"You and your wife. Where is she now?"

"She died. Two years ago. Breast cancer."

"I'm sorry. Really. You coming in?"

"I'm in a lot of trouble I guess."

"Some. Not reporting your kid missing can be a felony: depraved indifference et cetera. But depends on the details. And if the DA's got a hard-on. But not my call. I'm Homicide. I need to know what happened."

"My wife . . . " He faded off.

"June." More silence. Clem hated leading. But it was that or grind his teeth to powder while Nichols meandered his way to the truth like a still-water creek. "She the one hurt Cindy?"

"Yes." He paused. "She was always sort of wound up. But she went downhill after she got sick. Had an operation, chemo, it didn't work. She got bitter and withdrawn. She was only forty-two when she died."

"And she'd take it out on Cindy."

"Sometimes. I mean, she loved Cindy, but normal kid things would make her crazy. But I was really shocked that she'd hurt Cindy so bad." His voice thickened, the sound of someone fighting to maintain composure. One of those little things that was hard to fake.

"Cindy had a condition where her bones could break easily. I don't know much about it, but it's Osteo-something or other. Normally I'd think you were lying, and I'd be tearing you a new one. But it could've just as easily been your wife who broke Cindy's arm. So what led you to fly the coop?"

"The last time she broke Cindy's arm. It was before school. I wasn't there."

"Tuesday, June 5th. The day she went to the hospital. What happened between your wife and Cindy that morning?"

He paused. "It was so stupid. Just so stupid." Then nothing.

"Mr. Nichols?"

He sighed painfully. "Cindy got up early. Tried to make my wife scrambled eggs. She didn't know how, burned the pan, stank up the house. June came down and exploded."

"And you were . . . ?"

"Visiting my brother in Fort Bragg. I got back Tuesday morning, went straight to work, didn't go home. They called me from the hospital. Cindy gave them my number."

"Not your wife's. Because she was afraid of her mother."

He paused. "Yes. I went to pick her up. She begged me not to take her home, so I took her to work with me."

"And the hospital asked some questions, I take it."

"Yes, the doctor. The one in the wheelchair. Doctor . . . "

"Parcell."

"Yes. He didn't believe what Cindy told him. And I guess I looked guilty. I was so flustered."

"Anything after that? From the hospital? They said they hadn't referred it to the police."

"Nothing. Parcell said we'd hear from the hospital's outreach program. If we didn't cooperate, they could refer us to the police or Social Services. But no one called."

I'm shocked, just shocked, thought Clem. "And after that?"

"When she . . . disappeared . . . June called me about two, said Cindy hadn't come home. I left work; we started looking. She didn't come home that night. We kept looking, for days."

"But you didn't report it. Why not?"

Nichols hesitated, then continued in a more emphatic tone. "My wife was afraid. She thought she'd be blamed. She didn't want to die in prison.

She just went fetal. To be honest, I doubted any jury would believe her."

Clem's ears perked up. Sometimes a change in inflection meant that what followed was rehearsed. A lie, or the truth but not the whole truth. "You might've been right," he said. "And she wouldn't have lasted a month in prison if everyone thought she'd killed her own daughter. Local code of honor."

"I've heard. Anyway, after two weeks of looking and waiting for the hospital to call, she begged for us to leave town. So we went east. I kept coming back to look for Cindy."

"What was her date of disappearance?"

"June 14th. A Monday. I'll never forget."

"Well, honestly, there wasn't anything you could've done. She probably died within a day or two of her disappearance."

Nichols paused, trying to choke back emotion. His voice was almost a whisper. "That's what I always thought."

"Look, if it's any comfort, she didn't suffer, far as we know. No torture, sexual stuff. She went with him willingly. He gave her an injection; she had no idea what was going on. It could've gone much, much worse for her."

Nichols loosed a cavernous sigh. "Thanks. That does help. More than you know."

Clem was perplexed. Nichols's reaction sounded like colossal relief, like he'd been nursing the hope for years. While most fathers would take solace in the knowledge that their child hadn't died a nightmarish death, they would still be devastated at losing hope that their child was alive somewhere. Nichols seemed as if he'd long accepted Cindy's death, the only question being how she'd died.

Clem finally spoke. "So. What now?"

"I just don't know. Now I'm afraid."

"Look, I can't say for sure, but you've lost your wife and daughter. Long as you're telling me the truth—and you'd better be—what you did was way stupid but not something they throw the book at you for. But get a lawyer and come in. It'll go lots worse if they collar you."

"It's the truth, I swear. And I'll think about it. I mean it."

"Don't wait too long."

"Okay." He took a wheezy breath. "I'll talk to a lawyer."

"Good move." Clem paused. "Now, why don't you tell me what you haven't yet." A gambit, but there was something Nichols hadn't come clean about.

"I . . . " His voice choked away to nothing.

Clem continued gently, "Mr. Nichols. I don't read you're lying. Just not telling the whole truth. I get the feeling you just don't want to go there. But I'm trying to catch this ghoul. If we're not copacetic, there'll be some pissed-off guys combing the Sierras for you an hour from now. Let's not do this the hard way, okay?"

Nichols snuffled thickly. "Late afternoon. The day she disappeared." He stopped, but Clem let him continue on his own. "I'd come home. June was driving the neighborhood, I was calling to see if she was at one of her friends. The phone rang . . . "

Clem's heart sank. "Cindy's killer." After they'd returned from the pet shop.

Nichols's voice tightened. "Yes. He said he had Cindy."

"And you were certain, because no one else knew Cindy was missing."

"Yes, that and . . . " He halted again. His breathing shallowed and quickened, as if he were having a heart attack. He let loose the low moan of a suffering animal.

"Mr. Nichols?"

The moan continued to half-throttle his speech. "I could hear *Sesame Street* on the TV. In the b-background. The theme song. Cindy was s-*singing along*. She always did, ever since she was four or five. I'd have known her voice anywhere." He paused. "Even now. He asked if we'd reported her missing yet. I said no . . . " The line went silent.

"Mr. Nichols. I need you to get this out on the table. Now."

There was a long pause. "He s-said, good. That Cindy would die quickly and peacefully. The next day. At noon. If we didn't say anything, report her missing . . . "

Clem froze. The reason Matthew had drugged her a day before killing her. "And?"

His voice became hoarse. "That she would still die the next day at noon if we did. But he would torture her to death. *With his knives*," Nichols sobbed, then slowly regained control, as if putting the unspeakable into words had lifted some of the burden. "Then he just hung up. He never called again. It was like he was just stating facts, not trying to taunt me."

"And I imagine you never told June."

"No. It was better for her to hope Cindy was out there alive somewhere."

"So you kept coming back, even though you were certain she was dead. For the sake of your wife. And you've spent four years wondering if Cindy's killer had kept his word. Until today. That's why you called me."

His voice was a brutalized, confessional whisper. "Yes, Inspector. That's why I called you."

Angie took Highway 280 back into San Francisco, oblivious to the mist-shrouded coastal mountain range and the sparkling inlets of Half Moon Bay. She was shaken from being at close quarters with Matthew's past. In some way, even seeing Cynthia pulled from the tank hadn't hit her so hard. Back then, the killer had been a man made of fog. She called Clem.

"I'm stuck here waiting for someone important," Clem said. "You should probably meet him too."

Half an hour later she parked at the Hall and worked her way upstairs.

Clem started things off. "So. Finally a motive. He killed Sis because she rejected him. Interesting, though. He was out of commission for days. Not the reaction I would've expected."

As she pondered Matthew's behavior, she heard an unfamiliar voice from outside Clem's door, a sonorous basso with a deep-south lilt: "Popping his psychopathic cherry." A long hooked nose edged into view in the doorway.

Clem grinned. "I'd know that beak even if you had four nose jobs. Billy, get your 'Bama ass in here. And stop teasing the women."

A balding head appeared with a pair of twinkling, crinkled eyes attached to the nose in question. Equally noticeable were his overlarge ears, which stuck out from his head in Mr. Potato Head fashion and were fringed with long hairs at the lobes. His threadbare, ill-tailored navy jacket was fatally rumpled, probably savaged by an overhead bin.

"Angie, my peckerwood buddy, Billy Rankin. FBI." Clem looked him up and down and scowled. "J. Edgar is spinning in his grave. Your wife promised to dress you herself before you got on the plane. Last time you were here six years back, I *begged* you to spring for a new jacket."

"She's busy putting up the peaches. And I *got* a new one, right after I left last time," Billy replied, proudly stretching his arms out for inspection.

"You check in? Or they just send you out back for kitchen scraps?"

"No, figured I'd set up housekeeping in your supply closet. Anyways, I'm up on things, 'cept Angie's adventure today."

Angie went through her lunch with Bridgett. "You were saying about a cherry?"

Billy nodded. "Even what was probably Matthew's first kill—Cynthia—was pretty antiseptic. His sis was his first in a way. Cynthia was probably a preparatory step."

"Like he knew he was going to kill Claire," continued Angie, "and created this alter-ego of her before he did?"

"Something along those lines. Even *he* probably wouldn't know what jumble of fantasies created her. Far as self-awareness, these folks are plain cattywampus."

Angie grinned. "Translation?"

Billy gave her a smile. "Sorry. In Yankee: off-kilter, like a picture you can't get to hang right."

Clem threw her a wink. "The Jethro shit's a put-on, but I have yet to prove it. So why the shock reaction to burning Claire?"

"At the time, killing her was probably the last thing he wanted," replied Billy. "Anyway, let's do us some prognosticating. We got us two 'primary' targets we know of: the doc who got him fired, and the girl who reminds him of Sis. I read the doc's next to go. But his ultimate target's Joanne."

Clem nodded. "Killing Joanne first might make Roderick anticlimactic."

"Goes back to Claire. Sis committed the ultimate transgression. Way he sees it, it was normal for his sexual attentions to zero in on her. Deep down, he had to resent the hell out of her, even downright hate her."

Clem considered it. "Because his father would beat him, humiliate him, and wouldn't lay a glove on her."

"Exactly. Kids in abuse situations often get through it if they have somebody they can do some commiserating with, a sibling who's also being abused. But Matthew's totally alone. Maybe Claire gloats, the way only kids can. She becomes the enemy; rape evens the score. And then she turns that topsy-turvy. Labels him a pervert and thwarts his dominance, two worst things she could do. Matthew's as narcissistic as a deb flouncing down the ballroom steps, anything impinges on his self-image and unveils the ugly truth'll set him to rage. She's forced his hand. He even feels a sense of grief, though only the most self-indulgent sort."

"So the tears on the Plexiglas. And Joanne?"

"She like as not symbolized an answer to his being 'forced' to kill Sis. It's 'supposed' to happen; he's 'supposed' to meet Joanne. And she spits in his salad. His rage must be something fierce, even more than towards Sis. Least Claire played her 'proper' role, then went 'bad.' Might could be he even blames others for her rebellion by now. But Joanne took away his vindication. That'll spiral into a new blood fantasy."

"But I think he's been intimidated," replied Clem.

"Well, it was months 'fore he built up to killing Sis. Maybe couldn't do it before he 'constructed' Cynthia. It made him feel more ready, even we don't know why. And those lunchroom antics with Joanne. And how intimidated he must've been by Sneezy, who'd tormented him for years in school.

"But it also ties in to his dying. He's had two stressors in his recent life we know of. First Claire's rejection four years back. He responded by doing whatever it was with Cynthia, then killing Claire. Then maybe hibernated for a while. And he learned he's dying, what, four months ago?" Clem nodded. "So mid-January. He likely had to construct some spiritual justification for his death. Nothing you or I'd see as spiritual. We'd think it was whacked. But after, we know he poisoned Daddy—February fifth, right? And killed Rohde in the tree . . . "

"Valentine's Day," interjected Angie.

"So he's taking care of business, longstanding fantasies first. Papa since before the training wheels came off his bike, Rohde since high school."

Clem eyed Billy. "And the cardiologist with the worms in his brain? My bunions say Matthew did it, but we don't have a clue as to why."

Billy shrugged. "I'd check out whether the guy had any business at San Francisco General while Matthew was there. Some altercation?"

Clem shook his head. "Nothing in his hospital file."

"At this point the guy's turbo; could just be the doc pissed on his shoe in the men's room. Anyway, he's on a timetable. Next two'll come quicker'n a sailor on shore leave. Protection?"

Clem bowed his head in disgusted defeat. "Call 911 and update your will."

Billy held his breath, as if stifling his anger. His voice came out hoarse and strained. "Lord, these people are pee in the fucking gene pool. We'll lose one, maybe both."

Clem nodded grimly. "Big week for motorcades."

"Give me a minute," Billy muttered. He disappeared out of earshot and returned a few minutes later. He handed Clem a slip of paper. "We've got a condo free on Cathedral Hill. No bodyguard, but the entryway's locked, and he'd have to get past lobby security. Get them in there tonight. Don't take no for an answer."

Clem nodded. "One question. Do we go public about Claire? Rattle him? We've leaked every other killing except where he poisoned Dad. I don't want that out 'til I sort out things at Soledad."

Billy thought it over and shook his head. "Not this time, Clem. Claire was a huge part of his life. She has a profound effect on what winds his clock even now. With serials, first kill almost always forms the kernel of everything comes after, and I think that's Cynthia and Claire, like two Janus heads. Each kill plugging up some ulcer in his soul. And that maybe held him for a while, but his impending death's torn 'em open again. I'll warrant that something you know about their life and death—something he won't know you know—will be the thing that trips him up."

Billy stood and picked up a black leather satchel that looked as if someone had used it for bomb disposal. "Well. Time to check in. But thought I saw my ol' pal Grunt outside. Let's stop by and be sociable."

Clem answered with an incredulous stare.

Billy's eyes twinkled. "I brung him a present." His drawl was off the cornpone scale.

Grunt was indeed at his desk in the far corner of the room by himself, shuffling files in the manner of someone skilled in the art of looking busy. He overflowed his police-issue armchair like a soufflé gone berserk. Angie caught a sour whiff of beer breath from a yard away, and his bushy mustache sported beernut husks.

Billy waved at Grunt as they approached. "Hey ol' buddy!"

Grunt looked up, spotted Billy, and buried his shock under a belligerent glare. He puffed out his chest and growled, "What the fuck do *you* want, asshole?"

Billy shook his head sadly. "Now, Grunt. That how you greet someone you ain't seen in six years?" Grunt's cavernous nostrils flared like a rhino's. Angie gathered that no one called him Grunt to his face. "And here I brung you a present all the way from Virginny."

With an officious bow, Billy presented Grunt a gift-wrapped package Angie took for a framed photo. He eyed it suspiciously, then snatched it away and unwrapped it.

Angie leaned over. It was a photo of Grunt standing with his arm around a balding, evil-looking man in glasses. They were both wearing the white robes of the Ku Klux Klan with the hoods pulled back. Behind them a huge cross burned in the night. It looked shockingly real.

Grunt looked up at Billy and gaped. "What the fuck . . . "

Billy gave him a shit-eating grin and lowered his voice almost to a whisper. "Hey Grunt, that's you with Ernest Clements, Grand Dragon of the Invisible Empire! See, I got me this old fishing buddy defected from FBI to spook land. And I'm talking spooks I mean spies, not the nigras like *you're* thinking. Anyways, he's in this hush-hush *dee*partment makes gag photos same like these. Like say there's someone we don't take kindly to in Iraq. Well, these guys, they do a spread to where he's maybe diddling this other guy we don't like neither."

Billy's smile became sly. "But here's the kicker. See, if it's a half-ass job, any discount wedding photographer knows it's fake, right? But *these* guys, they got a zillion-dollar gadget can make 'em a photo where no one can tell. Hell, even *they* can't tell when they's done. Shit, it even makes negatives."

Billy tossed several photos onto Grunt's desk, all shots of Grunt with the Grand Dragon: at a restaurant table, standing at a bar, sitting in a car. "Nice touch, that cross, huh? Anyways, *another* funny thing 'bout these guys: Ask to speak to 'em, well, guess what? No one's ever *heard* of 'em! No, they'll tell you they just don't *make* no fake photos, for that would be unchristian."

Billy paused. "Oh. And in case something bad happens—dog pees on 'em, whatever—now don't you worry. I'm giving Clem a whole extra set 'fore I go." He turned and strode toward the elevators, trailed by Angie and a smirking Clem.

Angie laughed so hard her eyes watered. Clem now had a set of gloss-ies of Grunt cheek by jowl with the country's most vicious racist, photos that any expert witness would conclude were genuine. And the Klan would probably roll out a tongue-in-cheek "no comment." They'd be tickled that the world thought they'd infiltrated the San Francisco police, even if they didn't have a clue what was going on. Add to that the previous complaint by brother officers and Billy's letter on file. Even Grunt's union pals would run for cover. He'd be pounding a rent-a-cop midshift a week after the photos hit the *Chronicle* crime desk.

Of course, Grunt could always tell Chief Jackson—the only high-ranking black man on the force—that the CIA did it.

Roderick folded two handkerchiefs and wiped off the door handle of her white Jaguar sedan, an exercise by now so routine that she'd occasionally blown it off. Still, she'd breathe easier when Matthew was dead. Just her luck that the only person she'd really screwed in her whole life happened to be a psycho killer.

The new Jag was the only luxury she allowed herself, and she loved peeling out into the purpled evening with an attention-getting whine. She worked eighty hours a week, much as she'd done for thirty-seven years since her fiancé, a med student who'd gone for medic duty at the tail end of Nam, had died screaming in a pit of shit-caked punjees in Cu Chi.

She still lived in the cramped, low-ceilinged duplex flat she'd rented for fifteen years. Truth was, she didn't much care for the place by now. But what with rent control, she was paying less than a third of market and couldn't bring herself to leave. The landlord would put out a contract on her if rents skyrocketed again.

Her most recent date had been more than a year back. And what with the gaggle of women stalking the wards, she was only halfway to the next one. A lot longer if the Parkinson's really kicked in, she thought with a shudder. She'd glanced at the web dating services, even hazarded a trial membership, though without posting her picture for fear they'd be howling hospital-wide the next day. She'd surmised that the men were seeking women twenty years their junior. Those willing to date someone in her mid-fifties seemed too near death to risk an attachment.

She tooled through the park with the windows gapped to take in the scent of eucalyptus and was soon thumbing the garage opener. Maybe a nice change of pace to get out of town, she thought as she trudged up the stairwell. Maybe Santa Monica. It would be good to walk on a real beach again. Not like the tiny pocket beaches of the North Coast, where the water was so chilly that you couldn't go in past your ankles.

She wasn't sure about taking Joanne, hesitant at trying to relate to someone young enough to be her daughter. She'd never had a child, and kids always seemed to shy away from her. And for that matter, there was the minor issue of whether Joanne would want to spend a month cheek by jowl with her authoritarian boss, Matthew or no Matthew. But at least she should sit down with Joanne and ask about her situation. Maybe even in the tech coffee room.

She couldn't suppress a smile. The staff would be aghast. She'd never set foot in there in twenty years.

The bulb at the top of the stairwell had burnt out a week before. Ever since the tremors, she'd been terrified of standing on stepladders and had put off replacing it. She passed the door to the Millers' downstairs flat in the dim light from the base of the steps. The crackling of something frying behind the door made her grind her teeth in irritation. Sometimes they whipped up a batch of fried chicken that left her flat smelling like a KFC for hours.

She reached the top of the stairwell in the dark, slipping the skeleton key in the ancient kitchen door lock by feel. It turned over with a familiar clink. But the door now opened into a flat that was, surprisingly, pitch-black. She always left the kitchen light on in the morning. She cursed it, quailing at the unavoidable ascent up the stepladder to change it.

She plunked her satchel in the doorway, leaned into the kitchen, reached out blindly and grabbed the countertop. She began to edge through the kitchen, sidestepping timidly towards the dining room arch, the location of the nearest light switch.

Her eyes had adjusted, but something was wrong. The flat was still utterly dark. By now, there should've been enough faint light coming through the front living room windows to make out the outlines of the dining table and chairs. She'd left the shades half-opened every day for probably five years.

A withering fear ripped through her, and her hands trembled uncontrollably. The kitchen light could be coincidence. But the shades meant someone had been here.

Or was here now.

In panic, she groped for the light switch and flipped. Nothing. And then the silence was broken by a hollow, humorless chuckle inches from her ear, and a harsh whisper full of ire.

"Hello, Scarecrow."

As the ice-cold towel slammed her face with the dizzying reek of chloroform, and the hand behind it jerked her head back until she thought her neck would snap and the arm pythoned her chest tightly enough to crack her ribs, it wasn't fear she felt.

What she felt was grief. A soul-scarring grief that there was no merciful knife slitting her throat, no bullet tunneling a bloody swath through her brain. Because it meant he wanted her alive: alive to face a universe of torment that would gape before her like the steaming jaws of Hell when she next awoke.

Clem called Corrections to get a list of Haitians and Haitian-Americans in Soledad but learned that ethnic profiling didn't cover them. Yet another call to the warden, only to find the scumbucket had left for the day, pointedly ignoring five messages. Larsen was running out of time.

He called Dr. Roderick on her cell and on her home land line for the second time, but no answer. Ditto Joanne. His desk clock hit 7:15, and Grace made her presence known on his cell.

"Clem, you'd better be putting your key in the ignition as we speak."

"Umm . . . almost there."

"Now look. I've put up with the table-for-one anniversaries. I've even gotten used to the fact that I can conjure up a homicide call just by leering at the knob of my lingerie drawer. And your only child has almost forgiven you for bugging out on her first piano recital."

"Look, I'm still sorry about that, okay? At least I caught the first half."

"The only reason she hasn't asked me to file for divorce and sole custody. I even tried my hand at gefilte fish tonight. Though I don't know how it'll work with the General Tso's."

He froze. General Tso's chicken. Grace had never accomplished a successful General Tso's, and she never ordered out. Only one person he knew could make decent General Tso's. He gritted his teeth just as he heard a shrill voice in the background.

"Fish? You call that *fish*? Even cat don't eat. See?" There followed the distinctive sound of a feline hiss.

"Mom, stop torturing the cat."

"Feh, I don't torture cat. Same like bird in coal mine. Cat don't eat, you don't eat."

"Resorting to weapons of mass destruction, huh?" Clem grumbled.

"You have only yourself to blame," Grace said curtly. "Twenty minutes or your fate will be hideous."

"Okay, twenty-five max," he replied just as a girlish background voice chimed in.

"Ewwww, Mom, do I have to eat that?"

"No, dear, it's just for your father."

He took the opportunity to hang up. When he'd first married Grace, she and his mother had spent years quietly despising each other. They'd worked out a grudging truce when Jenny was born, one that had somehow blossomed since then into an unholy alliance. He sometimes wished they still weren't speaking.

And although Grace usually laughed off his frequent absences, he knew she was dead serious; she'd brook only another year or two of Homicide before lowering the boom. But his resistance was limited to affectionate grumbling; the truth was, she'd been far more accommodating than most wives would be about having a husband whom you didn't dare ask, "how was your day?"

In part, even though she made twice what he did as a freelance graphic artist, she still had a traditional Han woman's respect for a paycheck with a pension at the tail end. Probably a genetic upshot of centuries of famine and flood in her ancestors' Hunan Province. And although most cop marriages were doomed, older Chinese couples seldom divorced; in fact, so far he'd even avoided the sexual desert creep that afflicted so many of his relatives' marriages. One cousin had told him that Chinese marriages never die, they just fade away.

To be sure, he'd faced down his share of come-hithers, especially from groupies who prowled the bars frequented by off-duty cops, where homicide inspectors were at the top of the food chain. He'd been jolted out of marital torpor more than once, and six years back, as a newly minted detective, he'd spent a month choking on a diet of agonized fantasies and marital guilt until the object of them gave up in disgust and took up with someone from Vice. But he'd never taken the fateful step of straying. And although he'd never asked, he somehow knew she hadn't either.

He tried Roderick for the third time at the hospital, but she didn't pick up. He made a mental note to stop by her place on the way home, mother or no mother. Then he called Joanne, also for the third time—this time on her home phone line. To his relief, she picked up.

"Joanne, you home?" And to think they said there were no stupid questions.

"Umm . . . yes. I just now got your cell phone messages. The battery died. I just recharged it."

"So are you packed? There's a squad car parked outside ready to move you into a secure FBI condo. Sorry, though, no bodyguard yet."

"Yup, I've been getting ready since I got the message. So why the new digs?"

Clem hesitated. "Look, Joanne, I hate to tell you this. But if I don't, we may both regret it. We're not letting this out, and I'm asking you not to say anything. But we're certain Matthew killed his sister."

Joanne gasped audibly. "*Jesus. Just Jesus . . .* "

Clem cringed as he heard her phone clatter in the cradle. One of his self-commandments was never to hide bad news from a potential vic. But he hated those moments of infuriating helplessness.

Clem assigned Angie to escort Billy to one of the storied meat and fish places near the Embarcadero, where the waiters wore white aprons and the dark wood booths—many of them with curtains—had entertained the city's elite for the better part of a century. She spent an hour grilling him about his cases, finishing with a laundry list of serials he'd helped bring to ground, along with a few who were still out there and would probably stay that way. The repartee was visceral enough to induce the touristy-looking couple in the booth across the aisle to change tables. It stayed empty, despite an 8:00 p.m. seating line snaking out the door.

"So why did you switch to this from Kidnapping?" Angie continued.

Billy grinned. "We don't tell anybody, but truth is, there's precious few ransom kidnaps."

"Most of them are custody snatches, right?"

"Exactly. Hell, even some ransom kidnaps turn out to be custody. Last one I worked, turned out the father arranged his son's kidnap, paid the ransom to himself and everything. Then, when the kid wasn't dropped off, his mother figured he'd been killed by the kidnappers."

"So she'd stop looking sooner or later. Christ, what a scumbag," replied Angie.

"And the Feebies tend to shy away from pedophile-type kidnaps 'cause the success rates are so low. Doesn't make for good press. But on the other hand, at any one time, there's maybe three or four hundred serial killers lurking around out there."

Angie's eyes widened. "Really? But I thought the number of serial kills per year was much lower."

"It is. Lot of 'em's in hibernation at any one time, waiting on some stressor to set 'em off. Others kick the habit as they get older."

"So what's it mean to be a profiler?"

"God's honest truth? Jack shit," Billy scoffed. "Half my colleagues have advanced degrees and they've never interviewed a witness. When they *do* interview someone, it's usually a serial killer in prison."

"Like Clarice and Hannibal? From *The Silence of the Lambs*?"

He chortled. "In their dreams. They come back to the office all starry-eyed carrying buckets of bullshit. Psychopaths are shameless self-promoters. I wouldn't waste an hour on one. Key to catchin' one's the stuff he never figures out for himself."

Angie raised both eyebrows.

"Most of these shitheads are cunning in a shallow sort of way," Billy continued. "They're good at burying the surface patterns where we'd catch 'em easy. It's the underlying stuff trips 'em up."

"What do you mean?"

"Well, when a serial buries one pattern, he almost always subconsciously creates another one to replace it. We're all creatures of habit; psychopaths far more than most. Let's take it to the ridiculous. Suppose we've picked up that each time a woman's killed with an identical MO, some time in the next two or three days some fella always goes to a bowling alley and bowls high-scoring games for eight or nine straight hours."

Angie nodded. "So somehow, that's his way of coming off the high of killing."

"Right. But let's say now the guy worries he's going to get caught. So he takes his show on the road, starts hitting other cities."

"Find a kill with the same MO, then check out the bowling alleys."

"Exactly. He can maybe change the city at will, but he can't do without his cool-down bowling. And he figures it's too innocuous for anyone to catch. He may even bowl in a different city than the one where he just did the deed. But somewhere, some guy's going to be spending eight hours rolling 250 and up."

"So what about Matthew's pattern?"

Billy shrugged. "If we knew what it was, we might already have him. There's two things worries me here. First is, he seems to kill with motive. On the one hand, it's easier to ID that kind of killer than someone who's random. Sounds callous, but we usually dredge up these patterns as he keeps killing. He stops following his killing pattern, we may lose the trail."

Angie grimaced. "Meaning we might not figure it out until after he kills Roderick and Joanne."

Billy nodded grimly. "If at all, much as I hate to say it. But even more, it's not even them that concerns me so much."

Angie's mouth snapped shut as she weathered a burst of indignation.

Billy smiled gently and held up a palm. "Hold it, hold it. Remember I live in a world of 'shit happens.' It's like being a heart surgeon. You stake a lot on saving someone, it'll eat your psychic lunch down to the parsley." He sighed. "What I mean is, what worries me most is what's next. After he either kills Roderick and Joanne despite our best efforts, or writes them off as untouchable because we can jerry-rig enough protection."

"You mean the poison."

Billy nodded. "And our protecting them may speed him up."

Angie shuddered. "The devil and the deep blue sea."

"Yup. One of those weird situations where the opportunity creates the motive. He probably wouldn't think of setting out to kill a couple hundred random people; he's not a Tim McVeigh in that sense. But the opportunity's been dumped in his lap. He'll see it as serendipity. And if he stays true to form, he won't be random. He's probably been putting all kinds of thought into drumming up a good reason to use it. Some group that 'deserves' it and becomes the focus."

"And once he builds up a head of steam—"

"Then we're looking at a body count on a scale this city has never seen. In the end, Matthew Larsen could be the country's biggest mass murderer since Osama bin Laden."

He checked the hangman's knot, grinning as he recalled the woman who'd brought his espresso at the café. She'd given him the oddest look when she'd seen the morbid image splashed on the screen.

The rope extended to the ceiling, looping through the planter hook in the corner. The other end was tied to the heat pipe of the radiator six feet from where Scarecrow stood. A piece of drawing paper was taped to the floor beneath her. She was naked below the waist, stripped to her bra above, her hands secured behind with duct tape, her mouth taped the same way.

She roused herself when he let go of her, throwing her weight on her trachea and constricting her breathing. Her eyes bugged as she reflexively balanced to keep from choking. He sat on the floor in front of her and focused the powerful xenon flashlight up onto her face in the dark.

"Hello, Doctor. You're looking well," he said quietly.

Her eyes widened as her predicament dawned. She tried to speak, but her voice was a moan behind the tape.

"I'm sorry, Doctor, it would be unseemly to listen to you beg. Death with dignity and so on. To cover the basics, we're doing a messy together. You're going to die by asphyxiation." *Her eyes bulged as she strained at the tape gripping her wrists. Her jaw fluttered crazily up and down.*

He smiled at her muffled cries. "How sweet. Our first 'moment.' You know, all of us have this fervent hope buried in our guts that death will come easily and quickly. And some pull it off. This one slips off like a baby to slumber. That one creams a telephone pole in a drunken stupor. Others drag it out, perhaps with some debilitating disease, but have the compensation of being able to set things right with God and man.

"But Doctor, a very few wake up one day to find they face a death so monstrous that even the most grizzled coroner will weep with rage at what he pieces together. And I wonder sometimes what it must feel like, as that terrible knowledge boils through the bloodstream."

He smiled gently. "But not enough to want to change places with you."

He stood up. "I'll give you the history of your messy. Honestly, I'm kind of jazzed about it. During World War II, there was a failed attempt on Hitler's life. The SS rounded up the culprits. He instructed the SS to torture them to death by the most fiendish means possible. Most of the stuff was pretty prosaic, the usual meat hooks and so on. But one participant, a Lieutenant Schleicher, arrived at an inspired means of hanging his victims. One so grotesque that the SS gave him a commendation." *He watched her eyes tear as she frenziedly shook her head.*

He set the flashlight on the floor. Then he walked over to where the rope was tied to the pipe, untied the knot, and pulled tightly, watching as she bridged up on tiptoes to keep from strangling. He tightened a bit more, so the balls of her feet strained for the floor, barely finding footing. He nodded with satisfaction and retied, then set the flashlight on the radiator so she could see him.

"Perfect. Hey, did you know you have to boil a hanging rope? Or it stretches and causes no end of problems." *He grinned.* "I've spent hours over a hot stove today. Anyway, what happens is that your foot muscles slowly give *out, producing excruciating agony when you try to stand. On the other hand, when you rest your feet, you'll begin to strangle. For a while it's a trade-off. You let yourself strangle while you rest your feet, then bridge up to stop strangling. I'll keep lowering the noose so you can keep at it. But eventually, the foot muscles reach failure, and you'll strangle to death. The time varies, but for someone of your body type, oh, say, eight hours. Amazing, the urge to stay alive as long as possible, despite the most hideous suffering as a result. So much easier to let oneself die. Which I urge you to do if you can. I won't interfere." He gave her a sad smile. "But you know? It never, ever happens."*

He took an adult diaper from a package on the floor and began taping it onto her. His tone was apologetic. "Sorry to invade your privacy. We're going to do a little painting, and this is a practical necessity. I mean, hey, I'll be wearing these myself in a few months." He secured the diaper tightly around her groin. "Comfy?"

She glared at him in defiant rage.

He stepped back to the radiator, picked up the long box of finger paints resting on top, and walked over to her. "I bought these for Cindy four years ago. But she just wanted to watch Sesame Street. Hey, you remember Cindy, right? Spiral fracture? Right humerus? Funny, just like mine." He unscrewed a green jar, fished out a glob, sat down in front of her, and wiped it onto the paper. She swung a feeble kick, connecting with his chest and knocking him backward.

He stood up and grinned. "Oops! Silly me. Look, no hard feelings, I'm not the vindictive sort. Though I admit I thought about having you stand on a hot plate instead of the floor. But a moot point." He walked over to the wall and flicked a switch, then shrugged. "No power."

He sat down again, this time to her side. "Some more green here." He opened another jar. "And yellow here and here."

She wrenched herself into an attempt at a clumsy side kick, to no avail.

"And some red here." He looked up at her. "Shouldn't be next to the green, right? Or it mixes and turns black. Too depressing. There, that's about right. Don't want to overdo it."

He stood up and walked over to the taut rope stretching to the pipe. "Oh. The diaper's because when people strangle by hanging, they usually lose control of their, well, their bodily functions. I'd almost missed it."

Her body spasmed and a high-pitched wail escaped from behind the tape. He leaned on the rope, carrying the balls of her feet into the air. She flailed and thrashed, her muffled cries now chuffing and guttural. He eased off and her feet began sloshing grotesque paint spatters onto the paper. He leaned and she lifted again, swinging like a pendulum, spreading the globs toward the edges of the paper, then finding foothold in the center as he eased her down again.

He sauntered to the edge of the paper and eyed it critically. She was breathing in choking heaves, mucus bubbling thickly down the silver tape. "You know? That's about right. If it's overdone, it'll lose the textures."

With one arm, he encircled her just below her hips and lifted her off the floor. With the other, he bent and pulled up the paper, then let go of her, leaving her flailing.

He taped the paper on the wall and eyed it in the beam. "Hm. Not bad for a first outing. I'm still wondering what to call it. Incidentally, Schleicher called this method of execution the Puppentanz, that is, the Puppet Dance. What a cut-up, huh?"

He took a marker from his pocket and wrote underneath, then nodded approvingly. "Fascinating what happened to him. The Russians caught him and sent him to a camp in Siberia. Moscow ordered his execution by firing squad. But the camp commander apparently had a reading deficit and instead buried him up to his neck in a lime pit for a few days. He just sort of melted."

He shined the light on his wrist. "Well, goodness. Here it is, going on nine. Look, if it's okay, I'm going to grab a burger." He held up her keys and gave her an apologetic smile. "Hope you don't mind; I don't get to drive a Jag too often. I'll be back in, oh, let's say, half an hour. You want anything? Burger? Fries?"

She looked at him with loathing, twisting in pain to keep her feet bridged up.

He nodded understandingly. "I didn't think so."

He headed for the door, then turned and faced her. "Oh. And in case you need it." He pointed at her hips. "The bathroom's right there."

CHAPTER TWELVE

Jojo sat at his desk, fending off discouragement. The search for garage apartments had been hours of door-to-door stuff that had him fantasizing a career change. Unlike last time, a canvass of video stores hadn't produced anything, other than sullen stares from a few staffers roused from an afternoon snooze. The Brazilian connection was their best bet. He'd tracked down the head of the civic association—a downtown lawyer—and passed along the sketch of Matthew.

This morning, he'd started by pulling a DMV list of recent title transfers for cars under the names "Matthew Larsen" and "Robert Larsen." What with his new orange ride, he'd likely ditched his old Toyota and bought something else. But Jojo came up empty. He expanded the search to transfers under the letter L, in case of a screwed-up data entry, and began running down the huge list. Chances were Matthew had put down a false name, but you never knew.

As he'd thought, no purchases in the name of "Robert" or "Matthew" or anything similar. But one thing did stand out. A '93 Subaru, purchased by one April Larsen two weeks back. He wondered why Matthew had put the car in his mother's name. He could've written down any name if he'd bought it through the classifieds. Dealers checked ID, but private owners seldom bothered.

It hit him as he flagged the car. Matthew knew he'd be dead soon enough. He couldn't put down a false name and leave the car to his mother.

But if it were in her name, it might revert to her after his death.

Such a nice boy, he mused, shaking his head.

Bernadette checked her watch as she turned into the driveway. Almost 8:30 a.m. She heaved a sigh of relief. Yesterday with her mom had been impossible. Before she'd headed to work, the old lady had started genuinely babbling, some outlandish tale about her renter from four years ago giving her a Tijuana snow globe. She even whined that Bernadette might be in danger. Bernadette finally picked the damn thing up off the coffee table, slammed open the sliding doors at the back of the house, and pitched it into the woods. It shattered satisfyingly against a tree trunk.

Not only that, she'd been besieged by calls from Angie. After the first one, she'd realized to her shock that she'd never cancelled the agent agreement in writing. So the bitch had pieced together that she had a shot at selling the place and was trying to horn in. Maybe the doctor had said something to someone. She'd refused to answer the calls, thanking her lucky stars she'd never signed up for voice mail.

She was happy to see that the yellow tape had been torn down. And she'd watched the San Francisco news last night for hours, flipping channel to channel. Not one shot of the house, just the little girl. She grabbed her purse and the envelope of documents she'd drawn up at the lawyer's, and waddled into the backyard. Spotting the huge trench and the yard-high pile of dirt a few feet away, she hissed an epithet. She pondered what to say about it to the doctor and decided to dole out a smidgen of truth: an old fuel tank she'd decided to remove before selling the place. No sweat, he couldn't know about the city's screwball UST regulations.

She unlocked the back door and went in. There was gray fingerprint dust everywhere but nothing that couldn't be explained away. As she stood at the foot of the steps, she debated whether to check the three upstairs bedrooms and the master bath. It would mean two trudges upstairs, one now and one later with the doc. She decided to be thorough, took a world-weary breath, and set out on the arduous climb.

As she conquered the landing, breathless as an overloaded Sherpa on Everest, she smelled something unpleasant. She continued doggedly toward the summit, the smell penetrating farther into her nostrils with each ponderous step. It became painfully recognizable as she reached the second floor hallway.

Some jerkoff hadn't flushed the damn toilet. Even if she flushed now, the place would stink to high heaven a while. She panted to the top step, mouth-breathed her wind back, walked down the hallway, and turned left into the bathroom with the offending toilet, hoping to God it hadn't overflowed. She held her breath, took the few steps past the ramshackle particleboard cabinets, and turned towards the Depression-era toilet bowl to the right. To her bewilderment, nothing was wrong. She bent over and sniffed. Everything seemed fine.

The smell was coming from one of the bedrooms.

She cursed her luck. A dead animal. She'd have to clean it up—and quick. She made a face. If it smelled this bad from twenty feet, it'd be unimaginable at close quarters. She clomped out of the bathroom and past the two bedroom doors towards the master bedroom at the end of the hall. Its door was half-opened inwards. She reached it and furtively edged it open.

The room was strangely gloomy. For some reason, the windows were covered with blankets. And what she saw in the faint light coming from the window edges didn't make sense either. In the left corner of the room stood a tall, gaunt, short-haired woman in bra and panties, her hands behind her back, her head bent forward. The smell seemed to be coming from her.

My God, thought Bernadette. A squatter.

"What the hell are you doing here? You get the fuck out of my house!" Bernadette screeched. She took a step closer. She could now make out the hangman's noose, the ligature bands, the suspiciously dark hue of the stranger's face, the swollen tongue. She cast her befuddled gaze at the woman's bare feet. She wasn't standing, Bernadette now saw. Her toes touched the floor, but her heels were suspended an inch above it. She looked up at the ceiling, jaw slackly agape, and saw the rope looped through the big planter hook and tied at the other end to the radiator pipe. She absently recalled selling the huge brass planter. She tried to remember how much she'd gotten for it, but drew a blank, and let her empty gaze wander down the woman's scrawny torso.

The woman wasn't wearing panties, as she'd first thought. She was wearing a light blue diaper, like a gigantic Pampers.

All at once, the various parts of her brain started chattering like monkeys. Her mouth slowly opened and closed like a goldfish in warm water. The room danced with flashing white fireflies, and her legs collapsed like rolling logs beneath her.

He watched with relief as she slowly emerged from the chloroform stupor, stretched out in the ancient clawfoot bathtub, the water covering her to her neck. A hell of a job getting her undressed and into the tub. He'd had to knock her out twice, a real fighter. And her greasy odor had sent him into dry heaves. But there she was, her hands secured behind her back with the ever-handy duct tape, her feet similarly bound. A rope was looped around her neck and secured to each of the tub's rear claw feet.

He wiped the sweat from his brow as her eyes opened and she looked up with vacuous puzzlement. "Umm . . . Doctor?"

He smiled pleasantly and leaned over. "Why, yes. Hello, Bernadette. I must say, the house is really quite lovely. Well, except for the dead woman hanging in the master bedroom. I'd expect you to take care of that before closing, of course."

"The dead . . . " Her memory began to trickle back through the chloroform fog. "What the hell am I doing in the bathtub?"

He went down on one knee and gave her an affectionate poke on the shoulder. "Oh, let's just call you a little ad lib of mine."

"Ad lib? Umm . . . ad lib to what?" It was sinking in that her hands and feet were bound. "Why am I tied up?" Her eyes filled with fear. She tried to sit up, but the loop around her neck tightened and gagged her, and she flopped back with a splash, gasping for breath.

"Well, not to quibble, but you're mostly taped up. As to why? Long story, but you're an ad lib to the Puppet Dance."

"The . . . the Puppet Dance? What the hell is a puppet dance?" she asked hoarsely, gingerly testing the rope again.

"The woman in the bedroom. She danced last night. The Puppet Dance. A bit disappointing: she lasted only five hours. Way off the mark. I mean, I even gave her two rest periods," he said with a shrug, then smiled. "Though the last hour was just magnificent."

Bernadette went pale. "Then . . . you're not . . . "

He laughed softly. "No, I haven't come here to get chiseled for half a mil. I'm the one who buried little Cindy in your backyard. And I made the doctor dance herself to death last night. Look, is all this starting to sink in? I'm kind of on a timetable."

Her eyes bulged and she began to shriek. He stood up. "We have ignition. Though I doubt anyone will hear you. No one's home next door, and all the windows are closed."

She continued to scream. He disappeared into the second bedroom and then reappeared, slowly dragging a large plastic barrel into the bathroom. He followed that with a second one. Bernadette stopped screeching.

"W-What're those?" she stuttered.

He pried the tops off, precipitating a hideous cacophony of clicking and scratching from inside. "Well, after talking with you, I decided I just had to add a San Francisco flavor to my messy. A local delicacy, it's usually us that eat them. But I wanted to see what happened if I let them turn the tables." He hefted a barrel and tipped it into the tub by the faucet. Dozens of enormous dark gray crabs tumbled out, each with a carapace six or seven inches in diameter and two razor-sharp claws. Bernadette began shrieking again, heaving and splashing waves of water out of the tub.

He emptied the second barrel. "Fifty all told. Species Cancer magister, *Dungeness crabs. You'll recall you asked me to get some for you," he said over her screeches. "Cost me more than four hundred bucks, actually. And let me tell you, what a job hauling these babies up the steps."*

He twisted the faucet, turning on a thin stream of cold water, then rested on his haunches and spoke over her squeals. "Your timing was impeccable, I'd just finished untying their claws. Now, the only problem is that they like dainty morsels for breakfast. Clams, little squiddies. I wasn't sure they'd feed on something so . . . well, big. Then again, they haven't eaten in a day and a half." He studied their behavior, eyeing Bernadette's sudden spasm of pain with an approving smile. "Hey, guys, that's the spirit! Okay, button it."

Bernadette stifled her wails, though rolling and whimpering with each savage pinch.

"Sorry I can't stay and watch the fun. Aside from this being a crime scene, I really need some shut-eye. So I'll be leaving you to your own devices."

He studied his watch. "Nine a.m. on the nose. Now, here's the fun part.

There's a clue visible from the street that someone's been here since the police finished up. If San Francisco's finest are sufficiently observant, they'll find you before the crabs eat enough of you to kill you. If they're not, well . . . " He smiled sympathetically and shrugged his shoulders.

"H-how long is that?" she whimpered, wrenching back and forth as a claw speared her calf.

He pondered her question, then grinned and shrugged again. "You know? I haven't got a clue."

She shrieked as one of the great crabs clambered up out of the water onto her flabby right breast and brandished its claws in her face. It reached out for her lip with one of the huge pincers. He teased it away, wiggling his fingers and distracting it until it lunged at him, nearly snagging a pinkie. He shook his head, giggling as she thrashed around until the crab gave up its perch and slid back in the water. "Why? Why?" she moaned.

He stood up, walked to the door, turned, and smiled broadly. "God's honest truth? Because you look like a bulldog with impetigo. Ciao . . . "

Towards 10:00 a.m., Clem tried Roderick on her home phone and her direct office line but got no answer. He dialed through the switchboard and reached the Radiology secretary.

"I'm sorry, Inspector. She's absent and hasn't called in."

"That unusual?"

"Not to be absent. But not to call in? First time I remember."

Clem felt a twinge of anxiety. Her house had been empty last night when he'd knocked. "When she comes in, have her call me right away."

He dialed Roderick's cell, and a man's voice answered, with a metallic whine in the background. He glanced at the screen and his notepad. It was the right number.

"I'm looking for Dr. Francine Roderick. Inspector Clemson Yao of the San Francisco Police."

"Doctor . . . just a moment, Inspector . . . " He sounded sleepy. His voice came back on a few seconds later, level and monotonous. "Ah, you mean Scarecrow. I'm so sorry, I completely forgot. You see, Scarecrow's, well . . . dead."

The line clicked and adrenaline exploded through him. He called

Dispatch and sent a unit to Roderick's apartment. Five minutes later he was patched through, and the responding officer got on the line.

"I'm here. Two-unit building, upper unit. I knocked, nothing. Crowbar the door? "

Clem assented. The line went silent for several minutes, then crackled.

"Okay, I'm in." The officer went off-line, then returned. "Nobody. Kitchen door to the garage is open. A valise on the floor near the door. Nothing in the garage: body or cars. No forcible entry, but kitchen door lock's Tinkertoy. Same with the door from the garage to the backyard. No one downstairs."

Matthew had probably cased the place ahead of time and learned how to pick the locks. She'd made it home, and he'd kidnapped her, probably in her car. "Yellow-tape the door."

He ordered up a crime scene team and rang Jackson. "Looks like Dr. Roderick bought it, Chief." He went through the morning's events.

"Shit. Just shit," Jackson spat out. "And we turned her down for protection. Clem, I don't know how long I can hold off the vampires. And guess whose Cantonese corpuscles are the main course."

"No surprise. I'll get a guard on Joanne, filch someone from Frazier at Taraval. Big mystery is, where's Roderick's body? Where's the crime scene? If not at her flat, we don't have a clue where it is."

Jackson grunted. "I'm hoping Nevada."

Clem put a "stolen" flag on Roderick's car, called Frazier, then called Joanne.

"Joanne. You at the hospital?"

"Umm . . . yes."

"You'll have a bodyguard within the hour. Sorry to tell you this, looks like Matthew got Dr. Roderick."

Joanne gasped, "Jesus."

"But we don't know the situation. My FBI honcho here is certain you're Matthew's next target. You're on 24-hour protection."

Her voice was taut. "My God. What in God's name did he do to her?"

"Honest, Joanne, I don't have a clue yet. I'm sure I'll know within twenty-four hours."

"Umm . . . now that I think about it, I'm not sure I want to know."

She paused. "I guess you must feel terrible too, since you tried to get her protection."

Clem's answer stuck in his throat.

"Inspector, I never thought I'd say this about anyone and mean it, but please make Matthew dead."

"Trust me, number one on my to-do list."

"And I'm sorry I hung up on you last time. Honest, I was just rattled."

"Joanne, we *all* are. At the moment I feel like the ass end of a diamond-back."

He hung up feeling a deep admiration for her. He'd seen plenty of pro-spective victims—even the most macho gangsters, ex-cons, and Mafia wise-guys—collapse into blubbering, hand-wringing twenty-car pileups in the face of being pursued by an implacable killer. And she was putting them to shame.

Angie was startled out of her morning coffee ritual by the sound of a heavy footfall on her wooden front porch. She entered the foyer and looked out the small glass door windows just in time to see a pair of baggy, porcine eyes register shock nearly equal to her own.

She opened the door and glared at Grunt. He looked like he'd slept in his suit. "Umm . . . did I have some sort of psychotic episode and invite you for coffee?"

Grunt reddened and shook his head. He waved a manila envelope at her. "Actually I was just droppin' these off. But since you're here, maybe we oughta sit down and talk." His stare ping-ponged between her face and the cleavage revealed by her terry cloth robe. She decided not to wrap it tighter; he would enjoy her discomfiture even more than the view.

"Sure, if you'll consent to being cuffed."

Grunt did his best to drum up a smile, but his eyes shot holes in it. "Hey, sorry we got off on the wrong foot. Trust me, you'll wanna have a look at these." He waved the envelope again.

Her heart lurched. Something was very amiss. She glowered at him. "Wipe your feet."

He followed her to the kitchen table, and she gestured him to a chair.

She was about to offer him coffee when he grinned and piped up, "Hey, that coffee smells great. I could use a cup." Now serving him would give him some sort of psychic upper hand. Since the glass coffee press on the table was half full, she couldn't figure out a way to refuse. She handed him a mug and contented herself with not offering cream or sugar.

He poured a cup, maintaining his ersatz smile. He rested a meaty palm on the envelope. "Gotta admit, Billy really fucked me royal there." He shook his head. "The friggin' Klan, who'd a figured? Anyway, guess Clem'll take me down."

Angie half-expected him to beg her to intercede. "Inspector, this is none of my business."

Grunt's smile darkened. "What, you thought I was gonna ask you to get Clem to call off the dogs?" He shrugged. "I get my pension in nine months. They won't pull that unless I push the Chief in front of a train or something." His smile vanished, and his eyes narrowed into slits. "And trust me, it definitely *is* your business." He thrust the envelope across the table at her.

She half-knew what it contained as she opened it. Twenty pages of photocopies of newspaper articles from twenty-two years back. The shooting and its dire aftermath.

The blood drained from her face. "You work fast."

He shook his head. "Not *that* fast. I started checkin' you out after I saw you at the pretzel cart. *Thought* you looked familiar. I probably saw that old pic of yours in half a dozen cop bars. I stopped by one, two nights ago, and got the whole spiel from a couple old beat buddies. One of 'em told me he thought you were Reserve now. I checked it out, found an Angie in the rolls. Only you were Dietrich then, not Strackan. So the bleeding hearts never caught on that you were back. And cops keep shit like that to themselves."

"But you won't, I take it."

He smirked. "Day I show up in the papers, you'll be right there the next column over." He paused as if for effect and held up a stubby finger. "By the way, did you know that if you've been dismissed from the Force, you're ineligible for the Reserves?"

She nodded slowly. She knew exactly where he was going.

He leaned forward and leered. "So if I don't miss my guess, you filed a false application five years back. I'm sure the old boys told you, 'no sweat.' I mean, who'd a thought it would matter? But *you* signed on the dotted line. Am I right?" He didn't wait for an answer. "And guess what? That DA who tried to fry you in your own blood way back when? Calloway? Now on the Board of Supervisors? Well, I hear our current DA owes him a few favors."

Angie felt numb to her toes. She'd not only be publicly kicked out of the Reserves, she could net a felony charge to boot.

He smirked. "Hey, don't sweat it, you'll probably get probation." He aped a look of surprise and banged a fist on the table. "Well, holy shit! It just come to me. Funny, I seen you twice lately with Clem. And then I come to find you're the Realtor on that house where they found the dead girl. Now, what am I bet you been working that case with him against the regs? Union'll *love* that one. If I'm *really* lucky, they'll put him out to pasture right next to me."

He stood up, reached in a suit pocket, and took out a pack of Camels. To her shock, he tapped out a cigarette and lit it with a Zippo. He leaned back against a tile counter, smugly enjoying a few deep drags, throwing in a smoke ring for good measure. Angie eyed him with cold fury. No one had smoked in her house since she and Roger had moved in nine years earlier.

He finally stepped up to the table, took a last slurp of coffee, and flipped the butt in the cup, ogling her cleavage a last time. "Well, it's been grand. Guess I'll head on down to the Hall. You have a great day."

Angie glared at him as she opened the door.

"Hey, look," he continued. "No hard feelings, okay? Honest, I don't like pulling this shit. I got a lot a respect for you actually, gunning down The Beast and all. Took some brass balls. After all, I'm still a cop, right?"

"Yeah, way way down there somewhere," she muttered.

His face flushed as he barged out the door. "Fucking cunt," he spat out as he tripped down the steps, turning his head back toward her to make sure she caught it.

She opened the kitchen windows to air the place out, then sat down at the kitchen table and took some deep breaths to quell her trembling. Her cell chirped.

Clem's voice was taut as a bowstring. "Angie, Matthew got Roderick. Last night or this morning. I'm at her place now."

Thoughts of the confrontation with Grunt vanished as Clem briefed her. She hung up stunned and afraid, pondering the new twist. Roderick had been a target, her fate probably horrific. Not knowing what it was or where it had transpired only added to the grimness.

Unlikely he'd choose some venue where the crime wouldn't be discovered. He had a bizarre streak of flamboyance. Far more likely he'd done the deed right under their noses. Billy had stressed that you looked for repetitive elements in crime scenes—not necessarily the most obvious ones, for example the staging of the girl in the tank. It might be something much more subtle. In Matthew's case, the only thing she could think of was the purposeful placing of a clue—like the two pipes in the wall—where someone observant enough would realize something had happened.

After an hour mulling over the possibilities, she settled on what seemed the only place that offered something: Janine's house. Forensics had finished two days ago. She dismissed the idea that Matthew would have the temerity to stage another killing there, until she thought about the reckless brinkmanship of the oak tree. If it were the crime scene, there'd be something she'd see from outside that would tip her off.

She pulled into the driveway and looked up at the house. At first glance, nothing seemed awry, but a closer look was more revealing. She couldn't see through the two windows on the upper left, the master bedroom. They were covered with dark blankets. Like the pipes, a tip-off, but a subtle one. Only people who'd been to the crime scene might notice. A patrol driving by wouldn't have a clue.

She tried Clem twice on her cell but got voice mail. She stewed for several minutes, knowing that what she was contemplating would have him steaming like a Calistoga geyser. She still had the house key, something that had slipped Bernadette's attention as well as her own. She pulled out her .357 from the door compartment and chambered the rounds. As she circled the house into the backyard, she looked up and saw that the side windows were also blocked. The master bedroom had been cut off from view. She unlocked the back door and stepped gingerly into the kitchen. Nothing amiss.

Everything was as she remembered as she kicked off her wooden clogs and edged into the living room, other than the gray powder that mottled the striped red wallpaper, the slate fireplace and mantel, the built-in plywood bookcases, and the wobbly banister leading upstairs.

As she worked her way up to the landing, the beginnings of a stench hit her amidships. Another step and she heard a faint whimper from upstairs. Creeping to the top of the steps, she heard an unmistakable groan. She peered into the gloom through the wide-open master bedroom door. In the dim light from the hallway, she could see a tall woman standing in the corner, completely still. Her saliva salted up as she ran to the doorjamb.

Angie now recognized the gaunt figure of Dr. Roderick hanging from a planter hook. She was convulsed by a shiver that ran like a tiny animal up her back, but there was nothing she could do. She checked the closet, then turned back into the hallway towards the bathroom to the sound of a low, anguished moan. The doors to the two other bedrooms were wide open. Someone was alive and suffering in the bathroom, but she couldn't risk Matthew coming at her, so she scoped out each one as she moved down the hall. Finally, she edged into the bathroom.

She stared down to the left at the bathtub and drew breath. A woman's bloody, ravaged face below a shock of matted, reddish-brown hair stuck up out of the water at the head of the tub. Skin hung off her gouged cheeks, nostrils, and triple chin in long bloody strips. Her lips were completely missing, revealing two rows of yellowed, crooked teeth in a hideous bloodstained leer. A rope looped about her saggy neck had notched its way into livid flesh, evidence of her Herculean efforts to sit up. The water was an opaque, pale red, and roiled with violent eddies. It reminded Angie of a scene from a TV show she'd seen about piranha, in which they tumultuously gorged on a peccary.

She let out a shriek as a huge dark gray crab spidered out of the water onto the woman's chest. It worked its way sideways to her face, eyestalks rotating, mandibles kneading in hunger, enormous claws at the ready. The woman began lolling her head, jaw slack at the waterline, eyes still clamped closed. Angie smashed the crab with the butt of her gun, bashing it against the wall of the tub and pinning it there. Its carapace cracked open, its legs flailed, and it went still. Angie let it drop into the water, which started boiling with voracious activity.

The woman's eyes, miraculously untouched, now opened and stared into space, startling Angie into recognition. It was her longtime nemesis, Bernadette, but in a condition Angie hadn't wished on her even in her most self-indulgent fantasies.

There was no way to haul Bernadette out of the tub, so she untied the rope from her neck and pulled the drain plug. Then she glanced around for something she could use to smash the ravenous crustaceans. She settled for the porcelain lid of the toilet tank and began bashing it up and down around Bernadette's torso, sending crab after crab to anguished death. For a second, Bernadette's eyes locked on her, and her look of terror suffused into one of burning fury, as if her predicament were somehow Angie's doing. She finally blinked into unconsciousness.

Minutes later, drenched with bloody water, arms aching from wielding the heavy lid, Angie stared down at the mashed shells, guts, and claws submerged in the few inches of water that refused to gurgle down the choked-up drain. She averted her eyes from the revolting hummock of minced, bleeding fat breathing in heaves above the waterline. She dialed 911 and secured an ambulance once she'd worked her way past the dispatcher's skepticism. Then she called Clem. This time, he answered.

"I found Roderick. And Bernadette." She filled him in on the mayhem.

"Jesus. Billy and I'll be there in twenty. I'll send a uniform to secure."

The ambulance arrived shortly, the black and white moments later. The two paramedics were aghast but quickly had Bernadette out of the tub and hooked to a bag of plasma. She was soon a mass of butterfly bandages. Once they had her carted downstairs and into the van, Angie approached one of them.

"Okay, what's the verdict?"

The six-foot, thirty-fiveish EMT shook his head in disbelief. He answered in a distinctive Rio Grande twang as he ran a hand through dishwater blond hair. "Damn. She's a mess, but she'll live. Most of the wounds were to small vessels. Once they're out of the water, they stop bleeding. No vital organs 'cepting her lips. Guess her brunch guests had a jones for soft tissues."

Angie cringed. *"Omigod. Did they . . . "*

"Nope, thighs were clamped tighter'n a nun's at a frat party." He glanced into the van and grinned. "Still are I think. She lost a couple pounds, but mostly looks like fat." He shook his head sadly. "God, I just *hate* these do-it-yourself lipo schemes. Will they ever learn . . . "

Angie couldn't help a belly laugh. "That's cold. You've got to be from Texas."

He gave her a broad smile. "El Paso, ma'am, born and bred."

"How long you think she was in there?"

"Like two hours maybe? Hard to say, I don't get many calls for hauling women out of tubs full of Dungeness crabs."

"Was she in a lot of danger?"

"Another hour or two, she wouldn't have made it; she'd have bled out. As it is, she's a plastic surgeon's wet dream. Not my department anymore, but who's the other one? The unfortunate missy suspended from the ceiling?"

"A doctor, from San Francisco General."

"Didn't know they made house calls," he replied laconically. "Y'all the police?"

"Real estate agent."

He gazed up at the house. "Tough listing?" he asked with rustic bemusement.

She gave him a sick smile. "Trust me, my worst ever."

The siren began to trill. He nodded to Angie. "Well, ma'am. It's been grand." He turned to take a seat next to Bernadette, then swiveled back and smiled, a bit bashfully, she thought. He was about to ask her out. Her bladder tightened.

"Umm . . . timing's never good in this biz. Any chance on meeting under less homicidal circumstances?"

Angie dredged up a mischievous smile and hid her trembling hands by clasping them behind her back. "Hm. You single?"

He held up a ringless left hand. She lowered her eyes in disappointment. "Oh dear. See, I only date married men."

He nodded, crestfallen. "Same here. Just looking for a walk on the wild side . . . "

Angie laughed and dug out a scrunched-up card from her jeans. "Give me a week though. I'm trying to catch the guy who screwed up my listing."

He shook his head in amazement. "Damn. You Realtors are a feisty lot. Gotta run. Oh." He pointed a finger to his chest. "Will Murdoch." He hopped into the van, and it sped off.

She felt the beginnings of vertigo at the prospect of sitting down across a table from a single man and was relieved it would be at least a week away. But he'd made her laugh under the most horrific circumstances. Not a bad start.

The beefy blond uniform ambled out and sat down heavily on the steps just as Clem and Billy screeched to a stop in front. Clem handed the uniform a roll of yellow tape, and Angie escorted them inside.

Clem's eyes narrowed. "This isn't my idea of 'help-out stuff.' May I at least assume you entered with the assistance of a key?" Angie nodded. "And that you're still the agent for the house? The correct answer is . . . "

She nodded again emphatically. Bernadette had never cancelled in writing.

"Good. See, that way I have some explanation to Jackson why this Angie character keeps turning up dead people. Last one, okay?"

She scrunched her head down like a turtle and nodded.

Upstairs, Billy shook his head as they stepped into the bedroom. "As my daddy used to say, well knock me down and steal m'teeth. Double feature."

Clem tried the lights, but Angie remembered that Bernadette had shut off the power despite her protests. He and Billy switched on Maglites.

The hanging body was suddenly bathed in their cold glare. Angie fought back a burst of tingling numbness and leaned against the wall. The pitiless light revealed half a dozen reddish-brown stripes of livid rope burns, the purple-blue lividity of her face that contrasted oddly with the pale hue of her shoulders, her puffy, lolling tongue, and swollen, hemorrhaged lips. Angie noted the exploded capillaries of her protruding eyeballs, the brown stipples on her eyelids and around her eyes—evidence of prolonged strangulation— and the absurd blue diaper taped around her bony loins. For an instant she transposed herself into the doomed doctor, saw herself choking and shitting in the noose at the hands of a pitiless, leering monster. The image pounded her, caving in her insides.

But just as she felt her knees giving out, she was absurdly reminded of a plucked wild turkey she'd seen hung by its scrawny neck from the awning of a cabin in the Blue Ridge Mountains when she'd stopped and asked directions, and she had to stifle a burst of sick laughter. A full-tilt attack of cop humor.

Billy snapped on latex and poked Roderick's arm. She swung stiffly like a grotesque pendulum, one toenail rhythmically brushing the floor with a hideous skritch.

Clem eyed Billy quizzically. "Rigor top to bottom. So she died yesterday sometime?"

"Early this morning. Poster child for accelerated rigor. Thin body type, and she probably struggled for hours, flooding herself with lactic. So onset's much faster. We often see it in torture vics." He pointed to her feet, their color by now a deep purple from the settling of blood in the lower extremities. "This one's a flabbergaster. Strangulation's a serial's MO of choice. Gives 'em that feeling of control, lets 'em prolong things if they want. But she could keep from strangling by standing on her toes, took her hours to die. See the multiple ligature marks, deep at the base, shallow up here? Resting, strangling. To die quicker, she'd have had to pull her feet off the floor, constricting the blood flow to her brain until she lost consciousness. Defeating the most primal instinct, the urge to breathe."

Clem nodded grimly. "Nearly impossible. Most hanging suicides don't fall far enough to break their necks and change their minds as soon as they start strangling. You'll see their fingernails embedded in the rope from trying to hold themselves up. And those people *want* to die. Imagine willing yourself to strangle to death when what you want is to *live*."

Billy peered at her face. "Started with duct tape. Pulled it off toward the end."

"It was on her a long time," Clem added. "Adhesive on her cheeks, skin burns. Lips torn up too. Probably tore it off so she could breathe through her mouth, to keep her going. By then, she couldn't muster a scream."

Angie couldn't look any longer and pointed to the far wall. "Look at this." A piece of paper was taped to the wall, covered with garish blotches of paint. In the center she could make out two smudged green footprints. The title was penned underneath in black marker in block letters.

SCARECROW'S PUPPET DANCE.

Clem walked over, gave it a once-over, and looked back at Roderick's feet. "Jesus wept. See the paint on the floor? And her feet, the paint. He had her sloshing around while she was strangling. It's over there," he finished, pointing to several covered jars in the corner.

Billy nodded grimly. "And he diapered her, so she wouldn't ruin it by losing control of her urination or defecation." He looked Clem in the eye. "Friend, he's just beat the fool out of you. Fact, a big part of why he did Bernadette. She's not a real target herself."

Angie brooded. "He did her more for effect, not revenge. That was an excuse."

Billy nodded. "That's why he didn't bother to set it up separate, so he could stick around and enjoy her suffering. She's a prop; he's just strutting his stuff at departmental expense."

Clem continued, "And he's on the money. Public doesn't get that we don't post guards at old crime scenes to make sure the guy doesn't come back and do it again. It'll look like the Three Stooges." He shook his head in disgust. "Y'know, I'm really getting sick of this guy."

Billy muttered, "Thank God his days are numbered."

Clem shrugged with resignation. "So are mine."

Angie looked at him wide-eyed. He shrugged. "I'll be off the case. This time tomorrow they'll be shoving me in the Iron Maiden on the steps of City Hall."

The news infuriated her. He would get masticated as part of somebody's political agenda, just as she'd almost been two decades before by the DA. And the city would probably shoot itself in the foot by assigning an incompetent. She stomped through the other bedrooms, tight-lipped with anger. Finally, she filched a pair of latex gloves and a Maglite from Billy and distracted herself checking over things she'd skipped while looking for Matthew. In a bathroom cabinet, she found a huge sky blue patent vinyl purse tacky enough to shame trailer trash and a sheaf of papers in a legal envelope. She couldn't imagine he'd kidnapped both women. He'd lured Bernadette somehow. She fetched Clem and he nodded permission.

She rifled the purse. "Bernadette's wallet, but no keys. I didn't see her car, so he probably drove off in it." She slid the papers from the envelope onto the shelf: ninety pages of boilerplates for the sale of the house, prepared by a Booneville attorney.

She paged through them. "He got her here under false pretenses. Called her or met her, told her he wanted to buy the place. Papers are a cash deal. That would've had her doing the Macarena."

"Just goes ta show ya," replied Clem, "never try to sell yourself. Always use an agent."

Angie took a deep breath and told Clem about her encounter with Grunt.

He took it all in and finally shrugged. "Well, to tell the truth, I wasn't sure I was going to pull his plug anyway. Far as Homicide goes, he's pretty harmless. Jackson won't give him a live suspect unless the guy's drenched in his wife's blood at the kitchen table sobbing, 'I'm so sorry, take me away.' Right now I mainly want him to stop fucking with me."

"So you'll both just declare victory and leave it alone?"

Clem nodded. "As long as I don't lower the boom, he'll leave you be. Sort of like the old days with the Soviets. Each of us with the big nuke, but nobody's stupid enough to push the button." He smiled thinly. "Of course, that doesn't mean I can't find some other way to make his life a living hell."

Jojo's phone rang. "Paulo Carvalho here." The head of the Brazilian civic association.

"Mr. Carvalho. Good to hear from you. So, you've got something? On the tenant?"

"Maybe, maybe not. A friend of a friend says we may have your boy."

"Do you know who the landlady is? Her address?"

"Not yet. Friend of a friend wanted to be sure she won't get hassled over her illegal unit."

"Don't worry, not my department. Does she know her tenant might be dangerous?"

"That I don't know either, but I doubt it. My friend just told me that his friend knew a woman from Rio in that neck of the woods who'd picked up a new tenant four months ago. White guy, thirties, glasses. But he doesn't know what the guy looks like. Even the landlady has seen him only a couple of times."

"So maybe a false alarm."

"Maybe," replied Carvalho. "But compared with, say, Chinese, there aren't too many Brazilian owners in San Francisco. They're mostly working-class renters. And most owners are from São Paulo, not Rio."

"Okay, maybe something to it. Get me that name and address. And better if nobody tipped her off. If he hasn't done anything to her so far, he probably won't. But if she freaks, he might pick up on it and react."

The phone rang again. It was Clem. "Well, we're running on vapors." He described the carnage at the Maury house.

"God, I hate to see you become the village leper," Jojo said. "But we may have a lead on where our monster's holed up." He relayed Carvalho's information.

"We'll meet there soon as you get the address. And no derring-do shit. Don't go in without backup. Meaning me."

"Wouldn't think of it. I'll bring the throwdown; it'll be a good shooting."

"Shooting's too good for him, now he's stuck me with dreams of giant crabs eating my face off. I'm gonna scalp the little Norwegian fucker alive and hang his goldilocks on my mantel."

Again he tossed and turned on his little bed. On the way back to his apartment, he'd looked forward to sinking into slumber as he entertained himself with replays of Scarecrow's hippity-hopping death rattles. Maybe indulging in a round of playtime once he'd zeroed in on the best ones, especially at the end when she'd started chuffing like a cat with a hairball. And he'd amused himself laying bets on whether Stink Woman would emerge from the tub to tell the tale.

But the landlady had chosen today to clean, and to boot had thrown some bossa nova on endless repeat, loud enough to hear over the vacuum. He liked some of it, especially avant-garde singers like Gilberto Gil. But her tastes ran to the Lawrence Welk variant, heavy on wheezing accordions. It was driving him batty.

Usually it wasn't a problem; he could go out for an hour. But now, all he wanted to do was fantasize and sleep, and he'd been trying to pull off first one and then the other for three hours. Even dissing Yao on Scarecrow's cell had brought only momentary pleasure. He looked at his watch. After noon already. He debated whether to go grab a sandwich.

But just as he gathered himself, the phone rang upstairs. The vacuum clicked off, the music turned down, and she answered. Her phone was in an alcove between the kitchen and the dining room over a corner of the garage, and he'd heard her gossiping away in Portuguese a dozen times. It might give him a shot at some shut-eye. The vacuum didn't faze him, nor her chattering, only those wretched, bleating accordions.

But now her words came quicker, and in a higher register. Her voice was tight and hoarse, as if she was trying not to speak too loudly, unaware that he could hear her almost down to a whisper through the floorboards. Might be nothing, but he needed to check it out. The attempt at secrecy was ludicrous, since he didn't speak Portuguese. But she was subconsciously trying to keep him from hearing.

He threw on his clothes, grabbed a foot-long kitchen knife, and bolted out the door, taking the flight of steps two at a time into the backyard. He edged up the rickety steps to the back door, keeping to the banister to avoid being seen from inside. The door was open, as usual, only the screen door locked. He leaned and peered into the kitchen. Her massive buttocks jutted into the hall from the alcove fifteen feet away. Her words were rapid and strained. His gut heaved as he caught the word "policia." He'd been made. He pulled back from the door. If she saw him and screamed, whoever was at the other end would call the cops, if he hadn't already. The thought crackled through him like electricity. He felt the urge to get in his car and drive.

And then it came, just like it had each time before. When he'd captured Sneezy, when he'd grabbed the doctor from the trail, when Scarecrow had stepped into her dining room. He was bathed in a steely calm, as if he were floating in cool, clear water. His anxiety evaporated and his deductive reasoning began firing like a machine gun. His picture hadn't shown up in the papers yet, so the caller had found out some other way. And he probably wouldn't call in the SWATs unless he was sure she'd left so she wouldn't get caught in a bloodbath. Yes, something was holding things back, so it paid not to cut and run. He had time to at least dig out his money and fetch the bird, the notebooks, and the poison.

He carefully ran over the Brazilian equation. Then it hit him like a jab to the chin. His thoughts scurried back to a call to his mother three months ago. He'd gone out of his way to tell her his landlady was from Rio, something she'd be sure to remember despite her usual bourbon torpor. She'd always wanted to go to Rio. He cursed his oversight. So the cops had questioned her and were sniffing around the Brazilian community. The landlady would probably call them now. But he could still bail out in orderly fashion if he could stop her.

The phone clattered in the cradle. Her broad shoulders and the back of her head with its frowsy, tangled black hair emerged from the alcove. She stood there a moment, as if debating what to do. He took the huge knife and slit an inch in the rusted screen by the handle, reached in with a finger and flipped the lever, then stealthily opened the door and crept in. The huge arc of her behind protruded again from the alcove. She'd turned back to the phone.

He ran the last few steps and grabbed a fistful of hair. Any greenhorn ninja knew that the proper technique was to come up behind, reach around her, grab her hair and jerk her head forward, forcing exposure of the jugular and carotids to the blade and negating the protection of the windpipe.

But damned if it just didn't feel right.

He jerked back as hard as he could. Her knees bent and her huge, round eyes bulged in shock at the ceiling. Her jaw gaped so hugely that he could see the glint of her silver fillings. He reached around her neck, and the finely honed steel began its journey in a slow, deliberate circle across her throat almost to her spine. She drove back into his chest and slammed him to the wall in an effort to evade the terrible blade, to no avail. He felt a grim satisfaction at the viscous sucking noise he more felt through the handle than heard as he worked the blade through the cartilage of her trachea like a cellist bowing an arpeggio. Finally, she convulsed and sagged in jets of blood, her head waggling on her neck like a lampshade with a missing wing nut. He barely sidestepped a spatter that pumped from her neck like wine from a bag as her body crumpled. He snatched the sticky receiver from her hand and replaced it.

He now absently shook his head in disapproval at the indelicacy of her execution, just as she gave up a last ragged gasp on the floor. She'd never been a target. There'd of course been a lowbrow thrill in the blood sport, and he would savor the syrupy gagging of that windpipe for days. But it was an enormous, untimely inconvenience.

And certainly, he would never have chosen such an insipid finish for any-one, target or no.

A slit throat. Egad.

No matter how well slit, it was beneath him. Slasher stuff, triter than trite. Even the infamous Ling Chi of imperial China, the Death by a Thousand Cuts, was more bark than bite. Most of the incisions were made postmortem after the condemned died of blood loss, to make him unpresentable to Heaven. And they'd usually doped the guy up with opium to keep him from jerking around and bleeding out.

Jeez, what fun was that?

And his frightful admonition to Nichols had been for effect, never intent. Cindy had been an exquisite piece of broken pottery, painstakingly glued back together, not carved into fleshly ribbons like human stroganoff. He'd actually cringed at portraying himself as a child-slicer. But if he hadn't been firm with Nichols, the whole spiritual foundation of the Cindy ritual would've toppled like a Lego skyscraper.

Yes, he could hear time's chariots, but he had a reputation to uphold. He glanced into the dining room, his eye alighting on the bowl of plastic fruit on the battered table. He'd grab the bird, the notebooks, the cash, the poison, and a few necessities, then park at the door. He could allow ten minutes give or take to spruce up the landlady.

His thoughts flew back to his musings at the Laundromat. Round and around she goes . . .

He'd have one pass, and it wouldn't be easy. Postmortem stuff risked the ignominy of signature kitsch and didn't have that vital nucleus: the gut-wrenching silent narrative, as the viewer pieced together the fearsome an-guish of the sufferer, finally waylaid by his own empathy into becoming one with him. Like a novitiate before the cross, reliving the rip of the spear as it sliced through Godly spleen, but minus the redemptive pablum. A great messy sledged away the delusion of goodness in the world, unmasked the mirage for the scorpion-plagued desert it was. It laid bare the inexorable triumph of the bestial, pulverizing the bulwarks of even those who went home every day and scrubbed off the stench of gore and putrefaction.

So no, it certainly couldn't be up there with Scarecrow or Sneezy.

But sometimes you just had to wing it.

• • •

Jojo drummed his fingers, hoping for a quick call from Carvalho with the landlady's name and address. He checked his watch. Almost one. Finally, the receptionist buzzed him.

"I just heard back," Carvalho sighed in exasperation. "He called and told her the tenant might be dangerous. Thought he was doing the right thing."

Jojo cursed under his breath. "Did he call the police?"

"No. He told her not to, they argued about it. He called ten minutes later, got her machine. Her name's Maria Saraiva. Jojo, I'm worried to death here."

"Okay, let's not jump to conclusions. Maybe she just ran off. Give me the address and phone." Jojo headed for the motor pool. On his way, he called Clem on his cell.

Clem answered immediately. "I'm still at Janine Maury's place, I'll head over with Billy. I won't go in 'til you get there. No squads, worst case we have a hostage situation."

"Second-worst case anyway. I'm there in ten minutes, heading out now. You bringing Angie?"

"Not where there's a chance of flying lead. And she's fiercely pissed. Trust me, that's something you don't want to experience."

Jojo grinned in spite of the tension. He could hear Angie furiously jaw-boning Clem in the background.

At Motor Pool, he learned with relief that he'd snagged an unmarked. Homicide didn't even allot one car per inspector, and he often had to arrive at a crime scene in a taxi. Once he'd been short of cash and had to take the bus. He popped the cherry on the roof, sped out of parking, and tried the landlady's number. The phone picked up with a distinctive hum. But to his surprise, a man's voice answered on the recording, with an ersatz Brazilian accent.

"*Bom dia.* You have reached Maria's House of Horrors. She cannot come to the phone right now because she is dead. So, there is no point in leaving a message. But come and see us any time you like. *Obrigado . . .* "

Jojo cursed and floored the accelerator. He called Clem. "Well, she's dead, he's gone." He relayed the phone message.

Moments later, Jojo pulled up to the white stucco house matching the address. He drove up the steep makeshift dirt driveway into the landscaped backyard and parked in the carport. The air by the back door reeked of engine exhaust, as if a car had just idled there. Clem pulled up almost instantly with Billy and got out, pistol drawn. "No chance he's here, but keep an eye peeled."

Clem and Billy followed Jojo to the back door of the house. Clem pointed out the slit in the screen. "Left the door open, didn't want us to have trouble getting in."

Jojo nodded. "He's got something he wants to show us." He burst into the kitchen shouting "Police!" knowing there'd be no answer.

Clem eyed the upright vacuum cleaner on the floor next to the time-worn porcelain sink. "Thought I heard vacuuming when I got him on the cell. She was upstairs doing housework."

Jojo examined the sink. "Blood and water. Final cleanup."

Billy leaned into the hallway to the dining room, empty but for a lake of blood that glistened black over the floorboards. "She's gone, bled out. No one could lose that much blood and live. Maybe half hour ago, no congealing. Spray spatter pattern on the wall, probably took her out at the neck standing up. She was at the phone. Blood on the receiver."

"His first slice and dice," Jojo muttered.

"Our baby's all grown up," added Clem behind him. "Music's still on. Probably why she didn't hear him." They inched into the dining room, edging along the wall to keep clear of the blood pool. A trail of it smeared the floorboards from the narrow hallway through the dining room and around the battered dining table to somewhere behind it.

They followed the trail around the table to the back, first seeing her splayed, black-sneakered feet. There followed a blood-drenched white apron tied around her stained blue jeans. Finally they could see her completely: thick-boned, heavy-bosomed torso stretched prone, hammy hands limp at her sides. A small pool of blood had formed on the floor where her head should have been. Lying on the floor near her shoulders were a bloodstained carving knife and a spattered claw hammer.

Billy leaned on the table, his face flushed. "Used . . . the hammer to bang on the knife to cut through her vertebrae. Hard as hell to cut off someone's head with just a knife, even one that big."

Jojo grimaced and eyed Billy quizzically. "Why drag the body over here?

Lot of work. She's big, bigger than he is I bet. Head or no head."

Billy eyed him grimly. "Staging. Didn't want the decapped body in the hall, it'd make the rest anticlimactic. Display centers on her head; I doubt he's got it stuck on the hood ornament. It's somewhere ahead."

They walked away from her corpse and stopped near the living room arch. A piece of paper was taped to the wall adjacent to the archway, smudged with bloody prints. Written with markers in alternating yellow and green letters was the phrase:

MATTHEW DOES CARMEN MIRANDA!

OR

HEAD ON A PLATTER

"Signed his work this time," remarked Billy. "Something real special."

They entered the living room and looked to the left. No one spoke. Finally, Jojo closed his eyes, swayed, and mumbled shakily, *"Madre de Dios . . ."*

Soft music played on the CD, "The Girl from Ipanema," an old-fashioned band with an accordion warbling the famous melody. An ancient record-player turntable had been pulled from the stereo cabinet and placed on a small coffee table in front of it, the cables trailing back into the shelf. On top of the turntable, a large, dark-skinned woman's head slowly spun around and around. One of her eyes bulged obscenely wide, the other was tightly shut. Her jaw was pried wide open with a broken-off ballpoint pen, supporting her head on the rotating platter and giving her cocoa-colored face a look of astonishment. A heap of plastic bananas, apples, and pears rose a foot above her head, nesting in her curly black hair. Rivulets of blood streamed from the raggedly hacked neck and dripped onto the table, where they collected in puddles on the oak-colored wood.

The room stank with the coppery, sweet reek of blood and an oppressive electrical smell. Wispy fingers of gray smoke began curling from the turntable; the blood by now had worked its way inside, boiling and scorching on its innards. They all started as a bluish spark finally shot from under the turntable with a low-pitched zap, followed by a billow of gray smoke. The platter slowly stopped turning, halting with the woman's hideous head facing them. The pall of smoke engulfed them, and the stench of ozone and fried blood choked the house.

The three detectives staggered as one out the door and vomited.

• • •

In the cool of the afternoon, he mused over an espresso at an umbrella café at the edge of the Mission and allowed himself a moment's gloating. He was more than pleased with his impromptu Brazilian sketch, along with his renewal of the severed head as objet d'art. Choppers the world over would kowtow like court eunuchs before the Son of Heaven. Fourteen minutes all told, four more than he'd planned, but he couldn't resist changing the phone message. And he'd bogged down on the turntable speed, sixteen rpm versus thirty-three and a third, switching back and forth before settling on the faster. It was still needling him, but he knew he was just being neurotic.

A mischievous grin twisted his lips. Not quite up there with Kemper, who'd buried the head of a victim in his mother's front yard, with the face angled upwards towards her bedroom window because she liked having people look up to her. Still, it would land him his own website.

But the exhilaration over his artful dodge vanished as he pondered his dicey situation. Like surviving an Andean plane crash only to find there was nothing to eat but dead passengers. He had to give Yao credit, even if the stunting at the Maury house and the landlady's would see him reassigned, if not cashiered. Yao had been a worthy adversary; he'd known that all along. But he'd never imagined that his offhand remark about Rio could've led to his near-capture.

He'd been saved by the goddamn accordions of all things.

He'd need new lodgings quickly. He had a candidate, a garage available two weeks back. On the basis of "just in case," he'd taken a look and met the crotchety landlord. It was overpriced, so probably his for the taking. He'd call, then head over after he tailed Honeypie from the hospital. It was in the Sunset, a long way from his turf, but he'd overstayed his welcome in the Castro anyway. Probably time to rotate cars too.

The Rio thing made two big blunders, though the other one—that surly cat of Claire's he'd neglected to exhume—hadn't come to anything. Dispatching the little beast hadn't even given him the nostalgic jolt he'd hoped for, even though he'd waited until weeks after Claire's death, feeding him and changing his stinking box. But he had to admit, even with all the hissing and growling as he jammed Speckle down on his haunches and swept in the dirt, his heart simply wasn't in it.

Nope, just one of those things you grew out of.

He'd only recalled the phone number on the collar after the yellow tape had gone up, but it didn't faze him. He'd been front-page news for two weeks, but not a word about Claire. Like any bureaucracy, the police department leaked like an off-brand condom. If they'd discovered anything, it would've made headlines. The notorious girl-killer now suspected in the death of his sister, blah blah blah. Claire's whore friend — he couldn't remember her name, no telling what it was anyway, all the girls had booth names like Bunny and Trashy — had maybe even left the life. By now, she was getting a bit long in the tooth for the peep.

B-something. Brenda? Brittany? Well, once he cleared the decks a bit, he could take a trip down memory lane and look her up. The Khmer Rouge thing with the acid and paint sprayer would do wonders for her complexion.

He indulged in a moment's wistfulness. For years he hadn't allowed himself to, after he'd reluctantly brought Claire to judgment. Only recently could he view those terrible days from a contemplative distance.

He'd offered her up, as Abraham had his son, the only time he'd ever received an unmistakable commandment. One misty afternoon after he'd finished Cindy's tomb, he'd been clicking through some links on California history. He'd just thought to distract himself from the bubbling of his indignation over his rejection by his sister. But as the tale of the minister spooled down the screen, the bustle of the café whited out as if engulfed by a blizzard, and his ears heard nothing but the tap of the terrible pendulum. He felt like a huge blowfish had inflated itself in his guts, its spines piercing him with a hundred ulcers. He read the story again and again, hoping he'd misconstrued, that it was just some impotent, anger-driven fantasy you never acted on.

He'd been tempted to beg forgiveness for her, time and time again. Even as he doused the pickup cab with gasoline, snaked the fuel-drenched cord through the driver's side window to the wad of gasoline-soaked paper towels filling her mouth, and locked the door, he'd silently hoped for a shred of mercy. But he had not asked. Instead, he surrendered Claire to the flames.

Because Tom Nichols had shown him the way of sacrifice.

He'd sworn not to look at her as she died. He bowed his head and tremblingly touched the match to the cord, watched the flame course the ground like a serpent of fire. But then he fell into the grip of a dreadful force, felt his neck wrenched up so his eyes riveted on her in the dim beam of the flashlight. As the flame reached the window, her eyes suddenly gleamed luminously in the dark. She banged desperately on the windshield as her mouth spewed torrents of liquid flame and the cab exploded in a fireball so intense that it blew the passenger window twenty feet into the brush.

After seconds that ticked off like hours, he staggered like a zombie down the overgrown byway to the side street where he'd parked, nearly forgetting the box holding the mewling Speckle. He drove to Gilroy in a fog of stupefying grief, relieved to find his mother passed out in her chair as expected. By the time she'd come to, he'd set the clocks back and pulled the fuse on the TV. She groggily made it halfway through her freshened drink and passed out again.

The sacrifice plunged him into a howling wilderness. But in those days when the sun came up like a blood blister, when he thought himself unable to clamber up the slick walls of his pit of horror, Cindy was always there.

Not that he was some delusional crackpot. She didn't flit around with a wand or anything. But in the blackest hours, when he would plant himself at the tank face every night, she was a beacon, hauling him back from the abyss.

Not until years later, when Honeypie began working his shift, did the fragmented events of his life begin to mesh. At first, he assumed Honeypie had been offered up as a substitute for Claire. A Claire perfected, not a drugged-out hooker who would spread her legs for any dick backed up by sufficient cash, even in the face of his offers to rescue her from her whorish life. But Honeypie? She spat in his face, with an emasculating contempt he'd never known.

And at first, he'd been blind with wrath, his soul shriveled up like rotten fruit. He hadn't understood why redemption should be dangled in his face, then jerked away when he reached for it, like when that scary fat Guatemalan kid used to steal his lunchbox. He'd already suffered so much, his despair echoing off the tunnel walls by the hour.

But it had been his own obtuseness that confounded him. He hadn't been offered redemption. Redemption implied he was less than whole.

No, what was offered was much greater: the healing balm of vengeance.

Oh, yes. Honeypie would grovel, as Claire had. She would puke and piss herself before his remorseless blows, as Claire had.

And finally, like Claire, she would die. But this time, he wouldn't glut on his own horror. No, this time, he'd exult in her exquisite debasement, savor every bone-cracking blow as he hammered her into whimpering jelly, luxuriate in every grisly detail as she blew blood bubbles and cursed her God with her last, tortured breath.

Honeypie had never been meant as a replacement, no, not for anything. She was to be his play toy. And oh, how he would play.

Clem and Billy returned to the Hall at five, haggard from the mountain of reporting work covering several murders and near-murders. Waiting on Clem's desk were two message slips asking him to see Jackson in his office, the last with exclamation points. By now, he was numbed by the assaults on his coply ego. For the first time in his stint in Homicide, he had to admit he might half-enjoy smugly watching Matthew mow down some other hapless inspector while he worked a nice, low-profile Man Two.

Clem waved the slips at Billy. "That one about the wolves? That's me."

Billy threw him a sardonic grin. "Like I've been eaten by wolves and shat off a cliff. Gang Task Force?"

Clem nodded. "Well, let's get it over with." Gang assignment was a backwater for homicide detectives. They were mostly intergang splatter fests, and rival gangs never talked to the cops. Instead, they avenged their honored dead themselves and tagged their names and colors on walls like frescoes of martyred saints, walls the unlucky owners were understandably hesitant to sandblast. The few witnesses who came forward often died for it. Even if you *did* finagle a solve, the result was a yawn from the powers that be, especially because half the killers got nothing more than a quick tour of Juvie until they reached majority. A third of the city's homicides were gangster, mostly in minority communities. And, like most cities, San Francisco had noisily proclaimed the formation of an antigang unit, which any homicide inspector worth his salt deftly avoided having anything to do with.

Clem trudged the fluorescent-lit hallway to the HQ Office of Investigations and waved a flaccid hello to the secretary. To his surprise, he wasn't made to cool his heels but was ushered in immediately. Jackson was parked at his desk, a tall, wiry, elegantly dressed black man with a full head of hair so snowy white people wondered whether he took Clorox to it. He stood up and shook hands. The formality was not a good sign.

"Sit down, Clem. Lot to talk about." Clem took a chair and cocked an expectant eyebrow. Jackson continued, "Mason called an hour ago."

"And cauldron bubble," Clem grumbled. Drew Mason, senior crime reporter at the *Chronicle* and their main leak channel. He was sympathetic to the Department, and was Jackson's *Monday Night Football* buddy, but couldn't avoid hanging them out to dry by now.

"Asked me if we're expecting any more murders at the Maury place. Said maybe he should just camp out there and wait for the next one." Jackson mustered a cynical grin.

Clem reddened and shrugged. "What can I say? Our boy's got *huevos*."

"Ostrich sized. And by the way, who's this Strackan lady keeps shoveling deadsters up my bunghole?"

Clem winced. It wouldn't do for his Police Reserve slumming to come out right now. "The Realtor for the Maury house. Every time she walks in there another corpse pops out."

Jackson eyed him over his glasses with the tired smile of someone who instinctively knew when he didn't want to know. "Tough line of work, realty. But maybe she can find something else to do with her time. Morgue's stacking up."

Clem grinned in relief. "She's already switched to macramé. Hey, you in the market for a place? Such a deal . . . "

"I'll ask the wife, she loves a bargain. You don't *get* between her and a yard sale. Anyway, Clem, you and I, we've cleaned the puke off each other's shoes a time or two. And I sure as hell don't blame you. Larsen would de-*huevo* any inspector we've got. Certainly worse than you." Clem nodded. The "but" was circling like a vulture.

It finally landed. "But City Hall, in their infinite fucked-uppery, they don't see it that way. They've already 'suggested' I consider another inspector. Tomorrow"—Jackson held up an eight-by-ten of Maria Saraiva's fruit-topped head—"it won't be a suggestion. I can give them an excuse about it taking a day to pick someone, getting his cases reassigned. And then"—he gave Clem an almost imperceptible wink—"word might not get to you for another twelve hours. These things happen." He glanced at his watch. "So say forty-eight hours. Stay away from the Hall. You strike gold, you'll get a tickertape. You don't . . . "

"Gang Task Force."

Jackson smiled thinly. "Just do it." He nodded, and Clem began to rise from his seat to go.

"Oh. And Clem?" Jackson lowered his voice. His eyes narrowed. "I don't take kindly to being shat on. Collar or corpse, your call. ACLU won't squawk, even *they* know when to pick their battles." He held up the picture again. "Gloves off, we'll back you up." He paused. "Even that asshole, Grunt. Racist fuckwad gives me shit, it's skin-slipped, liquefied decomps here on out. He'll blow beets 'til his first pension check," Jackson finished, referring to two especially nasty habits that decomposing flesh was heir to.

"I don't think you'll hear a peep out of him." Clem didn't bother to suppress an evil smile. "But the decomps would still be a nice touch."

Jackson's eyes twinkled. "You're right, they would." He jotted a note on his yellow pad.

"Of course that means he'll have to start testifying again," noted Clem.

"Not a problem. DA's springing for two months' lessons in . . . what's that word? Like the rain in Spain."

"Elocution?"

"Right. For him *and* Mumbles, three times a week. Fact, I just interviewed the instructor. Talks just like, umm, the guy from *Lawrence of Arabia*? Not Omar Sharif."

"Peter O'Toole?"

"That's the one. He gives them a passing grade or they both go to Traffic." You had to spend a decade with Jackson in the trenches to know he was smiling. Even his wife missed it sometimes.

"And?"

"I told the instructor to lighten up on the feather boas."

Clem's eyes widened. "Drag queen?" Grunt's bigotry was exceeded only by his homophobia.

Jackson paused. Another invisible smile. "Temporarily."

Clem gasped. "Jesus. Pre-op?"

"And loving it. Get him started, it's all he talks about. I told him Grunt was overseeing our gay outreach program next year. So, you finally got something on him. You taking him down?"

"Not for now. I wouldn't miss this for anything."

"At my age, better than sex. And this never happened." He shooed Clem off.

Clem pulled out his cell, crossed his fingers, and dialed Angie. "Now, is that my very favorite amateur homicide detective?"

"Hah. Don't even *think* I've let you off the hook yet."

"Just think, you could've been barfing breakfast in the yard with us."

"Hey, it's not like I've never yakked before. Anyway, I know it wouldn't be kosher to bring me to a potential shoot-out. So, they punch your ticket?"

"I have two days to bring back a body. So put on your most fashionable thinking cap. Tonight's a night off from mayhem. Matthew's finding another garage, picking up a few odds and ends. Napkins, silverware . . . "

"New kitchen knife . . . "

He winced and tried to think of a snappy cop crack, but it didn't come. "Sorry, off my feed. I feel kind of shitty about the landlady at the moment."

"You feel like you sicced Matthew on her?"

"He wouldn't have done her otherwise. She must have done something to where he sensed her fear. The lawyer who gave us the tip is howling bloody murder, talking a wrongful death suit. But it's like being asked if you want fries or the vegetable medley with your shit. It was our only lead." Clem sighed in resignation. "Anyway, change of subject. Let's meet at Matthew's digs tomorrow morning at nine. Forensics'll have some goodies. And I'm under instructions to steer clear of the Hall. Sucks there right now anyway."

"Too much *Schadenfreude*?"

"Schadenwho?"

"German expression. Taking a certain twisted pleasure in someone else's pain. Everyone feeling sorry for you, but they're actually sort of enjoying it."

"Yeah, my Jewish friend says that's why God gave them Israel instead of Florida." Clem hung up and dialed Joanne.

"Hello, Inspector. Thank you for the fine young officer following in my footsteps. I feel a lot better. Especially with that cannon he's got in his holster."

"You home now?"

"Getting there. I'm in the back of the squad car on my way to the condo. It's a weird feeling. Everyone's looking at me like they can't figure out if I'm a VIP or I'm under arrest. I told him to put on the siren, but he says he's not allowed. Can you talk to him about that?"

Clem grinned. "Don't push your luck. Anyway, there'll be another guy on tomorrow morning at five. He'll take you to the hospital and follow you around until five. Et cetera."

"I've got the hang of it. Umm . . . did you find out yet what happened to Dr. Roderick?"

Clem paused. "We found her. Forensics is still piecing things together, and I'm not allowed to release anything until they get through, even to you. But you'll be the first to know." The truth was, he had the feeling that Joanne was achieving a much-needed equilibrium, and he didn't want to rip it raw with a blow-by-blow of Roderick's grisly death.

"Okay, I understand. And thanks again. Now, kindly let me enjoy my chauffeur in peace . . ."

He tailed the black and white only a short way. He was getting butterflies about the Subaru. Tomorrow he'd find some new wheels, get long-term parking for the Subaru someplace near the airport. He'd called the old coot, and the Sunset place was still available. Amazing how easy tonight's move-in would be. The bird, forty-two notebooks, microwave and TV, a hundred or so bags of popcorn, two-suiter of clothes, fourteen thousand bucks, and, near as he could figure, three hundred doses of dimethyl mercury.

He should've expected the protection. Funny they'd never assigned it for Scarecrow, who anyone could figure was on his list. Honeypie would've taken some digging. He puzzled a moment before it came to him. It had taken Yao a strangulation murder to get the overtime.

Not that it fazed him. He knew where the chinks in the armor would be, while the uniform wouldn't have a clue. Showing her a good time under the noses of the gumshoes would even put the chief's job on the line. Tonight, he'd follow until he knew whether she was going home or not. That would tell him a lot about tomorrow, when he'd begin the hunt in earnest.

And after he'd wreaked justice on her, he'd spend some time refining the Big One, the one that would burn him into San Francisco's memory. And it would give him the numbers. Not that he was obsessed with quantity. But when you were talking centuries, boutique killers simply didn't have the shelf life. He'd be on it full time after past-tensing Honeypie.

He knew it would be the whores. Legions of them, like the ones who'd sucked Claire into their sleazy, stinking universe. He would touch them, one by one, and they would die. Die by the hundreds. Die until the few left alive had fled back to where they'd come from in quaking fear.

He'd spend a month of days and nights in the neon-walled, Pine Sol–scented dark of the city's girl clubs. He'd buy lap dances, squeeze their fake tits and cup their ass cheeks, sneak a dab of quicksilver in their infectious pussies for an extra twenty. And once in awhile he'd fuck one, the tip of the condom smeared in the garish cabana light with the faintest oily smudge, his liquid death pounding half a foot inside her to the tune of her perfunctory cooing. He'd be the house favorite, the overpaying geek. They'd laugh contemptuously behind his back as they jiggled away with wads of his cash.

And then, he'd just disappear. Maybe they'd wonder what happened to him as they zeroed in on the next mark. And not too long after, they'd begin to numb, and shake, and shuffle, and drool, until they couldn't find a john willing to let them suck him off for a crack hit.

He could almost see the hordes of tongue-speaking Bible thumpers pouring from church buses, caterwauling "Onward Christian Soldiers," and waving their placards in front of the clubs. Trumpeting another plague of vengeance on fornicators. The loonier ones would proclaim him some latter-day Old Testament hero, even if poisoning whores didn't have quite the Mosaic pizzazz of pouring molten gold down the throats of calf-worshiping idolators.

But the final irony would be sublime. Hundreds of twitching whores dumped like bags of rancid garbage on the steps of San Francisco General, the only place legally bound to take them. Roth would need a whole wing for them, along with a budgetary supplement he'd never get.

And truth was, he'd never been able to get up the oomph to do Roth à la Roderick. Scarecrow may have french-fried his brain, but she was also the most brilliant person he'd ever known. And in every great messy there was an homage to the victim, that they'd been worth that much effort. Even Sneezy. A lout, but somehow even his father hadn't inspired such raw fear. Roth? Just another pathetic, blowhard bureaucrat. Not even worth a nickname.

And he'd always known he was strictly hetero. The idea of debasing and destroying a man—even Sneezy and Dear Old Dad, not to mention the Early Bird messy he'd pulled off on that doc Honeypie had the hots for—didn't give him that prickle in the groin he'd gotten from Scarecrow, the one that would mushroom into a bloom of heat while he hammered Honeypie into living red muck. He grinned at the swelling that hadn't been there thirty seconds ago. He might have to adjust his plans, have a go at that promising little ass before grinding her into unrecognizable gore.

In fact, now that the thought struck him, it was a must.

The anticipation made him lightheaded. He'd only done Claire that way once, when she had been in a drug-laced coma, had at that ass long and hard enough so she'd come-to limping and hemorrhaging. Like few things on earth, reality had eclipsed anticipation. But it had sent her over the edge, and he only belatedly realized it had been a tactical error.

Her own fault of course. He'd broached it a dozen times, and she'd always refused, even in a coked-out stupor. She'd had to expect he'd exercise his privileges eventually. But he knew right away he'd erred in doing her while she was out cold. What he should've done was mete out the necessary discipline. She would've fought, to be sure, but sooner or later she'd have accepted her duty. And anyway, he always enjoyed when she got a little ornery, even at the cost of a scratch or two. It reminded him of that first time so long ago, mere weeks after the long-awaited appearance of that first Playtex junior miss in the bathroom wastebasket.

He'd thought about having it bronzed.

But Honeypie would be something else entirely. He would show her his hardness, rub himself all over her cheeks and hair, let her know exactly what he would do to her, and—of course—what he would do to the rest of her as soon as he finished pounding at that delectable ass.

He grinned impishly. That way, she'd never want him to stop.

He nodded knowingly as the squad car with its doomed cargo turned down the street toward the new condo. If the pattern held, he'd have first shot at her tomorrow. Maybe catch them off guard, not expecting him to strike so soon af- ter today's bloodbath and eviction.

He checked his watch. A couple of free hours. Plenty of time to hit the Bangkok Theater on Market. Despite a couple of visits, he still hadn't quite settled on his inaugural mark. Cookie was still his best bet; after he'd anted up fifty for a nude lap dance, she'd promised him three songs, but had begged off to pee after two. But more important, she was no scabrous, dead-eyed skank. Those he would leave to their own horrific fates. No, she was a fresh-faced new- bie barely off the bus from Montana, not yet ravaged by booze, drugs, and the empty words of the rescuer types. Just the star quality he needed, anybody's daughter who took a wrong turn and found herself in the dragon's maw.

He sighed contentedly. After he'd merc'd them all, he'd pop off emails to CNN and the locals, naming Cookie as the overture to his magnum opus, the Bride to his Frankenstein. She'd learn of her grotesque fate when they shoved a brace of microphones and cameras in her face after her shift. There'd be in- terview offers out the nines. Hell, maybe even a group hug on Oprah if she got lucky. And everything capped by a tear-jerking candlelight death vigil. He'd have to triple dose her so she'd be the first to the finish line.

She'd be the most legendary whore ever to drop her panties. And after all, didn't everyone deserve their fifteen minutes of fame?

At the Soledad front desk, Jojo drummed his fingers and eyed the guard. "Anything?"

The guard scowled. "Well, let's just see. I mean, it's been twelve whole minutes since *last* time I checked." He dialed the warden's line, spoke, then listened and hung up. "Look, secretary says he's in a meeting the next half hour. Then he's got some dinner deal with the city council. She can't squeeze you in."

Jojo rolled his eyes. "I'll walk him to his car if I have to." He paused. "Hey, you guys have a water truck?" Clem had said not to tell any guards why he'd spent the last hour here twiddling thumbs. But no reason he couldn't snoop.

"You thirsty? Yeah, we got a water truck. Water from the wells tastes like it's aerated with cow farts. They say it's the septic tanks and pesticides.

Sometimes we truck in water for drinking, use the well stuff for flushing crappers and laundry."

"Any chance I could get a peek?"

The guard eyed him suspiciously. "Not a one. Last time I extended you folks a professional courtesy, we got butt-fucked for letting Larsen's kid poison him."

It was after visiting hours, and the place was empty. Jojo pulled out his wallet, sidled over to the desk, and passed a hand over the counter. "How about an unprofessional courtesy?"

The guard palmed the ten with the dexterity of a blackjack dealer. "Funny, I'm feeling much more courteous now." He broke into a snicker. "Have a look yourself. By now it's back, parked in the lot across from visitor parking. Water connection's outside the walls; we don't park it inside except for maintenance."

Jojo ignored getting his clock cleaned. "Maintenance. At the motor pool?" The guard nodded smugly and returned to his magazine.

Jojo passed back through the checkpoints into the lot behind a high cyclone fence topped with whorls of barbed concertina. The dusty forest green diesel truck with its massive water tank and valves was parked across from the visitor spots against the prison wall. Jojo circled it.

Then his blood froze. Three huge well-worn tires. And one new one, so new that little pieces of factory rubber sprouted from its treads like thick black hairs.

He hurried back to the desk. "What's with the new tire?"

The guard looked suspicious. "Had a flat this afternoon. Why you want to know?"

"Sorry, police business."

The guard's eyes narrowed. "Our friggin' water truck tire's police business?"

"Long story. So what happened to the flat?"

The guard seemed uncomfortable, probably undecided about how much he should say or not say to a homicide detective. "Guess it's still at motor pool."

"What'll they do with it? And when?"

"Buddy, I'm feeling some serious discourtesy coming on."

Jojo scowled and passed the guard another ten. "That's all I've got."

"It'll do. Tires we dispose of special. Environmental regs, so we don't send 'em out with regular garbage. They go to a tire disposal facility."

"When does it ship out?"

"That's worth twenty. Dispatch'll know." He called, asked about the tire, and hung up. "Tomorrow morning at seven, soon as the motor pool opens. There, you happy?"

Jojo felt like he'd stuck his finger in a light bulb socket. "Decidedly not. When does the motor pool shut down?"

"Locks down 7:00 p.m." He glanced at the wall clock. "In forty minutes, controlled from the security center. Nice doing business with ya."

The necklace was going down within the hour. If it hadn't already. He reached for the phone. "I need to call the warden. Now."

The guard slapped a hand on it with a stony glare. "As friggin' *if.* You've overstayed your welcome."

The guard was probably safe, Jojo decided. He was uncomfortable, not because he *knew* why Jojo was asking questions, but because he didn't. "I'm informing you now, we have strong reason to suspect that Robert Larsen is about to be burned to death in the motor pool. Keep me from using that phone and you *will* be charged, possibly with accessory to murder."

The guard went pie-eyed, handed Jojo the receiver, and poked in the extension.

The secretary answered levelly. "Warden Fallon's office."

"Inspector Locsin of San Francisco Homicide. I need to speak to the warden immediately."

She replied with the robotic tone of a seasoned gatekeeper. "I'm sorry, sir. Warden Fallon is in a meeting, then he's finished for the day. As I told the guard, it would be better to arrange an appointment."

Jojo's voice darkened. "This is a life-and-death matter. I insist that you interrupt his meeting, now, and put him on the phone with me."

Her tone took on a mulish edge. "It's an important meeting, sir. I can squeeze you in fifteen minutes tomorrow at ten forty-five."

The warden had probably told her to ignore their calls. Time to take an

ax to it. "Ma'am, if it hasn't happened already, in the next half hour someone's going to slam a tire around inmate Robert Larsen's chest, douse it with
gasoline, and set him on fire. Trust that your name will come up afterwards."
He slammed down the phone.

Two minutes later, the portly, balding Bud Fallon sputtered red-faced
into the room, wearing a dark gray suit that had clearly been tailored pre-
desk spread. His shirt buttons threatened to punch holes in his tie and ping
off the walls.

He scanned for witnesses, then locked eyes with Jojo. "Son, I don't know
who the hell you think you are, but I'm deciding whether I should kick your
ass *before* or *after* you give me an explanation." He walked slowly towards
Jojo as if intending to make good the threat.

DOC bureaucrats were accustomed to the mail-fisted quashing of scan-
dals ranging from medical negligence to inmates coerced into bare-knuckle
cage fights. The prisons were fiefdoms under the sway of the state's most
powerful employee union. While supervisors and the guards were often at
loggerheads, they all benefited from the union's massive political contribu-
tions to both sides, and the DOC wrote its own ticket in Sacramento. Jojo
knew he had to meet macho with macho.

He stood up. "Explanation? Just a hideous murder plot you won't give
us the time of day on. Ready to kick that ass now? Just a hint: I'm a sucker
for a right-hand lead."

Fallon rolled his eyes contemptuously but reconsidered slugging it out.
"Son, do you know how many hideous murder plots I hear about? They
never pan out. When somebody *does* get whacked, you don't hear about it
beforehand."

"So how many come from San Francisco Homicide? That's not worth
the benefit of the doubt?"

Fallon's expression said "shit, no" in caps. He listened contemptuously
as Jojo went through their suspicions about the necklace. When he was done,
the warden barely restrained a sneer. "And I'm Nelson fucking Mandela.
Look, I checked into it when I got your boss's Chicken Little letter. Larsen's
in isolation. And Nuestra won't fuck up their world just to off a nobody like
Larsen. Especially something that outlandish. It's not Soledad style."

"It's a contract hit. It wouldn't have been accepted without the grease to pry Larsen out of isolation. And Nuestra won't do it themselves; they'll sub it out, maybe to a Haitian. Haitian mobs have this thing for necklacing."

For the first time, the warden looked doubtful.

Jojo continued, "You got a Haitian in here? Certified bottom feeder?"

Fallon eyed the guard. After only two months, he didn't have a handle on his tenants yet. But the guards made it their business to know inmate jackets inside and out.

The guard nodded. "Antoine Lacroix, real blue meanie. Gang leader in Haiti; came over to run one of the Miami gangs. Put a hit on some retired Haitian political bigwig lives in Malibu. We extradited him from Florida. Now he's trying to get deported back to Haiti. Hard to imagine why. Everyone there's trying to leave."

But it made sense. Gangs in Haiti were in cahoots with the government or the opposition. He'd probably cut a deal with the Haitian government to request his extradition. The government would slap his wrist and quietly get him out on the street, doing their bidding. Maybe they'd even given him the Malibu hit.

And deported was deported. A free pass to do Larsen.

Jojo cocked an eyebrow. "So what makes him such a sweetie?"

The guard grimaced. "He did the Malibu guy Haitian style, with a machete. Took a while."

Jojo nodded. "That'll work. Warden, can you tell me where Lacroix is right now? And Larsen? If you can, and you can keep it that way for an hour, I'll leave you in peace."

"Lacroix would be in his cell, the day room, or at chow. Larsen in the iso block; they eat there." The warden picked up the phone to track down Lacroix. He was scheduled for dinner, so the call transferred to the cafeteria station. A silent moment passed, and then the warden darkened several shades. "So where the fuck is he? Find him! Now!"

He began to call isolation, but Jojo cut the connection. "Larsen will be at the motor pool or on his way there. Which is exactly where *we* need to be. They can't wait any longer; they'd need time afterward to tidy up the mess."

"Quicker to call the station covering the motor pool. Send them in."

Jojo shook his head. "There's guards in on this. At isolation and the motor pool, maybe more. We might just hurry them up. How far is the motor pool?"

"Five minutes double time."

"You pack heat up here?"

"Major heat," Fallon replied, and nodded to the guard. The guard reached under the counter, pulled out a menacing-looking combat-modified pump shotgun, checked the safety, and handed it to the warden. Jojo pulled back his lapel and displayed his Glock nine millimeter.

The warden gave it a dour glance. "Against regs to take that inside. Keep a hand on it at all times." Then he looked at the guard and said in a firm voice, "Open." The guard hit a button behind the counter. The great steel gate to the prison interior slowly slid open with an electrical hum, capped by an ominous, echoing clang as it locked open, a sound like no other.

Jojo and the warden passed through, fidgeted as the massive gate closed and a second one opened, then passed through and loped down a long, gray cellblock corridor a hundred yards to the next checkpoint. The next guard looked at Fallon curiously as he opened the gate, but without the panicked look of someone in on a deal about to go badly south. They ran down the next seemingly endless corridor. Jojo held back as the warden became winded.

As they charged up to the next checkpoint, Jojo asked, "Last one?"

The warden nodded breathlessly. His face was scarlet and beaded with sweat, his breaths coming in wheezy heaves. Seconds later, at the gate, a wiry, thickly mustachioed guard glanced at the warden with wide-eyed shock. A visible spasm shot through him as they bolted past him and down the gray hallway. The asshole was in on it.

Fallon signaled with a finger to take the next left. As they tore by the open steel door, Jojo felt a burst of dread at an unmistakable odor.

Gasoline. The air was rank with it.

He took in the horrific details as a dizzying series of freeze frames as his eyes darted throughout the cavernous concrete garage.

The bulk of a naked, blubbering Robert Larsen twenty feet away, held standing by a rope hitched under his shoulders and tied to a ceiling girder.

His meaty hands, one atop the other, on the battleship gray floor in a small pool of blood. The homemade machete blade, a small camera, and a pile of prison blue denims next to them.

The thick, balding tire clamped around his chest like a foot-wide anaconda, drenched glossy black with fuel.

His wrists tied with big dripping balls of blood-red rags.

The slim, lithe man in prison blues standing three feet from him, his face concealed by a ski mask.

The impossibly long, delicate, chocolate-colored fingers that held, then tossed the lit match.

A plume of flame mushroomed six feet above the tire and enveloped Larsen's contorted face in a cone of fire and black, choking smoke.

He screamed. And then he began to spin. Whirling and whirling, faster and faster like a flaming top, bouncing around on the rope under his shoulders, trying to escape the terrible flames. He dashed madly this way and that until his feet lifted from the floor and flailed in the air. The tire dripped rubber down his thighs. Thick, glistening blobs sizzled and rimmed with blood as they met flesh and added the stink of burning meat and fat to the stench of rubber and gasoline.

Jojo looked for a fire extinguisher but saw only a pair of empty red wall brackets. He gritted his teeth, yanked out his Glock, flipped the safety, and drew down one-handed on Larsen's head spinning and jerking in the inferno. The poor fuck was dead anyway.

He snapped off two rounds through the thickening smoke, both missing the gyrating ball of fire and lodging in a pegboard tool panel on the wall. Larsen continued spinning and shrieking. Jojo went two-hand and stepped forward so close that the heat seared his knuckles. He fixed on the massive head cooking in the flames, exhaled, and fired. The head jerked and a spatter of red mist a yard in diameter drenched the pegboard. The fibers of the flaming rope parted, and Larsen teetered and fell backwards, still engulfed in flames as he hit the floor.

Jojo heard a bellowed "Holy shit!" to his right behind him, and turned in time to see the guilty-looking guard stumble through the doorway with a red foam fire extinguisher. He ran up to Larsen's prostrate, burning form and began pumping foam, reducing the fire to a smolder. Then he glanced furtively at Jojo and slinked back out of view.

Jojo eyed the Haitian. The guy stood there, tense and motionless, waiting to be cuffed.

Why hadn't the guard hauled him out of there?

Suddenly, he caught movement out of the corner of his eye behind him. He turned, looked up, and saw a camera panning on the wall a few feet overhead. The guard stood underneath, holding a white towel. He'd jerked it off the camera, which had been covered up during the necklace. It would've looked like a malfunction to a guy at the control center. He'd probably called the motor pool and checked; the guard had told him everything was fine.

Jojo glanced left at Fallon. He was purple with barely contained rage, eyes narrowed into slits, jaw jutting out and trembling. His finger jerked spasmodically at the trigger on the shotgun pointed at the floor as he battled the temptation to blow down the Haitian. He glanced back at the camera, then riveted his eyes on Lacroix in swallowed fury and disgust.

The Haitian exhaled in relief, gazed down at Larsen's charred, mangled head, then turned to Jojo and grinned smugly through the mask. His voice was a thick Creole patois. "*Bien*, good shot, eh?" He shrugged. "*Moi*, I still get paid."

Then a foot-long stainless steel crescent wrench arced through the air over Jojo's shoulder. At first he thought the guard had thrown it at him but saw the wrench was headed straight for the Haitian's head. Lacroix glanced up in surprise but caught it handily.

His eyes bugged wide as he realized his fatal error.

"I don't think so, asshole," said the warden with a grim smile as he leveled the shotgun at the Haitian's head and fired. Lacroix was scythed down by the impact, the mask shredded by the blast, unveiling a face the color and consistency of lasagna.

Jojo thought through it. The video would show someone out of view tossing a wrench to Lacroix, so the warden had acted in self-defense. Easy to claim there'd been a second inmate. Jojo glanced back at the guard, still holding the towel. There would be no prints on the wrench except for those of Lacroix.

The guard stepped forward, stood over the prostrate Lacroix, and sniggered. "Fucking moron, bringing a wrench to a gunfight." He gave the warden a sidelong glance. "Goddamn shit-thrower," he spat out with angry vehemence.

The warden nodded. To the guards, the worst prisoners were those few who got their jollies pitching their feces through the bars at the men in green, despite the fearsome beatings they received in retribution. The unspoken rule was that if you could find an excuse to kill a shit-thrower, you did it.

Jojo—and the warden too—had stepped into it. Nuestra had set up Larsen for Lacroix. And then probably given Lacroix to the guards. He never would've agreed to do the deed unless Nuestra had told him he had a free pass from the men in green. And then probably told the guards he was their meat. That way, Nuestra got out of paying Lacroix and curried favor with the guards at the same time—always a plus.

The warden eyed Jojo, waiting for him to say something. Jojo remained silent.

Fallon walked up to Larsen's grisly corpse and gazed down. Jojo moved up and stood next to him and shuddered. Burning alive probably did odd things to time. Larsen had been ablaze no more than ten seconds. It had probably seemed a lot longer to him.

But Jojo's sympathy was conflicted. He couldn't wish such a fiendish death on anyone, but Larsen's own brutality had nurtured the psycho killer who'd signed his death warrant.

"Nice shot," said the warden quietly. "We can have three rounds of Glock nine at the desk in ten minutes. Standard jacket?"

Fallon was giving him an out. Jojo could report the shooting to SFPD, or not, as he saw fit. If he didn't, everything would vanish behind the walls. They would melt down the rounds, maybe "reprocess" Larsen's body by totally burning him to remove evidence of the necklacing. Just another prison murder by an inmate gunned down when he attacked the warden. Page five stuff.

On the other hand, if he reported the shooting, everything would come out. The necklacing. The accusation that Lacroix had been killed in cold blood. And Jojo would become the enemy of the state's most powerful and vindictive bureaucracy, one that had its own clandestine gangs. The guard had been in on the necklace, which meant he was probably a member of the Green Wall.

Who might have no qualms about coming after Jojo, his wife, and his children.

And there was nothing in the manual about putting someone out of his misery. The kind of thing they'd bury in Wyoming, but in SF the brutality lobby would howl like coyotes. Not so much at him, but at the prospect of giving the cops new license to discharge a weapon. He'd be pilloried with a bad shooting to appease them.

All for the remote chance of winning posthumous justice for a guy who enjoyed chopping and burning people to death, who threw his own excrement at his captors.

He glanced down at the liquid mass of bone, blood, and tissue that had been Lacroix's face.

As friggin' *if*.

He nodded. "Yup. Standard jacket."

CHAPTER THIRTEEN

April Larsen never slept late, even under the urgings of a hangover. Not that she got them that often. Decades of rousting kids for school and working as a cashier had put her in the habit of drinking just enough to stay a step ahead of her long-suffering liver.

This morning was no different, though she shook her head in recollection of the day the Chinese cop had come sniffing around. After he'd left, she'd swilled herself halfway to kingdom come, spilling half a tumbler next to the La-Z-Boy as she passed out. She was greeted the next morning by the harsh perfume of Wild Turkey wafting up from the rug.

She tossed some water in the kettle and scrubbed the caked-on food off the top layer of dishes in the sink. She felt almost sprightly and made a pact to get down to the slicky stuff at the bottom by noon. The water boiled and she extricated a cup from under a pot containing the remains of some mashed potatoes. She set the pot to soak and rimmed the cup with the pad, its once-yellow sponge side now the color of burnt sugar. She prepped the coffee and planted herself in the La-Z-Boy. With a flourish as prideful as the day she'd gotten it, she hit the remote and settled back for the eight o'clock news.

She absently sipped as the news started. Usually it was local doings in Gilroy and Salinas.

But this morning, Matthew's picture was plastered on the screen.

The coffee spilled down her dress, but she didn't feel it. And she couldn't make out what the lady to the right of his picture was saying, as if her ears were stuffed with cotton like when she was a kid and had an earache. She leaned forward, oblivious to the liquid scalding her stomach. She could pick up snatches but couldn't make sense of them. The Cynthia girl she'd seen before on TV. The guy torn in half in the tree. Father poisoned in prison. Ex-boss tortured to death. Brazilian landlady with her head chopped off.

The topic changed and she cleared her head, swiveling it hard enough to hear her neck creak. Another channel. Maybe she was still asleep.

Matthew again. Only this time the words tunneled through the cotton and clanged against the bones of her inner ear. Cold-blooded child killer.

It didn't make a lick of sense, until she spun through half a hundred things at once, like a VCR going fast forward with the picture on.

The Garcias' cat, Mimi, in a burlap sack tied to a fencepost, Matthew batting her with a broomstick like a piñata until she was nothing but blood and bone chips inside her fur.

The loathing in his eyes when she'd Q-tipped the cat shit out of his nostrils and ears.

When she'd sponged the lipstick and eye shadow off his face.

When she'd sung to him a hundred times while she Ben-Gayed a hundred welts and bruises. His little messies.

Darker things flickered from beyond her emotional horizon like distant heat lightning.

The odd way he looked at Claire when she'd started getting breasts.

The empty three-pack of condoms she'd found in his closet with not a girlfriend in sight.

Claire's beloved Mittens vanishing without a trace, met not with girlish panic and nightly flashlight searches, but with a fearful resignation.

The scalding showers Claire'd taken to, where she once came out with first-degree burns.

Bob's tearful denial of her accusation at the prison, though she'd never seen him cry in forty years of marriage.

That odd rift in time the night Claire died. She'd groggily glanced at the clock at nine, slept for what she knew had been an hour or so, and awoken to find Matthew there with the clock at just after nine. She'd said hello, catnapped for what had to be only half an hour, and roused herself to find Matthew gone and the time pushing eleven.

The faintest whiff of gasoline when he'd kissed her.

Strangely, though, she felt nothing, even though her life had just detonated. Her son a psycho killer, who had poisoned her husband, and molested her daughter and burned her to death. She, soon widowed, sixty-two and penniless, a demon-spawning pariah in the town she'd lived in for four decades. People would cross the street when they saw her coming, break her windows, spit on her. She would eat the wetbacks' garbage, hoping for the Sunday when some church would take up a collection for the girl-killer's mom and furtively leave a bag of canned goods on the stoop.

Then she looked around and realized where she was. It was sort of like her pain dream. In Wisconsin as a girl, she'd seen a tornado close-up before her father had whisked her into the cellar. And sometimes she had this dream where she was spinning and spinning, watching cows and houses and cars bouncing around. Always when something bad happened, like when Claire had run away and when she'd died, then when Bob had gotten locked up and when she'd confronted him. She would whirl in the twister, always knowing in the end she'd be set down on her feet.

But this time was different.

This time, she was sitting in her chair, looking up at walls of wind towering into a billowing charcoal sky. Not that she was seeing things. She could see the TV, the fireplace, the stained Formica dining table. But it was like she had another pair of eyeballs rolling around inside her brain, like that crackhead girl's baby did in the *Enquirer*. It was like she could really see these howling walls hurtle towards her, then back away.

And she knew that when one of those walls hit her, it wouldn't be like always. Her brain-eyes would see the gritty winds flense the skin from her body. Whistling shards of glass would chop off her hands and feet. Grappling hooks would bury themselves in her poisonous womb. Her jaw would be torn off by stray rivets, her eyeballs drilled through with supersonic strands of wire.

She stood up shakily and stooped toward the kitchen, fearfully eyeing the walls of wind. The left one moved in on her, right through the bathroom, with the rhythmical pounding of a locomotive. She stepped to the right and the wall moved slowly back. The right-hand wall seethed closer, close enough to see not cows and houses and cars, but knives and axes and severed, skinless arms and legs and heads whirling with the wind. The wall itself was thickly red with a billion vaporous droplets of blood. She shivered and stepped left, hoping the left-hand wall would stay put. It slowly snaked back for her. She stepped into the kitchen, and the walls screamed towards her, closing together and cornering her with a clattering roar as metal met metal and bone met bone.

Knowing what was demanded of her, she grabbed last night's almost-empty tumbler from the counter, upended it, and bit down. It broke in her mouth, and she bit down harder, breaking off teeth and driving a razor of glass deep into her palate. The bourbon gurgled down, mixed with the salty taste of blood and flecks of glass that burrowed in her throat like insects. The pain staggered her, but she watched with relief as the wall whirled back a respectful distance, as if grudgingly paying her homage. She choked out spittle and blood, gripped the counter and teetered on her tiptoes, reaching for the top shelf of the cabinet.

There was just enough time.

Clem, Billy, Jojo, and Angie filed down the stairs of Matthew's garage unit. CSU was still poring over the landlady's gruesome demise. Clem turned back to Angie and grinned. "See my miracle of bureaucratic razzle-dazzle in the paper?"

She nodded. "Matthew's name and pic? God, about time," she added imperiously.

He gave her an indignant glare. "Hey. You don't know how many folks in Legal are nursing pulled tails this morning."

Billy glanced at Jojo. "Nothing about a necklace, I noticed." The paper mentioned only Matthew's poisoning of his father. Jojo reddened, but kept silent.

Two crime scene techs were downstairs. The frayed brown carpet was rolled back, revealing the concrete floor. The ratty couch had been dismembered, its innards stuffed into plastic bags. Clem asked a tech for a once-over. The tech pointed out a black leather glove tacked to the wall.

Jojo nodded. "A souvenir. Probably the one he used to poison dad."

On a small shelf next to the glove was a taxidermy of a snow-white fox. Clem pointed to it. "An arctic fox. The cardiologist with the tapeworms."

The tech walked them to a sheaf of drawings on the counter. "Stuffed in a drawer under the shelves." They circled around. The tech paged through them with latex-gloved fingers.

The first several drawings were sketches of Roderick's murder, showing her hanging from the planter hook. One showed the paper under her feet with dimensions. Another showed her hanging from a rafter in what Angie assumed was the Maury garage, an early reject.

She absently shook her head. "Interesting, seems he was always planning on doing her at the Maury house. Waiting for the tape to come down."

The next batch was a set of computer schematics for the tunnel and the tank, heavily smudged from use. Billy spoke. "What's nice is what's *not* here. Thank God."

Clem nodded. "Right, a whole 'nother set of drawings. Another girl, another tank."

The next set consisted of sketches for the horrific mural. All were on yellowed, lined notebook paper except one: a line drawing of the hideous, suffering woman with balls of flesh for arms and legs, her hands and feet a thalidomide nightmare. Unlike the others, it was on a large piece of apparently brand-new drawing paper.

Billy addressed them. "Last night I heard back from my oil-paint specialist. He did oxidation and solvent tests. Turns out the mural was painted at two distinct times. First was four years ago, back around when he killed Cynthia and Claire. But like a month ago, he scraped away part of it and added this image." He pointed to the new drawing.

Angie nodded. "So for some reason he suddenly decided to revisit killing Claire. Even to the point of adding this nightmare to the mural."

The tech turned over the horrific drawing. Written on the back in block letters was DIE LUDER SOLTU NICHT LEBEN LASSEN.

"I'll funnel it to our language lab," said Billy.

But Angie was puzzled by nostalgic familiarity. "My mom was a German war bride. I spoke it as a kid. The structure's old German, like from the Bible.

She used to read it to me. The phrase is familiar, but *Luder* doesn't fit."

Clem perused two books on a tiny shelf over the bed. "How convenient. A German-English dictionary. Right next to the *Elementary Sanskrit* he used for the sign at the oak tree." The tech handed Angie a pair of latex gloves, and she snapped them on, then took the book from the shelf and looked up the entry.

"Unpleasant woman. Slang, bitch." She paused. "So it means bitches shouldn't be allowed to live. But I remember the line from the Bible now. *Die Zauberinnen soltu nicht leben lassen.* Which in the King James becomes 'Thou shalt not suffer a witch to live.'" She shuddered at the verse that had justified centuries of slaughter. Thousands of old women were burned just for talking to themselves, a sure sign of witchery afoot in olden times.

Clem smiled grimly. "Thou shalt not suffer a bitch to live. Like at the oak tree, the word play isn't in the original; it's in the English."

The tech interjected, "We've carted a ton of books down to the lab. He had them in boxes. Pretty well read for a psycho. Vonnegut, Kafka, Shakespeare . . . "

Billy pointed at the shelf over the bed. "So these were the only books he had out?" The tech nodded. Billy eyed Clem. "First commandment of chasing psychopaths?"

Clem nodded. "Always wonder if you're doing exactly what he wants you to."

Billy winked approval. "So the bookshelf tells you . . . ?"

Clem pondered it. "That this is the Museum of Matthew. The drawings, the books, the leather glove, the stuffed fox, they're *exhibits*. He had things set up for after he died. Chances are anything we see, we're *supposed* to."

Billy continued, "Thou shalt not suffer a bitch to live. At the graveyard, he made it look like suicide because he had to. But here, you see his proclamation that he killed Claire. He probably redid the mural in the tunnel 'cause he's dying, to leave his testament. And 'named' his work on the drawing, just like the oak tree, Roderick's hanging, the cardiologist, and the landlady."

The final drawing was a map in pencil, also on yellowed, dog-eared paper, the same as the old drawings of Claire. Nothing was labeled, but

Jojo recognized it. "Where he murdered Claire." He pointed out the church foundation, the graveyard, the hillock, the pathways leading from the clearing, the little chained-up gate, even two trees near the clearing. A rectangle marked the spot where the pickup had burned. Another heavy line led down one of the pathways from the clearing to an unnamed street, noted as three-quarters of a mile away.

Clem spoke. "So this is the map he made to do the deed. And this line was his way out. So, say he drove to Auburn, parked on this street, took a bus to Modesto, got Claire and the pickup . . . "

"And Speckle," added Angie.

"Drove it to the clearing, burned her, and walked out to his car," Clem continued. "Then drove to Gilroy. That's why he took off the whole day the night she died. Needed time to set everything up."

Angie saw Jojo purse his lips, seemingly perplexed. She nudged him. "Something amiss?"

Jojo shrugged. "It's hinked out somehow, but I can't nail it down. I'll get back to you."

The tech walked them over to the single bed against the wall, picked up a UV light, and switched it on. Bright spots fluoresced on both sides of the bed. "Sheets haven't been changed in a few days. Lots of little soldiers on the sheets at the sides of the bed, like from fingertips. Probably same wine, different vintages. Nada on the girly juice."

Billy nodded. "Compulsive masturbation. Big time psychopath hobby. Just before or after he kills, five or six times a day. His sexual fantasies are knotted up in violence. Control gives him his jollies. He spent years 'owning' Claire."

"And Bernadette?" asked Angie.

"Maybe some self-justification, his pique over it taking so long to unearth Cynthia. But not an affront, not like Roderick or Joanne, where he has a gut-wrenching need to assert dominance. So more for an audience. Or because by now, he just plain adores killing."

"Right," Angie mused. "So when he fed her to the crabs, he was showing off, but it maybe felt better if he 'deserved' his pound of flesh. Well, couple of pounds."

"May mean if he does some mass killing with the poison, he'll dredge up some screwball rationale for it. Some group that 'deserves' it."

"And Cindy? Was that sexual?" Angie asked with a shudder.

"Not in the pedophile sense; we'd have ten more dead girls by now. I doubt Claire either; his shock and grief were too strong. Probably the sex and violence tie-in didn't mature until Roderick. But now, it's full bore," he said, nodding at the bed. "The merging of sex with violence he's feeling toward Joanne must be astounding."

"Fuckhead," Angie spat out vehemently.

Billy smiled thinly. "Not too clinical, but on the mark."

Clem walked over to the second tech, who was sitting on the concrete floor next to three cardboard boxes sealed with custody documentation. "Nothing in there we need to see?" His eyes riveted on the man's odd combination of a goatee and lambchop sideburns. He wasn't a tech; it was Rob Lyle from the crime lab, dressed in coveralls. He'd decided to work the scene to help out.

Rob's eyes were clamped shut, his face ashen. Clem tapped his shoulder. "Pal, you're looking none too good."

Rob opened his eyes and shook his head in disbelief. "Spend an hour reading what's in those boxes, you won't look so good either." Clem cocked an eyebrow. "Best I can tell, they're working papers for a huge set of notebooks. Every sheet's cross-referenced. Based on the system, like forty volumes. He took the notebooks but left this stuff behind."

"Stuff? What kind of stuff?"

Rob blinked rapidly. "First I saw was a method to induce gas gangrene in someone's limbs. Techniques to keep him alive as long as possible. That's like four days, by the way. Some secret police ghoul in Argentina came up with it twenty years ago."

He paused, stifled a gag, and took a deep breath. "Let's see. Then there's the one about using a titration thing to control the flow of chili-laced vinegar into someone's nostrils. The mouth is gagged, the nasal passages swell up, and the victim suffocates. The valve lets you stretch things out a while. That's from some place named Moldava?"

Rob clamped his eyes again and lolled his head, battling back nausea.

"Then a doozy from Indonesia. Something on the care and feeding of Komodo dragons. You know, those giant, man-eating lizards they have on one or two of the islands there? Like eight feet long?"

Rob continued, "Years ago, the government used to maroon condemned prisoners on this island inhabited by dozens of Komodos. Turns out his bite doesn't kill right away, his saliva's full of the same bacterial witch's brew you find in putrefying flesh. He gives you a chomp, then follows you around a few days while the flesh starts rotting off your body." He gulped. "Then he disembowels you without the nicety of killing you first."

He placed a hand atop one of the boxes. "And three or four hundred more goodies this city couldn't pay me enough to read."

Billy tapped Clem's shoulder. "I heard from my buddies. MO on Roderick's hanging looks like something from Hitler's SS."

Clem grimaced. "Jesus. We need to put this guy's brain in a capsule and shoot it into the sun."

Rob ran his hand through his hair. "Another thing. The guy's a stickler for sources, right? Almost everything has citations where it came from. Books, the Web, transcripts of judicial proceedings, whatever. Except . . . "

Billy looked down at him. "Except?"

"Some—maybe ten—just have a date and initials. And most of his handwriting's careful and deliberate. But these notes are much more scribbly."

Billy thought it over, then nodded grimly. "From interviews. With the rise of democracy, hundreds of professional sadists in South America, Eastern Europe, and the former USSR were granted amnesty, or their files vanished. For a hundred bucks and whiskey there's plenty'll schmooze with a fellow hobbyist. You'd find some exotic destinations in Matthew's passport."

Clem's cell phone chirped. He listened, then hung up and muttered, "Another link in the chain of chaos."

Angie poked him. "Huh?"

Clem frowned. "Someone once said a psychopath creates a chain of chaos, destroying the lives of everyone around him, even those he doesn't intend to."

Angie eyed him curiously.

"That was my friend, Grady Moore, with the Gilroy Police. Matthew made the local news. April Larsen, his mom. Neighbor heard a shot, called the cops. She just bulletized her head."

Officer Harry Voight of the Colma Police Department took the driver's license from the gangly man in the decrepit orange Subaru. He gave it a glance, then slouched back to the squad car. His partner, Jenny Speiser, sat at the wheel with a bored expression. She glared at him as he opened the door.

"Burnt-out taillight? And you're running a check?" It was a continual point of irritation. The city had put in whiz-bang car computers that did everything but make donuts. But with the hilly terrain and radio interference in one of the most densely populated areas on the California coast, you often couldn't even raise someone on the push-to-talk, never mind get two computers to chat over the airwaves.

"Yeah, I don't like the guy's eyes. They creep me out," Harry answered as he poked in the license number on the unit's tiny keypad, absently contemplating flame-broiled or fried for lunch.

Jenny rolled her eyes. "Christ, you're not marrying the guy. If nice eyes meant anything, I wouldn't be filing for divorce."

"Give it a rest. Tell you what, we don't get a blip the next minute, we blow it off." She rolled her eyes in acquiescence, and Harry poked a button. The machine signaled it was transmitting. And transmitting. Nothing came back.

Jenny drummed her fingers on the wheel and tried the microphone. She could hear Dispatch, but they couldn't hear her. "Dead spot."

"I mean it, his eyes look like a frigging moray eel's. Let's go with the ticket. But let the contraption whack away one more time." She poked the button while Harry pulled out his ticket book and took down the data off the license.

Finally, he glared at the computer and growled, "Fucking message in a bottle." He trudged back over to the Subaru and handed over the ticket with a flourish.

"Compliments of Colma's finest. Get that taillight fixed."

"Certainly, officer," replied the man levelly. "I can go now, right?"

"Sure can. Live long and prosper." The Subaru's engine sputtered, and the car drove off. It took the nearby exit into the maze of shopping malls that made up most of the city's square miles.

Harry watched him turn left and disappear, then shrugged. "Burger King?" Jenny nodded and revved the black and white, and they merged into traffic. Five seconds later, the gadget's receive light blinked and it began beeping. The report scrolled across the black screen, not in the usual green, but in an angry red.

Harry gasped. "Holy shit. No *wonder* I didn't like his eyes." He pulled a newspaper from the door compartment and held up the front page to Jenny. She glanced over and eyed the two-column photo and the banner headline, and her jaw dropped.

He had to be satisfied with his recovery from yesterday's debacle and his near-miss today at the hands of the Colma police. Two p.m., just over a day since he'd fled with the landlady's head slowly spinning behind him.

He was already settled into his new place. The owner was an asshole and had demanded two months' deposit plus first month's rent. At eight hundred a month, he'd shelled out twenty-four hundred for the privilege of moving into yet another five-hundred-square-foot shit hole. But on the other hand, the guy didn't seem to get the paper, so he hadn't seen the picture in the Chronicle *that accompanied the lurid tale of yesterday's bloodfest. The glasses and the thin beard still offered some protection, but things would be riskier.*

Still, he smirked at the consternation that must've reigned at San Francisco General this morning. It was almost worth it.

He'd managed to sniff out another clunker by eleven, a white Hyundai four-door with a suspect transmission. His confidence was buoyed when he saw the morning Chronicle *sitting right on the guy's table while they did up the payment and title transfer. You just didn't expect a psycho killer to come waltzing into your house and buy your car.*

He'd driven the Subaru to Colma, a town fifteen minutes south of San Francisco consisting of malls, cemeteries, and parking lots—things you couldn't squeeze into the city because of real estate costs. He thought he was dead and buried after the cops pulled him over. His eyes were riveted on the rearview as he wondered if he should just give up the charade and carom down the highway.

But he sat and stewed, desperately hoping that the flag San Francisco must've had on his license hadn't made it to the megamall provinces.

He drove away with his heart doing a samba and headed for the lot fully expecting to see a squad car careen crazily onto the street behind him. He paid three months parking and hopped the BART train back to the city. From there, another train out to the Sunset for a breather. On the way, he'd taken out the ticket and snickered.

His first moving violation. And he wouldn't even have to pay it.

There was one other thing he needed to do before tonight. What with Honeypie's protection, he'd need to pack heat. There was a chance the cop would sniff out the snatch before he was clear. He could sneak his dad's gun out of the house, but he wanted to have a play tonight. So he decided to pack up the car, head downtown, and scare up his old drug connection, certain the guy could pull it off on the quick if he greased things with a twenty. Assuming the gun buy went kosher, he'd be at the hospital just in time to tail Honeypie. Sixty-forty he'd have an opening tonight.

Not that he was in a hurry—he'd have one or two runs a week at her over the next month—but this late in the game, it paid not to miss a shot. He held up his hand. The tremor was now obvious. It didn't bother him when he picked up heavy stuff for example. But he was starting to have the tiniest bit of trouble eating with a fork.

He shuddered. Two months hence some nurse's aide in a prison clinic would be cooing at him, "Okay, Mr. Larsen, here comes the airplane . . . "

He put a last item on the list. Time to send Mom a money order. And, what with his picture pasted on the front pages from San Diego to Seattle, he'd need to give her a call. Let her know it was all just a case of mistaken identity, that he'd have it straightened out in a few days.

She'd buy it. She always had, after all.

Joanne hit the elevators. She couldn't help noticing that she was the talk of the hospital's female population by now, especially since Scott, her 5:00 p.m. consort, looked like he moonlighted at Chippendale's. She was relieved to find that much of her churning fear had worn off. She was living in a fortress and escorted everywhere else by heavily armed peace officers. In fact, she was almost beginning to enjoy the spotlight, especially the company of her bodyguard. He was shy, solicitous, and deferential in a way she found endearing, a relief from the sophomoric come-ons of the interns and residents, who believed that an "M.D." after a guy's name was enough to charm any girl out of her bloomers. She'd dated a few and found them self-centered and sexually loutish.

In fact, she'd sworn off them entirely after the last one, a visiting resident from Pacific enshrined as a Future Cardiologist to Watch. The whole thing had been a minor fiasco; six months before, he'd introduced himself in the lunch line. She'd allowed him to join her for the sole purpose of pissing off Matthew, who glowered at them the entire half hour. She'd played it to the hilt, tossing in some blatant goo-goo eyes for good measure.

She hadn't heard from him again until he finally called her at work three months back. After a one-way dinner conversation that revolved around triple bypasses, she condescended to a good night peck at the door to her flat. She extricated herself from his grip just as he tried to thrust his tongue in her mouth, evading it with the dexterity of an aikido black belt. It was still waggling wetly in the air as she vanished behind her door.

She grinned at the irony of it. The date had been a yawner, and she'd half-dreaded hearing from him again. But she also found herself just the slightest bit indignant when she didn't.

Scott opened the car door for her, and she slid into the backseat. As he took the wheel, she bent forward and smiled through the steel mesh. "Twice around the park, Jeeves."

He grinned back. "Yes, Miss Duffy. Clockwise today? Or counter-clockwise?"

"Actually, we're going to meet some of my girlfriends at my main haunt. They've heard all about you and my bad-ass wheels. I need to quell any speculation that I'm hallucinating."

Scott looked away nervously.

"And if that's not enough," she continued, "I'm going to go postal on you if I don't get some time away from work and that Bastille of a condo."

"I guess it's safe enough. But keep it to an hour. And no alcohol."

"Not one measly beer, promise." She gave him directions. After a few turns, she poked his shoulder through the mesh. "Here we are: Cooper's. Park in front of the hydrant."

"Sorry, only in emergencies."

"*Clem* did it. And I can't think of a bigger emergency than making my three best friends insanely jealous."

They found a legal spot and walked into the café to the sound of three boisterous screeches. Scott blushed, and she gave him a reassuring pat on the shoulder. "Now don't you panic. They think you're gorgeous. They're all the prettiest shade of green."

Scott spent thirty minutes alternately blushing and grinning under the ribbing of Joanne's girlfriends. Finally, she stood up. "I have to use the restroom. Why don't you entertain my friends for a few?" She eyed them suspiciously. "Don't even think it."

He walked away with her and lowered his voice. "I can't do that, Joanne. I'll have to stand outside until you're finished. That's God's law. Well, Frazier's, and I'd rather piss off God."

She blushed furiously as she walked towards the back, then stopped abruptly and turned to him at the foot of the short flight of stairs up to the women's room. She poked him in the chest with an insistent finger. "Now look here, Mister. These are one-horse bathrooms. Assuming you don't object, I wouldn't mind seeing if this protection deal gets a bit more personal once Matthew's pushing up daisies. And one thing that *won't* help that along is having you stand there listening to my catalog of bathroom noises. So, you can just plunk yourself here and watch the door. But out of earshot, okay?"

Scott went red as a hothouse tomato. "Joanne, for God's sake. Your bathroom noises won't make any difference to me."

"They will to me. Now you plant your butt right there. You can see the door, it's only three feet away. Okay?"

He rolled his eyes. "Okay. But I knock in two minutes. Deal?"

She rolled her eyes right back at him. "Deal." She walked upstairs, turned, saucily stuck her tongue out at him, then retreated before he could retaliate. As she opened the door, she glimpsed him leaning against the wall, eyeing his watch.

• • •

Adrenaline flooded him as he watched the unit turn onto Valencia. He'd have his first go at her. Honeypie met her friends there once or twice a week, most often on Fridays and Saturdays. He hadn't been sure she'd continue her routine, but suspected they would see it as pretty low risk.

He circled around to the service alley and parked in front of the café's steel back door. Like many restaurants, they kept the door unlocked so busboys hauling trash to the dumpster wouldn't get locked out. He pocketed the gun, took out a hammer, slipped it under his shirt, and walked in. The women's room was a few steps down the hallway and to the left. The place had been built out from the downstairs of an old house, and the toilets were the originals.

He'd mapped out the scenario before, but it hadn't included a vigilant bodyguard. It wouldn't make much difference unless the cop happened to stand right outside the bathroom door while he was doing the deed, where he might hear something and try to barge in. Problem was, he wouldn't be able to see if the cop was standing there or not. He'd finally decided simply to go for it, and fire through the door with his glorified popgun if the cop started breaking in.

The bathroom door was ajar. He scanned the hallway and the flight of stairs down into the restaurant and slipped in. It consisted of a single white toilet, discolored and scratched from years of use, and a tiny corner sink on an ancient hexagonal tile floor. Behind the toilet was a large window with clouded glass that faced out on the back alley. He pulled out a nail, opened the window about two feet, and hammered the nail most of the way into the frame, so the window couldn't be closed without pulling it out. He edged open the door and slipped out, then out the back door into the alley.

He trotted around to the passenger side of the car, opened the front door, and pulled out the length of thin white cord, the hand towel, and the bottle of chloroform from the paper bag on the passenger seat and laid them on the ground. Then he knelt down and adjusted the side mirror so he could duck below the car window but have a clear view of the bathroom window through the cantilevered mirror. He could view anyone in the bathroom, but she couldn't see him.

He remained kneeling for the next half hour, watching a parade of seven or eight women enter and leave the bathroom, until he began to wonder if *tonight would be a dud. Purely a numbers game. If he did it enough times, he was sure to strike gold, but he might have to endure a few false starts. He glumly began to think about closing up shop.*

Suddenly, he caught movement in the mirror and adjusted his head to center the view. She was wearing a white pantsuit. Honeypie, in her tech uniform, he was certain of it. He tensed, picked up the cord in his right hand, and worked it with his fingers like worry beads.

The woman hesitated at the sight of the open window. Almost all the women wavered in just that way, then peered out the window to check if anyone was in the alley, and finally turned around and sat down. The woman did just that, leaned over the toilet tank and scrutinized the alley. He couldn't see her face clearly, but the long blond hair was a giveaway. He held his breath, heart thumping in his ears. Finally, she pulled her face from the window, turned, and sat down. He exhaled in relief, doused the towel with chloroform, and launched himself headlong around the front of the car.

It was just past six-thirty. The afternoon had been uneventful, with nary a corpse within the city limits after yesterday's doubleheader and a half. Billy, Jojo, and Clem had spent the day fruitlessly checking out garages. Angie had visited Bernadette at the hospital in search of any insight she might have, only to find her staring into space, muttering a lipless version of "the crabs . . . the crabs . . . " They decided to brainstorm in the bar at Billy's hotel.

Clem drew an icy brew to his lips, took a languid sip, and winked at Angie. "Well, our last twenty-four hours. Looks like you're back to rousting homeys for crack pipes."

She gestured with her vodka tonic. "You're too pessimistic. Tomorrow Matthew's toast. My intuition's never been wrong. Well, excepting my first husband," she finished with a cynical grin.

Jojo wearily leaned over. "Consider yourself lucky. In the Philippines, you're allowed one shot. Get it right the first time."

"No divorce?" asked Billy incredulously. "What's the world coming to?"

"Latin Catholic deal. We have 'legal separations' out the ying yang. So half the country is separated but never gets divorced. Keeps the bishops happy."

Angie guffawed. "Talk about the elephant in the living room."

They laughed as Clem's cell rang. He listened, then shook his head with a disgusted grunt. "Get this. Colma police stopped Matthew. At noon, for a taillight. But they missed him."

"Huh?" exclaimed Jojo, astonished. "But they're on our grid. They should've had the flag. From the license or the plate."

"They did. Two minutes too late; car computer didn't work. Six squads and a copter prowling the malls for three hours, nothing," he finished with a fatalistic shrug.

The phone buzzed again just as he put it back in his shirt pocket. He let it ring three times in annoyance but finally answered. He listened intently, waving off their chitchat. His face became ashen, and he shook his head in slack-jawed disbelief. They turned towards him, hearts filling with sickening dread.

Clem hung up. His hands were trembling. Angie had never seen him so distraught. "Matthew kidnapped Joanne. From a bathroom at a restaurant in the Mission. Cop's in the hospital. He tried to break in; Matthew shot through the door. One in the spleen, one in the lung. He's in OR, may or may not make it. Happened forty-five minutes ago."

Angie's drink slipped from her fingers and spilled on the red carpet. "Jesus Christ," she whispered huskily. "He's got her. I never thought."

Clem's voice was little more than a croak. "We've lost her. He's got forty-five minutes on us. And we don't know where the fuck he is."

"Why so long?" asked Billy in disbelief.

Clem heaved a sigh of frustration. "Took them that long to track down the cop was on protection. He wasn't officially assigned. Frazier detailed him on the fly. That's probably why he took her to a café instead of straight home. No one told him not to."

They sat in impotent anguish. Angie vainly fought back tears. Joanne would die in some unspeakable way, a way that would haunt her dreams once she came to know the story. She cursed Matthew from the depths of her soul. There was no cavern of Hell too deep for him.

Billy gave Clem a sidelong glance. "Thirty years and I'm still not used to this part."

Clem's eyes wandered about in bewilderment. "Yeah. This one hurts," he whispered.

Jojo sat inert, his eyes closed, his head leaned back over the edge of his chair in exhaustion. Suddenly, he shook it woozily. "Wait a minute," he murmured. His eyes went wide. "Wait a fucking minute!" he exclaimed, loudly enough to draw a stare from a couple at a nearby table. "Matthew's going to burn Joanne, just like Claire. In the same place. He's going south. To the graveyard in Auburn."

Clem looked at him fixedly. "Huh. Not impossible. But what makes you say so?"

Billy shook his head briskly. "Not now, saddle up. Whatever Jojo has, it's probably our only shot. God willing and the creek don't rise, we'll catch up some; he can't do ninety on the shoulder. Call in the locals as a last resort. Jojo, explain on the way."

They tore out of the hotel and jumped into Clem's unmarked black and white, brazenly parked in a handicapped spot in front. The siren screamed, the cherry light whirled, and Clem hauled the car in a way Angie hadn't encountered yet from anyone.

Clem turned to Jojo in the passenger seat, simultaneously cutting off a huge SUV. Angie gripped the seat with both hands. "Okay, so why are we driving two plus hours to Auburn?"

"Well, first of all, those drawings of Claire. We assumed the later drawing—and the recent painting in the tunnel—meant he was revisiting the Claire thing, but they could just as easily be Joanne. In fact, I'm *sure* they are." He stopped as they flew over a bump and went airborne.

Billy waited for the car to bottom. "Maybe that's why he redid the mural a month or so ago. But nothing more than that? Not much to go on."

"Lots more," replied Jojo intently. "When I was looking at that map he made before he burned Claire, something was wrong, but I couldn't put a finger on it. Well, I finally figured it out." He paused as the tires whined through a turn.

"You waiting for an invitation?" growled Clem. "Lose the drama."

Jojo exhaled sharply as they straightened out. "Okay. On the map, all the features were there. The church foundation, the graveyard, the pathways, the hill, everything. One thing that was marked was this little chained gate blocking one of the paths. But that gate? They didn't put that gate in until six months ago, *years* after Matthew burned Claire. So Matthew took the map he made to stage Claire's murder and went back there again. Within the last few months. And marked the change on the map. It was the only thing different."

Clem nodded as he rammed through an intersection. "Right. And he didn't just visit for auld lang syne. He marked the change because he was going there again. To make sure he didn't show up with his load of barbeque and find a strip mall."

Billy spoke. "And it'd be catharsis to burn Joanne alive, same's he did Claire. Only this time, he'd enjoy the hell out of it."

"But we have the map," Angie pointed out. "I assume he doesn't need it. But wouldn't he think twice about going there now?"

"Not an issue," asserted Jojo. "The map didn't have any markings. No highway number, names, exit signs, nothing. He did that on purpose. It'd be impossible for anyone to know what it was if they hadn't actually gone there. He thinks we'll never figure it out."

Angie mulled it over, then started. "Of course. He left it behind to rub our faces in it. So later we'd find her body, and we'd figure out there was the map all the time. Just like the blankets in the window. A single clue that only someone in the know could get. And as far as he's aware, we don't know anything about him killing Claire. Nothing's gone public. While every other murder has." She gave Billy an affectionate nudge.

But just then, Billy's eyes glazed. "My God." He collected himself, then spoke. "We've missed the whole point of the clues. He wasn't setting 'em up so we'd discover the vic after he was done with her. It was so there's some small chance we'd discover her *in time.*"

"Huh?" interjected Clem. "A 'somebody stop me' thing? I don't buy it."

"No," Billy replied. "In fact the opposite. He's measuring his omnipotence."

Angie shook her head. "Okay, I'm clueless. So to speak."

Billy nodded. "Think about the blankets. You saw 'em the morning after he killed Roderick, figured something's wrong. But there was also a chance—a much, much smaller one—that someone who knew the crime scene might've driven by the house the night before, *when it was happening*. Shined a light on the windows and seen something amiss, right while he was up there strangling her."

Angie shuddered. "Right, even if he was set on killing Roderick at the house, it would've been much safer to do her in the garage. No view from the street. And seems he thought about doing it that way, then changed to the bedroom."

"Exactly," agreed Billy. "Look at the oak tree killing. He chose a tree in plain view of the trail, in earshot of the road, when he didn't have to. Now, he knew there's almost no chance someone'd be hiking the trail at night with a whomp-ass storm rolling in. Or driving by on a cold, rainy night with the windows open, where they could hear Sneezy screaming. But still the smallest chance someone'd catch on."

Angie nodded grimly. There *was* a pattern.

Billy continued. "And now, he had to know there's some small chance we'd piece together that he'd murdered Claire at the graveyard. And that we'd figure out in time from the map that he was going there again tonight, with Joanne."

Clem took over. "He chloroformed the doc right out in the open and injected him just off the trail. Of course the landlady doesn't count, because that wasn't planned. Even there, he stayed and staged the scene after he killed her, even though he sensed something was up. But what about his father?"

"Think about it," insisted Billy. "If Roth had reported the poison theft to the cops, it would've been immensely risky to visit Dad at the prison."

"Right, we might've given them a heads up. So he went to the prison not knowing whether he was a fugitive, but calculating Roth would never tell. But it doesn't hold for Claire, right? I mean, where's the clue there?"

"Well, we're short on details on what led up to killing her. But I view killing Cynthia and Claire as two sides of the same crime."

"Okay, but there wasn't anything . . . Shit," Clem spat out. "So when he went to the pet shop, he wasn't just sizing her for the tank."

"Didn't need to. Could've gotten her height and weight off her hospital chart."

"Right," answered Clem. "He lets Mike see her at the pet shop. Even at the house. Then he calls Nichols, tells him he'll do her noon the next day. If Nichols calls the cops, we slap her picture in the paper, put up posters. Mike recognizes her and calls us. She's still alive. And Matthew's toast."

Billy nodded. "But her rescue depended entirely on Cindy's father risking condemning his daughter to a horrific death. Something Nichols most likely wouldn't do because he had no idea Matthew'd let her be seen. Nichols thought the cops wouldn't have a snowball's chance of tracking her down in time." Billy put a hand to his brow and continued in an agonized whisper. "Dear God. It goes deeper than even that."

Clem's voice thickened. "I know where you're headed. Cindy's linked to his killing Claire. Killing Claire was the hardest thing he's ever done."

Billy took over. "At least consciously, he didn't *want* to kill her. He was *forced* to. Had to give up the only thing he 'loved,' least in his self-indulgent fashion. Couldn't bring himself to do it."

Clem spoke. "So he spins out a Greek tragedy beforehand, where Nichols offers up his daughter to Matthew rather than calling the cops. And gives himself a twisted role model for 'sacrificing' Claire. He may not have even known he was doing it."

"And after Claire's dead, Cindy's still there for him," added Billy. "The symbol of another man's sacrifice. A bizarre sharing of grief." The car went silent with horror.

After a moment, Clem continued. "And that's the last we'll say on this. Nichols'll turn himself in soon. He's finally gotten some peace knowing Cindy died a quiet death. Last thing he needs to hear is he might've saved her with a phone call."

"Jesus, what a fiend," Angie said. "So he was leaving it to fate, but stacking the deck so it was certain he would kill Cindy and then Claire. So ever since then, each time he leaves a clue so he could get found out in time, and then doesn't—"

"He becomes more godlike, more assured of his 'mission,'" Billy finished. "And waiting round the bend is some mass murder with the poison, some terrible retribution, where hundreds'll die. And all, I bet, still tied up with Claire somehow."

"Okay," agreed Clem. "I figure we've got it right, but the question is how to save Joanne. He can just torch her and surrender. We have nothing to bargain with."

"We surely don't," agreed Billy. "She's his Holy Grail. Probably wouldn't care if he takes a slug in the chest; it's just sooner or later."

Clem glanced at Jojo. "What about the locals? Best I can guess, Matthew will get to the graveyard in about an hour and a half if he's doing the speed limit. We'll make up some time but not enough to get there first."

Jojo shook his head in resignation. "Trance is a decent sort, but he's your basic bumpkin. I can't see these guys doing a night vision sniper takedown. Matthew'll cook her before Trance gets through 'Now put the gun down, son, and nobody'll get hurt.' If we can't figure something else, call them in an hour from now. But she'll probably come back in a body bag.'"

Clem pounded a fist on the steering wheel. They broke onto the highway and started weaving south at ninety. The car stayed silent as the landscape changed from low-slung corporate parks to rolling hills. The sky suffused into purpling twilight.

Finally, Clem spoke quietly, more to himself than anyone else. "Way I see it, our only chance is, if he kills her, what happens to him will be so frightful, even *he'll* think twice."

Billy looked at him askance. "Like we'll torture him if he kills her? Not something to gladden ACLU hearts. And he could always pop a round up his nose."

"No, nothing like that. He'd never believe it. It'd only do the trick if he believed it." He paused. "No, it would have to be someone he'd know could take him alive even in the instant it took him to kill Joanne. Someone who'd make him shit himself."

That anyone could be fearsome enough to loosen the bowels of a serial killer made Angie shudder. "Clem, is this idle speculation? Or an option? We're not rolling in alternatives here."

"Just gimme a minute," answered Clem with an edge of irritation. "I've bent the rules into pretzels in my time. But this is over even *my* edge."

They all fell silent. He finally turned to Angie. "Look. I'm trying to find something that'll give us even a small chance of bringing her back alive.

Me, I'm finished if I bring her back in an urn, and I've got a free pass if Matthew shows up with a toe tag. So I've got nothing to lose rewriting the rules. You guys do." He riveted his eyes ahead. "So what I'm going to do is leave you all off at the next motel. The only way I have a shot at this is going someplace you really don't want to go."

Angie stared at him in stunned disbelief. "*Fuck* you," she finally spat out raggedly. "Just *fuck* you, Inspector."

Clem bit his lip. "Look. There's a guy down south owes me a big favor. But he's scarier in some ways than anyone I've met. If I do this, the whole thing is out of my hands. And in his. We piss him off enough, we could even be dead ourselves."

Angie's jaw tightened. "I've spent two weeks chasing a guy who takes all night to strangle a woman so he can jerk off. I'm staying."

Billy leaned forward and tapped his shoulder. "Clem, let's say that at the moment, the Bureau will not look altogether negatively on unorthodox solutions. We've danced with a few devils ourselves."

"All for one and one for all!" exclaimed Jojo.

"Christ," muttered Clem, half-disguising a thin smile. He finally sighed. "Okay, devil take the hindmost. Agreed?" They all nodded.

Clem took his cell out, dialed, and spoke in Chinese, but enunciating carefully, as if the other person wasn't a native speaker. The discussion continued for fifteen minutes. Clem had Jojo write down the location of the graveyard. He gave it to the person at the other end, repeating several times.

He signed off. "Okay, last chip's on the table. Assuming we're on the mark, there should be a reception committee waiting for Matthew. They should just make it in time. And understand this. Tonight, you follow orders. Not mine, his. You don't argue, you don't even cock an eyebrow. Especially you, Angie. He comes from a place where the word for 'daughters' translates as 'other men's women.' And far as he's concerned, he's still there."

Angie nodded gravely. "So how was it talking to Mr. Frightful?"

"I didn't talk to him. Just a loyal sidekick who speaks Chinese. The guy speaks English. But he was too busy to come to the phone."

"Huh?" exclaimed Angie. "I'd think this is pretty urgent."

"He was watching TV. Doesn't like missing his favorite shows."

"Sounds like my son," replied Billy. "Okay, Inspector. Care to clue us in on just what world of shit we're stepping into? And don't worry, this never happened."

Clem rolled his eyes. "Buddy, you don't know the half of it."

"Whatever it is, it won't matter. Because I don't think that hellish image in the mural is some opium fantasy. With all his frightful expertise, he's conjured some gruesome fate for her. Just how he'll do it I don't dare contemplate." Billy gulped back nausea. "But when he's done, that's exactly what she'll look like."

He rode the middle lane, keeping to the speed limit. After all, his backseat cargo wouldn't pass even the most casual scrutiny. Now that he was out of the city, he was actually enjoying the drive. Not too bad going south. He checked his watch. Going on seven, another two hours or so. He'd arrive at his long-intended destination under cover of darkness.

He felt lightheaded as he gloated over the spectacular events of the last two hours. He'd snatched Honeypie right out of a bathroom, even drilled a cop the first time he'd ever fired a gun. Amazing, since a hundred bucks didn't buy much firepower. He'd had doubts that his pea shooter would be able to perforate a beer can in the unlikely event that he could hit one. He wondered whether the guy was dead. It would give him an extra treat tomorrow morning when he went to get the paper. Though nothing would approach that moment when he awoke, memories of Honeypie's spectacular mutilation and death slowly displacing the vestiges of sleep.

A pair of feet bashed against the rear driver-side door, and he glanced back at the blanket he'd wrapped around her. "Hey there! Coming to, are we? And spunky, too! Well, great, I wouldn't want you to miss a minute here on out. Comfy back there? Hope I didn't scrape you up too bad hauling you out that window." He heard a muffled moan. "Let's see. To keep you posted, we're headed for a town called Auburn, forty-five minutes north of Fresno. Ever been?" He paused and cupped a hand to his ear. "Oops! How could I forget: I taped your mouth. Anyway, shouldn't even be two hours. So just lie back and enjoy the ride."

She thrashed against the two seat belts securing her. "Oh. By the way, I may have whacked your bodyguard. First time I ever shot a gun, so call it fifty-fifty. We won't have a chance to catch the evening news, but it'll be in the papers tomorrow."

He paused, looked back at her, and lowered his voice. "Oh, but that's right. You won't be around tomorrow. See, when we get to Auburn, I'm going to fuck your ass to bleeding, smash your bones into splinters, and roast you with a gallon of high octane. And girl, it's gonna be bitchin'."

Clem took a deep breath. "Best to start at the beginning. At the peak of the Vietnam War, the North Vietnamese Army—the NVA—began a massive infiltration into the South. Soldiers and supplies came down the so-called Ho Chi Minh Trail. NVA weren't particular about what countries they went through. Especially since the U.S. was constrained from letting the war bleed openly into Laos and Cambodia."

Billy nodded. "So a big hunk of the trail went through Laos and Cambodia, just over the border from Vietnam. Ever so convenient."

"Yup. The CIA came in and began a secret war in Laos to try and shut down the trail. They enlisted support from one of the hill tribe minorities, the Hmong. Some say they're from Tibet centuries ago. There's another branch of the same ethnic group in Thailand."

"I saw them hawking jewelry when I went to North Thailand," said Angie. "They look more Chinese than the Thais do. And darker."

"That's right. See, the Hmong had emigrated from southern China, and they had a history of persecution under the native Laos. Like, if a Hmong wanted anything from a Lao official, he had to crawl up to the guy's desk on all fours. When the CIA came in, the Hmong soon had an irregular jungle army of about ten thousand called the Tai Da'm, the Black Thais. They were the fiercest, most ruthless warriors in Indochina."

Billy shook his head. "And that's going some."

Clem continued. "They killed NVA by the thousands. Pure *Apocalypse Now* stuff, mountain camps with severed heads on the fence posts. CIA worked with a Hmong general, Vang Pao, who ran the Hmong army, and a legendary CIA maverick named Tony Rogers, who did the covert stuff. In fact I've met him; he used to live in San Francisco 'til he died a few years back. Paid ten bucks for every pair of NVA ears the guys turned in, then shipped a huge bag of 'em to the U.S. Embassy in Vientiane to show them the Hmong were doing their job. Drove the secretaries nuts."

Angie grimaced. "And to think I get pissed at junk mail."

"Anyway. There were also clan chieftains who worked with Vang Pao and Tony Rogers. One of the more notorious of them—well, maybe *the* most notorious—is our prospective helpmate. You sure wouldn't know it to look at him. Looks like a potbellied, jolly old grandpa. I even forget his real name. But everybody calls him Uncle Haha."

He took a wrenching right off the access road onto the gravel. With grim satisfaction, he listened to her sobbing in the backseat. She'd figured out they'd arrived and was quailing in fear.

As well she should, he thought with glee. A mighty surge of adrenaline tingled from head to toe. God knows he'd gone out of his way to give them their chances. And they'd failed, time after time. All just to create this one moment of righteous vengeance. The planets had aligned yet again, and he was unstoppable. He stood astride the earth, a juggernaut.

He drove slowly so he wouldn't miss the turnoff leading to the graveyard. The rutted dirt road loomed ahead, and he switched to high beams. Another minute of jarring bumps and he pulled into the clearing behind the hill, the familiar nest of gravestones beckoning in the headlamps.

Hearing another bout of whimpering as he switched off, he turned to the blanket. "Well, just think, another two hours and it'll all be over. And then, you'll be famous—at least in forensic pathology! You'll be the slide they slap on the screen the first day when the class is too large."

He'd decided to execute her in the graveyard, on a patch of ground in front of the largest monument. When he burned her, the flames would be almost invisible from the highway, blocked by the stones. That way, he'd be able to indulge himself in languor as her limbs steamed and bubbled and popped. Careful not to overdo it. Say a pint of Super Unleaded for starters, then add every minute or so. Cooked through, not seared.

Just as in the fearsome finish suggested in 1508 by a tenderfoot witchfinder in southwest Germany. In one case, he was faced with five suspiciously ugly spinsters living in the Black Forest who were accused of conjuring a plague outbreak. He gleefully informed his superiors that if one subjected the arms and legs of an unconfessed witch to slow burning, the malefactor's limbs would take on a pose of penitence, kneeling with the arms bent to breast in prayer shortly before she died.

Probably figuring on an "attaboy," he'd been miffed when they'd rebuked him, noting that per Malleus, *verbal confession was recommended "so that the truth will be had from their own mouths and they can be given to the flames." Indeed, the prayerful pose might even be a ruse of the devil to distract the witch-hunter from securing the confession that would save her soul when combined with the cleansing of fire. They admonished him by quoting the manual:*

> . . . if after being properly tortured she declines to confess the truth, he should have other implements of torture brought before her, and tell her she will have to endure these if she does not confess. If she is still not induced by terror to confess, torture must continue on the second or third day . . .

Of course there was no Marburg miracle. Slow burning would make the largest muscles contract, tightly folding the arms and legs. Fire vics were often toe tagged in a fetal position. But as he'd depicted in the mural, with the bones shattered to bits, Honeypie's appendages should roll into big balls of flesh and calcium at each corner of her torso like a human dune buggy, though a bit of coaxing would likely be necessary. A freak show even by forensic standards.

He pulled the trunk handle, took the flashlight from the glove compartment, opened the door, and scanned the waving grass and brush. Then he got out and opened the trunk. He cast an approving eye on the new sledgehammer. He'd done his homework here, too, though there hadn't been too much. One treatise on the procedures for breaking on the wheel in Peter the Great's Russia, but mostly common sense. Start with hands and feet, and slowly work inwards to the hips, groin, and shoulder blades. Wrap up with the jaw and lower rib cage, avoiding the sternum lest an errant rib fracture spear the heart and ruin the fun.

Of course, he didn't have the huge wheel to strap her to, but four stout tent pegs and cord would make for a perfectly adequate spread eagle. And he couldn't match the fiendish fanfare of those grand old Russkies: by tradition the condemned were publicly carted to the scaffold, followed by a tumbrel right behind bearing the hooded executioners, who proudly brandished each hellish implement of slow death one by one at the cheering crowds.

Everybody loves a parade.

He hefted the sledge, then eyed it disapprovingly. It still had the price label stuck on the handle. He'd completely forgotten to remove it. He cursed and picked at it, then left it on so he wouldn't get the sticky stuff on his fingers. He beamed the flashlight again over the meadow, then stuck it under his arm, picked up the red five-gallon can, and the bag with the tent pegs and cord, and trotted everything over to the bare spot in the graveyard.

He returned to the car, opened the rear driver-side door, unbuckled the belts, and hauled her out in the blanket, letting her drop heavily on the ground. She moaned, first desperately trying to worm her way back into the car, then shivering in a fetal position in the blanket. He lugged her away from the car, got in, started the engine, and parked the Hyundai in the entrance to the dirt road, facing outward for a quick escape.

He pushed her along the ground with bruising kicks until she rolled clear of the blanket. Her snow-white pantsuit seemed to glow in the moonbeams, il-luminated by its own phosphorescent light. He grabbed her by the hair and dragged her ten feet into the churchyard. She writhed on her back, vainly try-ing to scramble back from the killing ground. He reached the spot and let her head thump hard against the packed earth, then gazed around a last time, satisfied that no one would disturb the revelry.

He grinned and shined the light in her contorted face. "Well there, you. All set for our messy. See?" He gestured with the flashlight. "I mean, would I kid you? The gasoline? The sledge?"

He shook his head sadly. "You know, it's too bad we didn't hit it off. What was it Paul said? 'It is better to marry than to burn'? Bit of an understatement. From everything I've read, burning really, really sucks."

He reached into his pocket, pulled out a small knife, and turned it over in the bright beam. "This is just to get you into the right mode of undress. By the way, you'll be pleased to know you're wearing the most becoming ruby ear-rings. I've been waiting for months to give them to you. So rest assured your ears will come through unscathed. They'll be in your personal effects." He paused, then grinned. "The earrings, of course. Not your ears."

He leaned, pulled the waistline of her pants out, then slit the pants from waist to calf, rolled her roughly onto her stomach, and peeled the pants down as she heaved and choked in terror. He crouched over her, a hand planted hard on her back, lips to her ear.

His voice was a deadly whisper. "Before we begin, Honeypie, I'll admit, you're not my first. I did my sister just like I'm going to do you now. But I want you to have a good, long look first." He slid up so his groin was level with her face. "Now you be a good girl," he whispered with hoarse arousal as she desperately turned away. "Close your eyes or look away and I break bones until you do what you're told. Of course, I'll break them all anyway, but not for fifteen or twenty minutes yet. I'm led to believe that someone handy with a hammer can keep things going for an hour or so."

He reached for the zipper of his jeans, then paused. "Oh, by the way. I burned my sister to death on this very spot. After I beat her into marmalade, of course. So not to worry, I certainly know my way around a woman's body."

"I hear that right?" asked Billy. "Uncle Haha?"

"'Cause he makes corny jokes. But don't be fooled. Story from Laos is when he was a teenager, a platoon of Pathet Lao—Lao Communists—killed his whole family in front of him."

"Jesus. What could be more horrible?" gasped Jojo.

"Over the next year, he hunted down the whole platoon. Kidnapped them one by one, dismembered each guy over a week, down to his 'extra' kidney. Then he'd strap what was left of the guy in a tree outside the Pathet camps, rigged with grenades so they couldn't take him down without blowing themselves up. When they came out to shoot the poor fucker and put him out of his misery, he'd pick them off with a crossbow. So most of the time they'd give up and let the guy hang in the tree, whimpering until he died."

"A crossbow?" asked Angie in disbelief. "Sounds positively medieval."

"They usually used guns, but they liked crossbows at night. There's guys could put an arrow in a bird's eye at fifty feet. Anyway, last one he got was the commander. Guy tried to slit his own throat when he realized he was caught, but Uncle Haha got to him first. A week later, when the Pathet went out to shoot him in the tree, they hit a tripwire and set off a gasoline bomb. Guy lit up like a Christmas tree, twenty feet up in the air."

Jojo grinned sickly. "Just deserts. But I guess I'd rather have Uncle Haha standing next to me tonight than Mahatma Ghandi."

"We won't be next to him. We'll be behind a rock somewhere. Matthew has to know Uncle Haha's the boss. Which believe you me, he is. Matthew shouldn't even know we're here."

"Right, or he'd think it was a hoax. So how'd Uncle Haha end up here?"

Clem's features became a mask of anger. "We gave him and his kind the royal fuck. When Nixon pulled out of Laos in '73, we left the Hmong high and dry. Communists took the capital, Vientiane, in '75 and began an extermination campaign. Thousands died in massacres. Others hid in the jungles and died of starvation, a few made it out living on bugs, ended up in Thai refugee camps. These were people who saved thousands of Americans by making a stand against the NVA. And nobody gave a shit. I mean, remember '75? The copter lifting off the Saigon embassy roof? Our boys were home, so just slopes killing slopes, right? Shit, we had better things to do. Like working on our fucking disco routines," he finished, waving a Travolta-esque finger in the air.

He sighed heavily. "Anyway. We moved like a hundred thousand of them to the States. Lot of 'em are down south in Fresno. But plenty were left behind. Lao government's still slaughtering them in the mountains, but nobody gives a fuck."

"How'd you happen on this character?" asked Billy.

"When Laos fell, his wife and kids were killed. He got out with a few war buddies, rotted in a refugee camp for two years, finagled a get-out-of-jail-free card. He came to Fresno, married again, had a son. A few years back, his kid was slumming on Viet gang turf in the Tenderloin. Just being a teenage smartass, but he got kidnapped. Would've been carved up — Hmongs and Viets don't like each other. Long story, but let's just say I reinterpreted a few regs and got him out. So the old man feels like he owes me a blood debt."

"So tonight is an act of gratitude?"

Clem shook his head. "Strictly business. Especially since I'm a cop. He doesn't like cops much."

"Oh? He some kind of organized-crime godfather?"

"No, not much Hmong involvement in that; it's mostly Vietnamese and Chinese. He has a grocery in Hmongtown, spends his days selling veggies and cracking jokes, his evenings watching old TV reruns."

"Living the American dream. So why doesn't he like cops?"

"Most Hmong don't trust them. These people were catapulted out of the Lao hill country right into mainstream America. Most of them don't speak English even now. They try to raise their kids in the old Hmong ways. Like Uncle Haha told me, he'd never even seen a pencil until he made it to the refugee camps. And then someone had to show him what it was for. Their kids are embarrassed at their 'backward' parents. The upshot is Hmong gangs, boys who reject the old ways and find a 'family' in the gangs. Only time Hmongs see cops is when they come to pick up their sons."

"Makes sense. But far as you know, he's clean as a whistle."

"As far as the blotter. But there's things people whisper that never make it to the courtroom."

"Such as?"

Clem's eyes narrowed. "Such as, let's just say gangs cross the street when they see him coming."

The car went silent. Suddenly, Angie recalled their second visit to Roth's office, and everything meshed. "Uh-huh," she said smugly.

"Uh-huh?" Clem repeated suspiciously. "Like what uh-huh?"

"Uh-huh. Uncle Haha calls this Tony Rogers CIA cowboy. Tony calls you. And you? You reinterpret the rule book on the gang leader, and voilà."

Clem growled, "Somebody please shoot that woman."

Jojo turned back to Angie with a thin smile. "That gangster? In San Quentin, they call him Claw."

She cocked an eyebrow at Clem. "Huh? Claw? So what did you do to him?"

Clem remained silent.

Angie poked his shoulder. "C'mon, you're talking to someone who put an extra five bullets in a psycho."

Clem sighed. "Okay. If you really must know, I broke four of his fingers, bent them back one by one to his wrist until they snapped like twigs. Fishing trick I learned from my dad; told me nobody makes it past five. And he was talking tong boys who'd spend their last moments watching the boss's Pekingese chow down on their intestines for giving it up. Claw and company were shitbird punks, no match for jungle fighters. Given my flexible techniques of persuasion, I didn't bust Claw, just let him know what a near-miss he'd had at the hands of Uncle Haha. Uncle Haha doesn't know who he is; he knew he couldn't ask me if I got his kid out. But even now, if he ever finds out, Claw'd be well advised to emigrate."

He paused. "So just as I did for him, tonight Uncle Haha'll do whatever he needs to, to get Joanne out of there. And whatever he decides in the process, that's his business. Don't forget it."

Suddenly a faint rustling reached his ears above the breathing of the wind through the brush. He crouched down. It had come from behind the church ruins. Maybe a dog or a feral pig. He held his breath, listened, and heard it again. He pulled out the pistol. With his attention focused on the foundation, he was startled by an identical rustle from off near the hill. He glanced over and was caught by another rustle, and then another, from right behind the churchyard.

The noises grew more frequent and distinctive, coming from all sides like a pack of stalking lions, the rustling of sleek, lithe bellies slinking through the brush. It couldn't be the cops. It wasn't their style. They'd have galumphed in with sirens and megaphones by now. And in any case, they couldn't possibly know he was here.

He snuck a glance at Honeypie. If it were the cops, he would reach over with his knife and slit her ear to ear. They'd never reach him or cut him down in time; he'd still get the chance to hear her life gurgle away, to feel the fountain of thick blood spurting all over him. Then, he could surrender. It wouldn't be the delight of hammer and flame. But not too shabby either. He could bask in the memory of wallowing in that blood until he became a comatose ward of the state.

But he now saw that the rustles were accompanied by movements of the thick grass and shrubs, all around him and back into the meadow. Whoever or whatever was stalking him, they were closing in. He decided to take up a defensive position. He hauled Honeypie up by the armpits and backed against the monument, holding her in front of him. Then he laid the gun next to the flashlight on the edge of the monument for easy reach. He held the knife to her neck with his right hand and gripped her so tightly across her chest with his left that she fought for breath.

From somewhere behind him, he now heard a low, long whistle, one he knew could come from no bird on earth. He had no idea what it signaled, but it filled him with dread. He leaned past the monument to look out over the meadow. As if in affirmation, shadowy figures loomed straight up from the brush and behind the trees, emerging as if from Hell. He tried to count them: first two, then four, then eight. The closest was perhaps twenty feet away.

He peered at them in the moonlight. The closest ones—four or five of them—were zeroing in on him with crossbows. Enormous crossbows, two or three feet across. He turned his head back towards the clearing and drew breath. Three more bowmen had materialized there as if from the air, fifteen feet away, their arrows glinting balefully. To a man, they were Asian, of small, powerful stature, the tallest maybe five eight. Their faces were empty of emotion. They were each standing absolutely still, as if the clearing and meadow had been decorated with a dozen statues of medieval Burmese warriors.

His heart pounded as he realized that these unearthly men had not come here by chance. They had come because he was here. They'd known he was coming. He grasped with dread that whatever would happen to him now would be, for the first time, completely beyond his reckoning. For the first time, someone else—he knew not who—was shuffling the shells.

They looped around an overpass onto the access road, found the gravel road, and turned, jostling half a mile in the dark. Clem switched to fogs and inched forward. "Shit. Where are they?" he whispered. "If they're not here, Joanne's dead. Or worse."

Just up ahead, a flashlight beam waved. Clem sighed in relief, pushed the car to the right into the brush, and stopped. A short, crewcutted Asian man in jeans and an Oakland Raiders T-shirt walked up to the car, wielding a huge curved knife like a scimitar. He scrutinized the occupants, his eyes showing a glint of annoyance when he saw Angie. Finally, he motioned them out.

They exited. The Asian, who looked about fifty, addressed Clem in halting Chinese and handed him a cardboard box. Clem looked at Jojo. "Side arms and cells."

Jojo eyed him askance. The first cop commandment was you never handed your gun to a civilian.

"They don't want us doing anything stupid, and I concur. It's their show."

Billy, Jojo, and Clem handed over their holsters and phones. Angie pulled her Ruger and cell from her purse and handed them to the Asian. He palmed the gun in surprise, then gave her a sly grin. He turned to Clem and spoke a few more words of Chinese.

Clem translated. "Matthew's here with Joanne. She's still alive."

Angie couldn't restrain a sigh of relief.

"We made time," Clem continued. "They've only been here ten minutes. They have him surrounded in the graveyard. This guy'll take us to a vantage point so we can see what comes down. But don't show yourselves. And keep it zipped."

They walked down the dirt road, following the Hmong and his ghostly beam. After five minutes, the road circled to the right around a small, tree-covered hill. The man left the road and surged into the heavy brush to the left of the hill, and they followed. They forged through brush and scrub that thinned to dry grass as they approached the base of the hill. As they finished circling the hillock's edge, the Hmong held up his hand, and they stopped.

A powerful flashlight beam came from just inside the graveyard thirty feet away. The man dropped his arm, and they crept up onto the hill, so they were looking down onto the cemetery. Angie could distinguish a dozen men surrounding it, eight of them bearing huge crossbows. Three of these bowmen stood in the large dirt clearing in front of the graveyard, lit by the beam. She squinted: she could now spy a pair of dark figures standing in front of the largest monument, a mausoleum about four feet high topped with a cross. The flashlight rested on top of the monument.

The edge of the graveyard now lit up brightly as three more Hmong walked briskly around the white car at the road's entrance and abreast into the clearing, all carrying powerful flashlights. They halted a few feet behind the three archers. The men on each side were thin and wiry. The one in the center was portly, with the beginnings of a paunch.

Clem leaned over to Angie and whispered. "Uncle Haha. The one in the middle."

Their escort signaled them to edge around the hill, closer to the graveyard. They crouched behind a bush, twenty feet from the nearest gravestones. Uncle Haha and his escorts beamed their lights straight at the monument.

Angie waited with pounding heart. And suddenly, there he was, lit up in front of her, the twisted creature she'd pursued since finding herself face-to-face with a dead little girl. Her skin crawled at her first sight of Matthew, and at the knife playing back and forth at Joanne's neck. But too, she felt relief. There was a chance, something she hadn't imagined a scant hour before. And it rested on the shoulders of the pot-bellied little man in the clearing.

Matthew's voice came, high-pitched and threatening, from the graveyard. "Whoever you are, get the hell out of here now! Or I'll kill the girl! I've got a gun!"

Uncle Haha trained his flashlight on Matthew. One of his escorts focused his light on Uncle Haha so Matthew could see him. He had chipmunk cheeks, large almond eyes, a pug nose with wide nostrils, and a broad mouth with heavy, elf-like lips.

He spoke with a voice strangely deep for his stature, in a machine-gun staccato. "Hm. So you this Matthew. Everybody call me Uncle Haha, 'cause I make jokes. From Hmongtown, Fresno. Laos in old days. Hey Matthew, you ever hear about Hmong?"

Matthew shook his head rapidly in annoyance.

Uncle Haha nodded knowingly. "Most don't know." He peered at Matthew, leaning forward and studying him. His mouth finally formed a wide grin. "Hey wait! You remind me someone . . . Aha! Lurch from *Addams Family*! Amazing, just like him! Anybody ever tell you?" He spoke to his escorts in Hmong. They looked baffled. Then Uncle Haha droned in a perfect imitation of the macabre butler, "Youuu rang?" The escorts grinned and nodded. Uncle Haha turned back to Matthew. "Haha! See? Anyway, Matthew, maybe you wonder why you standing in graveyard looking at old Uncle Haha. So I tell you. I'm paying debt. I get girl, no debt. No girl, still debt. First I think simple, then I do homework." He gestured to one of the escorts, who handed him a newspaper.

He glanced down at it in the flashlight beam. "Hm. Turn out you one famous guy, Matthew. Kill little girl. That one in tank, right? Everybody hear. Hey, even I never kill girl." He read on and shook his head. "Wow, poison father too. Very bad in Hmong culture, even if father bad guy. What else. Hey, guy in tree: I *like* that haha! I do bunch of those, maybe we compare notes. Hm. Hang lady doctor boss, put other lady head on record player. Huh? Head on record player? Make no sense." His brows knitted in confusion.

He finally looked up at Matthew, incredulous. "Hey Matthew, you one funny guy. Head on record player, like spin round and round?" Matthew nodded slowly. "Haha, remind me of old days. We play game: roll enemy head in sack through Pathet camp from hill. We call it Tai Da'm Bowling. Roll head in camp, get spare. Roll head through camp then out other side, get strike, haha." He spoke with his escorts, pointing at the paper. They smiled thinly.

"See, Matthew? We all think you too funny guy, make us laugh. And hey, seems you busy guy too. Lot busier than old Uncle Haha, I'm just little grocer in Hmongtown. That why I get so fat, haha, always eating! Wife nag me, say better we don't carry Ben and Jerry's," he said with an impish smile, pointing at his ample stomach.

"So anyway, first I think, well, I just tell you to give me girl, I let you go. Then I don't like. Three reasons." He held up three fingers. "First, you sorta guy who like to kill, sure kill again. Then I see on news and feel bad, like my fault. Second, maybe you never think I let you go, even people tell you I never lie, always tell truth. So not much use telling you, and you don't believe, right?"

He pointed the flashlight in Matthew's face, and his inflection darkened. "Right?" Angie was jarred by the change in his demeanor. Matthew nodded as if hypnotized, his knife still tight at Joanne's throat.

Uncle Haha counted off one and two, brows knitted in confusion. "Oh, right. Three. See, maybe more important that you kill girl than live. Stupid, yes: no girl worth it. But I see hammer, gas can, guess you thinking real party night. So then I think, well, you want to kill girl so bad, what can Uncle Haha ever do?" He finished with a huge shrug of the shoulders, palms upward.

Matthew spoke again, his voice harsh. "That's right! You can't do a damn thing! So you and your Hmongs get the fuck out of here! I don't want any trouble. This isn't your business."

Uncle Haha smiled patronizingly and shook his head. "Matthew, Matthew, Matthew. You think I come all the way from Fresno, go back empty hand? Miss favorite shows just to meet Matthew in windy old grave-yard? Hey, what I miss?" he asked, turning to his right-hand escort.

The man answered him. Uncle Haha turned back to Matthew. "*Knight Rider*. Well, wife tape, I catch later. Hey I like that one! You ever see? One with talking car? Great stuff." He turned to the man on his left. "Later *Dukes of Hazzard*, right?"

The escort answered slowly, "Boss Hogg."

Uncle Haha turned back to Matthew and grinned. "Boss Hogg fat like me. We love that guy, haha. Anyway, Matthew, old Uncle Haha *never* do anything for no reason. Me, these other guys, we getting old, right? Meaning no time for bullshit. So now we negotiate. Pretty simple. Let girl go, you die one bullet in back of head. Quick, painless. Girl die, these guys take you alive even in time it take you to cut her throat. Arrows hit but don't kill. These guys Uncle Haha's old buddies in jungle war. Guy to your left we call William Tell. Two months back I dare him put arrow through belt buckle thirty feet, cost me twenty bucks. Double or nothing, twenty more, haha." He spoke to the archer in Hmong. The bowman grinned.

Uncle Haha turned back to Matthew. "Anyway, Matthew, I take you alive, you go down old mine shaft in Mojave. Ten miles off road, fifty feet down, scream loud as you like. It take you thirty days to die."

Matthew's head jerked as if he'd been slapped.

"Let's see. First eyes, tongue, lips, teeth, ears, fingers, toes, dick, balls." He conferred with the escort to his left, then nodded. "Yup, that take about two weeks. Then get *way* ugly. Feet, hands, legs at knees then groin, arms at elbows then shoulders. Wind up with kidney, maybe lung." He threw Matthew a wink. "Actually truth? I never do lung, but always first time. Maybe I try day thirty just in case, haha."

Matthew began to sway, as if dizzied by the terrible vision. He blinked rapidly, and his mouth opened, but nothing came out.

"Anyway, Matthew, chitchat all done. Pick one, pick other. Door number one, door number two, haha. Like *Let's Make a Deal*, right?"

Matthew stood as if petrified. The escort on Uncle Haha's left handed him a pistol and he held it up. His intonation darkened. "Hey, Matthew, I don't hear you. Cat get you tongue? Tell you what, you got ten seconds. Start now."

The scene became deadly quiet, the only sound the low groaning of the wind. Matthew seemed frozen like an ice sculpture. But suddenly he sneered and ran the point of the knife deftly down the length of Joanne's neck, etching a thin line of blood. Joanne writhed, trying to escape the blade. "I'm just getting started, asshole. I'm not stupid. You can't shoot me without risking killing her. So just sit back and enjoy the show."

Uncle Haha answered with a half-nod. One of the men behind the grave-yard out of Matthew's view swung an arm. A small projectile whizzed with a warbling, unearthly whistle just to the right of Matthew's head. Angie gasped as he jerked the knife off Joanne's neck toward the sound.

Then a deep thunk, and three arrows launched with an instantaneous whoosh. One razor-tipped shaft bore deep in Matthew's right arm. The feath-ers of a second protruded from his right shoulder. He gazed at the knife as it slipped from his twitching fingers. The three archers drew knives and tore for the monument. Matthew let out a frantic cry and grabbed for the gun on the ledge of the monument with his left hand, releasing his grip on Joanne. Just as the pistol was almost in his grasp, one of the Hmong swept it off the ledge into the darkness.

Matthew groaned and dropped to the ground, bowing his head and cov-ering it defensively with his left arm. As Joanne began teetering, two of the men dropped their knives, caught her, picked her up, carried her away from the graveyard, and laid her out in the clearing. One retrieved his knife and began cutting her tape. The other two stayed over Matthew, brandishing their weapons. The rest of the Hmong moved in, their lips set in grim smiles.

Clem quietly exclaimed "Holy shit . . . Holy, holy shit . . ." He, Angie, and the rest emerged from behind the bush and moved toward the graveyard.

Uncle Haha approached Matthew, sprawled with his back against the monument and quaking in pain. Matthew looked up with a glare of undisguised loathing and fear.

Uncle Haha grinned down. "Hey, three shots, only two hits. Who miss?" He made a face of disgust, then leaned over, studied Matthew's mangled arm closely, and grinned again. "Ah, I got it. One pass right through." He slapped one of the archers on his back so hard the man nearly went sprawling, then turned back to Matthew. From his pocket he drew a small wooden ball carved full of holes. "See Matthew, we play a game we call 'Watch the Birdie.' You know, same like when you take photo? Only trick is, if you watch birdie, you lose haha."

Angie, Clem, Billy, and Jojo congregated around Joanne. She sat on the ground, head bowed between trembling knees. One of the Hmong picked up a blanket from the edge of the graveyard and offered it to her, but she waved it off in horror; Angie guessed from her reaction that Matthew had wrapped her in it.

Joanne's eyes seemed to blank, and she slowly brought her left hand up to her earlobe. Disgust etched her face as she yanked off an earring and threw it into the brush, then did the same with the right one. Angie was perplexed until she remembered what Clem had told her after his interview with Matthew's mother: that Matthew had bought her earrings.

Angie went down into a squat and draped an arm over her shoulders. "Hey. You're safe now. You all right?"

Joanne closed her eyes tightly. "I guess," she said in a tremulous whisper. She paused. "It'll take some time not to visualize fifty times a day what was about to happen to me." Her eyes suddenly opened wide. "What about my bodyguard?"

Clem replied. "Last we heard he was alive. But critical. Wait."

Clem approached Uncle Haha, who was standing over Matthew and joking with his henchmen. Clem took him aside and they spoke for a moment. Uncle Haha called one of his men, and he fetched the box of cell phones and firearms. Clem took his phone and made a call.

He rejoined the others. "Well, that kinda night. Critical, but out of danger." He eyed Jojo. "We get our guns and cells back. No bullets, no batteries. They'll call later and tell us where to pick them up."

Uncle Haha signaled to them, and they walked to the entrance of the graveyard. He handed Clem the box and pointed a finger at Angie. "No spare rounds right? I don't pat down."

Clem shook his head. Several Hmong frisked Jojo, Billy and Clem. Uncle Haha glanced at Angie and smiled. "Hey, Yao, this one meanass lady. Dragon Talon hollow points."

Angie glanced toward Matthew. The Hmong were wrapping his arms and legs in binder's twine. One of them picked up the sledge from the monument wall and walked away. She suspected it would hold court with the hacksaw in her darkest nightmares.

Boys and their toys.

Several Hmong walked up to escort them to their car. Joanne suddenly broke from the group, stumbled up to Uncle Haha, and hugged him, breaking into wrenching sobs she'd probably held back for as long as she could. He grinned in embarrassment at Clem and patted her back with both hands for a moment. Finally, Clem gently pulled her off him.

Uncle Haha slapped Clem on the back. "Hey, maybe we see each other again, Yao. Hope not though. Every time I see you, mean somebody in deep shit." He held out his right hand. "Paid in full, right?"

Clem gripped the offered hand firmly, nodded, and smiled grimly. "In full."

A shock hit Angie as Clem walked toward the road with the rest of them in tow. She glanced back at Matthew; seemingly it hit him at the same time. He twisted his head up from the ground and glared after Clem, his eyes glazed with panic and rage. "What? Where do you think *you're* going? You're not leaving me here with this Laotian lunatic, are you?" He paused as the truth sank in. "Yao! You can't do that! It's the law! This is America, Yao, not the fucking Indochina jungle!"

Clem turned back and stared at Matthew. "Good-bye, Matthew." He looked at Uncle Haha again, then back at Matthew a last time. "And welcome to the jungle."

Angie and Clem filed down the dark dirt road ahead of the others. She felt tension mount with each step. Then a sudden shudder twisted her spine.

"God, I can't believe I'm doing this," she whispered hoarsely. "Presiding over yet another monster's execution. Is Uncle Haha taking him to the desert to butcher him?"

She felt Clem glance her way. "I don't think so. I asked him to make it quick. He sort of nodded."

"*Sort of?* You know, long ago I was thinking husband, kiddies, a nice long police career like my dad. Instead, I'm frigging Van Helsing chopping off vampire heads," she spat out.

"Your point being?"

She sensed he was steeling himself for a mutiny. "Relax, I'm not going to do a human shield." She stopped and turned towards him. "But last time, I didn't have a choice. This time, we could put Matthew on ice for three months until he's a living corpse. But you don't *want* to take him in. Uncle Haha's doing you a favor, right?"

"Keep walking or our Hmong friends get nervous." After a pause, Clem continued. "I didn't ask him to, if that's what you're wondering. There's a difference."

"Not fucking much of one." Angie strode ahead.

Clem followed her and continued. "Look, Angie. This isn't about revenge." She turned and glared at him. "Okay, not mainly. But even if Uncle Haha handed him over—and I admit, I think he would if I pushed it—say I took him in. Ever chat up a guard in lockup?"

She shook her head in annoyance.

"Guys who can't read a bus schedule," Clem replied. "Almost nobody in there tries to escape. They figure bail, maybe a decent plea. But not Matthew. There'll be trips to the clinic, psychiatrists, maybe a gooney bird nurse with a jones for sweet-talking psychos. In a week, he'll find the weak link in the chain. And he *will* try to escape. It'll be all he thinks about. You can bet the farm he'd take at least one more life even if he fails. A month from now I'd be consoling some minimum-wage schlemiel's family. And if he succeeds, he could take a couple hundred down the toilet with him. The poison's still out there."

Angie pondered it. "And just as I did with The Beast, you're not willing to risk that. Okay, point taken. Bundy escaped the first time they caught him."

Clem nodded. "And beat a few girls' brains into ketchup before they caught him again."

"Still, I'd rather they didn't spend the next month carving him up like a side of beef. An hour ago I might've said different, but I can't live with that."

"As I said, I doubt it. But I'll track down Uncle Haha tomorrow morning."

Angie gasped as a thought spun into place. "Maybe that's why Uncle Haha took our weapons. So you wouldn't have to make that choice. Part of his favor to you."

Clem shrugged. "Could be. I'm not about to ask."

She walked a moment in silence. "So in the end we'll both sleep better, knowing he's dead? Is that what all this is about?"

Clem gave her a sidelong glance. "No, the point is that other people will. I doubt we will, but we don't count." He paused. "How'd you sleep after The Beast?"

"Just fine. After, oh, two or three years."

Clem mulled it over. "Yeah, sounds just about right." His voice carried a wisp of humor. "And by the way. If this hideous blood-guzzling locomotive starts showing up in your dreams, let me know."

"Umm . . . rest assured, you'll be the first."

He watched Uncle Haha perch wearily atop a gravestone a few feet away. Any further bellowing would avail him nothing. Yao and the others were gone. A torrent of helpless fury flooded him at the memory of watching Honeypie walk away while he lay pierced by arrows and trussed up like a turkey. The pain in his shoulder screamed with each breath, and he fought back the icy fear of what horrors lay in wait. But he tensely watched the man signal to one of his people and speak to him. All the Hmong began to exit down the dirt road.

A flash of hope arced through him. Maybe the guy had gotten rid of everyone so he could do a shakedown. Matthew took a deep breath and the shoulder pain tore through him, but he kept his voice steady. "Look, I won't play games. I've got five thousand dollars in my apartment in San Francisco. You let me out of this, it's yours. No games. I mean it." He had almost ten thousand, but he'd split it into two hiding places, one so well hidden they'd never find it. He might just emerge unscathed, except for a few holes in his arm and shoulder. He'd still have five grand and the poison. He'd lose his shot at Honeypie, to be sure.

But his whores. They were out there, this minute, waiting for the harvest. Even now, he found himself gazing off into the night, enthralled by the grim majesty of his vision.

Uncle Haha smiled and shook his head. "You think this about money? That I sit here? No, Matthew, no money on earth get you out of this. I just rest a minute."

The bile rose in his throat and bitter fear froze his heart. The vision shattered into shards of glass before his eyes.

"You know?" continued the Hmong slowly. "Almost I give you to Yao. Like not my department. Even until a minute ago, still I wonder. Since I come to America, I never kill. But I don't give you over, and I explain why.

"Long ago Pathet Lao come to my village, ten of them. My father was clan chief back then. Pathet, they hear my father don't like Commies, so send platoon to scare him. Only scare. This I hear later through grapevine. But this commander and men, on their own they line up my whole family, hit them with flamethrower one by one. Make me stand there and watch like half hour. Mother, father, every brother, sister. Wait for one to finish burning before they do next." Uncle Haha clamped his eyes closed, as if battling back the hideous memory.

He opened his eyes and continued. "In that half hour I look into eyes of that commander twenty, thirty times. Each time he burn one, he look at burning, screaming child, then at me. Eyes like I never see before, hungry to see this pain in little boys and girls. And in me. So then I know why he leave me alive. So pain live on and on, fifty or sixty years, even they dead. I see lots of eyes in my life, some in war, some here. I see rage, horror, fear, grief, contempt, so many times. But never again after him I see eyes like that, Matthew."

He leaned over. "Not until tonight. First I think maybe I'm seeing things, but with hammer, gas can stuff I look closer." He eyed Matthew. "Then, a minute ago before I talk, I look close and see for sure. One minute not there, then there. That same hunger. Hunger for blood and screams, breaking bones, burning flesh. Like you don't have it, you starve and die.

"Anyway, a year later I kill him. And I swear then, if I ever see those same eyes, that same awful lust I act again. So you see, Matthew. No choice. You a dark evil, and only a man who see before can recognize. Maybe even old cop like Yao cannot, because he never see one like you kill. See that light in your eyes like torch of Hell when you hammer and burn. Only old Uncle Haha." He sighed, shrugged his shoulders and stood up.

"Honest, Matthew, at first I think to break you like you want to break that girl. But Yao ask me to make it quick. And others down the road waiting. So, Matthew, you one lucky guy. We skip hammer. Finish now." He leaned over, picked up the can of gasoline and unscrewed the top. "This is for the little girl in tank. And all my brothers and sisters."

They reached the car and boarded. Clem started the engine, switched on the lights, and looked at the dashboard. Then he leaned back and laughed. Jojo joined in.

"What's so funny?" asked Angie, leaning forward in the backseat.

"The police radio. That cagey old bird." There was a rectangular hole where the radio should've been. "It'll show up with the bullets."

They drove the bumpy half-mile to the highway access road and turned. Clem was about to speed onto the highway ramp when Joanne shouted, "Wait! Stop!" Clem slammed on the brakes.

Joanne got out and stood at the edge of the road. Angie joined her, followed by Billy and Jojo. As her eyes adjusted, she could dimly see the tallest monument in the churchyard. Joanne trembled beside her and Angie threw an arm across her shoulder.

Joanne finally spoke. "I just can't believe I'm alive here instead of dead there."

Angie shivered with the thought of the tragedy that had almost come to pass and hugged herself against the night wind. She turned to slide back into the car. But then her ears picked up the echo of a harrowing scream floating thinly above the moan of the wind across the meadow. She turned back toward the monument just in time to see a yellow-white fireball mushroom with a deep, distant roar right at the spot. It settled into a flickering blaze that seemed to move back and forth across the ground like a will-o'-the-wisp. She could just see the figure of a man walking away into the dark.

Clem glanced at Angie and sighed. "Well, *that's* gotta hurt."

She nodded grimly in reply.

They all slid back into the car. As they tore onto the highway, Clem opened the window, threw the light on the roof, and hit the siren. He turned to the backseat. "Joanne? I believe you escaped from Matthew at the graveyard, wandered around in the woods a while, found a pay phone, and called me, right?"

She slowly nodded.

"Good. Come to the Hall tomorrow. Jojo will take your statement. In the meantime, it reminds me: *I'll* need to stop pretty quick and find a pay phone."

Billy leaned forward. "Umm . . . you going to call this in? Guess we'd better get our stories straight. And to tell the truth, I haven't got a clue."

Clem glanced back at him. "Uncle Haha knew why I left Matthew behind. How could I turn around and collar him? Anyway, the DA would be my worst nightmare if I shoved this up his ass. Guy fights for the CIA, loses his family, comes to America, saves a beautiful woman from a psychopath? And he's up for Murder One? Worse yet, he looks like one of Santa's helpers. Pray tell, what jury would convict in this lifetime?"

Billy grinned. "'Specially when he starts his 'Me, I just fat happy little grocer' routine."

"Tell me about it. No, what I'll do tomorrow is call in an anonymous tip to Trance about the fricasseed serial in his churchyard. Then I'll go knock back a few with Jackson. Rig some damage control."

Billy eyed Clem quizzically. "So why the pay phone?"

"I need to call Grace. I'm screwing up the courage to tell her I'm two hours from home. The news will *not* be well received." He glanced back. "And Angie, you're hereby discharged from the Homicide stint that never was."

Angie replied, "Back to playing tag with Pee Wee drug runners in the project parking lots. And I need to find another house listing." She leaned forward. "Unless, of course, you guys can swing me something with pay . . ."

Clem glanced at Jojo and smiled thinly. "We'll talk . . ."